REINCARNATION

REINCARNATION

Also By Brad Mathews

Thousand Branches Series
The Thousand Branches
The Venom Storm
The Satyr of Fulton Manor
Tomb of the Phoenix

Era Sinistra Trilogy
Era Sinistra
Era Sinistra-The Shadow
Era Sinistra-Skyglow

Decay
The Girl from South Track
Revelation Trilogy
Revelation (Book 1)
Reflection (Book 2)

REINCARNATION

REINCARNATION

REVELATION SERIES
BOOK 3

BRAD MATHEWS

Unity Star Books

Dedicated in fond memory of Susan Shirley, the kindest, most loving mother and Nana a family could ever pray for. She has blessed all who knew her.

I am confident that there truly is such a thing as living again,
that the living spring from the dead, and that the souls of the
dead are in existence.

Socrates

Contents

The Laws of Interdimensional Time Travel

(As described in this series)

1. Memory cannot work in reverse. You cannot remember events from a future dimension and your reality belongs only to you.
2. When you travel to another dimension of time, you disappear from your current dimension and replace your future self in the new dimension.
3. If you die in a different dimension of time, you cannot exist in any of them.

I

Phobos War

Heavy red iron beams slam into concrete decks thirty stories high as shattered glass shards rain from the sky. Dozens of tourists and workers huddle under overhangs, shielding their eyes from the falling debris. A single shard strikes a suit-clad man in the forehead, impaling him with a particle descending at forty miles per hour. Howls and moans echo from a few blocks away as another building succumbs to a similar fate.

The sky blazes red with the fury of scattered orange light, as the shadows of distant clouds jostle in front of the sun, casting the city in hues of despair and hate.

I had entered the collapsing high-rise before. The home offices of Maxwell and Sons Architects and Engineers, which contractors usually abbreviated as MSAE, occupy the eighth floor, spanning the glass-clad exterior. Their office is decorated in neutral hues and utilitarian themes: Photographs and renderings of prized projects are anchored to the untextured white walls on stainless-steel pipe backing frames, tethered to steel tensioning cables, which bolt into the metal studs behind the sheathing.

Seeing it falling to the horror of what I can only describe as a terrorist attack chills my heart with a scarring regret that rocks me to my core. The steel beams, each coated with a foam fire spray, match the vermillion patina of the sunset.

The screams intensify while sirens begin to blare in the distance. What remains of the building smolders with thick black smoke and a plume of concrete dust mushrooms into a wave that will douse the entire down-town area in cinders.

Running, I catch up to the impaled man. High overhead, the twisted steel shifts and sags, signaling that the building may collapse at any moment. His eyes shoot from side to side as blood pours from the wound above his temple. There may be no chance to save him now, but I try anyway. Removing my shirt, I tie it in a bandana around his forehead to at least staunch the bleeding, but it is hard to calm his tattered nerves. After trying to stem the flow of blood, I drag him away from the settling edifice, which could kill us both if it falls.

Inside, the stairwells empty as architects in short-sleeved semi-casual shirts and clip-on ties scatter in every direction, a few of them hefting the limp bodies of their coworkers. The last man to exit carries a set of rolled-up prints as though he's made it his mission to save a memory of his proudest creation.

With the T-shirt tourniquet pulled tight, I try speaking to the victim.

"What happened? How do you feel?"

"Darkness. And ... oh my God!"

"Stay with me, sir," I plead, too busy with my own thoughts to read his nametag, which has gathered clots of blood where the lettering is etched into the plastic.

"The ... they said they're going to blame Allah."

My heart sinks. "Arabs did it? Are you sure?"

He groans as the torturous pain squeezes his eyes shut, allowing a single tear to gather in the corner of his eye. "No—no one saw it."

"Hold on," I pant, squeezing his arm tighter than I should. "The ambulance will be here in a minute."

Two women gawk at us from the sidewalk across the street, both wearing matching patterned stretch pants and colorful clips to hold back their frizzled hair.

When I meet their eyes, trying to ask for help, they dart across the street as idling cars back up for blocks and start honking.

"I saw the whole thing," one woman says after sprinting to the yellow center line from across the street.

"Tell it to the cops," I say, waving them over the rest of the way to join me.

"Not that it makes any difference now," the taller of the blondes says, "but there was a shadow that flew over a second and a half before it happened. Sort of looked like a bolt of lightning, and then a big bang. Thought an airplane had dropped a bomb at first."

"Lucky it didn't take the whole building down," her partner says, eyeing the structural steel and kicking away the scattered shards of glass.

"Think anyone's died?"

"I don't know," I yell. "Help me hold his head up."

"You know, on the crime shows," the first woman chimes in, "they always tell you not to touch the injured—just leave it to the professionals."

"That don't mesh with doing the right thing," her partner counters.

"True enough. You're not sure what you saw or anything?"

"Saw it a second after," I say, my words hurrying and slurring together.

"Why didn't it take the building down?"

Although my knowledge of structural engineering covers only the basics, and I can't calculate loads, stresses, or tension, I can make one or two assumptions, which won't help this predicament in the least. The cause of the destruction might not have carried enough force to demolish the entire tower, but even then, steel-framed structures are both rigid enough to absorb unforeseen external forces and pliable enough to flex should the conditions arise. The twin towers in New York would have withstood the planes slamming into them had the thousand-degree jet fuel fire not weakened the steel, which may or may not have been manufactured within current industry standards. A lot of ifs, ands, or buts, but no real answers, at least none that were an acceptable excuse to the thousands of grieving families.

"Doesn't matter," I shout, gazing into the stranger's eyes.

He scans the skies, searching for something that may never arrive.

When his eyes finally gloss over, I let out a desperate exhalation, and watch a fire engine roll to a stop at the curb. A half-dozen EMT's unload supplies and hurry to his aid, speaking in clipped sentences to one another as they conduct the rescue operation.

"Smart move," one paramedic says. "Might have saved his life. You ok, Mister?"

"I doubt that," I say, wheezing in the dusty air and letting the orange-glinted glass shards that litter the street reflect the sunlight at my eyes, which have begun to burn from the dust and sweat.

"God—God be with me," the injured man says.

"What's your name, sir?"

"Charles … Chuck—they call me Lucky. Tell my daughter I love her."

"I'm Dawson," the first EMT says. "Tell me your daughter's name, Mr. Lucky. We're gonna make sure you go home and see her tonight. How's that sound?"

"My sweet Vanessa," he sputters.

My heart thunders with inexplicable agony. It hammers inside my chest, and memories race through my brain, none of them making any sense.

My hand flares like a glowing orb as I gaze at the Big Dipper, awed by the vastness of space.

"How old is she?"

"B—augghh—born a week and a half ago."

I linger beside them, retreating into the overhang of the neighboring building, which has escaped widespread damage. More sirens blare in the distance, and when my heart settles, I try to reassemble my composure. I've been in this version of Philadelphia for less than a week as far as I know. I don't remember how I got here or why, but I recall something Secretary Harley told me.

Look for the shadows.

"You know, legend has it that in Colonial times, they had a way to cure people who had been possessed…"

"Sir, what's your name?" a police officer says, jogging toward me and glancing at the injured man.

I introduce myself and wait for his reply, which he hurries through so fast that he misses words and entire parts of sentences.

"Got a list … a mile long, no doubt. But that was some quick thinking there. You saw what happened?"

I tilt my head sideways. "Talk to the blondes. If you can catch up with them."

"Who?"

"Frizzy hair, matching stretchy pants." I point along the sidewalk in their direction but see no one. "They went that way. Might have entered a shop or something."

"They saw it?"

"Said they did," I say. "But their story doesn't make much sense."

"I'll track them down," he says, and as he turns away, I read his nameplate. Officer Hartman.

"By the way, if you're *the* Kerry Gearhardt, you should visit the station when you can. We got a detective searching for leads involving a missing woman and your name came up."

"*The*—" Only the one word escapes my lips before Officer Hartman jogs along the storefronts, dodging gawking pedestrians, dogs, and debris as he goes.

My throat goes dry as I try to assign meaning to what he's just said. What does he mean by "*The* Kerry Gearhardt?" I'm not famous, have no desire to be, and I haven't been here long enough to witness someone dealing with the consequences of a sneeze.

"*The* Kerry Gearhardt?" I repeat it to myself just to hear the cadence again. This is getting out of hand. If I ever see Secretary Harley again, I'm going to slap him for not telling me what I was getting into.

At least I remember that much. Years and years ago, I met him on Market Street on a winter's day, and he started going on about physics. I like to say I learned something from him, but I didn't expect him to alter my life's course so completely. In some respects, I should thank him for a hundred lessons that have taught me never to take mortality at face value.

I ignore the pain and limp along the sidewalk, stopping to notice that I'm bleeding from stinging cuts on my knees, and then continue past a dozen storefronts advertising everything from spellbinding mystery books to masterpieces of the occult.

I've been wandering Philadelphia in search of purpose for a week. Every time I pass an unusual shop, I stop and look inside, just to confirm that what I've seen is real. Sometimes my eyes play tricks on me, making it difficult to discern which of the many horrors I've seen is real. Every horrid memory congeals into a soup of heartache and dreams, tied into a dysrhythmic knot.

What does the detective think I've witnessed? I rack my memory until my head hurts but can't come up with anything viable. I might have only shrugged and kept walking, but the occult shop has caught my eye.

"Whatever," I grunt to myself. "Got nothing to lose but more time."

The storefront window displays a leather-bound book with a golden, upside-down cross etched into a pentagram. I don't know symbology well enough to glean more meaning than the masses, but sometimes it isn't the reality that sells—it's the mystery. The bigger the mystery, the more chance it has to expand into an urban legend, and conspiracy theories always spring from urban legends. There are probably enough true believers for a steady clientele, and the location attracts both tourists and casual browsers.

My heart snags in my chest when I peer into a set of tiny, glowing eyes behind a black curtain. The glass door sports the business name The Philadelphia Witches' Club, established 2033.

A flier taped to the inside of the glass promises an exciting night-time street fair, where fans of the paranormal can assemble and showcase everything from books to homemade crafts.

Inside, a glob of purple crystals hides within a down-lit glass display case. I push the door open and try to find the eyes I'd seen. When a lady wearing a colorful knitted skirt saunters behind the counter, I allow my eyes to wander.

One aisle sports a wide variety of candles and crystals, while another carries haunting tales and eyewitness journals, encouraging buyers to write their strangest memories and keep them safe. If anyone's in the market for an item like that, it's me.

On the other hand, I have no money to spend.

"Hear about what happened down the street?" the black-haired woman says, making small talk.

"I was there," I say, meandering through the aisles until I spy a skull painted with roses and Mexican patterns.

Next to it, a quality-forged cast iron dragon figurine breathes plastic and ceramic fire. Its serpentine head glows with a hundred ruby eyes and its wings spread mayhem and darkness across the shelf. A distinct feeling of déjà vu creeps over me as I stare at it for several minutes.

Swallowing, I return to the register and gaze down at the glass display cabinet containing gemstones and glittering watches between tiny skulls and bones.

"What can I do for you?" she asks, raising her eyebrows and looking sideways for a split second.

"I actually have just one question," I say, glancing at a pentagram tattoo on the back of her right hand.

She waits and regards me with a thoughtful expression on her face.

"Have you ever heard of *The* Kerry Gearhardt?"

She furrows her eyebrows, indicating she's searching her memory and coming up blank. "Not that I know of. What's she known for?"

I gulp. "No idea. Someone I met today mentioned *him*. I was wondering if there's an urban legend about him."

"I know most of the big ones from Philly," she says. "Perhaps it's something new, or incredibly obscure, only found in library books. Maybe you should try there."

I allow myself to grin. "Are you actually pointing me to a resource of truth and knowledge? Doesn't seem on-brand for this sort of place. No offense."

She shakes her head. "I'm merely giving you access to another point of view. You don't think I know everything, do you?"

"Well—"

"Didn't catch your name, by the way."

"I—uh, Larry."

"Well, *Larry*, you got any itching desires to get in touch with yourself on a more intimate level?"

That might help me. "Matter of fact, I do. I also have an itching desire for money. I don't suppose you know a place I can get a few thousand bucks just so I don't starve to death trying to find the reason I'm here in the first place."

"I'm Marissa," she says, pulling a strand of black hair behind her ear. "And to answer your question, I can't give you a legal way to do it."

I nod and turn to leave. I feel sullen, bleeding with a yearning for truth, or at least an explanation of why I'm here and how I'd gotten here. But not even an occult dealer with a love of witchcraft and mystery can give me anything.

"Now about that disaster," she says, calling after me. "Reports say no one can explain what happened. I'm betting you can."

"Betting, as in a few thousand bucks?"

"Call it a hunch, *The* Kerry Gearhardt. You come back here in two weeks, I'll give you the 'I told you so' spiel in real time."

She knows. I flush red and flee the store in embarrassment.

Outside, the city is embroiled in chaos.

2

Deimos Mania

People are running into the street outside the shop, all hurtling in the same direction while glancing back at the thing that chases them. Terror scars their faces. After sweeping a child into his arms, a man collides with a woman exiting a nearby shop. In the aftermath, I hear the child howling with pain and shrieking with terror. My heart sinks when I see two more people dressed in casual business attire exit a high rise building across the street to join the frenzy.

"RUN!"

"It's gonna kill us!"

A woman emits a blood-curdling scream, and when I gather the nerves to look back at the 'it' they speak of, I can only gape in disbelief. A hole the size of Rhode Island has opened in the sky, letting darkness reign, and when it expands, I try to guess the culprit.

"Are you crazy?" a passing man shouts.

The hole in the atmosphere oozes blackness, pulsating like an infected sore, and behind it, a thin wisp of galactic space dust coils into a blue nebula. And beyond that, a dark planet scoots into the hole. Rather than fear, the scene might elicit awe, but in plain daylight, everything about it brings terror.

Conspiracy theorists point to a supposed rogue planet that will one day destroy the earth, and if this is the end, I'll never understand why. More people scurry through the streets as the void expands, and when one man cuts off another, they roll around on the pavement, hurling bloody fists at one another.

A building two blocks away has caught fire, belching thick smoke into the yellow sky. As the smoke bleeds into darkness, I can hear something whispering to me.

"Kerry, Conveyor of Light and Shade, carry on the legacy."

The *Kerry?*

I gulp, pace into the street, face the void, and stare into the interstellar abyss amidst the piercing screams. The flaming building groans and shifts, and when a sizeable chunk of its glass sheathing shatters, a blazing steel cross juts into the sky. Dangling from one of its red iron arms, a narrow rope connects to the head of a woman whose blood oozes from open sores across every inch of her body. She looks skyward as the rope saws the flesh away from her neck, leaving her to tumble ten stories to the sidewalk, where onlookers scream and run.

The masses won't assist the woman, but I'm no ordinary man. Galloping toward the flaming edifice, I try to imagine the victim's face. She can't have survived the fall, but I don't consider running to be an efficient use of time.

Rolling on the concrete and vaulting back to their feet, the street fighters chase one another at full speed. Behind them, a tempest of dust and smoke erupts into the air and spreads outward like a mushroom of smoke following a gargantuan explosion. More screams. More punches.

"Get off me, you psycho!"

"You idiots," I mumble at a volume so low they can't hear me. They're all going to die—I can see it coming before they do.

Something big and black swoops down from the cloud of smoke, looking like an angry, puffing haze of soot. It settles lower toward street level. The men, at least five of them now, hurry toward the industrial district fronting the river. Shouting slurs and launching tirades, they glower at each other as another threat filters through the venting slots of a manhole cover.

Entrails of sooty smoke drift upward and coalesce into a soupy cloud that flutters a few feet above the ground. Running headlong into it, the men scream as they are vaporized by it one by one. Nothing remains, not even clothing. Only one entity could have erased them so—a Shade.

More Shades emerge from the manholes along the street. Having seen the men dissolve, two women steer clear of the Shades by sprinting under the cantilevers of tall buildings. But the Shades have not gathered into an organized mass. They seem to be prowling the streets in pairs, stalking easy prey. This disorganization allows many terrified runners to escape, but when I step into the street and stare them down, a few confused people stop, as though I'm exemplifying courage.

I don't want any of the onlookers to die, so I wait for the Shades to notice me, stare me down, and drift toward me, overlooking over a dozen innocent people.

"You will not devour any more," I command them.

The Shades flutter and gather into an army around me, ready to absorb me one atom at a time. Their delay is their worst nightmare: My bones vibrate and my extremities glow with a power I don't understand. A ball of intense light surrounds me, and the army of Shades hesitates to attack. They settle lower, backtrack, and dissipate into black particles that slink back into the utility holes as I watch.

When a man approaches my side, he pants in disbelief. "How did you do that?"

"Get out of the city," I say. "More will come."

"Not afraid of a little smoke," he scoffs, flexing his biceps and lengthening his stride away from me.

"It's not just a little smoke."

"It's—what the hell is that?"

A dark, muscular figure hovers below the hole in the sky as if ready to command an elite attack force intent on destroying the city. His shoulder-length hair, knotted at the ends from years of neglect, sways in the breeze. The troops he commands materialize around a corner. An army of the undead, many missing their eyes, pours through the streets to strike down anyone who moves.

Social media zombie apocalypse memes seem lighthearted and funny when you're safely tucked away in your own home with only your phone's light to accompany you, but when the undead are actually ravishing the city, your blood freezes into ice in your veins.

The zombies scream as they march, smashing glass doors, gripping innocent bystanders by their necks and tossing them aside like broken dolls. Most victims survive the assault, but when I notice what advances behind them, my jaw drops.

The thickest cloud of soot I've ever seen mushrooms into the abyss, obscuring the hole in the sky.

I'm no match for the army of eyeless zealots, but that storm cloud alone might make me cease to exist. Buildings large and small disappear into its shifting dust one by one, leaving bits of splintered steel, broken concrete, and shards of glass to fall like a cascade of confetti a thousand feet high.

The motionless silhouette hovers in place, but his followers are ransacking the city block by block. Terrified citizens flee their cars and scurry toward the river, screaming as they go. A pulse of energy gathers in my fingers when I see the floating man casting his eyes down at me. He's going to kill me himself.

I have less than a second to react. A blob of fire shoots out of nothingness, aimed straight at my head, speeding through the air faster than the speed of sound.

A sonic boom rattles the windows of the neighboring buildings nanoseconds before it incinerates me. But something inside me has erupted to counter it. The flaming orb vanishes as it passes through a black cloud that envelops me, and within, my entire body glows. I can sense the energy pulsing through me as it shields me from the attack. I continue to glow as I wander toward the floating man, ripping apart any of the undead unwise enough to get in my way.

The hovering man, sensing he's met his match, floats down and stands in the street behind his advancing forces. The zombies scatter when they near me, some disappearing into an invisible veil a few blocks behind me.

He wavers as he waits for me to approach, folds his arms across his abdomen, and glowers at me.

The skyscrapers flank him on both sides, gathering the yellow sunshine into a canyon of hazy light in the abandoned street. "You didn't think you'd win, did you?" he growls.

"Whoever you are, your reign of terror ends now." My nerves vibrate with the halo of energy around me, but that does not deter him.

"You're one step behind—and only one. You don't have your six wizard friends to help you now."

I frown. He's got the wrong man. "Don't know what you're talking about."

"That's right," he says, his voice booming and his muscular body shimmering in the sun. He gathers a ball of flame in his hands and sends it aloft, where it vanishes into a puff of smoke. "You won't have remembered it. Best get out now, Larry, because powers you can't comprehend are emerging as we speak. They will destroy it all, and it'll be because of you."

Rage splits the energy in my veins, causing my stomach to tighten. I pour out every ounce of anger I can muster when I bellow at him: "YOU DON'T EVEN KNOW WHO I AM!"

He counters by growling at me and narrowing his eyes. "I know what you did."

"Yeah? What did I do? Piss off the wrong people?"

"You don't understand, do you?" He raises his eyebrows and surveys the surrounding destruction as the venomous black cloud vanishes. "No one escapes Hades, except you. And when you did, you created the mother of all paradoxes that will unravel the universe you know and love. I'm fighting to save it, and you can join me or suffer."

Such a corny line might leave me thinking he's watched too many Star Wars movies, but he's dead serious.

"Right," I say, frowning. "I'll just have to trust you."

"You are the one who freed me, Larry."

"How the hell do you know my nickname?" I raise my voice and sparkle with energy. I swear I can hear a humming surrounding me as though I'm an overloaded power transformer.

"Shall I call you Ker?"

I crack my knuckles and stare at him. "There's only one woman—"

"—in the world, who dares call you that," he recites. "It's too bad you'll never see her again. You can deny it now, but you don't know who you are."

"I know I will escort you the hell out of my city."

"You can doubt me all you want, but I came to warn you." His voice flickers like energized flames pouring out sparks.

"How noble of you."

"Come with me," he growls, "or watch the destruction of your city while you die."

"You know what?" I say, casting aside all doubts and allowing myself to level with him. "I'm not in the mood for that. I have a few things I gotta do. Can you schedule an appointment?"

He laughs.

Let him.

"I can delay them for a while," he says, relenting as he shrugs and builds a fireball in his hands.

Frowning is a natural reaction, but the energy that pulses in my bones falters when the emotion ebbs. I'm nothing but a man talking to a muscular fiend who can conjure fire using his own hands. "Who's *them?*" I ask. "The gods?"

"Gods. Titans. All of them."

My heart sinks. "And it's my fault they want to destroy the universe? Tell me more about this grand paradox."

He shrugs. "All in due time. Go and do what you're planning to do. We'll talk later."

The hell we will. I will not let a monster like this guy command me. The ability to conjure fire doesn't elicit trust; it smacks of evil, the kind I'll never join no matter the consequences.

"Fine," I concede. "Meet you here at sunrise?"

He nods and floats upward while spinning the growing ball of fire as he disappears into the smoke.

A woman approaches from behind me as I watch him flutter aloft. When I spin to face her, my heart skips.

Having closed her doors, the occult shopkeeper strolls toward me, offering a smile. "I don't suppose you're convinced now?"

"I don't know what you're talking about."

She narrows her eyes, takes one step toward me, and blanches. "You don't know who he is, do you?"

"I've seen evil before."

Another smile creases her lips, making her look like a mirage. "Yes, you have."

Struggling to form a coherent sentence, I fumble the words and dangle my fingers at my sides as though she's about to attack. "What is it you know about me? This makes no sense."

"Let's discuss it over coffee," she says. "My treat."

"Nice offer," I say, "but I have a wife and I'm trying to get back to her, if I can find out how."

Frowning, she allows her tone to become flat. Her worn-out platform shoes disappear into the legs of her jeans as her heels scrape across the pavement. "I can help you with that."

"You're going to give me another ultimatum? I'm not in the mood."

"No ultimatum," she says. "But I can't say it's entirely strings-free."

"What's the catch?"

She tilts her head, considering how best to respond. "You'll find out soon enough. What's your plan?"

I watch the smoke rise from the damaged building, marveling at how the destruction has ceased. The chaos from an attack like this will be debated in the press for weeks or even years, as conspiracy theorists, paid alarmists, and media pundits point fingers at one another without understanding the real culprit, whom the Fire Guy has identified as me.

"First, I need to go to the police station."

She looks around and then fixes her gaze on my face again as sirens wail in the distance. "Can of worms right about now."

"Cops told me I'm a person of interest in something. I need to get to the bottom of it. If they arrest me, do you have money to bail me out?"

She smiles. "Depends on what they arrest you for."

"No idea," I say, letting my chin slacken. True enough; the police officer had been vague, but then again if they did have questions about me I would consider it my civic duty to offer the truth, even if it doesn't put me in the best light.

"I'll go with you," she offers.

"Really," I say, "I can handle it myself. At least I hope so."

"But you admit you need my help. Are you going with Fire Guy?" Her lipstick shimmers in the light, making her skin whiter in comparison. She has gathered her hair into a rugged ponytail that bobs near her shirt collar as strands of frizz escape from the rubber band.

I surmise that blocking the street will hinder first responders from doing their jobs, so I stroll to the sidewalk. Marissa matches my pace, and together we avoid the neighborhoods that have experienced the worst of the attack. Along every street, citizens huddle near the buildings, crying, escaping in their cars, or phoning loved ones to let them know they're safe.

The traffic grows denser every block we walk. Close to the tourist area, the police station bustles with stressed cops, angry individuals, and suffering. With flashing lights and police cruisers constantly coming and going, downtown has become a disorienting spectacle.

Clipped small talk with the shopkeeper isn't doing me much good, but it keeps my blood pressure from skyrocketing and allows a clearer head to prevail. Wondering where the conversation will go once we settle down to talk, I keep my replies short while watching the frightened people pass by.

One woman yammers away on her cellphone, inserting clichés and cusswords every sentence or two. She speaks in a genuine Philadelphia dialect, where speed matters more than intent.

"You didn't say that before," she shouts. "I want to know what the hell it's going to cover, and don't explain it to me like I'm five."

Another woman leans on a glass storefront, shaded by an abandoned office building that towers three hundred feet above. She holds a little girl's head to her waist as she wipes the tears from her eyes. A man gallops past us on the sidewalk and glances at them while making for a parking garage fronting the adjacent boulevard.

"Never thought I'd see this happen here," Marissa says. "This kind of thing only takes place in those comic book movies. You know the ones—bad CGI in your face to give viewers an unrealistic scope while the hero faces impossible odds, but still finds a way to win."

I haven't watched comic book movies in years. If you ask me, they all follow the same plot, which rushes through the hero's origin story before he identifies the real villain and goes into battle, only to suffer a humiliating defeat. He then trains harder than ever while learning heartbreaking truths, faces the villain who has become even more powerful, and finally defeats evil, at least until the sequel promises even more incredible action.

Becky likes films that provide thoughtful nuance, featuring interesting characters with relatable dilemmas and quirky love themes, which may be even worse.

Breaking eye contact with the suffering citizens, Marissa leans in closer while lengthening her stride to match mine. Her breathing has become erratic, and her voice has a trace of alarm. "Who was Fire Guy?"

I shake my head and consider explaining everything I think I know, but memory has been unkind to me and I decide to fake it. "No idea, and I don't want to know."

She raises her eyebrows and glances into my eyes while she steps around a drainage grate in the sidewalk. "Seemed like he knew you."

"Many people *seem* to, but I doubt it. Or maybe I don't know myself."

As if she finds my answer satisfactory, she tilts her head back and glances skyward to scan for new threats. For now, the city has grown quiet, except for the sounds of a stressed population's chattering teeth. If New Yorkers felt this way after Nine-Eleven, I'm relieved I wasn't there.

3

The Hostility of Eris

The Philadelphia police precinct's lobby sports a generous array of greenery to enhance comfort—a strange choice for a law enforcement agency seeking to unnerve criminals. Potted plants, most of them fake, occupy the long, uninterrupted wall facing the street. They take in sunlight from transoms and large windows with knee-high sills. Upholstered waiting chairs flank simple end tables holding smaller plants and magazines, while a square coffee table pulls the furniture arrangement together. A pair of coasters and a few scattered pens rest on the polished surface.

Picking up one of the pens and clicking it might seem counterintuitive, but it helps relieve the stress of being here.

The receptionist had faced an arduous task connecting me to the detective who'd been looking for me. Giving her only my name made me feel self-conscious and insignificant. After pinging every detective in the precinct with an instant message, she finally received a response from Detective Lana Williams III.

Despite her assurance of the detective's imminent arrival, she lets the phone's incessant ringing distract her.

When the phone sounds again, she waits five rings before picking it up, utters a single-word response, and transfers it. Ten seconds later, it rings again.

Detective Williams's stylish, open-toed platform shoes click on the beige tiled floor, clack on the chrome dividing strip, and then go silent as she strolls across the carpeted seating area.

I make no gesture of acknowledgement when she enters, but I don't have to. She recognizes me, and I can't decide whether or not that's a good sign.

"Hope you are well today, Mr. Gearhardt," she says. "Care to introduce me to your friend?"

Marissa extends her hand, obliging the detective to shake it before she leads us through the double doors toward her office. "I run a local business and I promised I would help him with some things. If you don't mind me being here—"

"Don't mind at all," Williams says.

Without small talk, she leads us along a central corridor whose tile floor echoes dull unintelligible chatter from open doors at both sides. As we walk, I scan the white block walls that display formal photographs of past and current officers who have achieved accolades. Although I've been in this dimension for just over a week, I recognize the chief's picture from somewhere.

The detective's office is one in a row of individual offices along the left wall, where painted blue text—"TO PROTECT AND SERVE"—interrupts the portraits.

As she opens her door, I notice a large collection of books and binders in a three-shelf bookcase, sorted by color and thickness. The top shelf holds a pair of forged iron bookends that look heavy enough to support a print of every case law in Pennsylvania history without sliding over. Next to the bookends lies a pair of steel handcuffs commemorating the detective's first arrest, which may have been on a domestic battery case.

Her L-shaped plastic name placard labels her as a domestic case detective, leading me to think she may be investigating someone I know. The file folder lying to the right of her keyboard has the most disturbing portrait imaginable. On the front of the folder is a small photograph of me from seven years ago, with a printed label showing the case number and a name—Susanne Gearhardt. When I see her name, I choke in disbelief.

"Thank you for coming down, Mr. Gearhardt," the detective says in a forced congenial tone. Her wiry hair is neatly braided tight to her scalp from front to back and the top two buttons on her blue blouse expose a small vee-shaped area of skin.

"What can I do for you?" I ask, trying to keep the nervousness out of my voice.

It's no use—she can detect it. Marissa sees my stiff reaction and nonverbally reminds me to keep my composure.

"Here's what you can do for me," Detective Williams says, again trying to keep the exchange sounding positive. "I've been trying to locate you for weeks. Not an easy man to find, which led me to believe you were hiding."

"You didn't send officers after me," I say in self-defense. "If you wanted to arrest me, you weren't trying very hard."

"On the contrary," she says. "I have no reason to believe you've committed a crime. Being a person of interest isn't always a bad thing."

"Not a good thing, either, when you've got a file with my face and my wife's name on it. What do you want with Becky?"

Williams tries to hide a curious smile, but her lip twitches when she realizes that she's erred. I'm terrible at exploiting visual cues, so I let her untangle her thought before showing any expression.

"She was reported missing three weeks ago when she failed to show up at work, and the Harrisburg School district could not contact her. They asked for my help personally, since you were allegedly in the Philadelphia area. I know you have a son attending Penn, but I couldn't locate him, either. Was hoping you could shed some light on her whereabouts."

Missing? I furrow my eyebrows, showing that I'm not going to be much help. "My—my *son*? I don't have a—what are you talking about?"

"Is Ian Reilly Gearhardt not your son?"

I frown again as my heart hammers in my ribcage. She can detect deceit from a mile away, and although I haven't lied yet, my body language can't be helping me. "Never heard of him."

"Mr. Gearhardt," she says, exhaling and leaning back in her chair, "I've examined your records personally; Ian's birth certificate lists you as his father. Susanne gave birth to him while you were married."

Another shock. "That can't be right ... I'd remember ... wait, did you say *were* married?"

"Since you never turned up to sign the papers, the state of Pennsylvania certified by law that her divorce proceedings were uncontested. Where have you been all these years?"

My heart slams inside my chest, filling me with a corrosive adrenaline that is destroying any semblance of innocence I hope to present. That's a question I can't answer, because it doesn't make sense.

"I ... uh ... I don't know how to explain it."

"Your right to privacy," the detective says, shrugging. "You're not under investigation yet."

"Is that where *The* Kerry Gearhardt comes in?"

"Excuse me," Marissa pipes up. She straightens her back and allows her hair to droop below her shoulders. "I might have some insight into that."

"Your friend's about to give you up," mocks Detective Williams.

"Sorry, Detective," Marissa says, looking at the case file on the desk, which has remained closed while the detective grilled me. "*The* Kerry Gearhardt is special. He's battled demons and can speak with the gods. I heard about him long before he stumbled into my shop."

I give Marissa an impatient side-eye. "You—"

"Friend of a friend said he saw him talking to a man on the street about gods and Titans before they both disappeared into thin air. The story grew by word-of-mouth until it became what you might call an urban legend."

"Games of Telephone are hardly admissible as evidence," Williams interjects.

"But you said yourself that you're not looking for evidence yet," Marissa counters.

Does she have a law degree? Because the detective just scowled when she blindsided her.

I take a moment to flash a smile before the gut-wrenching pain twists in my abdomen. The news of having a son, and Becky's disappearance, is unimaginable.

"They say it was like you disappeared into another dimension," Marissa explains, studying my idiotic expression.

"Well ... now that you mention it...."

"*That's* where you're taking it?" Williams asks, sounding incredulous.

"You want to accuse my friend of lying? She has a point. I *have* traveled between dimensions—dimensions of time. I'm from a realm where Becky and I are happily married, and we never had children. Look it up."

She doesn't bite at my sarcasm, but is showing no signs of believing it, either. "Handy alibi. No court jury in the United States of America would believe that."

"But you don't think he *disappeared* her," Marissa says. "Or you'd have arrested him already."

"True enough," the detective says. "It turns out you have another alibi, one that checks out."

"You just said I wasn't under investigation," I say, letting my impatience show. "Which is it?"

"You're not. Sometimes things explain themselves when you're working other angles. We know you cannot have kidnapped your ex-wife because video evidence puts you in Philadelphia less than an hour after she was last seen. It's in the file."

"Where'd you get the video evidence?"

"I was trying to contact you for your testimony," she recounts. "There was an exclusive street party where the organizer was permitted to use public cameras to record the festivities, and you wandered in uninvited and soaking wet with an unidentified individual."

The party—I remember. Which means that it's in the past for me. I'm saved.

But the detective isn't willing to throw in the proverbial towel. "I still think you *do* know something, Mr. Gearhardt, or you wouldn't be so cagey about everything I've mentioned, including your son."

I growl. Allowing myself to raise my voice only makes me look worse, but I can't hide the emotion that batters me now. "I don't *have* a son. Whoever this Ian is, I don't know him. And I don't give a shit about that fraudulent birth certificate you got."

"Legit birth—"

"What are you getting at? Charge me with a crime right now or I'm walking out of here."

"That could be used against you..." she begins as Marissa interrupts her again.

"Not permissible. Not legal. I have a friend who's a paralegal, and she knows her stuff. Kerry hasn't been charged with a crime, so Miranda rights don't apply."

"But if I do charge you, they do," Williams argues.

"Then do it," I shout. "Right now."

"I can't do that, either," the detective admits.

"Then it looks like you're in a bit of a bind." I'm seething and red with ire, but I don't care. It doesn't matter what the police are investigating, other than the fact that Becky disappeared weeks ago, although I could swear I saw her only one week ago.

Before walking out of the detective's office, my conscience stops me.

"Something to say, Kerry?"

"I just saw her at home, maybe a week ago."

"Is that true?"

Human memory is flawed and prone to internal and external biases, as Harley foresaw many years ago, rendering eyewitness testimony essentially worthless in courts of law. Traveling across dimensions of time has warped my memories, making my own assurances meaningless. In this dimension I may have last seen her years ago. I have no faith in my own recollections, and that means my brain will be affected even more severely. If my memory is corrupt, then I might be little more than a figment of my own imagination, and that thought makes me gulp while I'm stomping down the hall with Marissa on my heels. I could confront her for lying to me, but I'm too hurt to enforce it with emotion.

And Marissa can sense everything careening through my head. She stays silent until long after we've emerged from the police station, where the humid breeze and dimming sun make the chaotic streets even more disorienting.

Rather than forcing a conversation with someone I don't trust, I allow my mind to wander, until the sounds of an intense argument intrude on me.

A group of men in their forties is gathered in a loose circle, launching rapid-fire accusations at each other, probably with no evidence. The first man to speak is red-faced; he tugs his yellow-dyed goatee and sucks in his gut. "It's the damn Russians," he growls.

His companion, who might well be his brother, nods along while a man opposite him forms a retort before the other has finished speaking; his words are more polished. His attire suggests a career in something like financial planning or a related field, although more casual than I'd expect, and his tone shows he's well-practiced in the art of debate. "If it were the Russians, why is Secretary Arch doing this song and dance about the Chinese stealing American military secrets? He knows he's failed. Even the president does, but they won't do a thing about it because they're on the same team."

"Nice conspiracy theory you got there," the first man's brother shouts. "Be great if any of it were based on fact."

"It's all conjecture," the first brother agrees.

"What do you think?" he narrows his eyes as he turns to me.

"I don't do politics," I say, shaking my head.

"Then you're not patriotic!" the speaker accuses. "When you don't fight corruption, you allow it to fester until it rots the entire body."

"Don't listen to him," the brothers say. "Dude's a couple beers short of a six-pack."

"That's what they want you to think."

"Always with the '*they*,'" the first brother bickers. "No wonder you voted for our traitorous ex-president."

God. I walk away faster than my muscles want to allow, but once I'm out of earshot, I can tell that the anger in the streets has not abated. A woman across the street shouts into her phone, running her fingers through her long, dirty blonde hair, her face flushed from the strain of trying to keep calm.

"I won't settle until you say my son's all right. You incompetent—"

"The aftermath is harder to watch than the original attack," Marissa says, her voice ebbing with sadness. "This is what we've come to."

I don't want to discuss the state of society with her either, so I change the subject: "Tell me more about this urban legend."

"Tell me more about your wife and your son first."

The hell with this.

"I mean your *alleged* son."

"I don't remember everything," I admit. "Time travel destroys your perception of time after a while, and events sort of run together like wet paint in a hurricane. But I remember being pulled away from her into a different dimension, and then talking with a guy—probably the same guy I'm on video with—named Cy. Regarding the underworld or something—oh my God."

"What?"

"Becky died."

"Probably should have told the detective."

Memory crushes my skull with a weight I don't know how to distribute, leaving me breathless and dizzy. "It's not like that. I think she was looking for me, years after I got pulled away."

"Do you remember the funeral?"

I frown and shake my head.

"Then how do you know it's real?"

I sharpen my focus and watch a storm cloud building in the distance somewhere over New Jersey. I can reason with hard dates, but I don't have any.

"What year is this?"

"Twenty forty-six," she says, narrowing her eyes to express skepticism. "What a weird question."

"Twenty forty-six," I repeat. "This is her dimension. Son of a BITCH!"

"Kerry?" She might look sympathetic but she isn't ready to accept that I may be telling the truth, or at least what I believe to be the truth. "What's the matter?"

"It was twenty thirty-five. I know that, but I don't know how. That's why she's missing."

"I'm afraid I don't understand."

"She's missing because I left her in twenty thirty-five, eight or nine days ago. It's been eleven years. I left her in the wrong dimension."

"That can't be good."

"Which is why the Fire Guy accused me of opening a paradox. Because I did—it wasn't the Russians or the Chinese, or Former Mayor Arch's fault. It's mine."

"Sounds to me like you've decided to follow Fire Guy," she says, picking up on the emotions with which I'm littering the streets.

"He knows more about it than I do," I admit, "but I don't trust him. The universe might implode if I don't undo everything."

She grins. "Such dramatics. I'll help you keep your wits, that is, if you don't mind me trailing along."

"I'm afraid something bigger is at stake," I venture, trying to keep my voice steady. If my train of thought is to conclude somewhere in this timeline, the consequences could be severe, and it doesn't seem right to include Marissa in the wider scope of things.

"Bigger than the destruction of the universe? Well, when you put it that way..."

"No," I say, biting my lip. "You can't come."

"See, I have a history of sticking my nose where it doesn't belong," Marissa explains. "So yeah, you're not getting rid of me that easily. Might as well get used to it."

I turn my head to argue, but her face communicates an air of confidence I can't have matched in any dimension. Everything I think I know about my life is upside down, hanging by a flimsy string I may have installed myself. I can trust no one in this realm, not even myself.

"Which brings us back to that urban legend," she says. "My information is credible: A friend said he remembered you arguing with your friend Cy right before you both vanished. So he asked around, talking to frequent customers in the vicinity. And everyone who remembers it corroborates the original story. I connected the dots when you introduced yourself as Larry, asking me about *The* Kerry Gearhardt. There never was a name. The stuff about the gods and the demons, who knows if any of it's true? But that isn't really the point, is it?"

I swallow. "At least the 'gods' part is. Cy told me he was The Swan, sent to the stars after his best friend drowned. I don't know how, but his story is true. I never trusted him either, but I have no doubt about *that* part."

"And the demons?"

"I don't know," I say, my heart pounding inside my ribcage. "But I'll probably find out if this Fire Guy has anything to say."

"So you are gonna follow him?"

I gulp, frown, and close my eyes. Adrenaline is forcing shuddering waves of torment through my bloodstream. I'm on the verge of tears, but I've already resolved not to let them leak from my eyes. Disastrous mistakes may be commonplace in my life, but this is beyond every failure I've ever caused. "I have no choice."

4

Hunting for Artemis

The sunlight fades below the western horizon, reflecting off glassy towers a thousand feet high. Marissa matches my stride as we walk the many blocks back to her store. When the sun is too low to cast any shadows, her image fades into a defiant murkiness that punches a hole in the surrounding air. Keeping my eyes on her, I hurry toward a blinking red crosswalk in order to change our course.

Market Street and the historic district lie only six blocks away, and following Eighth Street might get us there faster than trying to battle the crowds flocking around Independence Hall and the Liberty Bell. Although the attacks might have coaxed the tourists to stay indoors, I doubt the insanity will have abated much.

That far away, the skyscrapers don't loom so large, especially when you're drawn to the sights and sounds of Market Street. Finding the spot where Harley used to watch it could offer me solace and focus my thoughts. Concentrating on solutions rather than problems is a trick I've employed throughout my life, leading to better mental health. But when the problems stack up this way, solutions become scatterbrained ideas that only lead to stream-of-consciousness narratives.

Harley excelled at highlighting key aspects of complex problems, which helped to map a coherent plan. In this dimension, he won't be there, but perhaps being in his surroundings will help me tap into his methods.

Marissa knows we're headed to Market Street before we make it a block in that direction, and she ushers me into the open floor of a high-rise office. Blue glass windows lie flush with an opalescent limestone exterior, presenting a sleek, contemporary ambiance perfect for corporate business. Square columns spaced ten feet apart support the lower floors up to the sixth floor, beyond which a ten-foot setback breaks up the wall of glass. Two giant cinder planters buttress the clean glass doors, providing an enticing view into the posh lobby, with its retro coffee shop, miniature deli stall, and a stylish seating area lit by rows of LED lights recessed into the twenty-foot-high ceiling grid.

"Any reason you're going there?" she asks, as if she hasn't seen Market Street in over a decade.

"So I can think," I reply.

She frowns, then raises her eyebrows. "My dad once told me that thinking is the opposite of doing."

"Did he?" I chuckle. "Then again, haste can be catastrophic. Something I wish I'd learned a lot earlier in life."

"Then perhaps a compromise is in order?"

Well, when she puts it that way ... I exhale and try to stitch a reply together while she waits. "Compromise is the heart of democracy. If it's twenty forty-six, I'm guessing it's been at least thirty years since our leaders made compromise a dirty word. Which means you're old-fashioned."

"Not exactly," she says, dismissing my reasoning. "I don't follow politics, only reason."

"That makes two of us. I just hope Fire Guy understands that."

She flashes a smile at me before looking along the perpendicular streets toward the orange and yellow sunlight scattered along the horizon. "Any idea who he is?"

I shake my head. Although Cy had mentioned Greek legends and Harley had said something about Titans, I'm no closer to piecing the man's identity together.

Two ideas smash into my mind the moment I remember the Titans. "Twenty forty-six," I repeat. "That can't be right."

She chuckles and furrows her eyebrows as she says, "Would you like me to get into my calendar and prove it?"

I change the subject. "Have you ever heard of Harley K. Whitworth, Jr?"

"Um."

I wait for her to concoct a response. Her mind churns, recognizing the name but unable to place it. "I don't see how it's relevant."

"Give me a moment to think out loud. I don't remember where I ran into Cy, but I remember a few things, and I'm pretty sure we never set foot in this year."

"I guess I'm not following," she says, tilting her head sideways. The curled ends of her hair are tucked close to her neck and over her collar.

Trying to explain it is difficult, so I try to break it down into concise pieces. "I've been to plenty of years, in no particular order. Different dimensions of time. You might think that's far beyond kooky physics, but it's real. I think I left Becky in twenty thirty-five. Our dimensions are intertwined, so we experience time in similar ways. We're married in twenty thirty-five, which means I was pulled away from her that year. To undo the paradox, I need to bring her to this dimension."

"Can paradoxes be undone?"

"I don't know," I gulp. "But I have a feeling I'll find out."

"Sounds exciting," she says, patronizingly. "Maybe we won't get lost."

A frown spreads across my face. "We? I don't think so."

She gives me a blank stare. "Look, if my store gets destroyed because this Fire Guy fails in his goal, I've got nowhere to go, nothing to do. So I might as well help you if it saves the universe."

"And then there's the logistics of it," I argue. "If you *can* even time travel, you're going to meet many dangers you're not prepared for."

"Right," she says, shrugging. "Have you seen the things I sell? I might be more equipped to deal with those than anyone."

"You know where we can get weapons?"

"Hello? Mysticism and the occult? I've got potions and spell books, staffs ... you name it."

"Not sure that's going to help us."

Her tone doesn't match her narrowing eyes, but it alters the direction I'm taking, which may cause further chaos. "Why's that?"

"Because Fire Guy insinuated that he has friends."

"Sounds like a party."

I exaggerate a nod for conversational effect. Embellishing emotions like that has never been part of my repertoire, but I pull it off this time. "Big party. Bigger than life itself."

"So, we team up with Fire Guy, save the universe, and then lead the missus back to this dimension. Sounds like a plan, albeit with a few pitfalls."

I frown toward Market Street. "Such as?"

She tilts her head, a sign she's acting defensive. "I don't know, you're the expert."

"Then maybe I should tell you the biggest problem. I don't remember much of it, because I can't. When you travel to a future dimension, everything you see and experience there disappears from memory after you return to an earlier time, because you haven't experienced it yet. Do you follow?"

She nods.

"Which leads me to the next problem in this paradox. I shouldn't remember Cy, but I do. And I have no idea why."

"Would you remember him if you saw him again?"

Trying to wrap my brain around it causes a knot to arise in the back of my mind, which spreads a pain across every synapse. "Maybe."

"Where would he be?"

"Not a clue."

"Good deal," she says, trying to hide the sarcasm in her voice. "Let's go get lost in time, run into untold danger, battle who-knows-what, and maybe we solve the case of your missing wife."

Without consciously breaking off the conversation, I lead her up Eighth Street while glancing into lobbies and the windows of various shops. Traffic can be a slog in this part of town, especially around dusk. Although a few hotels cluster around the famous historic park, they can't hope to house all the tourists that summer brings to the district—leading many into taxis and public transit. And that rush often coincides with the business rush hour, making matters worse. Tonight, an eerie calm has settled over the streets.

Twenty minutes later, we stand at the signaled intersection with Market Street, look both ways, and cross to where an independent bookstore with a built-in coffeeshop welcomes a smattering of strangers wandering the abandoned sidewalks.

Two blocks away, a saxophonist belts out a discordant tune, surrounded by a little band of brave patrons willing to toss a few dollars into his case. Across from him, I see the pastry shop Harley and I once visited. It may have changed hands a few times in the years since, but it still offers a cozy dining room where Marissa and I can engage in more purposeful discussion.

I've worn myself out with complex thoughts, so I opt to let her lead the way toward it, revealing several surprises.

"Does time travel give you a unique perspective on the meaning of life? I mean, it's not like sci-fi movies don't touch on it from time to time."

"My wife and I are close," I say, allowing my emotions to rise to the surface. "I gave her something I had made at one of those interactive science exhibits years before we ever met. You select two washers and place them in slots with their edges touching, then you crank a handle to build up an electrical charge, and when you're done, you press a button that closes a circuit, welding the two washers together without any heat. It produces an unbreakable bond—I gave it to her as a symbol of our eternal love."

She makes a gagging face. "Touching."

"It's endured all these years; in fact, I'm sure she still has it. I would do anything for her, and I suspect I've already done many things. I guess it allows you to transcend what you think you know about life, about love and relationships. But it doesn't eliminate the problems. It makes them worse. Sometimes I wish I'd never chased after Sarah at Bones Holdings."

Marissa perks up at the mention of the name but says nothing.

I pull open the bakery's clean glass door and sample the delectable aromas of baking breads and sweet treats. She studies me in silence as I stare at a giant Danish big enough for us to split and still have leftovers.

"Got your eye on that Danish," the attendant says. "Best in the area, and it's the last one. I'll make you a special deal."

"Sold," I say, digging into my pocket and gulping in horror at the realization that I don't have a wallet.

"Geez." Marissa coughs. "I'll get it."

She pulls her wallet out of her handbag and waves a credit card over a reading sensor while I gaze at the decorative chalk-lettered blackboard tied to the wall with hidden straps beneath generous track lighting suspended from the open-web steel trusses. It hides the backroom, which houses the kitchen and an adjacent office. The recently-cleaned domed glass display counter offers special deals on limited-time products, while a poster promotes an author and music event on an upcoming Saturday evening.

"Thank you so much," the woman behind the counter says, lifting the lid and using a sheet of wax paper to handle our purchase.

"Don't mention it," Marissa replies.

"And thank you," I drone.

"Why don't you have a wallet?"

I wrack my brains and come up empty, which makes her giggle.

"Well, in my defense..."

"There's no defense for that," she quips. "Macho men carry big, fat wallets stuffed with cash, pictures of nephews, and condoms, sometimes attached to a shiny chain that draws attention to the fact that they have a wallet should any sly pickpocket wish for a broken wrist."

"Is that your opinion of men? You and Becky would get along."

She breaks the pastry into rough halves, licks the jelly frosting from her fingers, and nibbles on the corner of her half. "How'd you meet her?"

I recount what I remember of our history, certain that I'm leaving out huge chunks of it, but not caring. The act of chatting about it offers a soothing sensation of peace instead of despair. I'm unprepared to let go of that emotion during this precarious time.

When I'm finished, I bite off a gigantic piece of pastry and wait for her to tell me her backstory.

"I was five when I got interested in witchcraft. A friend of mine had a Ouija board, claiming it gave her the power to hold séances with the dead. One night, we had a sleepover with another friend. Skepticism aside, it happened to work, and I wasn't sure how. I know what you're thinking; 'blonde girl with dyed black hair and black lipstick, with a bulldog collar who listens to goth emo music you've never heard of.' But Misty was smarter than hell, a redhead, got into Penn, with good grades, and had a wide circle of friends, including football players, music nerds—everyone. She died a few years ago when a drunk driver plowed into her, going ninety on I-95. Ripped my heart out, too."

"Sad."

"You don't have to patronize me," she says.

But I meant it. The longer I listen, the more my heartstrings vibrate. Before long, I might collapse into tears as the tension breaks within me, but when I remember her perking up at the contractor's name, my heart goes glacial.

"Misty introduced me to a girl with amber hair and smooth, dimpled cheeks that night. I remember her because we started chilling a few years later. She told me about this new job she was starting at a big contracting firm."

"Bones Holdings?"

She nods. "You'll never guess what her name was."

I choke and frown at the same time. "Sarah."

Another nod. "We lost track of each other soon after. I don't know where she went and never saw her again. I'm guessing you did."

"The inspiration behind my time-travel journey. She never really explained to me how it worked, but I can still sometimes hear her voice echoing in my head."

"You know how to find me."

The longer we chat, the more comfortable I become. I'm ballooning with excess calories by the time I've polished off my half of the pastry. She wraps the rest of hers in a napkin, stuffs it in her handbag, and wipes her lip on another napkin, smudging off some of her lipstick.

Tucking her hair behind one ear, she stands, makes her way toward the exit, and considers me before we step out into the darkness.

"I think I might know the reason you can hear her voice," she says. "Trying to explain it might break your brain, but I know someone who can help you make sense of it. She owns a shop down the block from here."

She points toward Harley's corner. The coincidences are beyond comprehension; I have no choice but to go with her.

"I don't tell this to everyone, but she helped me after Misty died. She's big on mythology in healing and she'll tell you what I'm going to as well; that our minds naturally want to connect with loved ones and people who are important to us. She's not a medium or anything, but she understands the bridge better than anyone I know. If you're willing, she can teach you how to cross that bridge."

"Is that a form of telepathy?"

She gives a faint smile. "If you want to sci-fi it up. You can hear traces of their voices, no matter how much time and distance lie between you. And it revives a spirit that lives in us all."

"My wife might say our meeting isn't accidental," I say.

"Education tends to block our minds with skepticism, making us deny that everything happens for a reason."

"That isn't true at all," I argue.

A ten-second pause hints that a life-altering revelation is coming; I cast my eyes downward, clench my fists at my side, and brace for it.

"Of course it is. Only it's not because some god dictates it, it's because all gods are familiar with the innate qualities of the human brain, which no scientist has yet unlocked, and they use those qualities in many ways."

Marissa studies my expression after finishing, biting her lip, waiting while I gaze off in silence. If she's telling the truth, many things might be possible, and the consequences are surreal. How can it be true? It warps my head until I hear the wispy echoes of Sarah's voice once again, as clear as ever. The bridge Marissa is talking about could be the key to saving the universe and returning Becky to her proper dimension. I don't know how to prepare for what's coming, which makes me nervous about meeting Marissa's friend. I glance down and notice my fingertips glowing with a subtle shielding of light.

5

Hestia and the Hearth

Marissa has not finished surprising me. So far, I've taken most of her ramblings in stride, but the odds of running into her were astronomical. An acquaintance of Sarah's, with more secrets than expected, in one of America's biggest cities? Preposterous!

While she lets the silence build between us, I begin devising a line of questioning. How does she know so much? Is she connected to some untold higher spiritual being I've yet to identify? And is our meeting as random as it seems?

Before I can utter a single syllable, and while leading me along the Market Street sidewalk towards the corner Secretary Harley used to watch, she pipes up, "When it comes to women like Miriam, you can't take everything literally. Part of it is performance, of course. A good act is designed to fetch top dollar, and Miriam's got the best one I've ever seen."

"You're into the occult," I remind her.

She tilts her head, allowing the dyed tips of her hair bob near her shoulder, and balancing simple thoughts with candor. If that's one of her strong suits, this will be a strenuous relationship. Indulging in simplicity is a good way to waste time, and candor, otherwise known as brutal honesty, is too oppressive for my tastes. I prefer wholesome, down-to-earth people who balance confidence with humility, which is what attracted me to Becky in the first place.

"So?" Marissa plants a vacant expression on her face as she waits for me to explain.

"You wouldn't expect a believer in the occult to consider mysticism 'a bridge too far,' if you'll pardon the expression."

"It's out of my wheelhouse," she says, shrugging.

"Then what about your occultism? Is that an act, too?"

She lets her arms slacken, a signal that she's ready to relent. She slows her pace and looks into my eyes. "You gotta walk the walk in some professions, even retail. It's amazing how conservative people get with the purse strings when they don't think you actually believe in what you're selling. I'm sure it's similar in your profession."

True enough. Although construction comes with various built-in stereotypes, I like to think I've broken the mold, even if I do entertain some of the more commonplace thought processes in the industry. Engineers warn us not to take shortcuts under any circumstances, yet sometimes the tension between schedules and budgets necessitates a creative solution that doesn't exactly adhere to the project specifications. The best of us can recognize the design's true intent, and if we then devise a practical solution with the materials and labor capabilities at hand, we can reduce our costs. Often, engineers will sign off on these tactics with some fine-tuning, but outright rejections are a rarity because of schedule constraints.

"How much of it is an act?" I ask.

"With Miriam, or me?"

"Both."

"Maybe twenty to thirty percent."

I frown. That's not a surprising answer, and by now a lack of surprise is a wonder in itself. Is she trying to be predictable on purpose now that she's blown her cover? If so, it doesn't fool me.

"So, do you care to give me a rundown on what this bridge is?"

"Miriam's never exactly called it that," she amends. "My terminology might not be too precise, so that's why you should listen to her. She sees some things that haven't happened yet, but it's not like prophecy or anything. And she specializes in healing. She's as good at that as any three-hundred-dollar-an-hour psychiatrist. She just takes an unconventional approach."

"An unconventional approach will get you disbarred in medicine and law," I argue. "Even in construction, it only garners rewards if you make your intentions clear with submittals. You'd be surprised how much leeway 'or approved equal' gets you."

Marissa offers an insincere, lighthearted chuckle. "Jargon. See what I'm talking about?"

"Or as we call it, 'clear communication.'" My point won't be made using common construction phrases. But she expects this, or she'd make her displeasure obvious. Getting away with everything will prove impossible, but as with engineers, a few hits will get past her.

"I won't say Miriam deals in jargon all that much," she says, allowing the smile to linger a moment too long. "From what I've seen, she prefers language that keeps you guessing."

I gulp. Having to guess what someone's *really* thinking is a game I can do without. Becky employs that tactic with enough precision to keep me humble, but some people wield nuance like a brick.

"Sure she's in there?" I ask, noting to myself how dark the windows behind Harley's former station are.

"Better than fifty-fifty," she says. "Plan B is that you find Fire Guy without understanding the true complexity of your mission."

"I'm good at winging it," I claim. "Even when it goes south, I know how to gain enough advantages to eke out a victory."

She peers through a narrow crack between the window jamb and the black felt liner partition that displays merchandise to would-be customers. The felt-topped display table sports a pair of decorative urns, a few glittering crystals, and an array of candles and beads. The urns' motif captures my attention for long enough to question their origin.

Red and beige strips zigzag around the rim. The 'hip' of the curve and a couple of inches above the base carry a simple geometric pattern of repeated right-angle like a Greek key design. At three-inch intervals, simplistic stylized flames lap at the blocky S curve fronting the pictogram. A figure with long hair and a detailed wreath tends to the flames before the pattern resumes. I've seen designs like this before, although I'm not sure where.

"She has an apartment above the shop," Marissa explains. "But she's usually downstairs until nine every night—cleaning, organizing, you know how it is."

Pulling open the door, Marissa tries to suppress the jingling of the overhead bells. Miriam is sitting in a chair behind a glass display counter. In front of her, she has a clipped-together spreadsheet, a pen, and a writing pad for inventory. On a small pink legal pad, she scribbles rudimentary math, as if she doesn't trust the formulas in the spreadsheet program she uses.

By the time she looks up, she's completed and checked several calculations. She tilts her glasses down her nose and drops the pen on the clipboard.

"If it isn't the time-traveler himself," she says. "And an old customer, Marissa, is it?"

I give Marissa a sideways glance while raising my eyebrows. "Customer?"

"Long story. I'll explain later."

"Whatever happened to your partner?" Miriam asks me. "I believe you called him Cy?"

My face sags as I wonder why she brought him up, and what she means. If I could get past the mystery of how this woman knows me so well, I would ask that question.

"No idea. Might have died."

Now it's Marissa's turn to gawk. "You had a partner?"

"Even longer story."

"Sad news," Miriam says, her tone suggesting contemplation rather than mourning.

I don't know what I'm doing here if she's being deceptive, but she's already captured my attention. She'll lose interest in me if I don't tell her why I'm here, although Marissa knows more about that than I do, so I nod while she explains my mission. "*The* Kerry Gearhardt wants to know how transitive mind connections work. Like how you can interpret someone's thoughts from long-distance without speaking with them."

Miriam pushes her glasses back up her nose and combs her fingers through the tips of her hair. While this may seem like a moment to focus on business, it appears she has other thoughts running through her mind. Her stern expression slows her reactions, but her eyes give her away as she studies me. "Transference can only occur if the connection is strong enough. Special bonds, lovers, twin siblings, many have claimed this power. And unlike the kind that unscrupulous professionals employ, it's the real thing. I would be surprised if you weren't capable of such." Her eyes bore into me like drill bits as I try to understand what she's saying.

Her use of the word 'unscrupulous' flashes images across my mind of a horned man cloaked in black. "What kind of special bond?"

She is prepared for this question, clearly. "Could be anything. Just not mundane. Tales of yore depict a relationship that forms over time and space, something like destiny or common souls in the universe. And having read antebellum writings, we know that slaves and masters could sometimes share this gift. This is Advanced Psychology for the Weird 301. You won't learn this from a stuffy Ivy League professor, or for that matter, even from reading Plato himself."

"Why is it so weird? Seems logical enough."

She lowers her chin, glancing down at her notes. "There's more to it than that. Some attribute it to God or the angels, but there's a complex interplay between various deities that contributes to it. You could describe it as a magical power few understand. But I can tell I won't convince you with words."

She's anticipating my thoughts before they can even form in my brain. I'd love to ask her how she's doing it, but I suppose she'll show me before long.

Marissa's eyes have widened at Miriam's words, but when silence resumes, she busies herself looking at the candles and the artistic, cloth-bound diaries that take up an aisle to the left of the display table and cash register.

"Let me finish up," Miriam says, eyeing her work. "In the meantime, please browse at your own risk."

She picks up the pen, clicks the end, and resumes scribbling on the pink legal pad. I peel my eyes away from her and stalk the aisles. One wall of the shop carries a diverse array of so-called healing stones, which amount to polished and rounded rocks 'to help manage stress, sorrow, or guilt.' The crystals and rarer gemstones garner higher prices, sometimes enough to make me scoff at spending that much money on a rock. The farther I walk along this wall, the higher the prices go. At the end, a collection of pewter and bronze figurines graces a higher shelf above an assortment of colorful gaming dice.

I gaze at one figurine for so long that my imagination fills in the holes. It has the curvaceous body of a woman, standing relaxed, wearing a loose-fitting, ankle-length dress and a crown of grains. She carries a book in one hand and a foot-long rod of wood or metal in the other. Her eyes are closed, and her lips are parted.

At the back of the room, beyond a rack of T-shirts, scarves, and canvas and hemp handbags, is an antique fireplace with a carved wooden mantle. Its fluted and beaded pillars rise five feet to thick wooden corbels, with painted and carved leaves that show the veins in detail. The mantelpiece ends at a dusty shelf stocked with eclectic decorations: everything from Christian saints to fire-breathing dragons.

The surround comes to an end where the wood meets the rough, chipped-brick hearthstone. The artificial gas fire invokes a weathered, ambient quality, warming the back of the room with enchanting and relaxing orange and yellow light.

Next to the hearth, a claw-footed ottoman covered in green felt riveted to a polished-oak frame holds a pair of leather-bound books with snap closures. Standing beside a matching, cozy-looking chair, the furniture evokes classic themes and comfort. Becky would curl up in that chair and read Agatha Christie all night long, and although she wouldn't utter a single word, I'd know she'd be on a high.

Marissa stops perusing and stands idly next to me as I consider the hearth. "You've been here before," she says. "Why didn't you mention it?"

I don't have an answer. Rather than admitting I don't know, I simply shrug.

"Different dimension of time?"

I can't express my feelings any better than by narrowing my eyes and rubbing the ache in my neck. "Makes no sense. If we had an interaction in a different dimension, there's no reason she should remember it while I don't."

Marissa frowns and gazes at the fireplace and its cozy splendor. "You'll have to ask her."

"Which brings me back to your dealings with her."

She sighs, clasps her hands, paces to the chair, and sits down with her knees together, her back hunched, and her toes on their tips. "Long day, long shift, before I opened my own shop. I was coming off a breakup. A guy I'd really liked had stolen my money, skipped town, and sent me a letter with a picture of him and his new lover, which I shredded in anger. I leaned on a friend who suggested turning to metaphysical help as an alternative to therapy. But it didn't quite lead there—Miriam started a conversation with me, and before I knew it, she had me in the back room, spilling my deepest, darkest secrets. And it was like nothing I'd ever experienced, including the séances. Talk of spirits, goddesses, demons, or, as she pronounced them, 'daemons.'

"It took a while to take hold. A few visits, I think. And that's when she mentioned the bridge. See, in the grand scheme of things, my ex-boyfriend didn't matter. Someone else did. And I never found out who it was until I met you."

I look and feel shocked. "Me?"

She shakes her head. "You weren't the last piece of the puzzle. It was Sarah."

I force myself to shake my head, grip my knuckles with my thumb, and apply pressure. "You and Sarah? No offense, but that doesn't make sense."

"She means something to you, too. Don't you understand why?"

"Not a clue."

"The bridge. You can hear her voice, because the three of us are kindred spirits. Only she's not the one binding it all together—you are. I can see it in your eyes."

I stammer out, "I don't know what you're talking about. Becky is the only woman who means anything to me. She's my wife."

"Then again, I keep thinking there's a fourth person. Do you know of anyone like that?"

"Negative. And I still don't believe in occultism."

She scoffs. "You've traveled in time, and you mean more than you let on. If that Fire Guy is a sign, you might be the center of the universe. If that's apparent to me, why isn't it to you?"

"Time travel," I guess. "It destroys your memory. You do it long enough, run into enough things, you can question reality itself. If you have a few days, I can explain why that's not good."

"I see."

"I don't think you do," I counter. "One of the problems I keep running into is that the dimensions you travel to are yours alone, unless they're intertwined with someone else's. It's a fundamental law, but some beings don't have to abide."

"They say laws are made to be broken."

I nod. "That's what Becky always says. God had laws in the Garden of Eden, but he preprogrammed Adam and Eve to break them. If the God of Christianity can break his own laws, then the gods of Greek lore can too."

"And then what?"

"War."

"You can't be serious," she whispers. "The Russians? The Chinese?"

Finally the truth hits me. My thoughts are straying into a dark and dangerous place, yet I can recognize a premonition when I sense it. I now know who the Fire Guy is. I haven't gotten to the point where I can trust him, but I will have to rely on him to help me prevent the universe from unravelling.

Unsure of the best way to answer her questions, I shake my head and bite my tongue. "The Titans."

6

Calypso's Knowledge

For over a minute, Marissa stares blankly at me as if what I have just told her has failed to initiate further thought or disbelief. Giving her a moment to think it over, I reverse course and try to explain, "I mean—"

"You can't be serious," Marissa breathes. "Titans, as in Greek?"

I can only bob my head sideways as though I'm offering sympathy. "That's who Fire Guy is. Titans are the progenitors of the gods. His name is—"

"Prometheus."

While my grimace doesn't elicit a favorable reaction, it alters her perception of me. She gapes for a moment and begins a whispered word starting with H, when Miriam emerges from behind the counter. She stands tall and straightens her neck. "Come to my den," she instructs us in a flat, assertive tone.

The backroom is twenty steps behind the counter. The path to it curves between a pair of rotating circular plexiglass racks displaying various knickknacks and memorabilia—everything from keychains to miniature personalized Pennsylvania license plates. The top shelf sports a collection of herbs and spices in tiny glass jars bearing sticker price tags. All part of the 'healing experience,' I presume, and I utter a sly cough when I catch sight of cannabis leaves promising medicinal benefits. Plastic-sleeved "I heart Philly" stickers are an exorbitant price; then again, on Market Street this near to the tourist district, customers worry less about prices than normal shoppers do.

When the sparkly beaded curtain comes into view, I make no remark. Miriam leads the way, drawing the drape to one side, ushering us through the opening.

A button-backed lounge chair faces a polished log-slice coffee table and a matching couch with soft, burnt orange cushions in a room of thick red and green wall-to-wall carpeting. The coffee table holds a thick leather-bound book, cork-bottomed coasters adorned in the same red mosaic pattern as the statue in the store, and a variety of fragrant candles, while the couch boasts tassel-cornered plush pillows and a few black stains. A pendant lamp hanging from the coffered ceiling creates a yellow circle in the middle of the lounge.

Miriam slips her shoes off at the curtain and nudges them with a foot against the waist-high wood laminate baseboard and waist-high 70s-style paneling. "It's been a few years since your second visit," she says, as though she knows the statement will confuse me.

"My ... how many times have I been here?"

"Only once," she says. "This is your first."

"Right," I scoff. "I guess in a crazy world with merged dimensions, that actually makes sense."

"About that," Marissa speaks up. "One thing I didn't tell you about Miriam. She's kind of a seer."

"Convenient," I say, suppressing surprise. "This is a realm where everybody knows more about me than I do."

"Lethe has clouded your memory," Miriam says as I sit at the edge of the sofa, and Marissa leans back beside me, looking proud. Miriam continues, "I cannot tell you everything you have experienced. I don't have a crystal ball that lets me watch your every move, but if legend is correct, you've been through a lot more than you know."

She grabs a pillow from the corner of the sofa and fluffs it before dropping it next to the table. I notice it has a hidden glass shelf a foot below the tabletop that holds many identical jars containing who-knows-what. Before she settles into a cross-legged yoga position on the cushion, I become aware of the perfumed air in this room, a delicate lilac scent with hints of cinnamon. An odd choice, but it seems to relax my brain.

Without speaking, Miriam relights the candles with a miniature steel cigarette lighter from the glass shelf. Then she flips open the book and thumbs through it until she finds a page that appears to offer a diagram of the procedure for this type of healing.

She uncaps a tiny bottle, empties a few drops of oil into her palm, and then rubs her hands together to prepare. Nodding to the edge of the table, she coaxes me into kneeling across from her. "Now close your eyes, Kerry Gearhardt."

When I do as she says, the room becomes dark, and not even the soft yellow light penetrates my closed eyelids. The floor transforms into weathered stone, causing a sharp pain under my knees. When I open my eyes, the room has turned into a dungeon centered around a fire pit with red coals. A woman's face appears next to me, and when I turn to look at her, I see glowing blue eyes and curly amber hair.

"*Sarah.*" My voice seems to make no sound, yet I can hear it echo inside my skull.

As I scan her face, the coals in the fire pit rise through the acrid air and hover over the floor, which melts away until we are hurtling through space in freefall around the glowing red orb.

"*You found me once before, Larry.*"

Her voice sounds ethereal; like mine, it does not disturb the void in which we're rotating. If Miriam has magicked this vision of Sarah, I will scold her with a vicious insult, some variation of "you suck."

"*I know, because you said so. Now I want you to tell me how I did it.*"

"*Have you ever heard your wife or son's voices inside your own head ... like a reflection of their personality?*"

"*Uh...*" This is weird, but I sense that Miriam's voice may crank up the intensity at any moment, which she will claim to be part of the healing.

"*We are all made of stardust. Each of us are particles and minerals mined from the same cloud of matter. The souls closest to us can lie millions of miles apart and the atoms that make us up are entangled. Think of it like a bungee cord connecting particles. When one of us speaks, the vibrations in the cord transfer to the other particle instantly, where the universal speed limit need not apply.*"

I croak as a dusty feeling coats my larynx. *"Have you been speaking with Secretary Harley?"*

"I know the truth, Larry. Think about all those church classes where the Bible takes center stage. Even armed with the sacred text, human beings can only understand a miniscule fraction of it."

The glowing red orb enlarges, and I sense our angular speed has increased, as though the object's mass has doubled within seconds. As I watch its curved surface expanding into a flaming inferno world, I see Sarah's mouth and hair melt in the heat, and behind her wavering image dances a shadowy horned figure wielding a flaming pitchfork.

Use the dark, it commands me, directly into my brain.

The dark swells, erasing the ball of flame cinder by cinder until only a spinning ball of soot remains. When I look back at him, the ball of soot morphs into a wispy cloud, inching toward me. Pain slices through my extremities as a knot throbs inside my head, just beneath my skin. The agony shreds me and I touch my fingertips to my sensitive scalp.

I can hear Miriam's voice, far away, yet crystal clear: "The shroud of memory must fall, great Circe. Bless this Titan with the knowledge he needs and nothing more."

"Titan?" When I emerge from this trance she's placed me in, I'll tear her apart with profane insults.

"There's no eternity in his spirit," she drones, still in darkness, even as the horned demon glowers at me. "Release him from his servitude at last, for those bonds shall devour and defeat him."

Now I don't know which way is up; I'm tumbling head over heels in nothingness, an expanding vacuum that is destroying all celestial light. The boiling pain in my scalp explodes into a shockwave that reduces me to rubble, wiping out my consciousness as it rolls through the limitless ether.

When I regain my senses, I see a barren, ash-covered wasteland that extends further than I can see. My entire body pulsates with torturous agony, and I hear coughing and heaving coming from my left.

There stands a young man; he is near my height, with a few of my own characteristics—a bony forehead, a small nose, and wide-set blue eyes. A younger version of myself.

"My son?" I breathe, not knowing how my brain is forming these thoughts. *"Are you okay?"*

"Not even a little bit." He coughs, spitting up blood and bile.

Another face appears, dissolving into a gray haze, her deep brown eyes pleading with me. I reach out to her as she disappears, mouthing her name. Before I visualize our relationship and its complexity, tears form in the corners of my eyes.

"Vanessa."

Miriam's voice: "The daemons have beaten and bruised you, but you are more than the sum of your weaknesses, Kerry. You are a Conveyor of Light and Shade—a power granted by a princess of Crete, from whom your great Titan ancestors descended."

I furrow my brow and swallow nervously. Somehow, I've known this already, deep inside. That knowledge percolates with an infusion of Miriam's stern voice:

"But I offer you a warning, Kerry, Titan of Light and Shade. Be not deceived. You must use this power for good, or you will no longer be able to wield it. And without it, you will fail in your noble quest."

"I'm going to bring Becky back to her true home," I say. *"And save the universe."*

Colors erupt in the blackness, first blues, then yellows and reds, then all run into an amorphous blur. When shapes gather around me, I sink into a bottomless ocean of sound, closing my eyes before washing up on the other side.

The purple curtain rattles against the paneled wall, shedding a single glittery bead that bounces to a halt on the thick, plush carpet. Marissa's eyes have glossed over, but as she refocuses her attention, she scowls at me before recentering herself.

Miriam still sits cross-legged on the pillow, pinching her thumbs and index fingers together and mouthing a strange, rhythmic chant.

When she opens her eyes, a fresh jolt of energy resides there, unclouded by the tremors of reality. Clarity has transformed her, or at least that's my observation. Then again, perhaps the newfound clarity allows me to see differently than before.

"Do you feel anything?" she asks.

I stammer out, "I ... I feel *something.*"

"More questions?"

My mind has become tense and rigid; I need to lie down before I faint, so I rest my head on the sofa cushions and try to make sense of everything she has shown me.

A Titan of Light and Shade. A younger version of me. A son. And Vanessa. I can only come up with a one-word sentence: "How?"

"Your journey has been revealed," she says. "You must embark on your journey, but don't forget those who have made it necessary."

"You *do* have a son," Marissa interrupts. "Why did you try to hide it?"

I cough and glare at Miriam. "I didn't know."

Marissa mocks, "Uh-huh. Just like that. The good man you are, you forgot the biggest, most important part of your life in search of heroism."

"Well..."

"So now we're teaming up with this Prometheus? What if he betrays you?"

I narrow my eyes. "I'm sure he will. And no, you can't come. I'm not subjecting more innocent people to this interdimensional shit anymore. I'm fairly sure it's causing mind-bending time dilation effects."

"I want to help you," she responds. "And you already decided to let me, because I know Sarah."

When I hear that name, I turn my attention again to Miriam, who grunts as she presses her palms on the edge of the table to lift herself up. The pendant lamp sways for a moment before letting its circle of yellow light settle above the coffee table.

"Can you explain how Sarah knows all this physics stuff?"

"I would think it's obvious," she snaps. "Miriam referred to it as entanglement. Riff on that a moment. Don't you understand what it entails?"

I glance at Marissa, gulping before I speak. "A ... bridge ... that connects us, and that is entanglement. It means we can read each other's thoughts. I just didn't know she understood physics."

"Perhaps she only understands the properties that connect you. You must find the root of that connection if you are to understand it."

Marissa clears her throat. "I can help you with that."

Shooting her a sideways glance, I gather my thoughts into a short sentence: "You must keep in contact with her. Last I knew, she lived in Portland."

"I believe she still does," Marissa says.

Before I'm ready to accept, I frown at Miriam and narrow my eyes. "I don't consciously remember a Vanessa, but she must have been important enough for tears. What do you know?"

"Only what your vision has showed me."

My brain has wild, dark thoughts that I don't know how to corral. If Vanessa is significant and I encountered her where I saw my alleged son, logic implies their fateful connection. I never knew I had a son until now, and there can only be one reason. If I put my thoughts into words my brain might explode. Even though I can't fully articulate it, I feel my heart breaking, and it is a powerful blow at my sense of self.

"Now what about Fire Guy?" Marissa asks. "He says he's coming back this way so you can decide to join him. How are we going to find Sarah and this Vanessa person before we meet him?"

"I have an idea," I say. "But you won't like it."

"Hit me," says Marissa.

Miriam listens with her arms folded as I explain the groundwork of a plan. "I'm going to use time dilation to my advantage. If I can find a portal, we can slip to another dimension, where I still remember this conversation. The only problem is that I have no control over where that dimension will take me. I can only rely on memory, which is still shoddy, even after this healing."

"I'm down for it," says Marissa, wide-eyed.

"You're not ready for it. You need to understand a few things about dimension-hopping."

"So tell me."

I let my mind focus on a single train of thought, and I'm barreling toward that destination at full speed despite any perils that line the tracks.

"Only a few can do it. But I think it might work differently if you're with me. The place we end up going will be my dimension, filled with people and events that have impacted me. If you react personally, you'll get confused about what constitutes reality."

"Hello? Occult dealer."

I fake a smile. "The future might offer you new memories, but don't indulge them, because they aren't real—to you. The past will erase memories of things that haven't happened yet."

She shrugs. "Makes sense, I guess."

"The biggest one: 'Be careful not to die'."

"Shit!" she yells. "Thanks for reminding me."

Suppressing a groan, I continue, "You don't understand. If you die, you cease to exist. You won't even be a memory to anyone. Your whole life is erased."

As I'm saying it, that dark thought begins to take shape in my brain. I allow it to fester there far longer than I should, and as it expands, it takes sorrow to a new extreme. I now know that the reason I don't remember having a son is that he died in a different dimension of time. The only reason I can remember him now is the same reason I remember Vanessa; Circe and Miriam's magic has reconnected me to their memories.

"Except in my case," I add.

And now I have a new task.

7

The Guardian of Io

The candlelight in the back room dims as a wispy puff of smoke curls and drifts toward the coffered ceiling and the pendant lamp. Confusion immobilizes me as I gaze through the smoke at Miriam, while she rearranges her bottles on the shelf beneath the table. She considers me for a moment.

There are so many things to ask her, but for now, a single monstrosity of a question makes my teeth chatter.

Marissa lays her hand comfortingly on my forearm, but her eyes suggest she knows it's not helping. I hope that she will speak soon as I scoot to the edge of the sofa in the smoky room. She stays silent instead, allowing my dark thoughts to continue.

"So what you're saying is, my friend and my son ... that somehow I can find them, bring them back, and everything will be fine? That I won't be guilty and alone for the rest of my pathetic existence? And I'm supposed to believe you've seen everything, like you're the Wicked Witch of the West, only you're the good guy. None of it makes sense, and I'm not sure I trust you."

"You saw what you needed to see," Miriam says, her tone unchanging. Locking eyes with me, she stands up straight, carefully placing the pillow in the corner of the sofa and patting it. "Healing sometimes comes with side effects."

"Such as generational trauma? Disorienting ... whatever the hell this is."

"Ker," warns Marissa.

"Don't you dare ... call me that." I clench my teeth with the tension in my gut while I chide her, even though her use of my nickname is little more than an accident from my cutting her off.

"You don't have to take it out on her," says Marissa.

"Who should I take it out on, then? Fire Guy?"

As I accost her, her eyes seem to gloss over. Her reaction would have made me even more enraged except I'm not prepared to go there. I calm down; I feel like I'm doing the right thing even though I don't know where I'm going.

"I don't think you understand what I'm saying. Miriam has helped you, but she's not the hero of this saga, you are. You know your next step, and I'm coming with you."

With a lump in my throat, I rasp an unconvincing response. For some reason, I can persuade people to join me without issue, but when I attempt to warn them of the implications, they either don't believe me or they don't care.

Adventure can be a fantastic change of pace, but if it kills you, you're no better off. Why can't people see that?

As if she can hear my thoughts, Marissa answers, "Some people would rather die from an enormous beast than from cancer."

"Cancer as in the Crab?"

She shifts her feet. "This might come as a surprise, but I don't believe in astrology."

"Same here." Breathing out helps calm me further as Miriam adjusts books on a shelf made of decorative carved slats behind me. I hear her dusting off one book and placing another next to it. If Marissa were serious, I'd criticize her. She doesn't understand my personal knowledge of Greek legends, which is probably for the best. If she did, she might lead me in too many directions, only hindering my goals.

"What do you think bungee jumpers fear more?" Her expression changes to one of humor. "A failed triple bypass or going splat on a rock?"

Frowning, I shake my head to show I don't want to hear the answer.

"Risk is its own reward."

As I glare at her, the smoke dissipates, leaving an enrapturing aroma with the brisk scent of cinnamon. Miriam dawdles at the end of the couch, and folds her arms across her ribs, as though waiting for us to leave.

Marissa carries on, "And it's not like you're so cautious yourself. You ran off to God-knows-where to do something you had no business doing. People who swallow swords shouldn't tell others to be careful with knives."

Miriam chuckles and she paces behind the table. At the end of the room there is a stack of boxes piled up to the ceiling, containing old paperwork, rejected supplies, or memorabilia she hasn't yet shelved. It makes the room feel less artistic and more utilitarian. But how had she balanced the boxes in such neat rows over ten feet high without them collapsing? I don't see a ladder anywhere.

I feel uneasy when I notice a black doorway; it feels like I'm being watched by a tall figure standing behind it, and I picture eyes in that darkness watching over me. I'm thinking it leads to Miriam's second floor apartment where she keeps her ancient relics.

"You know when I said that you'd get along with my wife—I take it back."

Marissa shrugs. "Thanks."

"I meant that as a compliment."

Her laugh signals closure; without a witty retort, she withdraws her hand from my forearm, presses her palms against the worn knees of her faded jeans, and stands.

I groan as I follow, and Miriam reacts like a chiropractor seeking payment. Right … I'm penniless. Perhaps I should have mentioned it before I had her fling me into another dimension.

"I'm sure you're ready to turn in for the night," I stammer, looking past her to the door, which now holds back a dim light.

"That your way of saying you're not gonna pay me?"

Damn seer with penetrating insight.

"We'll get it squared away in the future," Marissa offers.

Miriam hazards a knowing grin. "Of course you will. Right after you face the Giants and plunder their treasures. I give it eight weeks."

Is she being facetious or making a prophecy? It doesn't matter. She's letting me off the hook for now and I'll consider that a win.

"Don't want to keep you up," Marissa says, issuing a pleasant smile. "We've got to run anyway. See you in about eight weeks."

Miriam leaves her backroom, parting the curtains to let us through. Taking up a broom standing idle in a narrow slot between shelves, she whisks us past the rotating display stands. The glint of a gem catches my eye as I pass, and outside, a car with bright yellow headlights idles at the curb. We head towards the exit and open the door without speaking.

As we emerge, the car revs its motor, nudges forward, and lets its engine die. Clouds have covered the city over the last hour and a few sprinkles of rain splash onto the car's windshield as the door swings open.

The driver is wearing a black velvet bowler hat and has a newspaper tucked under his arm, looking as though he's just stepped out of a time machine. He might be quite presentable at a 1930s board meeting in New York. As he notices me, the rain intensifies, and the light from the street-lamps sparks a neat sheen in his eyes. He smiles and strokes his chin before pulling out the newspaper and leaning back against the brick wall under the overhang.

"Hello, Secretary," I say.

Marissa tugs on my forearm as if to escort me along the sidewalk. By the time we reach the end of the block, my heart has settled once again, allowing rational thought into my brain. Gazing back at Harley's station reveals that the old man is sipping a cup of coffee as he settles beneath the overhang, out of the rain.

Raindrops wet my hair and trickle down my face like solemn tears, as Marissa stares at me.

"You called him Secretary," she says.

"I knew a guy once who observed this corner. Smartest son of a bitch I ever met. Good friend. He moved on up after he dined with Mayor Archinson. Have you heard of him?"

She thinks, then shakes her head. The rain is straightening her hair and streaking her mascara, but she doesn't seem perturbed. Her spirit is still in deep sleep because of me, buried beneath the mounds of memory and alarm working through her soul.

Her dedication might lead to remorse in the future, but I'm grateful to have her now. I may share ideas with her when we're out of the rain.

The raindrops hit my flesh, feeling like painful memories of my fallen son. Walking to the corner by the bookshop, I try to create a plan in my mind.

A few blocks away, there's an alley, a narrow receiving dock between glass residential towers near the garage I parked in when I first came to meet Harley. It feels like eons have passed since then, and perhaps they have. In the last few weeks, I have noticed something troubling that is weighing on my heart. Time travel disrupts the normal flow of time and can cause paradoxes, because theoretical physicists claim that at scale, time is elastic. I need to solve this paradox to save Becky—and the universe.

When you're young, time flows in only one direction at a constant rate. You cannot change it or hurry it, no matter how often you ask your parents what's taking so long to get to your destination.

After the death of a loved one, spiritual advisers tell us that time heals all wounds, but now I understand how foolish that sounds. Time might heal old trauma, but it also creates additional pain.

"That's interesting," Marissa says, patronizing me. It takes me a moment to realize she's reacting to my description of Secretary Harley.

"Fascinating." I wait for the crosswalk to show the little illuminated pedestrian and cross the street. Marissa follows saying nothing, though I know the wheels in her head are turning. Overhead, the sky darkens to an ominous shade as the storm approaches from the south.

In ten minutes, we're both shivering. The alley offers little shelter; instead of creating a barrier from the wind, blocking the slanted raindrops, it channels the rain into a two-inch-deep rivulet toward a drain while the wind howls and swirls in the narrow corridor. Along the perimeter, parapet caps channel the water into gigantic beads that slam onto the cracked pavement like exploding water bombs. When one slaps my head, I feel the chill of the icy water trickling between my eyes before falling to my feet.

"We're about to get good and lost," I say, knowing where the portal will lead us.

The back corner of the brick, still stained black from neglect, invites me. Its energy tugs at me as I stalk toward it. Marissa hesitates at first but follows behind. I need only touch the rough brick, and the world will change.

Holding my breath, I reach out toward the corner, grasping her hand to take her for the ride of her life. The stars twirl around us.

The waves lap at the rocky shore in the moonlight as a solitary kayaker rows toward the center of the lake, a fishing rod anchored against the sidewall of the vessel. When I feel Marissa tugging at my hand, I lead her towards the water's edge, which reflects the moonlight with glimmering, hallucinogenic splotches of radiance, evoking dread. The island stands undisturbed a quarter of a mile away, shaded by a dense forest of deciduous trees.

"Beautiful," she whispers.

"You're probably wondering where we are."

She sighs, and I turn around to face her so that the lake house stands gray beyond her shoulder. As I gaze at it, a sense of mourning passes through me. This dimension has a trick up its sleeve, but I can't access it through the lake house. We must instead travel to the island, climb up the slope to the cabin, and vanish inside.

Weighing potential outcomes, I scan the shoreline for a canoe or craft so as to avoid wading through reeds on the way to the island. Standing tall, I wave my arm at the angler, trying to catch his attention. He glances up at me as his line disturbs the water and the rod curls under the weight of a large fish.

He grabs at the line, pulling it back over his shoulder and spinning the reel, which spreads a zipping sound across the tranquil lake. At any moment, he may haul in a monster catch so he can pose with it in a picture to be framed for his office cubicle.

When I let myself smile at the idea I become anxious, my emotions now heavy and sad, as if the rain is making them feel soggy. Looking beyond the dock, I see small waves in the water which are moving into the grassy reeds a hundred feet away. I stand straight to look in that direction, hoping Marissa will know where we're headed without me having to say anything.

An owl hoots behind us, deep in the trees across the road from the row of houses skirting the lakeshore. The hills beyond hide many of the secrets that haunted these shores since before Europeans settled here. Ancient Natives may once have worshipped and hunted here, stirring hidden magic.

Together, Marissa and I march past the pier toward the edge of the pebbly beach, to where the knee-high grass tufts sway. From there, the land slants upward through stands of wild grass until it reaches the tree line, creating a wide lake inlet where the reeds grow through the mud at the lakeshore. The grass is thicker now than I remember.

Marissa lets go of my arm and faces the marshland with me. Taking the first step feels natural. The ground gives a little beneath my feet as I wade through the waist-high grass, which thickens ten feet from the open water. When the grass reaches my face, I turn to make sure Marissa is following alright. A clump of mud has swallowed her shoe, and she pulls her foot out of the bog and shakes it.

"Are you sure you don't want to wait and steal the fisherman's boat?" she asks.

"Might be a few hours," I surmise. "I don't think we have that long. We need to hurry."

She grunts and slogs through the mud to keep up with me. Our pace is too slow. We should have reached the stag-horn tree in less than thirty minutes, but time is ticking by faster.

Expecting the journey to be easier the farther from the open water we tread, I try to keep up a good pace, but ten minutes pass before I spot the tree. We've wandered thirty yards off course, but the mud thins as the land slopes upward. After ten more minutes, we exit the reeds and I search the rocky bar, where I had once found a boat. Not this time.

Marissa shivers, understanding that we'll have to swim through the narrow channel between the bar and the island. The air is crisp, and the water will be hypothermic.

As we trudge toward the water, I wrap my arm around her to warm her up. She hunches her shoulders and tilts her head away from me but doesn't wrestle free. Aware of the time, I turn to look at where the angler was an hour ago. Having caught his prize, he is sailing farther away, past the end of the island toward the lake's other shore, where another row of houses looks out over the tranquil waters.

Marissa dips a toe into the water to gauge its temperature, shivers, and then says, "Not bad. Fine night for a swim."

"If you're okay with it."

She shrugs. "Don't see any other way. Besides, didn't you say we're on a time limit?"

I nod. "Want to know why?"

"I have a few ideas," she says. "But go on."

Describing my feelings makes me feel better. Using logic to describe things makes me less sad and more enthusiastic, a trait Becky had noticed long before we got married. I can't remember exactly what she said, but I can feel the icy water chilling me as I wade in. The water splashes to my chest and presses my clothes against my skin.

Marissa starts swimming before I do. The water seems to vibrate as we near the island, but I dare not look around.

It only takes a few minutes to cross the channel and reach dry land. I squeeze the muddy water out of my shirt and lumber up the slope into the trees. Marissa follows, and just as I start to speak, the ground begins to rumble.

"That might be one reason we need to hurry," I say.

"What is it?"

I gulp. In the center of the lake, the water bubbles like soda, spreading foamy ripples toward the island. I squeeze her hand and lead her deeper into the trees. Our wet clothes make the journey harder, weighing us down so we can't run.

"Don't want to know," I pant.

But then it shows itself; tentacles rise out of the turbid lake and the moonlight glints off their wet, leathery scales. The monster pushes toward the shore, crawling on the points of its outstretched appendages. We hurry up the slope, but the tentacles, shooting higher than the branches of the trees, reach the shore before we make it to the wooden porch.

It seems to have spotted us and lunges out of the water. I grasp the wooden handrail, squeeze my eyes shut, and remember the book on the table inside.

The Soul of the Baron.

Energy floods into my veins, causing my fingers to glow and the monster to roar. Trees topple in its wake as the beast lumbers through the forest toward us, its scaly tentacles slapping at the water's surface and lopping branches off trees as it climbs. It's big enough to gobble down the cabin in a few bites, yet it pauses as we back against the whitewashed siding boards.

My extremities glow brighter when my fingers curl. As Marissa clutches my hand, I can see the energy radiating through her wrist and her wet hair standing on end. When my light surges, so does hers.

We escape inside not a moment too soon, wheezing from adrenaline and cold. I notice the wooden table and the floors have been cleaned; someone lives here now. I gulp in warm air, hoping a hunter won't emerge from the closet wielding a shotgun. The book lies at the edge of the table next to a glass half-filled with water. I gaze at it for a moment, thinking fast as the floorboards tremble.

The monster hasn't given up. It roars in the humid night and the entire house vibrates with the sound.

With narrowed eyes Marissa observes as our clothes and feet drench the floor beneath our feet. The entire cabin creaks as the tremors loosen the nails on the floors, and shingles and roof members peel off, allowing the moonlight to filter through the gaps.

As I take up the book, hold it to my eyes, and watch the cabin spin, the monster pours out a storm of spittle and fury. A shining blue light hovers in the center of the hallway. Still carrying the book, I reach out, move toward it, and feel my navel tighten as light explodes around us and we are whisked through time and space.

8

Gemini Fire

The midday sun blazes overhead. A sticky humidity bathes my skin in sweat, sticking my clothes to my body. Flashing from hypothermic cold to humid heat is something I didn't prepare for. I wipe the sweat from my brow and look around.

The staging lot of Bones Holdings houses stacked cast-iron pipe lengths in standard lengths, each stamped with plain white lettering indicating the manufacturer and the standards it complies with. A semitransparent plastic tarp is draped over part of the stack, allowing a view into the ends, ringed with dry dirt and spider silk. The trailers are arranged in a horseshoe shape, where the subcontractors gather around them and the three interconnected doublewides serving as Bones's field headquarters.

During their lunch break on a typical day, hard-hatted workers stroll through the staging area with metal lunchboxes and clipboards, never removing their personal protective equipment. The only one examining the piled goods right now is a tall, bearded man in a flannel shirt. Without glancing up at us, he squints at the figures on his clipboard, pushes his goggles up his nose, and scribbles some notes.

Bones Holdings requires PPE inside gated areas during construction hours, a rule few care to break, but our lack of safety equipment doesn't even turn his head. I walk up to the diamond-plate ramp that leads to Bones's main trailer doors where an outside air conditioner runs nonstop. Since all the windows on this side are covered, I assume the air inside is cool, which would be a pleasant change from the summer afternoon temperature that heats up our sub's trailer.

"Are we going to discuss what just happened?" Marissa looks me over.

I raise my eyes to the rising steel skeleton two hundred yards away, standing a half dozen floors shorter than when I last saw it. I already know we've emerged into the past. And if my intuition is correct, Sarah will be here today.

"Not sure that would do any good," I reply, creeping up the ramp and clinging to the tubular steel handrails. "I'll give you three guesses where we are."

She looks around. Guessing the name of the general contractor can't be hard; the big red B with hex bolt shaped holes should give it away without the black block lettering spelling out the rest of the contractor's name. "She's here, isn't she?"

"Judging by the height of the building, she must be."

"Are they going to hammer us for not wearing hardhats?"

Explaining contractor policy becomes less important on the list of daily topics of conversation, and my head hurts to hear her inquire about it. "Visitors don't always come in wearing them," I say. "They keep extras on hand, just in case."

"Might protect us from whatever that thing was ... I'm sure there was..."

I clear my throat and pull at the door handle. "Best not to worry. The memory's going to be gone in twenty minutes anyway."

"You seemed like you knew your way around," she explains. "Like you've been there a few times."

I grunt. "Good eye."

The wall behind the reception desk welcomes all visitors to the field headquarters. Behind the wall, a printer zips out page after page of specifications or ASI instructions while a worker clacks away on a keyboard. Wheels rolling across spiked rubber chair mats are followed by the click of heels on the hollow plywood floor.

Christie's wavy blonde hair reflects the sunlight diving through the window. She combs a strand of hair behind the earpiece of her glasses and greets us without remarking on our appearance. Both Marissa and I are dripping wet and dirty, our matted and tangled hair sticking to our scalps. Christie's hair is neatly knotted near her shoulder.

"You're late," she says. "Jamal said he sent you here an hour ago. I have the specification update for Div 23 ready, if you'll give me a moment. ASI-326 doesn't change much, but you may also want 21 and 22, if you think Jamal will want them."

I've been away so long that this sounds vague and unappealing, so I simply nod. I notice Marissa's tattered jeans leg, and decide she probably caught it on a rock or thorn. Her once-white shoes are caked in brown dust and mud.

"Mind asking for Sarah, too?" I ask Christie.

"Of course."

"Jamal's the foreman," I tell Marissa as an aside. "My boss. I sure as hell hope I was on time this morning."

"I'm not following," she says, casting her eyes to the end of the foyer, where a blank wall exhibits before-and-during photographs of the construction site. Six eleven-by-seventeen sheets of paper display the colored bars of the official construction schedule.

"Not following what?"

"She says you were here an hour ago, but you were at the lake."

Frowning again, I explain: "Say you're working in your shop today. That version of you has disappeared, replaced by this one. Same with me. Good thing it's lunchtime or Jamal would give me an earful."

My voice catches in my throat as an amber-haired woman rounds the corner and grins at me. "Sarah."

"Oh my God!" Sarah squeaks, hurrying to hug Marissa.

She turns her head toward me. "Hi, Larry, thought I heard your voice."

I can't utter a single word. I let them catch up, sharing small talk I don't find all that interesting. Interdimensional time travel hasn't changed this version of my personality; I'm as pathetic as ever.

"It's so nice to see you again!" Marissa exclaims.

"Been a few years," Sarah says, combing her hand through her curly locks and placing a hand on her hip. "I didn't know you knew each other."

"Never seen her before," I mumble.

"What brings you over here today, Larry? Collecting that ASI revision?"

"Uh ... yeah, I guess. Among other things."

"Can I help you with something?"

I hesitate. Now that she mentions it ... I don't know where to start. Even uttering one word will sound crazy to her, causing her to grow even clumsier than I am, if that's possible. We'll need to let the conversation flow naturally, something this version of me struggles with. Having Marissa here might smooth it out.

"*The* Kerry Gearhardt," Marissa begins.

"Larry, you mean."

God. Telling Sarah the truth now will change the future. She's not supposed to know my real name yet.

"Yeah," I stammer. "Guess she heard it wrong."

Marissa gawks at me, smooths out her shirt, and tries to dry it. Sarah either hasn't noticed that we look fresh out of a swamp or doesn't have the nerve to comment on our appearance. That might work better than trying to explain it to her.

"Okay, *Larry*," she quips. "You were just telling me about this coworker you used to have, and when I told you I've known her longer, you acted..."

Unnatural.

"I thought you'd taken one too many laps around the pool."

Sarah scans our muddy, soaking bodies. "I see."

"Don't know what you're talking about," I grumble. My memory is already fading. We'll have no time to chat if we ever want to make it out of this dimension.

"Come to think of it," Marissa says, "I could use a refresher right now. *Larry?*"

Sarah beats me to it. "Sure—we can catch up after I get off work. You like Chinese food?"

Their voices trail away as I focus on a carpet stain under a potted plant, whose large plastic leaves glow in the afternoon sun. I must leave this dimension ... I have no time to revive old friendships for the universe's survival.

And that presents a monumental problem. I can't bring it up here without Sarah thinking I'm crazy, and I sure as hell can't escort her into another dimension where it will make sense. Doing so may cause yet another knot in the paradox.

And then I remember something, causing my heart to sink even further; if Sarah became invisible in the future because of a glitch in time travel, could it be that I started her on that path? A lump forms in the back of my throat. That can't be true, yet it makes more sense than anything else I can come up with.

"Sounds like a plan," I say catching them up and gathering Marissa's hand in mine.

"Wait, you two are dating?"

"Sarah," I say, frowning, "where did that stain on the carpet come from?"

She looks and smiles. "No idea. I think I noticed it on my first or second day. Bones uses this same trailer complex on every major job, so the stain could be years old. But when that plant sheds leaves I'm usually the one to vacuum them up."

A plan forms in my brain—I can't believe I'm going to do this. She could accuse me of kidnapping, and I could end up in jail. A large leaf is coming loose from the plant at eye level. I stroke its tender veins and feel the sweat burning on my forehead.

"You think you could hand me that stapler, Sarah?" I ask, peering at the various office supplies on the reception desk.

My toes are at the edge of the stain. When she hands me the stapler, I squeeze Marissa's hand tighter and shuffle to the middle of the stain.

Pressure tugs at my abdomen, and the office vanishes into a sea of stars swirling through the heavens. Adrenaline pulses through me as a knot of pain hammers at my scalp and my extremities are set alight.

The wormhole spins us through time and space before we land in the center of a narrow hallway where wooden floors shimmer in the pale moonlight.

Mist envelops us as stars flash before my eyes. We're being pulled out of the heavens through an opening rimmed in the hazy blue light of distant stars.

The blue catches fire as we rip through it, vanishing before licking at the walls or ceiling. All at once, Sarah's expression is unhappy and morose; she lets her arms dangle at her sides. She doesn't speak at all. Her face is now pale, and her hair is tinged with white.

"Now that's a trip," Marissa jokes.

"I don't understand," Sarah says. "How ... Larry? Please tell me I'm dreaming."

Choking on my words, I let it all out. "I'm afraid not. We just traveled through time. And I have a few questions now that we're in your future."

"My future?"

"*Larry* has been around the lake a few times," Marissa says.

"I have, in a literal sense," I explain. "What I want to know is how. Think about it."

Sarah shakes her head, looking around the well-manicured front room, where a thick log sits in the fireplace and the new furniture squares a seating area. A shirt and a pair of binoculars lie on a minimalist table. "*You* want *me* to explain?"

"How did you come to Bones? Where did you work before? Where did you go to high school? Do you have a past life? What did you do?"

Marissa fakes a smile. "Solid first date questions."

Sarah takes a long time to think about it, which makes me think she may be trying to concoct a lie. These questions may seem unfair, but deep in my heart, I know I trust her.

You know how to find me.

I've always known how to find her. But why is it so important? The answer might have a lasting impact on me and change who I am. I am afraid to find out as it may separate me from Becky, and that would haunt me forever.

"I was recommended for the job, I think," Sarah says, her voice trailing away into the dark corners of the room while I listen for the details. "When the company I worked for went under. My former boss said she knew a manager at Bones; that company was called Heartland Office Systems. I went to high school in Minnesota, and I don't think I've had a past life."

"Minnesota," I murmur. It can't be.

"For a few years, anyway, before my family moved to Pennsylvania, where I've lived ever since. I graduated from South Track High ... named because it's on the south side of town next to the railroad tracks."

Shockwaves spread through my body, chilling my flesh. "South Track."

That's the link.

9

Dreaming Hypnos

The longer Sarah stays in this realm, the more luster she loses. While I'm keen to keep this visit brief, I need answers before I can go ahead, and bringing her back to the office will have disastrous consequences. She frowns, perhaps trying to mask her authentic emotions, even as the starlight in her eyes fades away.

"I went to Ironside," I say, "your big rival."

The light blue mist swirling behind Sarah resembles a whirlpool suddenly coming back to life after being inactive, creating a feeling of urgency. Sarah struggles to speak, and as I anticipate her reaction, I notice a hint of an idea forming in her face. I am trying to control my emotions to avoid escalating the situation and potentially ruining our interaction.

"I don't have rivals," Sarah says in a melancholy voice. "Only allies."

"You went to high school in the same city?" Marissa says. "Quick, someone call the cops!"

I glare my displeasure at Marissa's derisive comment, and although she seems to want to double down, her posture eases, showing she's at least willing to listen.

I ask her, "My wife thinks everything happens for a reason—do you believe that?"

"Not if that reason is a higher power," Marissa says, shrugging. "Cosmic mysteries, however, often have an underlying explanation for anyone willing to look for one."

I frown. "Uh..."

"I mean, if you think about it, the bigger the coincidence, the less likely it seems to be organic."

"I want to go back," Sarah mutters, fidgeting. "Tell me why it matters on the way."

Nodding my head in assent, I respond in the only way that makes sense to me. "I don't have all the answers. It just seems like that was a huge coincidence." Turning to Marisa, I continue: "Do cosmic mysteries often unite people through time? I have my doubts; it could be the work of the gods."

"Why do gods always break their own rules?" Marissa quips.

"Of course I want to get you back," I whisper, turning again to Sarah. "I want to understand our connection and why we have it."

Sarah backs away toward the sparking blue nebula, her lips twitching. "Con ... connection? I don't feel comfortable with this, Larry."

"Do you ever hear my voice?

For a woman who's so easy to get along with, her body language catches my attention, helping me to realize that I'm being 'creepy.' So I alter my approach.

"I mean, do you ever feel like you're passing basic thoughts through space to someone who can understand you?"

"I guess ... I don't understand what you're saying."

"Sci-fi addicts call it telepathy or something similar, but I've recently learned that the phenomenon is real. Basically, chemical pathways in our brains can become entangled, like wave-particle duality, where all matter behaves as both particles and waves. Scientists claim that sub-atomic particles can share information, seemingly faster than the speed of light, because of the wave nature..."

"Lots of scientific mumbo-jumbo," Marissa scoffs in the background. "And you're butchering it."

"Yeah, my wife also says I get carried away."

"I don't understand," Sarah repeats.

Trying to explain it is difficult, and I'm sure to misrepresent the governing scientific theory, but I must share basic ideas with her if I want to convince her that we share a connection deeper than the city where we both went to high school.

I try again: "Think of it like a jump rope that takes the shape of a wave. A tiny vibration at one end of the rope transfers to the other end faster than light because both ends are part of the whole. The wave functions as both a particle and a wave."

"Are you really qualified to talk about particle physics?" Marissa asks.

I try to defuse the tension by offering a hollow grin. "Of course not. But you planted the seed yourself, and I'm just letting it germinate."

Sarah smirks at Marissa, asking incredulously, "Are you saying you're into science?"

Now I suppress my own smile, as I don't want to make Sarah more uncomfortable.

"You'd be surprised how the sciences influence the occult, and vice versa," Marissa explains. "Why do you think religions have conflated the two for thousands of years?"

"Maybe they have a point," Sarah remarks.

"Right, but it's more of a mutual symbiosis than a nefarious conspiracy."

The conversation has gotten away from me. In the tidy, dust-free hallway with spotless white walls, I gather myself in order to stop Sarah and Marissa arguing, which will benefit none of us.

"What's your point?" I try to read Marissa's expression, but she's gone rigid and pale. "The scientific connection—"

"Hypnosis," she interrupts. "Do you believe in it?"

"Just as fervently as astrology."

"Mental health professionals have advocated for it for generations, so this is an example of science cooperating with the occult. Sleep can have powerful effects we don't yet understand."

"Are you sure we don't understand it simply because it's just some sideshow garbage for magicians to use to dupe the easily deceived masses?"

"There's a difference between the sideshow version and the psychiatric version."

"And I don't suppose you can perform a real hypnosis," I say.

Marissa shrugs and rolls her eyes. "I'm not sure I'm qualified, but I know a few tricks to induce sleep."

"And I thought I already *was* asleep," Sarah rasps.

Croaking and clenching my biceps, I relent. "Then let's do it. I could use a good nap."

Marissa looks around to gauge whether this will be a suitable environment. An old-school fireplace of dark red bricks sports a black television screen set high over the mantle. At the hearth, a litter of woodchips and splinters meet a braided rope rug showing a moose motif. Fresh ashes suggest someone's imminent return to the cabin, possibly with a shotgun.

A crumpled throw lies over the upholstered back of a couch, which faces a sharp-edged coffee table and a rocking chair sporting a woven squab cushion with a floral pattern.

"Not sure this will do," she says. "Got any other alternative dimensions we can try?"

I shake my head, sharing an uncomfortable glance with Sarah. "Bad idea. Let's bring her back to Philly first."

"But I think she deserves to understand what's really going on," Marissa says. "If we go back to the construction site, it'll never happen."

"I think she deserves safety," I protest.

"And I think she's perfectly capable of making her own decisions," Sarah cuts in, irritated.

"Well ... do you trust me?"

"You're a good person, Larry. I've always seen it. I think it's because you're a good listener. Your eyes give you away if you try to lie; you're without any guile."

Weird explanation—is that supposed to make me feel encouraged, or mocked? Even though I've always followed my instincts, I try to listen to others as well because I don't have all the answers. Going against this might lead to distrust or even hatred, and conflict always ruins well-thought-out plans. I ask, "Is that a compliment?"

Her eyes light up at my question. "Do you want it to be?"

Whatever I try, I think I'm going to get away with it, and that might worry me in the future. A normal person might just go with the easy "thanks," and leave it at that, but I've lied to myself too many times.

I gulp. "I just have one question. What did you mean when you said you don't have rivals?"

She smiles although she knows she's about to embark on a terrifying journey through time and space. "You could say I don't subscribe to the notion that life is a series of competitions where you see adversaries everywhere. If you look for enemies under every rock, you'll find one in the mirror. I'd rather make friends than foes."

Such a sensible explanation might elicit a similar reply, but I need answers, and to get them, I need her consent.

"So you're saying you're okay with just one more jump? Then we'll take you back to the trailer."

My question seems to make the situation more mysterious than it needs to be. She relaxes her shoulders, gives in, and says, "Don't make me regret it."

I'm worried that I'll be the one to regret it first, but saying so might make her change her mind, thus ending our connection. If I'm correct, what will I have achieved? If I'm right, what will I gain? Understanding my life experiences seems insignificant compared to destroying the universe by breaking the time continuum. Then again, if this encounter doesn't leave me more enlightened than when I entered it, the entire affair will be time wasted as the Titans wage war on Earth.

"I know a place," I say, feeling the cool air bind with the saliva in my throat. "Just to warn you, we're going to fall onto a bed in a house across the lake, and I don't know what will happen when we get there."

"How do you know that?" Marissa asks.

"I..."

The muscles in my throat tense. She's asked a valid question, and the answer I'm about to give surprises even me. I can't explain why I remember, but I do. This revelation challenges everything I thought I knew about the rules of the universe. If I can break time, then what else can I break?

"I've done it before," I explain.

"I guess the rumors about *the* Kerry Gearhardt are true," she says.

Taking Marissa's hand in mine, I guide Sarah toward the closet door. Dust coats the door's hinges from being by the lake for such a long time, so it hasn't been opened in a while. Looking around the room makes me worried.

If someone lives in this cabin, the lake house may belong to someone else now, or Becky could still be using it for vacations. This side quest could lead to disaster.

Before I grasp the handle, I scan the living and dining rooms. The new owner has replaced every cabinet door with genuine oak slats and solid wood panels; the ogee edges shine in the dim light, reflecting a blue color like moonlight through a half glass of water that lies next to a copy of *Soul of the Baron.*

The empty pendant light fixture casts a rustic shadow, and for a panicked moment I can see the shadow move, sending chills through my body. At any second, the owner might return, carrying a rifle to shoot us for breaking in.

I swing open the closet door, curl my fingers around Sarah's dainty hand, and step backwards.

Falling. Again the weightless sensation between expectation and panic tightens my stomach, as we tumble through the stars, pass into a sea of darkness, and bounce onto the bed in unison and up to the textured ceiling.

A giant mirror hangs on the wall above an empty TV stand with seeded glass doors. Blue light from the moon fills the room, making it hard for me to see what happens next. I start to panic when I realize something is different. The unkempt blankets indicate a change of style. Becky doesn't like knitted blankets with tassels; she's always preferred a more modern look with clean lines. As an art student, she decorated her living space with paintings, books, and sculptures.

The dark bedposts and fluffy carpet reflect the stylistic flourishes of colonial decor, and the mix of designs in the room is not what Becky would chose.

Panicked, I realize we aren't alone. A door closes nearby, and down the hall a light flickers on, showing a tall shadow lumbering toward the bedroom. We have seconds to react.

There's nowhere to hide. I jump to my feet beside the bed, cueing Marissa and Sarah to do the same. When they predictably react slower, the shadow skulks past the open door, but then stops as though he can sense our presence.

The sudden attack catches me off guard. The stranger bursts through the door and head-butts me in the stomach. Taking advantage of his vulnerable position I strike back with my fists while the two women gasp in fear.

"I'm going to kill you!" the stranger grunts.

Twisting my hips, I grab him and throw him to the ground, kicking and punching him. He screams and spits, trying to defend himself by blocking my punches. Rather than letting himself succumb, he pelts me with defensive strikes to immobilize me. Once he has stopped my progression of punches, he knees me in the groin, pushes me off and, enraged, punches me in the head.

Howling, Marissa lunges to my defense. With two enemies to deal with, the attacker's assaults become more random. Feeling the situation shift, I circle round him like a boxer preparing to strike. He hesitates, gathers his courage, and glares at me. "Get out of my house now," he warns. "My neighbor is going to kill you."

He's unarmed, so I put up my hands, and back away toward the door as he lumbers to his knees. My muscles tighten in defense.

"We don't mean you any harm," I say, scuttling out into the hallway with Sarah and Marissa.

"You're going to regret it, you son of a bitch!"

Now would be a good time for the lake to do its thing, I think as I remember the naiads trying to drown me. I glance toward the bay windows as we sprint through the living room with the stranger hot on our heels. Hearing the squeaky hinges of the closet door confirms my worst fears.

My heart hammers in my chest.

Click.

Sarah gasps, throws herself at my back, and whispers something as the dimensions flash by us.

BOOM!

A storm rages over the lake, propelled by a powerful torrent of wind. Billions of icy raindrops plunge into the depths of the turbid water as the illusion transforms.

As the lake boils and splashes, a thousand dainty fingers dance on the surface, revealing inky, blotted arms that glimmer in the moonlight as they make waves scatter in every direction.

A flash of evil red light sets the lakeside aflame, chasing the tormented shadows of the helpless trees. Millions of limbs are clenched tight to absorb the heat. The fire glows brighter as the seconds wear on.

Lying flat on my back, I can't see anything, but I hear tormented breathing. Then voices whisper an incantation in an unfamiliar tongue.

Slowly, my brain begins to understand what they're saying,

"You are not alone, Kerry, Titan of Light and Shade."

My heart is beating fast and loud in my chest as I look up at the starlit sky. I open my eyes and see blood pumping from wounds on my body. The gunshot has torn red, bloody gashes across my leg. Sarah is next to me, struggling to recover from the shock. Splotches of blood stain her jeans leg crimson as she huddles over me, breathing my name. The last thing I can see is Marissa trying to disarm the stranger, and then I black out.

When the landscape transforms into a stunning view of downtown Philadelphia, the sun warms my arms and legs in a friendly embrace. The city is rotating as though perched on a Lazy Susan as my heartbeat settles in my chest. This time, the voices are clearer.

"You are a Titan, Kerry." Her voice exudes a familiar charm, branding the image of her long braids into my brain. *"When you look at the stars, you will find Callisto, the Great Bear."*

Tears leak onto my cheeks as the city continues to spin.

"You know how to find me."

"That's Charlotte Bronte, Kerry."

When I close my eyes again, a void of expansive black engulfs me, boiling over with a stain of oil-black sorrow infecting the scarred sky.

"I love you, Dad."

The words ring in my ears until they lose all meaning. Around me I am aware that the city stretches into darkness where reflective towers meet stacks of illuminated squares a thousand feet high. All that's left of my memories are fragments of old regrets, invading my every thought with despair.

10

Cronus Disorder

With the shotgun leaning against the sofa's armrest, its barrel tucked between the arm and the cushion, the occupant buries his face in his hands, looking through his fingers at his feet. He wears a pair of ankle-high black socks that show a few inches of skin beneath his red plaid pajama bottoms.

His long hair is still wet from the shower and drapes near his shoulders. He watches as Marissa stands with her feet apart, ready should he make any sudden movement. She has turned on a standing lamp in the corner, and the diffuse light paints a blotchy yellow circle on the ceiling next to a decorative bookcase displaying a diverse array of books and movies. Stacked firewood in the hearth creates a rustic appeal that lends the room an intriguing campfire aroma. But instead of peace, there is an atmosphere of chaos and dread.

"How was the nap?" Marissa asks without prying her eyes from her hostage.

"Uh…"

I look to my right and see Sarah lying on her side, her hair tangled and her shirt rucked up over her belly. Her wavy hair has tangled into a clump on the floor next to her head. Marissa has wedged a couch pillow under her head to make her more comfortable.

"What…" I gag when the pain tugs at my calf. "The. Hell—just happened?"

"You invaded my home," the man says through gritted teeth.

Without taking her eyes off him, Marissa relaxes her arms and speaks to me. "How does it feel? Can you stand?"

I can't move my legs. It feels as if they are welded to the floor. But in this case, feeling pain is a good sign. "I ... I don't know."

"Hope that shot makes you limp for years," the man grates out.

I glare at him. To take charge of the situation, he would only need to load the shotgun. And his muscular upper body appears strong enough to overpower Marissa. She's no match for him with me wounded and Sarah out for the count.

The blood seeps through her jeans leg, making an opaque circle on the denim and showing the gun's scattershot had grazed her leg before hitting mine. If either of us had been hit squarely, we'd both be incapable of walking.

A shotgun wound in the leg wouldn't be enough to knock us unconscious, so what happened? Marissa obviously knows but she isn't saying. Confusion crawls up in my brain while I wait. If her hostage is in the mood to talk, I have a laundry list of questions for him.

"This isn't even your house," I rasp, sliding my undamaged leg across the floor into a position I can use to get myself into a sitting position.

"It's mine." His voice is smooth and unperturbed by rage or aggression. "Bought it six years ago."

"That can't be," I say. "What year?"

"Would have been twenty forty-one," he says. "What do you care?"

I do the math inside my head. Since Ian was eight years old when Erebus or Cy pulled me away, and I'd met them again in this house when he was ten, Ian would be seventeen years old by now, meaning this man would have purchased the house from Becky.

"Realtor offered a great price," he says. "Single woman who owned it disappeared, and the bank foreclosed. Damn good privacy, unbeatable view. Until some goons invaded."

"That's impossible. The single woman who owned it before was alive in 2041. She would live here now."

"How do you know that?"

"Because I'm married to her. I think. If she's still alive."

My reaction makes him move his hands to show more of his face. A patch of gray stubble mars his chin. He draws his thick, black eyebrows into an angry frown, which makes him look older than he probably is. I scowl when our eyes meet.

"Then why didn't you make the payments?"

The question hits me like a brick. Rather than trying to cobble together a reason, I gather my knee closer to my midsection and turn my attention to Marissa while glancing at Sarah's sleeping body a few feet away.

When our eyes meet, Marissa shrugs. "Could be she saved your life—or your leg. And if I hadn't been here, he could have killed you both, then mounted your stuffed carcasses on the wall. Be a great conversation piece, wouldn't it?"

The idea that she could have overpowered him by herself is preposterous. I gape at her as though her explanation isn't good enough, but when she doesn't answer, I force a new round of questions.

"How did you manage to ... restrain him?"

"That I'd like to know myself," the occupant says, scooting his socked feet toward her and leaning back against the cushion. "She's right. I had another shell with your name on it."

"Let's just say I used a trick I learned a long time ago. You might call it a spellbinding curse, or a bit of magic. I call it leveraging your spiritual connections."

"Uh-huh. I suppose you have a bridge somewhere to sell me, too."

She flashes a wry smile and then frowns. "Occult dealer."

"Occultism is bullshit," the hostage growls. His fingers vibrate and his knees bounce up and down a few times before coming to rest on the ball of his foot. "Gonna take a better excuse than that."

"It was dark enough," she says, her posture remaining firm. She pulls her feet together as she speaks but doesn't look away from the hostage. "They say a magician never reveals his secrets, but I'm not a magician. I can connect with the spirits of the dead faster than you can blink. And it turns out, there are a lot of them in the area. You'd never think that, but anywhere you go, you're likely to have several nearby if they choose to linger."

"Unbelievable."

"Most people are attuned enough to feel it if they're alone and it's quiet enough. I think there's a phenomenon named after it."

Gulping, I conjure the phenomenon's name while eying the title of a movie on the top shelf of the bookcase. *Pride and Prejudice.* The same movie Becky and I had watched that night I disappeared. "The ghost in the room."

"So I spoke to them. And they spoke to you, mister." She addresses the prisoner. "Or should I call you Charles? They are still speaking to you. That's why your heart is at rest."

I gape at him. His body language suggests shock and disbelief. If his heart is at rest, he isn't showing any signs of submission. Going by his reactions to the surrounding situation, he has enough energy to leap off the couch and pounce on her with one motion, yet he stays still as though she wields an unbeatable weapon.

"Oh my God. I mean, if you believe in God."

She shakes her head and glances at me from the corner of her eye. "Did I say I don't believe in God? I don't know if he's real in the same way religious people do, but mingling with spirits can only be possible if there's a deity of some kind. I choose to describe myself as a spiritualist."

"But—"

"There are more of us than you think. And your experiences must make you certain that it works."

My heart sinks. The agony in my leg waxes and wanes, as though my brain is dealing with the pain by pushing at it, letting it swell, and then pushing harder. The same way you work your car free from a snowdrift. Put it in reverse, give it some gas, then ease off while someone helps you rock it back and forth. The tactic works unless there's enough snow to need a shovel to dig yourself out.

"Then how did I ... we ... get knocked out?"

A curious twitch of her facial muscles suggests she's working to suppress a coy smile. Tilting her head to the right, she is still regarding the prisoner. "Because I hypnotized you."

I push up onto my elbow, letting a shocked expression pass over my face. "What?"

"Didn't I promise I would? So you could both discover your connection?"

Her explanation causes a vague memory to prod at my mind. Where were we? The earlier scene loses focus the longer I stand here. We reached this house by traveling back in time, assuming 2046 is correct. But if Becky isn't here, the setting makes no sense. If this is my future dimension, Marissa's detainee shouldn't even be here. The timeline has become skewed, and trying to assign an explanation for the warping of it leads to myriad possibilities, each more absurd than the last.

"Did it work?"

I don't remember. As though sliced away from the rest of my consciousness, only a blurry black blob remains where recollection should provide clues to the past. Stuttering alerts her that the experiment has failed.

"But you were under," she protests, turning her head to look at me. "I could sense it."

Gathering a sense of humor, I prod her. "I don't think you're *that* boring. Maybe you put us to sleep, but the rekindling, or whatever was supposed to happen, didn't."

"That's not the way hypnosis works. You can't put someone under without a purpose because our brains are hard-wired to resist that. You have to convince them that the seeds you intend to plant will germinate first."

"Jargon," I cough.

"I might not be an expert, but I'm well versed in the how and why. Don't assume I don't understand how things work just because I went into business instead of getting a degree."

From the corner of my eye, I see Sarah's fingers twitching. Marissa and I break eye contact while I push myself into a painful sitting position with my damaged leg still outstretched. My muscles can only hold the position for so long before I collapse, unless I can move my hurt leg to offer better support.

Sarah's eyes blink open as Marissa watches Charles. Or as my mind is beginning to refer to him, Chuck. During the exchange, his eyes have glassed over as he looks back and forth between Sarah and Marissa. When Sarah is aware enough, she furrows her brows as though to massage the pain away.

"Welcome back to hell," I whisper.

"What ... you were ... Kerry? I thought your name was Larry."

"How are you feeling?" I use my arms to turn my body to face her so that I don't have to bend my neck as much, but my leg still resists.

"You were there ... sort of.... And now you're here. I heard ... your voice, I think. From a long time ago. But I don't remember what you said. It's—oh God, ow!"

"Hurts like hell," I agree. "Can you move your leg?"

"Uh ... I think so?" She pulls her knee up to meet her chest while wincing in pain. Better motion than I can tolerate might mean she's less injured than I am.

"We gotta get back to the cabin, if we can," I say. "Because this dimension is going to destroy your memory."

Which reminds me ... why hasn't it destroyed mine? Without knowing how long I was out, I can't figure out where along the timeline I am. But if time can twist so much that Chuck's story is possible, we're in deeper trouble than I thought. We won't have hours to limp back to the cabin or hike through the woods to that other portal. We're going to need a portal that is closer. I only know of one, and it leads to the same place we got shot, although a different version, where Becky might still be alive. The thought of seeing her again makes my heart murmur.

As I reach down to prod at the tender flesh around my wound, my fingers glow faintly. The blood boils when I touch it, sending spasms of pain through my leg and making me wince at the torture.

"I shouldn't even be alive," Sarah whispers. "How? I put myself in front of you."

"Why?"

"Wasn't thinking straight," she explains. "I knew he had a gun pointed at you, so I acted on impulse. Luckily it only hurt my leg."

"Did a lot more than that," I say, gulping down shame. She wouldn't have sacrificed herself for me unless we shared a deeper connection than I thought we had. "We just don't know it yet."

"I don't understand."

"There are consequences for everything you do," I say. "And in different dimensions of time, they're worse—much worse. Becky's alive now, somewhere, which means she'll know what just happened. And she's going to search for me. I think we just changed everything while changing nothing."

"Kerry? Why didn't you ever correct me about your name?"

Smiling is too painful. I can only let my heart sink deeper into my chest while averting my gaze from hers. "Guess I was just excited you were talking to me in the first place."

A knowing look crosses her face. She uses the pillow to prop herself up, leans back against the chair's legs, and rests her back. "I didn't know you felt that way. I'm sorry for not recognizing it."

"No need," I say. "We're meant for something else. Becky means everything to me."

"What's stopping you from going back to her?"

Frowning does nothing to chase away the demons. I can't fix this. As a physicist I used to read once said, "You can't create order from a state of chaos." He was describing time, and time for most of us marches forever in the same direction without slowing until the world ceases to exist. But scientists know that time is a separate physical dimension, that it links to the fabric of the universe.

I worry that time is going haywire because I've caused too many paradoxes, that the universe could collapse into one fiery singularity, compressing all matter into a soup of particles so dense that time and space cease to exist.

"A lot of things are outside my control right now," I say. "First things first, we return you to the jobsite. The problem is, I don't know the way."

"Kerry?"

Looking at Marissa and back to Sarah, I realize that my existence itself hangs in the balance; if my reality unravels here, everything does—Marissa, Sarah, Becky and I all go into the soup forever where neither memory nor premonition can survive. "We're lost again." The words feel like ash in my throat.

II

Theban Harmonia

Far from looking like someone in shock, Sarah seems pensive, though pale. Her eyes flit to me, while her brows remain unchanged, as though she has a million questions. She can only utter one: "Lost?"

"Big problem," I rasp. "The island is the only way I know back to the construction site. But we can't get there. We'll lose our memory and, therefore, our reality ... and possibly our legs too."

I scan her expression as I think it out, reason flashing through me. "Unless we can fly."

"I get that, and I agree," she says, swallowing. "It's just that if we don't make it, what's the worst that can happen?"

"We've already distorted the past and the future beyond repair," I say through gritted teeth as a white-hot surge of pain shoots through my calf. "We stay too long, we die. And then there's no way home because we'll no longer exist."

"Except—"

"The attic." The idea should offer relief, but the moment the word escapes my lips, a disturbing sensation of grief comes with it. "Except that won't work, because if I'm right, that portal has been sealed in this dimension."

Sarah rests her head against the wooden chair leg, an admission that she's flagging. I expect a frustrated sigh, but she makes no sound and only grimaces when another wave of pain hits her.

"Attic's a mess at the moment anyhow," Chuck says. "Started an insulation renovation project six months ago, never got around to finishing it. I was trying to convert it into a great room, lost interest, ran out of money. But maybe I'll start again."

I glare at him. Behind him, a tall side table with turned legs supports a potted plant, some of whose leaves have browned and crisped. The smooth tabletop has a thin layer of dust that softens the yellow glow from the standing lamp and casts a peculiar sheen into the surrounding air. Sarah and I must have narrowly missed crashing into the table when the shotgun blast rang out.

This simple piece of furniture matches Becky's sense of style more closely than any of the other décor; not too ornate or rustic, its sleek legs and thin top are more contemporary, yet complement the overall motif. If Chuck decorated this house himself, he did an impeccable job.

Picturing how it looked the last time I climbed up there, I lock my eyes onto him while Marissa stands still with her arms folded. "That square shaft up there made of CMUs ... is there still a hole in it?"

"There might have been once," he says. "Made me think it was a laundry chute or chimney flue from the water heater. But the water heater exhaust is routed to the roof next to the kitchen hood in a hidden wall cavity. You can look all you want, but you'll never know it exists without opening the cabinet above the range. It's shallower than the rest of them because there's a duct buried in it."

"I don't understand," Marissa says. "What does the water heater have to do with anything?"

Frowning, I try to explain it without the jargon. "Most household water heaters used to use a natural gas burner, but they created exhaust fumes, undetectable until you got sick. So now it's mostly electric for efficiency and health."

Chuck offers a nod to indicate he knows what I'm talking about. "Wanted to install a heat pump system a few years ago, but after I analyzed the cost, I figured it would take twenty years to pay for itself. They're supposed to be ten times more efficient than gas, but when gas is this cheap, it doesn't warrant the initial investment."

"Let's brainstorm," Marissa says, glancing at her wrist as though she's wearing a watch. "We don't have time to talk about water heaters."

"Good point," I say, looking over to check on Sarah and trying to drag my injured leg to sit up. "I should know this, but where is the water heater?"

"Crawl space," Chuck says. "They poured a concrete pedestal for it and the softener under the kitchen. Gas service comes in from the road."

"Might make a good portal," I say. "Although there's no way of knowing where it will lead, and that's a problem."

"If getting out of here is as dire as you say," Sarah says, the tension stirring just beneath her voice, "maybe it doesn't matter where it leads."

"I don't want to get you lost," I say, trying to hide my shame.

"You said we already are."

"If we can somehow find our way back to the island," Marissa reasons, "that's our best bet, so let's do it and quit wasting time."

"Couldn't have said it better myself," Chuck growls.

"We need to help them," Marissa says, narrowing her eyes. "I trust you won't try to kill us again?"

He offers a wry smile. "Better if you go willingly than for me to have to lug three corpses out, then have the cops asking questions when a fisherman hooks your collar. 'Sides, I gotta clean up the blood."

Marissa doesn't look amused. She shakes her head and helps Sarah first. Sarah offers her hand while grimacing and suppressing a groan. Although the injured woman stands several inches taller, Marissa is strong enough to help her stand while she steadies herself against the side table. Coughing in the dust she plants her foot on the floor, whimpers with the pain, and slings her free arm around Marissa's shoulder.

Putting any weight on her leg is more than she can bear, and I'm hurt worse. In fact, I still can't move my leg. My entire limb has gone numb even though I can still feel the pain. Chuck grunts up off the couch and holds out a hand for me. I groan when I grab it, and he pulls forward while I bend my good leg under my center of mass. I have enough leverage to hold myself upright and enough balance to stand on one leg.

"You have a background in home renovation?" he asks as he puts my arm around his neck and supports me toward the hall.

The window across the hall filters blue light into the room. As we avoid it, I mutter to myself, looking up at the black rectangle in the ceiling as regret pierces my brain. Every time I say goodbye to this house, tears well up in my eyes because this served as our temporary home. Even though I can't recall many of the experiences we've had together, Becky and I shared so many memories here, and though I can remember few of them, they still carry an emotional toll.

How does it work? I ask myself. Shouldn't memory and emotion work together, or are they served by different parts of the brain?

Twenty feet down the hall from the open doorway to the main bedroom is the second bedroom, which has a view of the lake. The arched opening supports a sliding rod with a roller wheel to guide the barn door along a track. How did I not notice that before? Becky made teasing remarks about "cow doors" during our Harrisburg house hunt; it's another design trait that clashes with her personality. Delving deeper into memory to assess whether the door had been there the last time, I limp along while Chuck supports me.

Sarah and Marissa pause at the door opening until Chuck forces me into the bedroom. The women follow us into a small room big enough for a single bed and a dresser that has wooden knobs that have faded over years of use. The covers on the bed are wrinkled, and a baseball mitt lingers on the pillow beneath a black-and-white photograph of a baseball legend. Such a shrine might look like an homage to Jackie Robinson, but I sense fragments of Ian's personality in this room.

Ian struggled with tee ball when he was young and never played, but that didn't stop him from admiring the greats.

The soft gray carpeting compresses beneath my feet as Chuck helps me sit on the knotted-yarn bedspread. Its curving pattern resembles the stitches on a baseball. Clever. Pinching one of them between my fingers, I watch as he slides open the slatted door to reveal a stack of boxes below a clothing rod. He hefts the boxes out of the way and restacks them on a toy chest. A shiny steel handle in the crawl space hatch glints in the soft blue light as he bends down and pulls it up.

Spider silk flutters as he fumbles for a flashlight on the floor and flicks it on to illuminate the dusty crawl space. Tremors walk up my spine as I can already feel the prickly little legs on me, making my skin itch as they drape their strands of irritating silk. If I make it into the hole without screeching in terror, I'll consider it a success. Need I mention that my number one mortal fear is not death or public speaking, but spiders?

I have nightmares about them. Big ones. Small ones. One or two, or in the millions. More times than I can count, I've awakened moaning in terror, reeling until the light clicks on and the present slowly washes away the gut-wrenching images.

Still supporting Sarah's slender body, Marissa mocks me with a sardonic grin. "You look like you've seen a ghost."

"Shut up," I croak.

"Come on, *Larry*. These little guys are an important part of nature, and I happen to like them."

"That's it," I say. "We can't be friends anymore."

"Gee, thanks."

"Get in the hole, miss," Chuck directs. "Can't say it's been fun with your spiritual warfare or whatever the hell you were doing, but I'll miss you anyway."

"Just jump," I say. "Sarah, protect that leg and I'll see you on the other side."

She glances back with a worried scowl. "Other side of what?"

They vanish into the black before I can reply. The portal works. I stare into the silky abyss, wondering how a portal in a crawl space access is supposed to work. No one would ever be able to service their water heater if the hatch transports them to a different dimension. But there's no time to worry about the implications now. Trying to swallow my terror, I teeter on the edge until Chuck gives me a shove into the pit.

The floor evaporates as I fall through nothingness.

The *Soul of the Baron.*

The words fly past me, swirling into a cloud of black ink as I rise out of the pages, growing to full size as I morph into shape beside the kitchen table. I shudder when I survey my surroundings.

Sarah and Marissa are huddled in a corner where the kitchen cabinets leave a foot-wide nook at the exterior wall. The painted wooden cabinets have yellowed with age. The musky scent overpowers my nostrils as I look around; dusty spiderwebs make dingy splotches of gray in the upper corners of the walls, while dirty strands crisscross the room. The island might be home to a million of Marissa's little friends. I retch when I look back at the open book's yellowed, water-stained pages, yet shining jewels crest the spine.

When I scan the rest of the dining room and living room, my fear grows; no one has entered this cabin in years, and I don't want to know why.

Rotted wooden furniture has collapsed into splintery piles of termite powder forming anthills, and stuffing puffs out of gashes in the sagging couch.

Beside the mantle, a gauze of webs covers a wooden coat rack, and a grimy, dust-covered stag's head peers down at me from a bare section of wall next to the rack. Dirt coats its antlers, burdening a nest of spider silk in its crown. The room seems to rotate as I stand here.

I hear a faint cry from the hallway, and it shreds my heart. Over in the corner, Marissa comforts Sarah as she sobs. Something sinister lurks here, and I struggle to understand its depths. Emptiness and emotional pain fill this abandoned place. I can sense the heavy sorrow spreading in the room as the whimpering crying grows louder.

I see footprints in the dust towards the end of the hall, disappearing into the filth as the black distance distorts everything. Nodding to the women, I try to encourage them to join me, but neither of them moves.

"What?" I ask.

More like who.

Those words pierce my mind with agony as oppressive as the cabin's interior. I can sense the anguish of her heart-wrenching cries. Everything in this space feels like an abyss of sorrow, deeper than I can fathom.

Go to him.

My feet begin to move before I am conscious of it. The memory of the pain in my leg still batters at me, but at least I can stand on both feet now. As the moans grow louder, memories tear me apart, cutting through the imaginary world I have created in my own mind.

MEMORIES:

Everything blurs. Trees, grasses, clouds, the sun, and the sky streak past me in effervescent colors, bleeding together like tears spattering onto fresh ink. The sounds are sublime, somewhere between eerie and serene, echoing like a distant train's horn in a tunnel.

Shape and form come into view as our car speeds along through Pennsylvania's forested backcountry. Becky pushes the accelerator, testing the car's stability and traction as she approaches a curve. A smile tickles the corners of her mouth as she leans into the turn while listening to the slow, sunny tune on the radio.

"You're awake," she says.

A pair of feet kicks at the back of my seat. Twisting at my hip, I can see his unkempt hair sticking up to one side; he mirrors everything I say and do. I gaze at him for so long that his image blurs and fades. He's safe in his own world, and more content than I can ever imagine.

My soul hurts, and energy fills me, making my fingers glow as I lace them together on my lap.

As the scene disappears, I can only mouth his name: "Ian."

I know his name. The whimpering sounds tug at my heart and tears stream down my face. My fingers grope through the dank air as if to grab his voice and massage the hurt away. Yet for every inch I move forward, the further away he seems.

Trying to understand this realm only deepens the emotion, and the ache drops lower into my heart while I try to put the pieces together.

The different route we took to get here should have given me an idea of how this dimension would affect my senses. It feels like we've fallen through that dark, cobwebby crawl space into a derelict universe as grim as any place I can recall.

Considering that this might be a parallel universe of our own dimension, I imagine that instead of getting better, this dimension has deteriorated, and not just physically. The moaning sounds coming from the nearby room seem to support this idea. If we don't find a way to reach Ian, and escape this decrepit world, we'll be imprisoned here in endless sadness.

After a few moments, Marissa and Sarah join me, wiping away their tears. Mascara has streaked its way down Sarah's face, giving her a haunted look. My heart races as I reach out for the voice, feeling it slipping further away. Time seems to stretch out and the closer I get the more the space expands.

And then suddenly everything disappears into a black hole that consumes me. Floating through time and space, I see stars rushing past in bands of white light as I orbit a red star. A cold hand grips mine and I feel icy needles piercing my skin. The darkness now glows white as the galaxy speeds by and the tears freeze on my face.

Now I understand what is leading me—the boy—his cries of sorrow and pain in the void, and I haven't been able to reach him. But I must believe that there's a way. Because without hope I'm nothing more than a Shade with a body inside of it.

12

Chiron's Death

The sun beats down on the staging yard of Bones Holdings, bouncing off prefabricated sheet metal parts and plastic-wrapped HVAC fasteners. The reflections off these items work into my woozy brain, giving me a blurry headache. Sarah and Marissa don't seem to notice my agony or that the world is spinning as I twist my ankle and yelp.

The world above me whirls clouds and distant wisps of smoke into a vortex of gray and white as my ankle binds on a dried clump of mud from a recent rainstorm. Yelping, I collapse before I can take another step. The world around me goes black.

Beep! Beep! Beep!

I feel nothing as blurred images pass my sight, like fragments of a dream shattered by restless sleep. When a face appears over my head, I close my eyes and let the demons chase me into uncharted waters.

I am lying half-naked on a pebbly beach, feeling the frosty air invading my senses. The surrounding forests are alive with the sounds of breaking twigs, hoots, howls, and the occasional splash of a fish jumping up to catch a fly.

I feel only dread and uncertainty for the future. I roll over and pick up a stone, pretending to throw it like a pitcher. The stone barely reaches the shore ten feet away. My arm has gone numb from my body's weight. As I look up at the sky, a billion stars are watching me.

Being here doesn't make sense. The soft yellow light glowing inside the lake house is enticing, but I know the way back to the trailer is through the cabin. I dread wading through the reeds and braving the icy water again. I wince with a fresh jolt of pain while I try to figure out my next move.

I realize that Sarah and Marissa should be here, but they are now just memories.

Another fish jumps, closer to the shore. I hear a screech and a humming motor but see only darkness and the forest's verdant backdrop. Cars don't often travel this road, so perhaps a large game animal has leaped in front of a weary motorist. I watch the roadside, for several moments, listening for more sounds and hear nothing else. But a movement somewhere to my right causes a shot of adrenaline to scour through my bloodstream. The sound of soft shoes on pebbles ... by the time I recognize the intruder, I can see her face. She looks like a ghost; her face has grown pale and her dark eyes look like craters in snow. She drifts in and out of focus for several seconds, while growing nearer. My heartrate intensifies as I watch.

She is a few inches taller than me, with long, lanky legs clad in dirty blue jeans and a sweatshirt draping her shoulders. Her long, bead-tipped braids move as she stops just out of my reach. I breathe her name.

"Va—nessa."

"Wondered when I might see you again, Kerry Gearhardt."

My head is spinning. Millions of miles away, her stars sparkle in the shape of a square ladle. "I don't believe it's you. You ... what happened to you?"

"Nothing you need to know about," she whispers, her voice solemn and patient. The glimmer of stars makes her eyes shine with an emotion I've never experienced myself.

"But you shouldn't be here. You can't be."

She pauses but doesn't smile. "You don't remember it, do you? This moment?"

"What?"

"I caught up to you. I've searched for you a long time, Kerry. Don't go."

"I have to ... gotta get back to wherever I was," I stammer. "They're waiting for me."

"You have a lifetime to figure it out, but at least you remember me now. Twenty-six years have passed since we last saw one another, but I was there at the very beginning, at the Pennsylvania Hospital. There was a rumor you were coming, but I didn't want to believe it. I knew it the moment I laid eyes on your tiny body. A Titan in Philadelphia. The fulfillment of an ancient prophecy—the Minoan princess searched the Labyrinth in vain."

"You never thought to tell me this?"

She hesitates. "It was never the right moment. But now you know; you must save the world now, Kerry."

I can feel myself frowning. "I'm only one man. And not a great one at that."

"You can't fail; the universe depends on you. Only you can unite the heroes, to stop the war and undo the paradox."

"I don't know how. I'm lost."

Her face flushes as she speaks her last sentence. "You have all the tools you need to invest in a brighter future."

"Hell of a broker line," I say as she turns away. The frayed ends of her orange and yellow sweatshirt shine bright in the moonlight and a gust of wind clacks her beaded braids together.

Beep! Beep! Beep!

Beep. Beeeep!

"Kerry."

"Thank God you're alive."

Marissa peers down at me through moistened eyes as my fingers feel the cold linen across my torso and I take in my surroundings.

The bed is tilted back opposite a small television mounted to the wall via black-painted metal brackets that allow the screen to swivel. I see a patterned beige wallpaper. My name is written in doctor-scribble on a whiteboard. There is an IV in my arm, leading to an elevated bag filled with transparent liquid. The bag is mounted to a rolling stainless-steel stand parked near my right shoulder. A long countertop with a white vitreous sink is on one side of the bed.

Sarah sits in a chair at the edge of my vision in a low-backed chair next to the bathroom door.

"What do you mean, I'm alive?"

"The doctor called it cardiac shock," Marissa says, keeping her head level. A square of sunshine glares off the vinyl floor behind her. "You fell. Don't worry, your boss—big guy with tattoos and a booming voice—said he didn't want to see you again until you've fully recovered."

"Jamal."

"He took those ASI prints you were asking for," Sarah says.

I crane my neck to look at her. Her hair is matted to her scalp, and mascara, tears, dust, and spider silk stain her face.

Her explanation for why I went to the construction trailer today fails to make sense; all the times over the decades that I've been there blur together, but it seems as though it's been decades since I've crossed the yard.

"You want to talk about what happened?" Marissa looks tired but tries to hide it as she straightens her back. "I thought we had died, but it was worse than that. Like all hope had drained away, leaving only bitter sadness. The most awful place I've ever seen, apart from those beautiful spiders."

I rasp at her: "Psychopath."

"Lucky the crawlspace brought us back to the cabin. Otherwise, your legs, and Sarah's, might have been amputated by now. Or then ... or whenever we were."

"Now do you understand why interdimensional time travel is so fraught with danger?"

She shrugs dismissively. "Works for me."

"But I might have predicted it would," I try to explain, my voice a croak. "Just not that version of it."

After a few uncomfortable minutes of silence, Marissa relaxes and glances at a painting in the hallway before refocusing on me. "Anyway, how do you feel?"

"About like you'd expect."

"I mean your leg."

I had forgotten that the pain still lingers, even when muted by time and distance. "Maybe I'll get to walk again."

"Pitiful," she says. "But the nurse can't help you with that. Lucky I'm trained to deal with fractured egos and bruised dreams. Spill it."

I'd much rather talk to Sarah. At least her aura gives off comfort, whereas Marissa seems to relish the darkness of my spirit. But then I don't have much to say—what I want hasn't changed.

Or has it? Perhaps I'm just not ready to talk.

"I see. Any more tentacled monsters I should worry about? I mean, apart from the ones in your brain?"

For a half-second, I can see Becky in her face, and I'm used to Becky's sarcasm. And I enjoy it because I know that despite it all, she has never ceased to love and comfort me. Going weeks or months without her feels like a lifetime, and by now I've lost track of how long it's been.

"He's awake!" the nurse chimes as her soft-soled shoes squeak on the floor. She also wears a cross-shaped pendant that sparkles under the fluorescent lights.

"Or at least I look like it," I say. Distinguishing reality from fiction has become increasingly difficult after so many dimension jumps have distorted time.

"Let's take your vitals," she says.

"So, cardiac shock? Is that doctor slang for heart attack?"

Her ponytail flops on her shoulder as she turns her head to look at the monitor, then yanks down the sheet covering me and rests the chilly stethoscope against the skin of my chest. "Take a deep breath, nice and easy."

"Well?"

"Not necessarily," she says. "They're related, though."

"Related as in father and son?"

"You'll have to ask Doctor Neechybaugh."

I gulp at her effortless pronunciation of a complicated last name. "Doctor who?"

"That's a good show," she says, grinning as I squint to read her name, Nichole, off the whiteboard. "One of the better British ones, in my opinion."

I wait as she creases her lips at the monitor. "Looks like you'll be able to go home in the morning, with the doctor's approval. We're going to keep you overnight just to monitor you."

"I'll stay with you," Marissa offers.

Coaxing sarcasm into my voice, I reply, "Great. Can't wait for you to Wicca the crap out of my brain while dancing around burning incense."

"You clearly know nothing about Wiccans," she says.

"And you do? Oh, forget it."

She repeats herself in a timorous voice, "Occult dealer."

It takes me several minutes to respond. I find myself feeling dizzy, and the reflections on the TV screen congeal together with the vicious memories into a confusion just before I pass out. It all goes black as time lurches forward.

Still groggy from the deep sleep, I wait the doctor examines me one last time while Marissa waits on the upholstered chair, leaning forward with her elbows on her knees.

She has brought a black T-shirt and a new pair of jeans for me to change into. Her expression morphs from pity to anxiety.

"Looks like you had a good night," says the doctor. "But do keep tabs on your own condition. If you experience similar chest pains again, get them checked before you collapse. That just leads to other injuries."

"I don't understand how it happened, really," I say. "It's kind of fuzzy."

"Take the rest of the week off work," he says, feigning warmth. "Don't rush going back, don't exert too much energy, and drink plenty of fluids."

After he finishes the discharge examination, he presses the button on the bed remote to lift me to a sitting position. He helps me up onto my feet. Pain rings my calf as I trudge toward the bathroom to change into the new clothes.

I already know I'm going to defy the doctor's orders; I can't wait the rest of the week. While going back to that horrible dimension of despair and sorrow, I must retrieve my son. No force on earth or in the underworld can stop me.

Although she protests when I explain what I'm going to do, Marissa drives me through the downtown canyons and back to the job site. Cars fill the parking lots, but there's an empty stall near the trailers and the diamond plate ramp.

As I swing open the door, I flush when I see Sarah standing behind the reception counter, a pained smile on her lips.

"You're not supposed to be here," she says. "Jamal sees you, he'll—"

"I know," I mutter, hurrying over to the potted plant. "Just need to get back. I don't expect you to understand."

"But I do," she says, her voice stretching. Her simple words eat through my confidence like acid. "Just be safe. And I'll see you on Monday."

Doubtful. Now that I know more about our relationship, I feel liberated. If I don't get hurt trying to get back home, I will meet Sarah on Monday, but the thought of getting trapped in a cycle of sadness and uncertainty weighs heavy on my heart.

When we reach the plant, Marissa squeezes my hand as I step toward the stain and let the vacuum overtake me. We whip past that red orb as the stars streak by as fast as lightning.

The cobwebs shift as a vortex opens, just long enough for us to step out onto the creaking floorboards. The color drains from my face and Marissa shrieks.

An eight-foot-diameter eyeball floats above the floor, sucking in strands of spider silk as the black hole pupil jolts from side to side. When it sees us, it emits a noise that vibrates the floorboards and loosens dust from the ceiling.

It growls and attacks, lunging toward us as though to suck us in. Inch-wide blood vessels cut jaggedly through the dilating pupil. Blue and red lightning scatters through the eye's white sclera, spinning like a black hole's swirling debris. The noise increases as it vibrates with raw power. Repelling us with a strong gust of wind, it turns to attack us again as tentacles slither through the surrounding darkness, in order to strangle us.

A powerful blast lifts us off our feet and pushes us about ten feet. The tentacles reach out in the dark, knock the stag's head off the wall, and wind around Marissa's body tight enough to squeeze the life out of her.

In the back room, the moaning returns as I leap over a spiraling appendage, and jump to punch the enormous eye in its pupil. Another shockwave, but weaker this time, causes my fist to fly inches past the iris as it moves to strike again.

Behind me, Marissa squeals as the tentacle coils tighter around her like a monstrous python inching toward her neck.

Pain slaps me from behind as one appendage smashes into my skull with enough force to cause acidic memories to slosh around in my brain. The jabbing sensation throbs at the back of my scalp as I grasp toward the only weapon I can see to fend the monster off—a double-pronged fire poker hanging next to the mantle—but the beast's tentacle twists around my arm and pulls it back toward the pupil, which intends to devour me.

"Let me go!" Marissa rasps.

I aim a wild punch at the whipping appendage, making it recoil just enough for me to get within a foot of the weapon. Its lightning blood vessels surge blue and red once again, as another powerful blast shakes me and another tentacle prevents me from reaching the poker.

It's squeezing my neck now, but the stain around my aura grows darker, and when it feels me eroding its appendage, the eyeball roars and releases me while one of its other tentacles drags Marissa across the dusty floor.

I howl with rage as my fingers curl around the poker. When the monster realizes I'm brandishing a weapon, it relinquishes its grasp on Marissa and draws me closer. Gravity sucks at my hair like a vacuum as the beast pulls me into its blackened maw.

When I'm within striking distance, a surge of energy flashes through my veins, powerful enough to shed the darkness that has covered me, and I radiate light through the dirty, cobwebbed room. One chance is all I'm going to get; if I miss, it will eat me for dinner and have Marissa for dessert.

I explode and swing the poker right into its dilated pupil. Rather than react like any other creature when poked in the eye, it growls and pulls me so close that my nose touches its slimy surface.

With the floor vibrating around it, it locks me into a deathly embrace and pulls at my arm. Lighting gathers in my fingers and transfers through the steel implement, which bursts into a shower of confetti sparks and blue streams of lighting, pulsing energy directly into the eye.

I realize that I won't defeat this monstrosity with light; it strengthens with every pulse. Summoning my most painful memory, I emit a wave of darkness that erases its tentacle.

The monster growls when I dance free of its grasp, hovering over the floorboards like a cloud of graphite. This confuses the creature, causing it to release Marissa, who gasps in relief as she scurries away.

My darkness leeches out to destroy the gigantic eyeball one atom at a time, yet just when I can feel it yield to my destructive power, it vanishes in a flash of light and sucks us toward the cavity in its wake. Marissa howls as she rolls away, while I groan and succumb to the darkness. My body becomes fluid as I hover above her and settle towards the floor to regain my form.

She glares at me for a whole minute as I anticipate the sounds of distress from the other room.

"What the *fuck* did you just do?"

"I don't know," I growl, sprinting toward the hallway.

"No!" she screams. "You'll—"

Do I feel suspended in the air, like I'm stuck in a whirlwind that won't let go no matter how much I struggle? It's squeezing me, cutting off the blood flow to my legs as the churning air bruises my flesh.

Light flashes around me, and before I know it, I'm sitting in the dark, alone, surrounded by construction materials and job trailers. Marissa materializes and trips over my feet, rolling to a stop on my head as her knees crash into my skull.

13

Key and Torch

Moonlight reflects off the shiny ramp, shooting partial star patterns up onto the cloud cover. The breeze whispers through the abandoned construction site, making a sad fluting sound as it swirls among the stacked pipes.

There is only one car in the parking lot and I know it belongs to Sarah. The lights are off in the Bones Holdings trailers. If she's here this late, I might be able to get her attention by pounding on the door. After she lets me in, I will go through the stain and once again try to rescue my son.

Catching her breath, Marissa presses a palm against her chest and spies the open pipe ends and the flapping plastic tarp covering that protects them from corrosion. Since the landscape contractor has already laid most of the site's civil infrastructure, the supplier might offer a refund for returned materials, but the longer they sit here, the more susceptible to corrosion they become, depleting their value.

"We gotta get back," I rasp, peering into the dark trailer windows.

"Don't you get it?" Marissa breathes. "There's no way we're getting to the bedroom in that cabin. Because the portal in the hallway leads us back here every time."

"Then we won't go through the hall. We go outside, find a rock, smash the window, take my son, and come back here."

She frowns as though trying to work out what I'm feeling. When she realizes I'm not going to change my mind, she sighs, showing that she's willing to go along with my deranged ideas once more. If we make it back to her home dimension safely, our friendship—if you can even call it that—will be changed forever and she may never want to see me again. I struggle to speak when I realize that whether we return safely or not, things will never be the same.

"I don't like it, but I'll see it through this time." she says, relenting. "Although it looks like we'll have to wait until morning."

I shake my head and my heart leaps in my chest. "Sarah's still here."

She scans the parking lot and glances into the dark window. "Right. You think she just curled up to sleep under her desk?"

"That's her car."

"What time is it? Maybe she went out for a drink with a friend."

My scowl makes her roll her eyes and shift her shoulders as though my argument has hit her like a playful fist out of nowhere.

"Oh. Sorry I suggested she has friends outside of us. What was I thinking?"

"She'd know we're coming back."

"Which brings me to another question," she says, a twinge of nervousness in her voice. "I don't understand how it's night. Last time we were here it was midday."

Shrugging, I meet her eyes and then look up to the flapping tarps surrounding the unfinished twenty-seventh floor of our incomplete sky-scraper. "Different version of this dimension. Or we took a different route through space."

"That could be a problem. At least if I'm seeing things right."

"Same dimension, different version," I explain. "It happens often when portals lead you to a specific time and place because of the Butterfly Effect. Otherwise known as Chaos Theory."

"Something you could have explained before we left."

I allow myself a moment to become calmer, but she can see through it while she taps her restless feet on the ground. It had earlier been tire tracks in dried mud and is now damp with the evening humidity. "Didn't think about it."

"Any other surprises I should know about?"

I'm unable to respond to her sarcasm, and even though there's humor in her wit, I want to avoid a more intense argument. "Even *I* don't know all the surprises. You gotta be prepared for everything."

"That's reassuring."

"So we'll need weapons."

"What are you getting at? You gonna knock off a pawnshop?"

I shake my head. "Back to the lake house. We steal Chuck's shotgun, jump into the crawl space, go outside and around the back and shoot anything that moves."

Drawing in a raspy breath, she leans her head back and flexes her fingers. "Brilliant plan."

True enough, the plans I make never go according to expectations, because there are too many variables involved. The Butterfly Effect in action. And although I'm more careful nowadays, I still can't predict the future. Things are never what they seem, no matter which dimension I find myself in.

"Then let's hear yours."

For a few moments, she scans boxes holding pipe clamps, fasteners, and various strut attachments in the construction yard. "I see plenty of things we could fashion into weapons here."

"You're suggesting we steal from the job site?"

"If we don't get caught, we don't get our heads blown off," she reasons. "We'll just borrow a few things, bring them back, and no one will know. And then your foreman doesn't sack you."

I raise my eyebrows as I look around the lot. The boxes contain nuts and bolts, washer sets, strut clamps, and base plates. Contractors use parts from strut manufacturers to build utility racks in many configurations, for a handful of engineering variables, such as weight distribution. Struts are lightweight, slotted steel members that can be cut to any length. Contractors order them in bundles of standard lengths, but I remember seeing approved purchase orders for lengths as short as three feet, intended to support multi-trade trapezes for several pipe services.

Plastic wrapping bundles the struts next to the stacked pipes, which someone has already ripped open. An idea comes to mind as I approach them, looking around to make sure no one is watching.

I see scattered wrapping insulation and tape next to an unmarked box and look around for insulation shields, thin sheets of metal we could fashion into weapons.

Marissa is right. I grasp a fragment of sheet steel and flex it in my hands. Wielded with enough force, the edge should be sharp enough to fend off whatever attacks us. If I can find a drill press and a pair of sheet metal cutters, I can fashion a dull blade to attach to the strut with the fasteners. Lucky for me, I know we store these tools in a supply cabinet behind our trailer, which Jamal has accused me of failing to lock more than once.

We can use the flat top of a cabinet as a workbench to build our weapons.

I clutch the supplies and make the trek to the storage cabinet, with Marissa on my heels. She folds her arms across her midsection while watching me assemble the pieces. I then use the cutters to slice a curved line through the sheet steel to create a six-inch blade. When I'm done cutting, I run my fingers along the jagged edge and draw blood. I use the drill to make holes in the sheet and then guide the bolts into the channel, tightening it with a wrench.

As soon as I'm finished, I hand her one contraption and swing the other around me to test its weight and durability. It's heavier than I imagine a sword should be, but it will do.

Marissa grasps her blade and slices it through the air until it collides with mine. I respond by backing away one step and swiping it directly at her face, which she parries with ease.

"Good idea," she says, shoving it toward me clutched in both hands.

"Right. We don't want to break them."

We spar for another moment before I return the tools and make my way back towards the Bones Holdings complex. I gasp when I see a light inside. The parking lot is still empty, save for Sarah's car, so she must be stirring.

"What do you know?"

Marissa nods and follows me across the yard. I hurry up the diamond plate ramp, kick the dirt off my shoes on the hollow structure and pound on the front door while shouting Sarah's name.

"She's going to think you've gone crazy," Marissa says.

A window nearby opens, and I can hear Sarah call out. "I just called the cops. I suggest you leave before they come and shoot you."

"Sarah, it's me, Kerry. And Marissa. Let us in, please."

From inside, I hear a hollow thud of metal on metal, perhaps the sound of a binding clip hitting a filing cabinet. Sarah has formed her own weapon. Her footsteps pound to the door and she lets us in.

"I thought you'd be back sooner," she says. "Come in, we'll tell the cops the intruders have escaped. I told them I'm alone, so you'd better hide in Riker's office."

Riker is the site foreman and project manager, a man whose job I used to envy before the time travel shenanigans began. He used to wear a sport coat and a tie every day and host coordination meetings to manage disputes between contractors and suppliers.

"We're going back."

"Nice weapons," Sarah remarks. "Should I report the stolen supplies when the cops get here or wait a week?"

"Funny," I say. "There is one person in our contractor trailer who tracks inventory. You want to guess who it is?"

She smiles. "Perfect crime."

"We'll call it self-defense."

"Defense from what?"

I shrug. "Whatever comes at us."

The hallway off the main entry to the trailer complex leads to offices and conference rooms, making it a potential hiding spot. Unless the police search for intruders.

I turn toward the plant and hurry over to it. "We're bringing him back this time."

Sarah stands aside and watches me grasp Marissa's hand. "Be careful. Unless you need my help?"

Her offer shouldn't surprise me. After all, she's one of the most generous colleagues I've ever had the pleasure of working with, but bringing her along would put her in a level of danger she doesn't deserve. "No. Can you stay here until morning?"

She smiles. Her hair, still tangled and dirty, complements yesterday's clothes, also caked with mud, dust, sweat, and spider silk. "Why do you think I'm still here?"

"Go home," I say, eyeing her like a prospective boyfriend. "Clean up, come back here and wait until first light."

She shakes her head. "Not leaving until you get back."

"What did everyone say about your appearance this afternoon?"

She shakes her head. "Nothing. Everyone in this trailer is a professional and we work together without the sexist commentary on a woman's looks."

Although she speaks with an air of empathy, the vigor behind her words stings. "Uh, sorry. Didn't mean to—"

"Just go already," she says. "Don't come back without the boy."

Marissa looks me in the eye and grips my hand tighter as we step onto the stain and vanish into a black void filled with stars that look like driving snowflakes in the dark.

Something has disturbed the cobwebs. Giant clumps of spider nests now hang from the deer's head while dusty strings lie strewn about the floor. At first glance, I see no fingerprints, but then my heart races when I see a pair of women's shoe prints scatter from a cleared clump and make their way down the hall toward the portal.

She could have been searching for my son, but I already knew she was searching for us, and the freshness of the prints suggests she's still here. A surge of adrenaline comes and I clutch my makeshift sword and tiptoe through the darkened room.

Still rotting, the furniture sags toward the floor, caked with years of filth and cobwebs. A huge spider scurries across the floor toward Marissa, who picks it up.

Holy shit. I could vomit in horror just seeing her holding it.

"You're so precious," she whispers.

"I know you're here," someone says. I recognize her voice in an instant. Dropping my weapon, I make for the portal and freeze in the center of the hallway.

A different version of Vanessa stands there with the wispy vapor head of a young boy clutched in the crook of her arm. She moves to strangle him if I inch any closer, and a serpentine of fear scours through her eyes and emits a dusty, forlorn smoke.

"Don't come any closer."

I rasp out, "Vanessa. It's me. Don't you remember?"

"You left me here to die!"

I feel intense pain in my stomach and my shoulders droop as I realize the situation. This dirty, spider-ridden place seems like a dimension that has been forgotten. Seeing her here confirms my suspicion, but I don't understand how the rules work in this place.

"Let me ask for your forgiveness, then," I gasp.

The fire in her eyes blossoms into an explosion, and within minutes the smoke towers toward the ceiling and fills the room with a billowing column of ashen smoke. Fireballs lick at her eyebrows and set her scalp alight as her braids transform into smoky snakes lashing at the dusty air.

No, this isn't Vanessa. I have no time to react. She drops the boy to the floor and launches herself at me, transforming into a spear to impale my heart. Her smoky remains flash through the air like pressurized steam, letting out a banshee howl. In a split second, she'll slice through me like I'm not even here, but Marissa stops her.

She hurls her blade in front of me but the smoke spirals around the weapon and slithers up to her neck. Diving for my own weapon, I slash it through the smoke near Marissa's knees.

Marissa, like anyone held captive, drops her weapon, clawing at the smoke that is coiled around her neck. Desperation fills her eyes as she goes pale. I power my way toward her, grasping at the smoke tail and pulling it toward my face.

With a metallic clink, the makeshift swords glance off one another and I realize that only one thing can stop the demon from possessing Marissa. Connecting to my inner darkness is easy here. I can feel it scarring and pitting the insides of my soul as I embrace its corrosive nature, harnessing it into a weapon only I can wield.

Shade.

My body becomes a cloud of heavy, black smoke as I home in on 'Vanessa,' drawing at her smoky tendrils with all the force I can muster. Screaming ruptures the silence, scattering in my own ears.

Now free, Marissa leans down to pick up her weapon, pulls mine away from my ash-tornado body, and crosses them near where my neck should be. "Let her go!"

I'm going to smother her. Anger and rage tower within me as my body twists her into a smoldering pile of mush. I have no time to react as Marissa slices the blades at me, hacking away with astonishing strength.

Whack! Whack! The weapons slap against the coal ash, knocking me off balance. Reaching out, I feel the blades slicing through me as I begin to erode them molecule by molecule. but Marissa pulls them away before I can reduce them to nothingness.

We'll need them for later. Vanessa howls in my ears as I tear her apart, and I feel her energy transferring into my veins when I let go.

Her body transforms back into a rigid form as she falls to the dusty floor before me, moans, and disintegrates into soot. A lone whimper in the hallway suggests the boy is still there, but when I lay eyes on him, panic flashes through me as I hover over the dusty floorboards.

Ian has transformed into a paranormal beast with rigid fangs six inches long, a black, gnarled nose, and tufts of mangled fur clumping around stegosaurus plates spiking up his back. Lunging onto all fours, he claws at the floor and snarls at me, and when I see the hole behind his lupine ear, dread rattles my bones.

Marissa launches herself toward the portal with her weapons held high, slashes them through the darkness, and then turns to look at me in shock as the subject of her rage disappears into a puff of blue smoke.

As she waits for me to come back to myself, she glowers with anger. And for a moment, I can hear her voice floating ethereally through theair around me as I reassemble into a body.

"Be here," she says. "*The* Kerry Gearhardt. Let him go."

Tears of frustration flow down my face when I see my aching legs appear beneath me. Marissa stands with both blades held like staffs, their blunt strut ends resting on the floor as though she's a sentry guarding a roomful of treasure.

"Another opportunity will arise," she says, the flutter of adrenaline in her voice fading.

The defeat feels crushing; I collapse into her arms when she moves to embrace me. Saying nothing more, she rests her head on my shoulder, wraps her arms around my waist, and waits for me to stabilize. Then we shuffle toward the hallway where the Ian-beast has disappeared, fling ourselves into the portal, and streak through the empty universe and back to the construction site.

14

Madness from Melinoe

I'm aghast when I survey what has become of the construction site. Orange and yellow flames are devouring the trailer complex Bones Holdings had constructed just over a year ago, while I hear calamitous voices in the distance. Black smoke twists skyward like a tornado above the embers and sirens scream along the nearby streets.

Moments ago, we were here. And when the authorities arrive, we'll be the prime suspects of the arson. Worst of all, we cannot escape; the fire has destroyed the stain, and we won't be able to go back.

But I remember that one other soul lingers here, and when I picture her face, my heart pounds in my chest with anxiety.

Searchlights wave through the smoggy evening sky like distress signals, but I consider that they may be drawing attention to a special car sale or a bash event. I scan the sky for helicopters, and when I see none, I turn my attention to Marissa.

Her eyes have a blank look; shock at what has just happened.

My face darkens as I watch her shifting her feet across the dried mud. I grimace and point my knee at her, knowing that I'm using body language to convey something she might misinterpret.

"I suppose you want to talk about this," she says, the impatience simmering behind her mask of indifference. "But I had nothing to do with it."

"But you know something, Wiccan Queen. Spill it."

She allows her gaze to slacken while I continue to stare. While she may appear disinterested, I can sense the wheels of analysis turning in her mind. "I don't know how to explain it. Not in the traditional occult sense anyway."

"Non-traditional? Make some educated guesses, goddammit!"

She glowers at me, straining her face with sadness, and although I've been called aloof a time or two, I am good enough at reading body language to understand she's trying to deceive me. I raise my palms and look around.

Red and blue police lights flash along a side street, reflected in the dark glass of the next-door towers. Their sirens mute as they approach the locked gates. If we don't move soon, we won't make it to the back fence without them seeing us. And if the cops see us, they'll launch a city-wide manhunt for the arsonists who destroyed the trailer complex. To complicate matters, a pair of fire engines are coming in from two different directions. Like it or not, someone will see us.

A good sprinter could retreat into the shadow of the cast-iron pipes stacked four feet high near the ramp before the police and firefighters arrive. If they're too distracted while the engines attack the blaze, we could slink between the trailers and hop the barbed-wire-topped back fence, which stops across from the adjacent alley that houses backdoors and dumpsters.

If we get that far, I'll consider us lucky.

We sprint toward the pile of construction supplies, and Marissa is moving faster than I expected. Since she's shorter and more petite, I should be faster, by my injury slows me down. If we weren't in trouble, I might question her athletic prowess.

We dive behind the pipe stack just before the police car squeals to a halt in front of the gate. I breathe in and out, preparing for the next leg of the run. I grunt and stop to catch my breath, frown, and prepare for the next leg of the run. Marissa wheezes and pants, rests her hands on her knees, and waits for the siren sound to stop before whispering, "What if we've awakened an evil entity and this is its punishment?"

"Couldn't have said it better myself," I rasp.

We can hear the fire department's metallic clinking as they break the hefty padlock and chains holding the gate, while the police officers egg them on. I don't dare waste this opportunity no matter how much my muscles are aching. Keeping my head low, I scurry toward the grassy mud pit between two of the trailers, where tradespeople regularly assemble to smoke and shoot the breeze.

Terror and my anxiety for Sarah increases when I notice a petite woman's shoe prints, and I dart around the corner out of sight of the emergency personnel. As though hollowed out, my lungs cannot admit enough air to keep my vision from growing gritty and blurred.

She must be waiting for me behind the trailer, where a boxy air-conditioning unit punctures the metal sidewall supported by graying two-by-fours with angled kickers.

I don't see the shovel. Sarah swipes it past Marissa's scalp as it collides with my skull. Muffling a yelp, Marissa drops to all fours as the excruciating blunt force nearly knocks me unconscious. But one well-timed foot to the back of Sarah's knees is enough to drop her without hurting her. Lying on her stomach, Sarah drags the blade across the dried mud while heaving obscenities at her attackers, until she realizes who we are and her attacks lose focus before abating.

Still wielding her makeshift sword, Marissa stands over Sarah and offers a hand, which Sarah slaps away. "Get away from me," Sarah grunts.

"Sarah," I wheeze. "It's me. What the hell happened?"

"I'll tell you after I kill you!"

Instead of fighting back, Marissa holds up her palm as though trying to propel her away using a mystical force field. It's the same tactic she'd used against Chuck seemingly a millennium ago, but it proves just as effective at dispelling the confrontation.

"We gotta run," I gasp as I hear the humming and clacking of diesel motors approaching.

The civil crews had installed and tested a new hydrant inside the fences to deliver high-pressure water to strategic points within the site. The nearest existing hydrant was too far away from the main, so they installed a branch main to the new hydrant, which helps to protect the trailers at the back of the lot. As the firefighters attach to the nearest hydrant on the site, I feel my adrenaline hit overdrive at the thought it would take them only a minute or two to reach us.

I can make out the officers' distant radio chatter as they communicate with the firefighters hoping to douse the inferno. They're not in their cars, so, even if they do suspect arson, we may have ample time to climb the fence.

Opportunity, however, arises in unexpected places. The fencing contractor seems to have saved money by installing the bare minimum of stiffening members and starting the chain links at least six inches above the ground. It's just enough space for us to shimmy beneath it. However, the relief that we don't have to climb is short-lived.

"Suspected arson, over," one cop barks into the radio.

"How can they decide that fast?" Marissa whispers.

"They've seen us. This neighborhood will be swarming with cops in less than five minutes."

Great.

"Get the hell out of here," Sarah says, terrified. Her knuckles twitch as she writhes on the ground, reaching for my shoes as her hair frizzles in the heat of chaos.

"You're coming with us," I say.

Her eyes dart back and forth as she grasps the shovel and climbs to her hands and knees. "I'm a witness."

"Or an accomplice," Marissa retorts.

"I'll be the hero today," Sarah says with less conviction than feels natural, and she follows us through the gap at the bottom of the fence, crawling past a splintered two-by-four and biting her tongue.

When we climb to our feet, I make for the shadows along the alley. Slinking in and out of dumpster shadows and odd nooks in the walls, I feel the same gloom invade my soul. The darkness may provide advantages, but those always come with consequences, some more severe than others. We must find our way to safety quickly before the next step in our journey. And with Sarah along, the stakes are higher. I don't know how to factor that in at the moment.

"We're not getting away," Sarah mumbles worriedly as we retreat into the shadows. But a single open door letting out the low hum of music provides an escape, and I slip inside, wait for Marissa and Sarah to follow, and then shut the door behind us. We've made it.

"I don't intend to get away," I say. "I wish to save the universe. If we must commit crimes along the way, so be it."

"What crimes?" Marissa asks. "It's not like we set the fire."

"We did, in a way. My need to save my son, which I now know is impossible to do the way we were trying to do it, led us to mess with the dimensions." As I guide them through a messy backroom full of stacked boxes with liquid stains down the bottom row, I rub my chin. The smug DJ promises another earworm, as the music breaks to delighted whoops. "And now we're trespassing."

"And in a sense, we were already trespassing."

"And that leads me back to why this is happening," Marissa muses. "Some ancient deity, perhaps? Someone who wishes to keep the secrets of the dead and will haunt the living to do it?"

"Ghosts," I say through gritted teeth, "are *not real.*"

"We're all ghosts, in a way. Almost every ancient religion believes in ghost stories of some kind. They don't make TV movies and fake documentaries just for entertainment. Are all major faiths real or untrue if the spirits of the dead are so central to them?

"I don't want to talk about religion with you," I say.

"You said you've had run-ins with Greek deities," she continues, regardless. "And the Greeks believe in it, too; they have goddesses that govern death, spirituality, witchcraft, whatever you want to call it. Doesn't seem like a stretch that a goddess might want to stop us from getting your son."

"Wait," Sarah barks. "*You* have a *son?*"

I can only nod as the DJ's shouts and sorcerous beats cause a ridiculous craving to dance. Around the corner, LED lights flash and the dance floor goes dark before the pulverizing bass breakdown. Disco smoke fills my nostrils as the crowd chants its approval.

A high wire-mesh rack along the wall of this back room organizes a hodgepodge of boxes and supplies, while a dark, unknown liquid drips to the floor and trickles toward a central floor drain. The rack also holds various bottles filled with diverse beverages for the expert bartender.

I spot a pinot noir and consider uncapping it to produce some levity, but urgency returns my brain to reason.

"A son he didn't know he had until the other day," Marissa quips.

"A deity being involved is bad news," I say, "but not unexpected."

"Why not?" Sarah asks.

"Because I've learned that if you can predict anything, it's that you're in worse trouble than you realize. We only landed in a different version of the cabin because we chose a darker path to get there. I believe that version is some kind of spiritual prison where every emotion destroys objective reality. That's a bad sign, because if a realm like that does exist anywhere above the underworld, then time and space may be unravelling at a record pace. We need to move onto the next task before it catches up with us."

"See?" Marissa says with a smirk. "You're capable of clarity, after all."

"Well..."

"Next move?"

I grit my teeth. "Finding Becky. She's going to try to find me in this dimension because she knows I'm alive. And I think I know where she'll look."

Marissa frowns. "Where's that?"

"The industrial wasteland; the side of Philly that the photographers never show."

She chuckles and then replaces it with a dead-serious glare when she sees that I'm not kidding. "What makes you think she'll look there?"

"I haven't worked it out yet. But I'll tell you when I do."

"Well, that about sums it up," she jokes. "We're just wandering in the dark, searching for a specific thing, and just happen to stumble on genuine solutions that don't turn out to work. A real masterclass in how to screw up spectacularly."

"It only makes sense in this dimension," I explain. "She's missing in *this* dimension because I left her where she doesn't belong. *That* version of her knows I've disappeared and I'm not dead. But *this* version of Becky wouldn't know that unless she learned from a news report that I had broken into a certain lake house she used to own."

"That doesn't make any sense," Sarah says, and I notice that she's tapping her foot to the dance music.

The concrete floor shines in the soft light. The only other door is that of a refrigerated storage unit, which eliminates that direction of escape. We need to disguise ourselves as ravers if we want to get past the police, because going through a portal will only hurt us.

But another disturbing scenario has entered my head; if swapping back and forth from the construction trailer to the cabin has warped time, allowing a god of witchcraft to attack, this version of reality is now bound to hold many horrible pitfalls—and confronting them will require a change of motives if we want to survive.

Rather than moving, I stand shaking my head in time to the music, forming the beginnings of a plan. Getting to the industrial district should be easy unless more monsters assail us on the way. But we won't be able to take our weapons through the dancers, or past the bouncers, and the police are likely searching for two arsonists armed with makeshift swords. Also, Becky may not show up for days, presenting yet another problem, because spending too much time in one dimension can have similar results to jumping through too many; we'd likely get lost and lose track of which dimension we belong to.

The one we're currently in may be an alternate version of the same dimension from which I'd taken Sarah, and I've already lost track of how many versions of it we've entered.

The situation now has despair written all over it, and I can't cope in my usual way with the changing realities. My world has been turned inside out, upside down, and shredded beyond repair. Deep in my heart, I question whether I'm still doing it for Becky, or is survival my sole motive? I decide that even if the odds of surviving are huge, they're still miniscule compared to losing the woman I love.

"It makes sense to me," Marissa says. "With the Triple Goddess as my witness, I swear to help you make it."

"If it makes sense to you," I say, squinting at another bottle of pinot noir atop the rack, "Then you're already farther ahead than I am."

"What are friends for?" she says with a genuine smile, and Sarah makes a small noise that doesn't have the same level of emotion as before.

Gazing at my unused weapon, I come to a grim conclusion: Reality is not only subject to personal notions, but also to the whims of the gods. If the gods and Titans are at war, I see no room for error.

I stride to the end of the aisle, careful not to trip on boxes. Marissa follows my line of thought. She stands behind me as I grip the door handle, and an ache slithers through me. I swing open the door, feeling the chilled air whisk between us. The refrigerator stores ice-cold beverages, food items, and various stainless-steel kitchenware. After we leave our weapons in the inside, we shuffle through the door Sarah holds open for us and out into the club.

Meandering through the crowd I feel a sense of dread, as the neon-clad front door flickers with hope within miniscule odds, and I can't shake the foreboding that this time will end in disaster again.

But we exit the front door at the same time as a young man with a wiry, green goatee and many piercings and tattoos of chthonic beasts on his arms. A row of hand-ripped slits are held together with shiny steel links through each hole in his jeans, and a black, steel-studded belt snakes through his beltloops. He greets us with a 'sup?' and continues on with his night of alcohol-imbued partying.

I grunt a garbled reply, trying to say 'hello.'

Keeping our heads down, we scurry past officers marching two-abreast up the sidewalk in search of us. At the end of the block, a major boulevard connects downtown to some midtown dwellings. Walking to the industrial district will take time, and I still cannot shake the idea something will go wrong—if it hasn't already.

15

The Offspring of Nyx

Less than a block into our journey, Sarah grabs my arm, and shoves me backward into the pillar of an office building, scowling into my face. Even though a thoughtful demeanor had covered her expression moments ago, a regressive dread now swoops through her eyes. When she has me pinned against the wall of a tall office building, she scowls and presses her face closer to mine.

Although she's close enough to kiss me, she snarls, "Why did you do it?" in a whisper.

I look over to Marissa for a split second, hoping she'll make Sarah back away from me, but she is gazing up at the glass towers a few blocks ahead. Those towers are reflecting a peculiar orange glow from an unknown source. With little time to assess the situation, I let my perception settle on Sarah again.

Sarah's nose flares inches away from my own, yet her voice is too calm.

"Do what?" I ask.

"It had to be you and no one else. There was nothing wrong—I was about to head home for the night. I smelled smoke, saw a flash from outside the window, and ran out of there with my heart racing as the fire alarm blared."

Her accusation comes as a shock, but I'm learning to take stressful events in my stride. Such a tactic offers a better route to solutions where few practical alternatives come to mind, and forces my mind to assign reason instead of letting adrenaline destroy my progress.

"Wasn't me," I cry. "Was already five-alarm status by the time we … God, I don't even remember where we were!"

My shouting causes her to flinch, but her expression remains calm. "I want to go back. To before it happened."

"Not possible right now." I'm sure of this, because when the fire destroyed the trailer, the connection to the cabin ceased to exist. And returning her to the moment before the fire may result in us trying to find a similar version of the trailer and losing ourselves in the dimensions.

"I don't know you anymore, Kerry."

An odd notion, seeing as Marissa just hypnotized her so she could find the origin of our connection and entanglement.

"A little while ago, you didn't even know my name," I say, offering a sympathetic nod. "Sometimes when you get to know someone in their own world, your perception changes because you get more information that either promotes or breaks down your attachment to them."

"Really?" she says, her voice sour. "Let's skip the guessing game. From now on, just drop the plans at the reception desk and ring the bell on your way out."

Does this make me feel better or worse, I wonder?

Of course, right now neither extreme takes place, but when I think about the implications of her suggestion, a sudden wave of panic hits me. If my assumption is correct, she'll soon get the news that she has to move to Portland. If this causes our relationship to fall apart, nothing I've experienced with Becky can come to pass—in fact, I might never meet Becky.

Yet another towering paradox.

"Could you guys maybe shelve the discussion for a minute?" Marissa interrupts.

When I look to see the subject of her attention, I gasp. I see the nightmare is about to crank into overdrive. The orange reflection now looks like an enormous asteroid hurtling through the earth's atmosphere, burning as it falls.

I only have a second to react. Marissa shields her face from the streaking fireball while I spin Sarah round to shield her with my body.

It's only marginally successful. A millisecond later, an explosion rocks the building fifty stories up, billowing smoke and fire into the sky. The building's cross-members give way, raining glass shrapnel down onto the sidewalk. As the first shards tinkle I sprint into the street, dragging Sarah by her right arm and collecting a shellshocked Marissa as I go.

The glass shreds Sarah's jacket into ribbons of flannel and faux leather, and a spot of blood oozes at her neck. I don't bother to inspect myself for damage as the building quakes from the impact.

Flames twirl skyward as the fire eats away at the steel members and fasteners. When the terrorists struck the twin towers, the jet fuel was hot enough to weaken the steel girders. The same thing may happen here.

Rumbling from the strain of holding its own weight now, the building shifts to the left, trembles, and belches a column of thick black smoke. The building will collapse on us in just seconds, flattening everything within two blocks.

Now alert to our peril, Sarah sprints off and Marissa and I follow, screaming for the shrieking bystanders to get away from the catastrophe.

Whatever has blown a hole in the office building doesn't stop there. The impact has spread to nearby buildings, shattering windows and engulfing neighboring towers in fire.

The sound of sirens ruptures the night air again as we jostle through the fleeing crowd. We make it less than two blocks before the upper floors fail. One by one, in slow motion, the stories crumble, and chunks of steel rebar join in the shower of falling glass and concrete.

The street shakes as screams pierce the night.

"TERRY!"

My spine and veins seize as I swear I've heard Becky's voice screaming my name. I emit a helpless whimper when we reach the next intersection, where a speeding car broadsides an SUV and both skid sideways, jump the sidewalks and crash into the corner lampposts, ripping them from their foundations and sending them toppling into the buildings.

The mushroom of smoke and thick clouds of dirt obscure our vision as each floor tumbles on top of another, until the building comprises fifty broken concrete pancakes amid the destruction.

My heart is racing. The rubble shifts as the fire spreads from the broken concrete, twisted pipe, and shredded insulation.

"Jesus," Sarah weeps.

"NOOO ... TERRY!!!" The woman's frantic cries emanate through the urban canyon as the neighboring buildings churn with fire and smoke.

Terry is flattened in the destroyed tower, and his distraught partner knows he's doomed. If the first responders ever find him while sifting through the rubble, they will encounter a smashed, unrecognizable body.

Together, the three of us sprint past the wrecked cars. Three passengers are climbing out of the SUV, while throngs of bystanders assemble around them. We shoulder through a crowd of people who want to catch a glimpse of the aftermath, while one courageous man shatters the driver's side window of the sedan and comforts the driver. The driver mumbles incoherently, though he shows no signs of intoxication. The surge of adrenaline seems to have clouded his judgement. Though everyone involved has survived, the miracle does nothing to ease our nerves.

People gather around the collapsed building as sirens wail in the night to signal the destruction. Some chatter and shout instructions to one another as they search for survivors. If Terry makes it out alive, it will be a miracle from the gods, but I already know who is to blame.

I shout his name in frustrated despair as I punch a stop sign six blocks away from the scene. "CRONUS! You evil *bastard!*"

This is *my* city. I've lived here for more than a decade by my most logical calculations and I have grown alongside it. The sights, the sounds, and the people mean a lot to me. Seeing it in this state causes me extreme distress. I only feel the pain in my knuckles a few moments after punching the sign, and I keel over, vomit, and pass out.

My soul wavers within my body as I erode into a dark cloud that hovers over the sidewalk. It seems as if I'm attempting to get a better view of the path ahead while the wind whips me into a cyclone.

"Kerry?"

"Jesus, Kerry."

Their voices echo and then die like vibrations being absorbed by soundproofing boards. I let myself sink toward the sidewalk, and then feel energy spark where my fingers should be. The sensation spreads throughout my body as it assembles itself from the cloud, and I pulse with radiant light.

Marissa and Sarah gawk at this performance, as shocked as if I'd wrought a trick no magician would ever dream of attempting.

"What the…?"

My radiating light dims as they both stare at me.

"Guess I didn't mention it," I say, wincing as pain courses through my hand. "I'm the Titan of Light and Shade."

Marissa and Sarah are speechless, even though I'd expected them to fire off accusatory questions while we make our way through the crowded streets. The sirens continue to rage throughout downtown.

But after twenty blocks, I begin to pant and my legs buckle under a dull, burning sensation in my feet. I can scarcely keep going towards the industrial district near the shipping yards.

"You know what happened?" Marissa says through labored breath. It sounds more like a statement than a question, causing me to rethink my automatic response.

"I'm almost certain of it. But you'll want to sit down for this."

"Good one," Marissa says with malicious wit. "Just three strangers enjoying a nice evening while the city burns."

"Let's start with that Titan bit," Sarah snaps.

I'd anticipated that question, but now that she's broached the subject, I am fumbling for an answer as I search the skies for flying objects. Turning back to look at the street, I focus on the rows of brake lights backed up behind a blinking red stoplight a few blocks away. "I found out about it when … well, really when Miriam healed me. It's all coming together piece by piece. But I think I knew someone once who called me a Titan."

"Doesn't mean you are one," Marissa says, settling onto a bench and waiting for Sarah to slide next to her as they watch me like an orator's rapt audience.

"How many other people have you watched turn into smoke and then emit light?" Marissa raises her palms while Sarah blanches and slides her feet together, putting her hands on her knees and leaning forward as if huddling against an icy gust of wind.

"Her name was Vanessa," I begin, telling the story as best I can remember. When I'm done, I let my shoulders unhunch as I watch the two women form questions they don't ask.

"I guess you could say she was a friend. But I'm the only one who can remember her now—because of entanglement, and probably because of where I've been."

"Care to guess where?"

I try to hide the sorrow in my voice but it doesn't lessen the ache in my heart. Tears well up in my eyes, causing me to squeeze them shut while I hang my head in shame. "To the end and back, and everywhere in between."

"You look like you've been through hell," Sarah says, letting her sympathy shine through. She turns her gaze away from a weed growing in a crack in the moldy sidewalk and toward my face.

The traffic creeps forward as I look back at her, allowing my eye to linger longer than it should. The sirens still blaze down the streets to deal with Cronus's death blow. That coward! His father should have castrated him and burned the severed bits after his betrayal, but with Cronus, it's always more complicated.

As I regard the sidewalk crack, I find myself astonished at how nature finds ways to thrive, even in a bustling metropolis. If humans continue to shun nature, do they deserve to occupy space on this blue dot we call home?

"I think that might be true in a somewhat literal sense," I finally say, directing my gaze at Sarah's sneakers.

"It's funny," remarks Marissa, her voice cautious. "Religions use the mythical place called hell as a warning, but maybe it's all metaphorical. Spiritualism doesn't depend on heaven or hell. I think we should adopt that way of thinking."

"Look around," I argue. "Two thousand years on, we're way past that now."

"So we continue to let religion dominate our lives to our detriment, because a mysterious robed figure in the sky presented himself to a sheep herder thousands of years ago?"

"Hardly time for a theological debate," I argue, bristling at her arrogance. I may not be the one to teach her the actual truth, but whenever that happens, she'll wish she'd never said that.

"Who's Cronus?" Sarah asks, her expression pensive. "Someone you know?"

I clench my teeth and nod. "A Titan—a real piece of work. Betrayed his father and took control of the cosmos, which led to his own downfall. There are twelve Titans, and they're renewing their war with the Olympians. You think that's bad? Just wait for what's coming." I say all this while I cast my eyes back towards the smoke in the distance, where red and blue lights swirl.

"And you're a Titan?"

I already knew Marissa would go there. "Not related to the original twelve. I descend from the Cretans under King Minos and his daughter."

"Fire Guy is a Titan, too," she reasons.

I give a matter-of-fact nod. "Prometheus."

"And he wants your help. You're going to help them destroy Philadelphia."

"Don't know who the real villains are anymore."

She frowns. "And the only way to find out is by working with him. All the collateral damage, lives lost, to save the universe. And your wife."

I have no retort handy. Now I'm pacing in front of them with my hands clasped behind my back, and I turn my attention to the shipyards a few blocks away. In the other direction, chaos has baked the clouds of dust with a smoky scent, rendering the skyline a murky shade of charcoal gray. The dazzling squares of yellow light blur into the individual particles, making everything look hallucinogenic.

Working with Prometheus will lead me to the truth. And when I uncover it, I'll kill him, unless he kills me first. As the rage plants itself into my soul, the darkness within me swells. And now that Sarah and Marissa know what I know, they'll either trust me or help to destroy me. I won't blame them either way.

But before I join Prometheus, I need to save Becky. That is my primary focus.

Sensing that the conversation has turned, Sarah and Marissa rise to their feet and follow me down the narrow streets approaching the historical district, where we will turn southward and make way for the harbor.

A rumble in the distance suggests that the destruction has only just begun. Flashes erupt at the edge of the surrounding area, raining down like fireballs. It just makes my anger grow. Clenching my fists and walking as fast as my bones can carry me, I lead them away toward the crowds around Market Street.

But before we've made it a block, a man with a greasy mane of black and gray hair in a ragged overcoat approaches us from the shadows. He staggers toward me and I smell alcohol on his breath as his eyes dart in every direction. He is carrying a leather-bound book, the shimmering gold foil edges of which have thumbnail cutouts to mark sections. Raising it high above his head, he stumbles forward, raises his voice, and slurs his speech: "Repent, before it's too late."

Too many mistakes and too little time. It might take me eons to settle the strife I've caused. Now that I'm walking with the woman behind it all, I can only frown at my own stupidity in risking the entire universe for her. I hope it will be worth it.

16

Pandora's Box

The historic district along Market Street is familiar territory—wide enough for street dining, entertainment, and tourist throngs, it is a festive yet traditional experience. It keeps the old patriotic theme intact.

In the central business district, the crowds have died down, and the pedestrians, museum patrons, and shoppers are hiding in the hotel rooms or rental condos scattered throughout Independence Historic Park. A few remain, filtering in and out of storefronts, loitering on sidewalks, and congregating around the Liberty Bell. A group of people are waiting at a crosswalk on 6th Street, looking towards Independence Hall a block away.

On a typical day in this part of downtown, you can see people from various backgrounds, including foreign visitors. Many people coming here hope to glimpse the origins of the United States of America, which might promote unity despite the differing viewpoints among the citizens. Although in recent years, cracks have begun to show.

Lately, political displays have become more prominent, everything from innocuous campaign signs to full-throated rallies accusing "the other side" of "destroying America."

But today no such displays are visible, which I take as a good sign. Perhaps the real destruction has changed minds rather than heightened tensions.

When a woman staggering off of 6th Street bumps into my shoulder, she makes eye contact for a split second before gazing at the riverfront, where the nightlife blossoms after sunset. She mumbles, "Damn asshole," just loud enough for me to hear.

"Look who's talking," Marissa says, grinning, a full thirty seconds later when the stranger is out of earshot.

"Maybe she's right," says Sarah.

I can only nod. Normally, I'd be indignant or try to defend myself, but now that interdimensional life is spinning out of control due to my own actions, I make no real comment in out of a sort of pensive humility.

She's right—everything that has become of this version of Philadelphia has resulted from my disregard for time's fragility. The building has tumbled, and Terry is a crushed corpse because of me. If I weren't in my own body, I'd accuse myself of far worse, and I'd still be right.

Apart from hitchhiking on Interstate 95, the quickest route to the industrial district near the port should be via Columbus Boulevard, which fronts Penn's Landing and the Delaware River. If I remember the area well enough, the correct building might be six blocks away from the shipyards. At this time of the evening, with sparse traffic, the walk should take another hour. By that time, we will have sore feet and droopy eyelids. Still, I can't give up—Becky and the universe at large are depending on me.

As we cross the I-95 corridor, Marissa and Sarah are beginning to discuss history; Sarah relays what she remembers about the signing of the Declaration of Independence, and Marissa regales her with more personal stories about nameless heroes with spiritual foresight.

According to Marissa, William Penn's descendant Hanna Oakley led a charge of women to support the troops during the Revolutionary War, using various forms of paganism and spiritualism, to the dismay of other Quaker descendants. While more temporal-minded women did chores such as cooking, cleaning, and laundry, Hannah devised spiritual means to protect the freedom fighters.

Whether or not her story is true, what counts is Marissa's spirit.

Afterward, we make it to the shipyards in forty-five minutes. In that neighborhood, blocks of low-roofed unremarkable industrial buildings stretch as far as I can see. Giant harbor cranes load and unload shipping containers on and off enormous freighters. One such crane specializes in transferring cargo containers onto freight trains, which wait along a dozen terminal tracks headed out of town. At over a hundred feet high, the cranes give the neighborhood a heavy industrial feel.

We walk down the boulevard for several blocks and then turn into a narrow street with sparse trees growing through red iron grates. I follow a crack that travels several blocks toward the curb.

The area has room for industrial uses and street parking, with buildings taking up extra space. Although the buildings occupy more area than necessary, the overall theme of the neighborhood seems accurate. Towards the shipyards, the district becomes poorer, and is choked with thick undergrowth between tall deciduous trees.

After deciding another street will take us closer to our destination, I lead Sarah and Marissa along a wider side street, populated with three- and four-story buildings. Behind the buildings, an alley of shipping and receiving operations hosts several parked vans, which are visible between the blocks of brick veneers.

I study a nearby building and look several blocks ahead, to where a five-floor apartment building rises. This building is fronted by an empty concrete planter originally constructed of old jersey barriers. It is full of weeds that are taking advantage of the sun.

Five feet from the planter, a concrete bench huddles in a bus shelter beneath a dilapidated shade structure comprising steel curtain wall members and panes of clouded plexiglass which blur the oncoming traffic. A tilted bus stop sign juts out of the sidewalk. I focus on it for several minutes before sitting on the bench and beginning to wait.

Marissa takes a seat next to me, places her hand on the cold concrete next to my thigh and sighs awkwardly.

"I take it this is the place," she says.

I offer only a silent nod.

"Think she's going to come?"

"I just hope she's not inside already," I say, peering at the paved driveway that links the street and the alley. A single lamppost rises a few feet away from the building's face, bolted to a round pillar surrounded by unkempt grass. Splotches of white and gray paint coat areas of the black steel. The sodium light flickers for a moment, echoing my uncertainty.

I don't know what will happen or how it will play out, but I sense the kind of foreboding that precedes dread. My mind always tries to plan for obstacles in new situations, but with unknown variables, I can't plan at all. This is stressful because I take little time to think through complex scenarios that require action.

Ten minutes pass while nothing happens.

Sarah is filling the time by humming a dreary tune and craning her neck toward Marissa, until a loud horn sounds from the shipyards. It stops her for a bit, then her humming continues, even as she meets my eyes for a half second.

Marissa sighs again. "You know an environment like this might not evoke spiritual feelings, but you *can* connect with them if you know how. Time and space conform to their whims. Most of them won't interrupt, or even so much as plant ideas in your head, but if you learn to quiet your mind, you can hear them."

"Really?" I say, squinting and offering a sheepish smile. "I don't believe in that mysticism stuff. Better things to do, no offense."

"Then again, it might help you."

"Maybe, maybe not. I'm just here to save Becky." Glancing again beyond the lamppost to the driveway, I amend my statement: "Her car's not here yet, so we have some waiting to do. I'd prefer to be paying attention when she arrives."

"How can you even know she will?"

"Because I know this is the right dimension. I've studied it every possible way, and there's no other time that makes sense. Because of what happened to us before, she'll know I'll be here. She'll come."

"What if our presence drives her away?"

That possibility never crossed my mind, but I take her words in stride and carefully think out a next course should that come to pass. "Mission accomplished."

"But you won't know it's accomplished," she says. "Even if we sit here for three days, which I'm sure the building owners won't allow, we might miss her. There are no guarantees. We can't predict the consequences. Doesn't that scare you?"

I have learned that I should fear many things that don't affect me; with that knowledge comes the illogicality of letting everything scare me, which scares me even more. And now that peril is around every corner, I keep expecting something to happen, which paradoxically deadens the fear. I could train myself to "fear not," but lack of fear makes surprises more dangerous—and if I don't prepare for surprise attacks, I die.

"It does," I say. "But it doesn't. I can't explain it so you will understand."

I expect her to cross her arms and say, "Try me," but her body language doesn't change. Rather than giving me a wiser-than-you look, she glances sideways past Sarah and peers at the planter.

I take a few seconds to realize she's studying something and also focus in that direction.

The eastern horizon has gone black as thunderclouds tower over New Jersey, but those clouds expand as I watch; making a sprinkle of rain.

Marissa is still eyeing the empty planter.

The soil inside the planter should contain weeds, but someone has recently tilled it, making room for flowers.

Sarah stops humming, leans forward and plants her elbows on her knees, allowing a clearer view of the planter. I can see shapes emerging from the soil, subtle at first, but becoming more complete with every passing second.

The thunderstorm arrives sooner than I'd expected, and the sprinkle turns to a drizzle, which quickly becomes a steady rain that soaks through my clothes and hair and churns the muddy soil in the planter.

Seconds later, the shapes form a column of smoke that twirls overhead and then pauses. Marissa closes her eyes as though to interact with spirits; the Shades should lunge at her, but they don't. Keeping their distance, they hover over the planter and then dissolve back into the soil. Dread circles within me, igniting the fear. I can't outrun it, but I can cope with it the best way I know how.

Marissa does it better. She has connected with the Shades on a personal level, thereby talking them out of devouring her. If she can do it, maybe I can too.

For her part, Sarah has sensed nothing. Her hair drips as lightning flashes in the distance, illuminating a vast confluence of clouds that may be a swirling Nor'easter. The showers drench us as we remain sitting here. Marissa breaks eye contact and looks away along the avenue to watch for approaching cars. A pair of headlights filters through the rainfall and flicks off before another pair of lights peeks from the darkness and turns onto a nearby street.

After a moment of precarious reflection, I close my eyes and draw in a deep breath while forming sentences in my brain, trying to push them out telepathically.

Feel me. I know we have a complicated history, but we work for the same entity. Or at least we used to. Please connect me with Ian.

My mind settles and my heart aches.

There is no Ian. There is only you.

My son, I beg, letting my heart grow darker. *I know he's there, trapped somewhere in a place I can never reach. Please tell me how to get there.*

Your end, the planter replies, *will inevitably lead to a new beginning.*

A new beginning. For Ian to live, I must die. My chest is filled with intense pain as the planter sends countless darts of sadness at me. If I die, I can never be with Becky again. Death brings darkness, and I can never fully escape it. Even if I manage to push it away, it always lingers, ready to resurface and overwhelm me when I least expect it.

Occasional moments of relief wash over me, but intrusive thoughts flood my mind like bubbling acid, making it difficult to resist the weight of despair. Somewhere in the soil, darkness is brewing a powerful mixture of failure and hopelessness, seeping into the air as an invisible mist that permeates my body and settles into the depths of my being.

I know you, Kerry.

"You're a Titan."

"Kerry, you're such a man."

"Dad. I love you."

Dad. Ian is real, and if that's true maybe I'm not. My soul reels as the misery feeds it, and my body grows lighter with every passing moment.

Agony devours me as the storm calls to me, even while it marches across the city, extinguishing fires and providing fleeting relief to the suffering. I give in to the anguish, mushroom ten feet above the sidewalk, and then twenty as the venom of memory and hallucination feeds the Shade within me.

The Kerry Gearhardt, Titan of Light and Shade.

Sarah leaps off the bench as I vanish, and that moment of panic causes Marissa to peel her eyes away from the end of the street to sense my spiritual presence. Her voice is a salve of tonic washing away the sting, but as my ashen tears squeeze out to evaporate all within me, a faint light glimmers on the horizon. I reach out for it with every fiber of my soul as it grows closer, filling me with a memory I can't quite pin down.

"You know who you are, Kerry Gearhardt."

Use the light.

MEMORIES:

My heart drums as I gaze into Becky's eyes in a room of white lace and flowers. A three-layered cake sits on a decorative tablecloth nearby, while an usher guides a group of men in suits into the room. The men take their seats, while the gentle piano melody fades, leaving a lasting memory.

The smell of simmering meat reaches my nose as the music fades, making way for the colossus of words that I've tried to remember—to recite aloud.

"Susanne Rebecca Freeman," I say, with tears in my eyes, "forever will I be yours. My heart will be with you beyond the end, because eternity has no end. I promise to help you through all life's trials. You have my complete love and devotion. No matter what life throws at us, as long as we can lean on each other, nothing can tear us apart."

She holds out her tender hand, spaces her fingers and I slip the glittering ring onto her finger as the guests applaud enthusiastically, and some weep joyous tears.

"Becky Gearhardt," I whisper.

And before the music swells again, I clasp her waist, close my eyes, and follow it up with a blissful kiss that I hope will never end.

The sorrow drains away as I wait in the rain. I feel my body reform out of the mist between Sarah and Marissa.

Sarah stares at me as I glance beyond her to the planter, where sadness and desperation lurk. No weeds or flowers can grow in its poison, which acts like a deadly toxin that renders all human emotion meaningless. Every bit of darkness within the planter consumes the life-giving nutrients needed for life.

Marissa opens her eyes, and smiles in a way that reflects the soft glow in my body. "Welcome back," she says as I begin to weep again.

Forever cannot end, and nothing can tear us apart—not even death. The memory of that helps me to commit everything I have. For Becky. For Ian. For the universe.

17

Clotho Weaves

Downpours on chilly nights can cause immense distress in Philadelphia, even when not accompanied by lightning and thunder. Learning to cope took some effort, but I eventually got used to them.

But now that the fate of everything I've ever known and loved hangs in the balance, the chill radiates deep into my bones. The rain might hide my tears, but Marissa can sense everything I'm going through.

How does she do that?

She answers my question before I can even ask it. "I felt you, and you heard me."

"That explains it," I mutter, with a shrug. Wiping my wet hands on my drenched jeans worsens the feeling of hypothermia.

A quick nod tells me she didn't intend for the conversation to go there, as though our shared understanding required a different dialog. Her eyes sparkle with sympathy, while her dripping hair channels rain down her chest.

"What exactly happens here?"

Although her tone suggests she already knows and wants my confirmation, acknowledging the darkness only makes the situation seem more bleak. I flick my eyes back and forth, a dismissive gesture that surprises her. "Is this why she's missing?" she asks until I shrug again, causing her to rephrase the question. "I mean, if this place doesn't hold any real significance, why are we here? If what you say is true, wouldn't the version of her in this dimension seek out a different building?"

"You don't understand," I say, not trying to sound accusatory. "This is where it happens. I don't know what gave her this address. But she's coming."

Marissa takes this in stride, glancing toward the downtown skyscrapers, where the now-extinguished fires emit twisting columns of black smoke. "Where what happens?"

I frown and mumble in sorrow, "It's where I find her."

"And also this," I add, withdrawing the tiny, fused washers from my pocket. The rain washes a trickle of black grease from them into my palm. The streetlamp reflects on this like an orb of yellow light. The continual waves of distress that are washing over me dim my glow. Even if Marissa can see the shine of my personality's light side, she can't miss the darkness that has always dwelt there too.

That's one of my many flaws. It didn't take Becky long to notice it, resolve to correct it, and use it against me before we ever started dating. The Shade part of me may draw from that darkness, but it also refuses to let the murk define it. If I could go back and find her now, I'd be better prepared to overcome it, but that won't matter if I can't be with her. She's the spark that ignites me.

"Those are washers," says Marissa, shivering in the chilly air. Her expression adds a playful enthusiasm to her straightforward observation.

"They are infinity," I correct her. "Two circles, two souls. And no matter how hard you try, you can't break them apart. It symbolizes our relationship. Unlike your pentagram necklace and tattoo, which might look cool—"

"It might mean many things, depending on how you look at it." she says, folding her arms. "You might choose to see it merely as good luck, or your wife might see it as representing the wounds of Jesus Christ, for instance. For me, it's a pagan symbol of protection associated with air, earth, fire, water, and spirit—the five elements."

"That's very elaborate."

"Then don't act dismissive if you don't want me to reciprocate. Tell me everything, and maybe its protection will work."

Although the memory has faded over time, the emotional impact still gouges at me. Trying to articulate it without revealing my pain is futile. She can see everything playing out on my face as I speak, until I finish with the card on the concrete floor.

Erebus, The One True God of Darkness.

Hearing my story at first makes Sarah's ears perk up, but when she senses the trauma her eyes droop, her shoulders hunch, and she gathers her arms across her torso to shield her from the damp, chill air.

"Do you hear her soul?" Marissa asks.

"She's alive," I snarl.

"But you're entangled. You said it yourself."

Half nodding and half-shaking my head, I respond in a way that doesn't affect her the way I thought it would. "Your idea."

"Your reality."

"Reality," I say, letting out a dry chuckle. "Every time you think you know what it is, the universe hits you with a demoralizing truth bomb. It depends on your subjective experience and always has."

"If you say so."

"Secretary Harley K. Whitworth taught me that one. Good man, good friend."

"Who's that?"

"The Secretary of Defense," I mutter.

Seemingly abandoning the line of questioning, she raises her eyebrows, electing to go with a different solution.

"What if your butterfly effect idea applies to this dimension?" She shivers but speaks with such passion that her hands attempt to convey additional context, as if her words are insufficient. "What if in this version, she doesn't come? Because somewhere along the way, we've altered her perspective. If she ends up going back to the lake…"

"Because we were there," I reply. The reasoning is strong enough against any argument, although carrying it out is a problem. If we return to that dimension now, cross to the island, and drop from the closet onto the bed again, it may create a looping timeline—and that's if we're in the correct version of that dimension.

"You see it, then," Marissa says. "She doesn't come here. She goes to the lake, where whoever it is won't get to her. If that's the reality, she's safe there and you don't need to worry."

"I worry all the time," I say.

"By choice," Sarah interposes.

I wait for her to explain.

She slumps her shoulders again and turns toward the planter, which has turned the downpour into thick mud, making the jersey barriers look taller by comparison.

When a car appears at the end of the street, I frown, reset my gaze, and determine she won't clarify.

"If you don't choose to worry about the people you love, you're a poor excuse for a husband and father. Even my awesome abilities couldn't save her." I'm rambling, but just this once, allowing my words to reflect the darkness of my soul feels oddly cathartic. "What evil grants anyone the right to determine who lives and who dies, who suffers—and based on what? The lottery of the gods?"

"I know it makes you angry," Sarah whispers. "Probably would for me, too. But you can't let that swamp you, because you embody the light."

"It was a gift," I interject.

"Doesn't matter. You choose to use it, just like you choose to use the dark. Your choices make you who you are. Not any god or Titan."

"What do you say we employ a different tactic?" Marissa says.

I know what she's alluding to, but I don't need any further healings from Miriam, even if she *is* the descendant of an ancient sorceress.

She frowns at my reaction. "I didn't even say it."

"You were thinking it."

"Thinking what?" asks Sarah.

"But it might work out," Marissa continues, disregarding the question. "Even the best plans are subject to the whims of nature, and if you're not adapting, you're defeated. Miriam is real good."

"Is she even open this late?"

"There's a chance. But I'm not the one in trouble here."

I remember another industrial building in this district has a portal. Where did it lead? I ponder it for several moments.

Marissa breaks eye contact and swivels her attention to the street, to where a car is ripping along the wet pavement. The headlights flash, creating a strobe of red light interspersed with a shadow that flips in front of it. She looks shocked as the headlights jump six feet off the avenue.

A split second later, a roar emanates from the docks as a powerful wave crashes through the maze of shipping containers, topples the cranes and surges through the neighborhood, flowing under the uplifted car. As the wave recedes, dragging mud and debris back into the harbor, the car bounces back onto the pavement, its undercarriage slamming against the asphalt.

The shadow lurks near the sidewalk, forms a fireball, and shoots it high into the sky like a firework. My time is up.

"Finding you was a challenge this time," he growls. "Made a decision yet?"

He won't let me get away this time. I stand up, feeling my muscles flex as I face the icy atmosphere.

"You could use a warmup," he teases.

"I just want to know why," I say through gritted teeth. "Why did you save that driver if you plan to destroy the city?"

"Never said I planned that," he says. "We're at war. I don't want more collateral damage than there needs to be."

Stepping toward him, I rear back as if to sprint at him and plow my fist through his face. Instead of deflecting my attack, he saunters toward me as steam rises off his rippling muscles.

"Mighty generous of you. But your pal Cronus destroyed that building, and where were you?"

"Fighting on another front," he barks.

"If you don't want to destroy the city, what *do* you want?"

"You and me, we're allies, Kerry, Titan of Light and Shade."

Biting my lip, I feel the nerves tear at my back, spreading shards of anger to my fingers. I'm no match for him, but that does not diminish my wish to crush his cranium. As if we're in a Wild West gunfight I stare him down with my feet spaced apart.

"You help me, I help you."

"What do you offer?" I shout. "I don't trust you."

"I can offer you what your heart truly desires. You can give me your support. I've seen your abilities."

The skyline glows orange. I am trembling with hate as I inch toward him, my fists ready, waiting for him to make the first move. "Do you expect me to believe some vague promises? I should have brought your sister to this negotiation."

"Let me explain later," he urges. "Come with me."

"Not without them," I say, gesturing to Marissa and Sarah, who are standing nervously behind me. He can melt all three of us with a single attack, sending a fireball sky high if he so chooses.

But instead, he says, "Let's get a move on. You know how to fly?"

"Damn, I must have forgotten that lesson at Titan University."

He remains calm, although he simmers with orange and red light that burns through his veins like streams of lava. "Then hurry."

We don't manage a single step before the sky fills with a million fluttering wings. Bats and birds and other winged beasts swarm above the industrial wasteland, blotting out the orange glow behind the business district towers.

Rage surges through me as I sprint toward him, ready to batter him with my fists. An enormous rock tumbles down from the sky, dispersing the beasts. A moment later, pain rips across my torso, causing me to lose whatever bile has accumulated in my stomach. Marissa howls with pain as Sarah doubles over.

Prometheus unleashes a burst of flames toward us, missing and spewing incoherent curses.

From the corner of my eye I see the streetlamp reflecting off an enormous ball of water, which is churning toward us. It drenches the industrial district as it soars over the buildings. Prometheus doesn't deflect it, but then, it wasn't aimed at him. It circles overhead like a watery enemy ready to strike. Suddenly, it empties over us with enough weight to crush three large oil trucks to ribbons.

"WHAM!!"

The water smashes into the concrete as we disappear in a flash of orange and red light. The maelstrom whips us high over the Southside residential districts, dodging skyscrapers as we accelerate to speeds that make our skin ripple and the wind tug at our hair.

You shall not get away, the menacing voice in my head says through rumbling vibrations in the air current.

"Let justice be done!" a woman shouts from several blocks away, launching herself skyward to join Prometheus in whisking us across the city.

Her long silvery curls taper between her caped shoulder blades and her tunic flutters at her slipper-clad feet. As she races through the air alongside us, she spits venomous words in Greek that I cannot understand.

The avians chase us across the city, and once we reach the outskirts of downtown, it becomes even more confusing. Prometheus erupts with a mushroom of fire just as the winged creatures attack us, trying to drag us down to the rooftops and the streets below. The rain intensifies, but the beasts can't escape the flames.

Feathers scatter as their wings fail, raining charred carcasses down on the streets—even as another horde of feathered animals attacks us. Winged fairy women join in the fray, cursing at us, rasping and hissing as they dig six-inch talons into our ribs.

A second later, the harpies release us, but before we can fall to our deaths, some unseen energy holds us aloft.

Prometheus sends another white-hot salvo, which flashes the rainfall into steam as it tears across the sky like a flamethrower. The birds scatter, clearing our path back to the Bones Holdings job-site. We streak toward it at speed as rain lashes us with heavy drops like icy needles sewing threads of frost through our skin.

Sarah screams as we descend. I see that Prometheus has sent us further than the job-trailer; we are about to crash land into the base of a hotel tower. I am furious; this kind of time warpage might shred Sarah and Marissa to pieces, but we have no choice other than to bring them along.

So far, Fire Guy has protected us from many enemies. A squawk erupts from behind us as our escort makes a perfect landing. Passersby carry on as though four people drop from the sky all the time.

He doesn't bother explaining himself. Shattering the glass doors as he flings them open, he leads us inside the trembling building. The marble floors ripple with the vibrations, shaking up the lobby's leather-upholstered reclining chairs, glass coffee tables, and fake potted plants.

We hurtle toward the elevators despite the ineffectual protests of the hotel staff. When they see what is approaching from outside, they freeze, transfixed. A wave of cars is rolling and tumbling toward the glass walls, and as the elevator dings and the doors open, the cars come smashing through the windows, demolishing the furnishings and crunching into the elevator wall.

Then the doors pull themselves shut, and the elevator rises thirty floors to the penthouse. But instead of lurching to a stop, the elevator walls disappear and we soar through countless stars, spinning like marionettes as Prometheus whisks us to a new destination. I am fuming.

As we collapse onto a rocky shoreline, I gather my fists and punch Fire Guy in the head. I am frustrated that my hands burst into flames instead of hurting him. I expect him to launch me like a flaming rocket, but he lets me down easy, wraps his hands around my fists, and extinguishes the flames. A patient, pained expression crosses his face as he gazes from the bluff where we are standing, over a calm sea.

For the first time in a while, I don't know what's coming next.

18
Ephialtes's Deceit

The coastline comprises broken, rocky outcroppings rimmed by arid steppe lands. Fifty feet below, waves crash their brackish water over jumbled boulders, spraying saltwater into the sky. When the waves ebb, the channels between the rocks create eddies that gather whirls of foam on the surface. Even fifty feet up, the wind-tossed spray makes the air feel humid, allowing the grass to turn green near the cliff's edge.

A small, craggy cape juts into the sea ten miles away, with a rock formation protecting it a hundred yards offshore. At low tide it might be a perfect place to gather shells, if one were able to brave the fierce, howling winds.

Marissa joins me, looking out to the whitecaps in the distance, shielding her eyes from the sun. I shiver in the chilly wind. Behind us, Sarah sits on a jumble of shattered basalt, her hair whipping in the breeze.

Marissa pushes her hair behind her ears, surveys the coastline, and seems to be attempting a guess at our location. I don't want to hear what she has to say; she often interrupts my tranquility with pithy bits of wisdom. It doesn't usually bother me much, but right now I'm in no mood for it.

I peer down to the base of the cliff, frowning at sheared-off slices of cliffside eroded by the turbid water. I glimpse a crab scuttling in the foam.

"We can still find her," Marissa says, keeping her voice placid despite her underlying concern. "We'll just have to look another way."

"There's no other way."

"A guy I used to date," she says, "used to tell me there's more than one way to skin a cat. I punched him in the face because I happen to like cats."

I'm unable to even lift my eyebrows. Understanding her meaning doesn't diminish the pain of giving up.

"My point is that sometimes the right path is hidden. Everyone assumes the beaten track is the safest, most direct route, yet you miss the scenery that way."

"You think I'm doing this for adventure, and sight-seeing? And I thought you were deep." My tone is sharper than I'd intended, and she frowns.

"That's not what I meant. Some things can only be found once. What if the way is hidden where no one will ever look?"

I scowl. "No one bothered to look for her. The building rotted on top of her for so long only her bones were left. Which means nobody knew where to look."

Marissa narrows her eyes. "She's alive, isn't she?"

Good point, but it doesn't make me feel much better.

"Maybe we just have to check a few different dimensions. Backtrack. Where have you been? Where's she been?"

Behind us, I hear sniffling between crashing waves, as though someone has allergies. Marissa walks away while I watch a flight of birds gliding on the wind and settling on the rock near the cape.

Get moving, the air vibrations command.

A moment later, Prometheus appears at my side. When I angrily turn to him, I see Sarah's bowed head and her face resting in her hands, and between her fingers tears reflect the sun's rays.

"We should get moving," he says, echoing The One.

So he hears it too.

Rather than reacting to my anger, his sentences stretch into an introspective tone. "I should tell you something ... if the timing is right."

"Could have started days ago," I growl.

Again, his voice lengthens. "I'm on your side. The rest of them don't know, and they can't. The Titans are wrong, and while the Olympians might be imperfect, they're the only chance to save this world."

"Choice isn't always binary," I say, gritting my teeth.

A pensive nod and a careful shrug of his shoulders suggest he's feeling his way carefully through, removing as much tension from his voice as possible, as if preventing The One from uncovering his true thoughts.

"It rarely is," he agrees. "But think of what options you might encounter while shopping for tools to fix your car. There are innumerable choices, but you need only one."

I haven't fixed my car in ages, having grown into the habit of taking it into the dealer's service shop every time it makes a funny sound that makes me suspicious. Becky chides me for it, but I tell her it's better to get it done right than to fiddle with it again in a month. The analogy is easy enough to understand but doesn't make me trust him.

Beside me, his bony elbow is stained black, either by a curious tattoo or by dirt, but similar markings on his bare biceps and chest indicate that he's changed his appearance by another means. He combs a hand through his tangled hair as he speaks, still purposefully muting every accent and pause in his speech.

I could call him out, but I'd rather observe the ocean. I wince at a sudden gust whipping a stinging blitz of sand on the ridge. While my eyes are half open, I swear I sense something out there, lurking beneath the waves.

"I've already made my choice. Zeus and Athena needed my services after I made the mistake of walking away. I deserved Tartarus, but now I'm ready to make amends."

"You're saying you turned traitor—for me?" If I'm trying to provoke just a single flare of emotion, I'm not trying hard enough.

He looks solemn but otherwise unmoved. "For the earth. For mother Gaia."

"Gaia's not an Olympian," I say, envisioning her as a bikini-clad athlete with a number pinned to her top.

"We made the Olympians; the Titans did. Gave them everything they ever wanted. Awesome powers and human traits. It's easy to regret when you're sitting in Tartarus for thousands of years, but sometimes you have to admit you were wrong."

"Humility," I begin, "isn't a power most would ascribe to the Titans. No offense."

"But then again, perhaps it makes us that much stronger. Humility was in short supply during the last war. And it cost us."

"Indecision is no asset in war," I say, glaring at him.

"And neither is admitting a failure after the fact. It might seem foolish, but the best tacticians decide whether actions are successful and adapt their strategies based on what they did last time and what the enemy is doing now. If you can't admit you made a mistake, you're going to repeat it. And that's the best way to ... forgive the expression ... go down in flames."

If I understand his choice of tone, inserting more emotion into the conversation can't be wise. Still, I have no other choice; I've never excelled at altering my own feelings at will. I've always depended on Becky to help me with that. Leaning on Prometheus instead makes me feel sick. "But what about your commitment to The One? He's still the one calling the shots, isn't he?"

"Interesting you still call him that."

"Meaning what?"

"Wasn't your debt to him fulfilled when you destroyed the tower?"

This accusation is a blindside. I clench my fingers, glower at him, and bark my response. "What debt? What tower? You're insane."

"That's right," he says. "You don't remember. That's not surprising."

"My memory's pretty damn good," I snarl.

"Not good enough to defeat nature. It's no failure on your part. A mortal cannot remember events in the underworld, even if he's unfortunate enough to travel there. Quite the feat when you consider that only a few have ever escaped in millennia."

"Is it supposed to work differently for Titans? Because from what I hear, I'm a Titan, too."

"Immortal ones," he says, watching a pod of whales breaching the waves.

I glance out, deciding that's what I'd seen a few minutes ago.

"Immortality is only for the gods."

"The Titans and gods play by the same rules," he admits. "Immortals can be killed, just not by disease, starvation, natural causes. Only by war. Or murder."

"I see."

"You might be a Titan, Kerry, Conveyor of Light and Shade. But you're still mortal. And I just saved your life back there. And your friends too—doesn't that count for something?"

"Probably had ulterior motives."

"Do you want my help or not?"

The tension rises in his voice, and when he hears it, he lets out a sigh to calm his nerves.

"I'm not fighting your war for you. I'm finding Becky, undoing the paradoxes I caused.

That's how I'll save the universe."

"Noble of you," he admits, "but missing the bigger picture. You might have released us from Tartarus, but the Titans have been planning this war for ages."

"Wait, *I* let you out?"

"On orders from The One," he says, shrugging. "You promised him loyalty in return for giving you a means of retrieving your wife."

"I'm still not interested in your war."

"The Titans have assembled vast armies that the Olympians can't match. If you don't join me, your entire civilization will crumble."

"At least I'll see the end with the one I love."

He offers a nod and turns to face me. "Provided you can find her and return her to her home dimension. I can help you there."

What the hell? I'd punch him again if I didn't think my hands would explode.

"You're thinking I'm just going to sell my soul for some false choice between doing one right thing or another?"

"What if you can do both?"

"I need her, dammit!"

For the first time, I can hear earnestness in his voice now that he's shed the cloak of indifference. "She needs *you*, Kerry. And so does your son."

"You leave him out of this, you bastard!" My raspy voice catches Sarah and Marissa's attention.

Sarah tilts her head back, allowing her matted hair to stick to her forehead and her neck. Tears have reddened her eyes and washed lines of worry down her cheeks. She looks beaten, yet not ready to give up the fight.

Seeing her in this state spikes my guilt even further, as does Marissa as she wraps an arm around Sarah's shoulders.

"I can help you," Prometheus repeats, his voice dropping an octave for clarity.

I'm done arguing with him. Why must everyone else always be right, and me in the wrong? This thought just makes me angrier, but I know that conceding is the only right choice. Fire Guy will betray me because he's good at that. And when he does, that will be the time to release my rage.

"I knew you would see reason."

"He's right, Kerry," Marissa says, tilting her head away from Sarah and widening her eyes at me. "You even said it yourself: You're going to join him for the good of everyone."

"Just hope you're ready for the consequences," Prometheus says. "War is the ugliest hell you can imagine. And you will see terrible things."

More terrible than stumbling on my wife's bones? Or realizing that my son is trapped in a limbo of my own making? All the time travel in the world can't undo those sins or relieve the heartache.

"Kerry?" Sarah wipes her face with her hand and her wrist, smearing the tears to her ears, where they drip down her neck. She quails in the sunlight, making her glow with a surreal grace I've seen only in Becky. "I want to go home—but I'm with you till the end."

I shoot an accusatory look at Marissa, who tosses her hair over her shoulder and grins.

Smooth, I give her that.

"We have seen nothing yet," I warn. "They say the Titans are more powerful than the gods. Especially when the god of darkness backs them. It won't be easy."

"Anything worth doing's gonna be hard," Marissa says, offering a lopsided smile. She's paraphrasing a vague platitude I've heard before, yet she makes it sound genuine. "Let's get ready to fight."

Behind Marissa and Sarah, the rocky landscape stretches over rolling hills, to dry mountains where boulders are scattered among golden grasses that have been flattened by the ferocious wind. Whirlwinds of sand rise and fall in concert with the gales and a flock of geese flies in formation over the shore. In a distant valley the shadows of clouds run over a shallow gully of jumbled boulders and rotting tree trunks.

I can't help feeling I've seen this place before, in another dimension. Even though it is hostile to permanent settlement, I can still see its stark beauty. Yet the tides of war gather on the horizon. We must travel through the darkness to reach the light.

Our odds of winning are just about non-existent, but if war is the only choice, I'll fight until I'm nothing more than space dust. With tears stinging my eyes, I whisper two words that will ring in my soul for the rest of eternity: "For Becky."

19

The Orphic Eschatology

Hours pass in near silence, save for Marissa's panting, Sarah's complaints, and Prometheus's fireballs summoned just for fun. We march along the rugged shore, skirting the shattered, occasionally mossy basalt columns. In our present location, a lengthy swath of the cliff's rim has eroded into fist-sized stones and car-sized boulders. Fifty feet below us, the waves roll towards the beach with little spray, allowing the rocks to keep their crusty black shape.

Bored with the hike, and without a definite destination in mind, Prometheus spins an orb of fire the size of a softball in his hands, lobbing it high in the air like a solo batter practicing his swing. When it reaches a hundred feet in altitude its flames die out, and it gives off pitch-black smoke. He sends its remnant flying over the broken escarpment where it explodes at the foot of the rockslide. A cast of annoyed crabs snap their pincers as a retreating wave drags several of them away from the beach.

"Good thing we're nowhere near civilization," Prometheus growls.

"Not really," I say, glowering at him.

"You're in deep thought, my Cretan friend." His expression slackens as he glances out over the waters. "Can't imagine what's troubling you."

I mumble through gritted teeth, "I promised to take part in your war as a means to an end. Your cause is secondary to me finding my wife ... and my son."

"Not *my* war," he says, all at once sounding rehearsed. "The Titans want revenge on the Olympians. They plan for universal domination ... a terrible deal for humanity."

"I still don't trust you."

"You probably shouldn't," he agrees. "But we're allies nonetheless."

"Allies don't betray each other," I argue.

Still trying to work out Ian's true fate, I can't make the story make sense. It's nothing more than a jumble of half-formed facts, and I hesitate to delve deeper. I scan the horizon, noticing a flock of black birds contrasting against the blue sea and pale clouds. Depth is Becky's forte, although she's taught me about nuance over the years. What has happened to Ian?

Prometheus continues, "I don't suppose you understand what really happened. I had to keep up the illusion of revenge, but I made a promise I intend to keep."

"That would be a first."

He exhales a wisp of gray smoke, which somehow makes him appear almost pensive. Then he says in a lowered voice, "You let us out, using your gifts. Untamed and raw, but no less powerful. Such a combination can be lethal."

"You don't know a damn thing about me," I say, trembling. "And save me the 'we're not so different' speech, because we're polar opposites."

"Your son was a fine young man. I see where he got it."

"From his mother, I guess—wait, what did you just say?" I gape at him, suddenly grasping that he holds a key bit of information.

"You were there," he says, "but I suspect you don't remember because you're mortal."

He can see the wheels turning behind my eyes and offers an explanation I've already decided to ignore.

"See, memory cannot escape with the few mortals who have left Hades. Whatever you experienced there will stay sealed forever. I can count the number of mortal Titans on one finger."

"If two immortal forces clash in war, can either of them win?" I ask, attempting to bring logic to the conversation, even if it won't make him see me as calmer or wiser, and may even earn me more pity. It's a price I'm willing to pay.

Sarah and Marissa are forty or fifty feet ahead of us, far enough to diminish our voices to a murmur of key bits of information and nuances. Sarah halts, turns her head, and frowns at us. Marissa puts her arm around Sarah's shoulders and looks toward the west, where the sun is descending into the gray horizon. She's paying as much attention as she can. When Sarah stops, she pauses with her and peers back at me.

"Some say war never has a victor," he says. "We're immortal. Impervious to disease and old age, but never at the hands of our fellow immortals. There are always stakes and wagers."

I summon a more detailed response to Fire Guy: "Then why do you fight? A few people who share a rare gift should exist in harmony."

"Look out there," he says, nodding toward the choppy seas. "Do you see harmony when you look closely? Some people say there's always harmony in nature, a mutual agreement between species not to wipe each other out, so long as humanity doesn't destroy it first."

"You could say that."

"But when you look closer? Do you see the constant competition for territory and resources? Lions will kill other lions to secure their hunting grounds. Sharks and orcas roam the seas, willing to eat anything that moves. It's a daily battle to exist out there. In this scenario, humans are superior at coexisting compared to other animals. A benefit of being *the* apex predator."

"Are we really better at it? Name one other creature that has devised a technology powerful enough to bring extinction upon itself just by rearranging a few subatomic particles; supposedly to protect themselves from rivals with the same capabilities. Compassion isn't a human strength. It's a weakness."

"Such a sunny outlook," he scoffs. "Where you see weakness, I see potential. Resilience. Qualities the gods themselves are willing to recognize. Give yourselves some credit—case in point, you haven't even asked what happened to your son."

"I don't need to know," I lie.

"You left him." His voice is stern and imposing, making me curl my fingers into a fist.

"By necessity," he adds. "But the gods have powers stronger than mortality."

"Right," I say, deepening my frown at the receding crabs. As another wave crests offshore, they seem to sense its approach, wading into deeper waters so the flow sends them higher up the sand to the base of the rockslide where green mosses and lichens grow. "The gods are immortal. And even if Ian has inherited my Titan blood, he has no powers. I bet the gods would be stingy in granting mortals that power in order to preserve a semblance of order."

"Wise man," he compliments me, which makes me want to punch him again.

"Reincarnation," Marissa calls out, moving away from Sarah and towards us. She steps carefully in order to prevent twisting her ankles in any hidden cracks, exhales and waits until she's no more than fifty feet away. "You might be surprised what Wiccans say about it."

"Not more of this mumbo jumbo."

"It's true," she argues. "Some Wicca subsects describe transmigration, a process where the soul takes various forms, climbing the ranks of life until we reach what the Buddhists call nirvana. Others believe in a similar concept where we are reincarnated as humans. It solves the question of eternity better than competing religions, if you ask me."

"Won't work," I say, letting my hopelessness show in my tone.

She takes this in stride, which may mean she hasn't committed to the possibility. "I don't know of a specific ritual, if that's what you're thinking. It just changes your perspective, that's all. Maybe the gods believe it, too."

Before I can utter a snort of laughter, Prometheus holds a palm up as if to give her a high five. Flames spark at his fingertips, emitting wispy vapors of smoke that twirl and dissipate five feet above his hand. "Some gods are more sympathetic than others. Not the all-powerful 'I'm better than you no matter what' type. The idea has merit if you can sell it."

"Marissa?"

She knows the various pagan traditions better than I do, and if she describes it to them in scientific terms, the gods might be more willing to digest the concept that they're not so special and decide to help. But even that presents a false hope. If I'm to retrieve Ian from the underworld, I'll have to go there myself.

Marissa takes two steps forward, and tilts her head as she investigates the possibilities.

"The Greeks are students of science and the arts," I say. "Think of a Venn diagram. Where those two circles intersect is your angle. Think you can do it?"

"Convinced you, didn't I?"

Her sarcasm comes easily even when she doesn't smile. Becky was dismayed at my skepticism; she claimed it stunts spiritual growth and faith. I find that ironic because now Marissa is begging me to have faith in concepts so foreign to me that they might have originated in another galaxy.

"And it's not like my livelihood depends on selling the secrets of the occult or anything." she says.

That's what I'd hoped from the beginning. Seeing eye-to-eye with someone as unique as her has never come naturally to me, but I'm trying to do just that. Ian's soul might depend on it.

I concede at last, issuing an exhausted sigh and peeling my eyes away from her to the skyline, where the grass touches against the horizon like a paintbrush dipped in gold. Prometheus might have ulterior motives, but I'm not seeing any deceit in Marissa's eyes. Should that alone mean she's trustworthy?

"None of that gets me home, Kerry," Sarah says, appearing behind her. Her lips are quivering and her jaw is drooping toward the broken basalts and grasses beneath her feet. "I want to help you, but now I'm starting to think I'll never make it back home."

If her fears are correct, it means I've created yet another paradox. If she can't return home, she can't disappear on me in the past, and I'd have had no reason to have found her in the first place. Saving the universe from destruction will depend on me finding a way to undo all these paradoxes.

But now that I've processed what happened when I abandoned the one place I was sure Becky would turn up, I'm not sure I can go through with it. Is Becky waiting to find me there? I might never know, and a feeling of helplessness invades my soul. Having lost control of time, I'm going to need divine intervention to get this done. Will the gods even agree to help? The only way I'll ever find out is by joining Prometheus to meet them ... if he doesn't double-cross me first.

"I know this is hard," I say, trying to summon courage. "It all depends on faith now. It might not be the outcome you seek, but I'll find a solution if it kills me. Because it just might."

"There's one thing I want to know," Marissa says, gazing into my eyes with genuine curiosity. "Could you feel me when you disappeared?"

I can't believe this.

She knew what she was doing. Depending on her skills and knowledge might be the difference between eking out a pyrrhic victory and succumbing to a devastating defeat. Laying my fate at her feet isn't fair, but then again, we might have to combine our talents just to emerge alive. And if Becky and Ian's fates rest in my hands, the risk is too steep to imagine. Only one path lies before me, and the journey will be the most treacherous of my life.

20

Secret of the Coronides

Wandering along the shore with no clear destination frays my nerves. While traveling years before I ever met Becky, I'd often considered the 'road not taken,' believing that an unconventional path might prove cathartic and lead to greater fulfillment, that it might smooth out the stress that ate away at my mental health. Although I've never read the words of Robert Frost or been a poetry-reader in general, traveling in this manner had always eased my mind.

But now it doesn't.

An ache spreads from the base of my spine, inching higher as we skirt the jumbled, broken basalt rock hugging the shore. Fire Guy is leading the party, and either he won't tell us where we're going, or he doesn't know.

Rather than asking him directly, I sigh while taking in our changing surroundings. Collapsed sections of coast provide treacherous routes to the beach, with vertical cliffs of triangular columns looming long shadows over the shore after sunset.

As the yellows and oranges on the horizon fade to light blue, it is clear that much of our journey will take place in darkness, which presents another set of variables. For starters, rocky, unpredictable footing has led to several near injuries; Sarah's ankle has turned the wrong way, sending her staggering forward before managing to retain her balance and simply wincing in pain. After that, I'd taken care to avoid a similar stumble, but when a broken root got in the way, I'd tripped and slammed my knees into the rocky soil. The resultant limp only wore off ten minutes later.

Thus the darkness presents further challenges; the shadows on the landscape transform the setting into an alien landscape populated with unfamiliar plants, and new animal species prowling in the dark edges.

"You think we'll find a portal out here?" I ask, not trying to sound urgent.

Prometheus pauses, closes his eyes, and recharges. "We don't need a portal. We're here to meet someone."

I shrug. "The gods? Shouldn't you lead us to the edge of certain death first so we can properly appreciate them?"

While I spar with Prometheus, Marissa and Sarah scramble across a wide gash in the rocks, huddling together as if to shield each other from the ocean chill. While I can't hear anything they're saying, I catch Marissa gazing skyward once or twice. "Not really..." Marissa says, trailing off at the end of her sentence.

"Not really," Fire Guy repeats with a curious grin. "Seems you're a novelty to them, rather than a threat, at least for now. But they question your loyalty, seeing as you've worked for Erebus."

"I never worked for him," I say, gritting my teeth.

"You set this war in motion. It wouldn't have happened without you, and you were the one who said you were acting on his orders."

His accusation hits me square in the chest, causing me to look down at my feet. Should a fight break out, I figure that studying the lay of the ground can give me an edge, and if I time an attack just right, I can send him plummeting over the edge so the crabs can feed on his carcass.

"You're a liar."

He shrugs. "Believe what you want, but be careful not to cross the Olympians."

"Why is that?" I growl. "They gonna destroy the world in retaliation?"

A cool nod says it all. He's arrogant, a sin I wish to punish him for, powers or none. "You don't even want to know what they can do to you."

"Hey, Kerry?" Marissa calls out to me.

Without shifting my feet, I twist round to face her. She wraps her arm around Sarah's shoulders, allowing me another glimpse of her tattoo with its shaped dagger-rays ending at hairs and moles.

Sarah's dirty hair curls its way over Marissa's arm. She looks toward the fading blue of dusk then bows her head into her hands. A pang of regret strikes at my stomach as I empathize with her.

On this trip, Sarah has seen and overcome more than she's ever encountered before, and it must have made a knot of grief in her soul. Does living free of such turmoil reward our spirits with liberty, or does it restrict our movement and growth? Her body language could indicate a mix of both ends of the spectrum, but there is something more pernicious lurking beneath. Where sadness and rage mingle, they can ravage the heart with conflicts.

Marissa frowns, glances upward, and then looks at me. She says nothing, but now that I'm better at reading her expression and I empathize, I simply look away.

The darkness between the stars retreats before a glowing white streak that stretches across the cosmos to obscure the Milky Way's bright center. The tail of it skirts a distant constellation in the shape of a spoon, and is growing into a luminous orb hurtling toward the darkening blue where the sun set.

Although this might be the most stunning celestial vista I've ever seen, I'm not happy about it.

"What do you make of that?" asks Marissa.

"Gorgeous," I say. "Be sure to thank the Triple Goddess for me."

She shakes her head and tilts it back to observe the phenomenon. "A bit unexpected. Newspapers everywhere should be publishing science articles talking about this once-in-a-lifetime event. And religious websites should be prophesying the Rapture. You know why?"

I offer a blank stare.

"Because countless cultures have a history of superstition about comets. They're said to be harbingers of doom."

Raising my eyebrows at her, I turn back to gaze at the stunning tail. If I had a camera right now, this would prove the perfect photo opportunity and a chance to share special knowledge with my inquisitive son. I ask her, "And you believe them?"

"Not exactly," she says, "But look at the facts. Philly in chaos, the mass media running stories twenty-four-seven, with speculations ranging from terrorism to the wrath of God? A media circus. Except for the fact NASA knows every major comet that has visited our cozy home in the cosmos in the last four hundred years. *Scientific American* will have predicted it months before it ever became visible."

"She's right," Prometheus says. "The Romans thought a comet brought about the death of Julius Caesar. Catholics and Protestants warned of disease, famine, and war associated with comets. Because the sun, moon, and stars are predictable. When something comes along and throws that order on its head, some interesting theories arise."

"Such as?"

He clears his throat, and after glancing at Sarah, shifts his attention to the sky. The comet's reflection undulates on the calming waves fifty feet below us, filling the area with glittery ribbons of light.

"Drought. War." His words stretch. "Two daughters of a Giant sacrificed themselves to the gods because of drought, and feeling pity, Persephone transformed them into comets."

"Oh, shit!" I yelp when the ground trembles beneath my feet. "Earthquakes. Drought, famine, pestilence, war."

The vibrations peter out. The four of us peer into the heavens, stunned to the core. Whether ancient civilizations were right about the chaos following a comet, everything here portends chaos. I brace myself for another tremor, more determined than ever to defeat this evil in its tracks.

Stars hurl themselves out of the sky as the earth shakes once again. Boulders shift at the base of the cliffside as a rogue wave pummels the shore, sending a plume of water vapor towering above us. Sarah leaps to her feet as I sprint toward her and Marissa, while Prometheus looks as though he's trying to piece together a greater understanding of why this is happening.

Before I make it to them, the sky rips open, spilling stars, asteroids, and traces of light into the gap. Light flashes as a vast section of the cliffside shifts, widening the radial cracks away from the coast. I feel my heart pounding in my chest as I scoop up Sarah and Marissa, paying no attention to where we're running.

Rocks and soil shift as the ground moves beneath our feet. The boulders rumble at the base of the cliff, and there is a thunderous roar as the ocean collides with the land.

I spot a wide crack fifty feet away, with dust and clumps of grass falling into it. I decide that if we hurry, we can make it. I take Sarah's and Marissa's hands in mine, forcing them into motion, and sprint as above us the sky folds in on itself.

A screech echoes somewhere beneath the cliff, sounding like the harrowing cry of a woman in distress. It builds in my ears as the earth crumbles away from us. Boulders collide as gigantic ravines open on both sides of us. When Marissa screams in terror, I clasp her hand tighter, and run as fast as my legs can carry me.

Prometheus, having decided not to run, floats above the ruins, taking a defensive stance in midair. My heart races when the gash before us opens wider as we get nearer to it. A one-foot leap we could have managed grows to an impossible three-foot one in the blink of an eye.

A titanic splash in the ocean behind us sets off a tsunami that speeds toward the shore. The explosive impact scours the air with a torrent of salty droplets that become a monstrous storm front, the wind whipping it into a swirling frenzy above our heads. When it rains down, the race becomes harder.

I have only one chance to bring the women to safety. As they sense the earth collapsing beneath their feet, they pick up speed and I lunge toward the fissure. With all my might, I leap off from the trembling edge, cycling my feet as though running in midair. We're airborne a half second before the ground we've jumped from crumbles into a caustic cloud of dirt, which the pressure wave flashes into mud.

Though we land on more stable ground, it slopes toward the new cliffside of jumbled boulders in a rising, frothy sea. Howling now, I am clinging to the root of a brush, expecting the earth to give way beneath me.

Instead, the mud storm pummels the grassland, plastering us with filth; a torrent wet enough to erode to rivers of grass, mud, and stones, creating canyons that flow into the broken shore.

Now the flash flood whips away the surrounding earth. Marissa gurgles in the muddy flow, thrashing her legs to swim to safety. The storm abates in seconds, spreading less water across the land while a strong pressure wave rolls inland like a powerful gale, uprooting shrubs and rocks the size of my fists.

Sarah flops into the water; the strong current pushes her to the edge. Though the fall itself won't kill her, broken bones and the inability to breathe will cause her to drown. I reach out a sodden hand as her hair tangles in a root. She lets out a gurgle, and her eyes dilate as a maelstrom of debris, shrubs and trees forces the water higher. I feel her hand slipping away. When the stone next to her shifts, she shrieks as I struggle to hold on to the root.

An enormous rock rolls inches past Marissa, diverting the water and trees around her. Not fast enough to beat the landslide, I try to swing Sarah into the void, but her fingers slip through mine, and she slides down the embankment with the muddy water and its debris.

Tears spring to my eyes as I see her reaching out to me and screaming my name. The tidal wave of mud, trees, and rocks flows over the precipice to crush Sarah. As I grimly hold on, I see the flood staunched; the trees have built a tenuous dam along the fault line that has taken her.

As the flow abates to a muddy trickle, Marissa huddles behind the rock at the edge of a brand-new canyon, clutching my arm with enough strength to keep me stable.

Above us, the defeated stars glimmer as the hole in the cosmos repairs itself. Gasping and spitting out salty, filthy water, I peer out at the tsunami rolling back out to sea. Agony now floods through me as Sarah's terrified expression leaves an indelible impression on my heart.

Heaving and whimpering, Marissa holds on tightly, gathering me into a frosty embrace as the tidal wave of defeat rolls over us.

"God no," Marissa moans. "God. She's just so ... so innocent."

I can't reply. My chest and shoulders heave as I weep. Pain and grief transform into rage; I'm going to destroy Cronus if it's the last thing I do.

"She's ... oh, Sarah!"

"You know how to find me."

"Tell me it isn't true," I moan. "You can't ... just ... leave. I barely feel like I know you, but I've known you forever."

"In life and dreams, Larry," she says, clasping a pair of scarred, dirty hands over her heart, "I'm always right here. There's nowhere else I'd rather be."

"I—I don't know what to say."

"You'll find Becky," she sputters. "It's in your heart. Your destiny. That bond is permanent. Tell her I'm sorry."

Agony bores through me like a rusty spear through my soul, filling me with regret. I cannot let her go. Nothing can erase the pain, and nothing can help me rise above it. The light from her energy has gone out, sapping my source of power. Now, with no energy to fight the Titans, humanity will lose. The last bloody battle of Earth will result in billions of dead; brothers, sisters, children, even people we've long considered enemies, all rolled into one cosmic destruction.

"I can no longer fight," I whisper through my tears. "You sustained me. Even when the darkness seemed impenetrable."

She laughs weakly in her anguish. A million miles away, a red giant bakes the vacuum of space with a particle soup of radiation and light as we settle into a permanent orbit. "You see it now, don't you?" she asks.

"I ... I see nothing."

"You know how to find me."

Her eyes close and her image dissolves into a cloud of tears and mud. Something hovers above me, holding onto something whose blurred shape resembles a human body.

Prometheus hovers above the ruins, settles in the muddy rill, and lets his shoulder muscles relax. "I tried," he groans. "I'm sorry. I know she meant a lot to you."

Her soiled amber hair falls over her swollen face. Her clothing is indistinguishable from her skin because of the thick layer of mud, and she flops in his arms as he sets her down over his knee and cradles her head in the crook of his arm.

"It's the end," I blurt out, feeling the darkness withing me swelling. "I can't help you in the war. I'm done."

"Looks like you now have no choice," Marissa sputters through her tears.

"You don't understand, do you?" I argue, my body trembling. "Without her, there's no me. No power, no Titan. Just a useless bag of bones that used to lead a construction team."

Prometheus gapes at me, curling Sarah's hair in his fingers. "You led a team? You're more fit for war than you imagine, my friend."

No one is fit for war. Always in the cause of peace, power, tranquility, or control, it destroys everyone it touches. Those who die with honor and those who perish in disgrace share the same destination—they can never win.

21

The Lost Pyre

Deformed and eroded, the broken jumble of rocks below us shifts as the larger stones succumb to gravity, rumbling as they settle. In the blackened void, cut off from the starlight, I can hear the sea's mournful song as though through a conch shell. Intermittent sloshing sounds interrupt the coda.

Sarah is lost to a different dimension of time, isolated from the memory of friends and family. She's alone in the cosmos, forever trapped in a realm that is erased from memory. Her fate is my fault; I must bear the burden and no further explanation can overcome that fact.

For every moment I sit stunned by my incompetence, Prometheus looks more and more perturbed. Even though there are only subtle indications of what he's feeling, I can sense a profound sadness building through him as he moves. Choosing silence may be the best he can offer in the way of sympathy, and it may help more than it hurts.

Marissa wraps her arm around my waist, gazing out over the retreating whitecaps before turning to regard me. Prometheus has made avoiding the sight of Sarah's defeated body easy by depositing her somewhere behind the large boulder and telling us to stay put, as though we could move if we wanted to. As I weep, Marissa squeezes me tighter as if to wring out every tear I produce.

Her mascara, all but washed away in the mud storm, carries residual streaks of black down her cheeks, transforming her expression into a forlorn pity that somehow breaks down what remains of my sanity.

Rather than trying to assign blame where it doesn't belong, I let the finality burrow deep inside, untouched by the light of day and hidden from everyone else. There, her memory can grow into something more profound. The images carry a weight that crushes my heart. Pointing fingers will come later, and I already know who the second recipient will be.

"I don't pretend to know what it's like," she says. "I'm afraid I'm not great at consoling. But if it's thought you need, I can help you."

I feel my lips quivering as I continue crying.

Our Titan companion returns before I can reply to Marissa. He is carrying an assortment of sticks and branches he's gathered from across the landscape. The forests are too far away for him to have walked, so I assume he used his powers of flight. Although he flaunts his fire-summoning abilities, he's hiding something else.

"At least you admit it," I choke, remembering the way a friend had attempted to soothe my agony when a family member had died.

"What do you think he's doing?" she asks when Prometheus drops the wood and turns away for more.

"Probably wants to experience s'mores for the first time."

She chuckles and relaxes her hand, leaning back against the rock and peering over my shoulder, where a few remaining shooting stars dart toward the darkened horizon.

"You know what religions did to people they accused of witchcraft in Europe? Most victims were innocent, of course. A tragic loss of sight from those who claim the power of vision. They executed more than a few Christians, but mostly, the church deemed it a way to destroy what they believed to be a scourge in Europe—pagans."

"Interesting how a person's status makes them believe anyone on their side is totally innocent. Except you said 'most,' as if there actually were witches."

"Of course there were pagan witches," she says, shrugging and running her hand through her hair. "I mean, there's more than one reason the Roman Catholics co-opted and desecrated our most cherished holidays. The very word 'holiday,' derived from *holy,* they designed to tear apart pagan customs."

"I don't see it that way."

"I didn't expect you to," she says, nodding. Her ankle twists into a muddy rivulet the flood had carved into the soil, a bit of body language that shows she's uncomfortable with the topic she's about to broach.

"My point is, whether the victims were innocent or not, is that many of them were burned. In America, they hanged them. Some Europeans found a crueler approach necessary. Ironic if you think about it, because pagans have practiced cremation for centuries."

"Sarah's not a pagan," I whisper, my voice sounding hoarse and unnatural. Touching my lip confirms that during the chaos, I've cut it, and Marissa has been avoiding looking at it.

"I'd say it might be time to consider the option."

"Her parents won't appreciate it," I argue.

Then again, her parents will never discover her remains or even remember her. Because she died in a different dimension of time, she can't exist in any of them, not even as a memory. Burying her won't be an option in this terrain, and no one could ever pay their respects in such a place, distorted by the laws of interdimensional time.

Sighing, I relent and accept her line of thinking, at last coming to realize what Fire Guy is gathering wood for. He already knows the only logical path forward, and gathering the necessary fuel without speaking is his way of showing remorse.

Watching my nonverbal agreement, she nods and wets her lips. "I don't suppose you're hungry right now. We could barbecue."

Biting my lip to avoid laughing at her dark sense of humor, I look away, toward the horizon where the sun has set. Now that the light blue sky has faded, night forms a black dome. This realm is isolation personified, even though the Titans have breached the border and rained destruction on us. If I was their target, how did they know my exact location without Prometheus playing both sides?

If he's being duplicitous, he's making no effort to hide it.

A moment later, he returns to the broken hillside, carrying another armful of twisted green root systems pulled up from the ground, lopped off branches carved into wooden spears, and flat strips of oak devoid of bark. He builds the monument, starting with dried grasses as kindling, overlaid with a thin cover of twigs before adding the heavier fuels. Constructing it like a log cabin a little over five feet long, he stacks the wood until he has nothing left.

I moan as I watch him hoist Sarah's body to the top of the edifice. Marissa looks away as he fastens her limp wrists to the oak boards and ties her frayed curly hair into a haphazard ponytail laid over her breast like a bouquet of wildflowers.

"Got anything to say?" Prometheus asks.

I don't have the nerve, but saying goodbye without pouring out at least some of my emotions seems like an insult to her humanity. So I scuffle my feet through the soil and wedge myself against the rock, feeling Marissa pressing at my back and holding my hand to steady me.

Then I limp six feet to the pyre, dig deep into my psyche to produce words that somehow can't describe the torment I feel, and hope I can do her justice.

"Sarah. I didn't really know you well enough to give you a proper sendoff, but somehow it hurts more than I can describe. We share an astral connection through time and space, and maybe that's enough. Except I know it isn't—we're here because of you. After I set off to find you, I found my wife, had a son, because of you. Without you, I'm neither man nor Titan; I'm nothing. I owe everything to you, to Bones Holdings, and the owners who contracted them. I commit to serving you, to ending the war and to saving the world. But I can't do it without you. I just don't know how to access your energy now. If there's a way to learn that, please guide me. I never set out to save the universe, only you. Yet I've found more than I ever dreamed, and The One no longer controls my destiny. In a way, you do. Saying goodbye is ripping away every piece of me. Knowing how to carry on without you is a mountain I can't scale on my own. I need my friends and my family. And my adversaries. Guide me through this journey, and I'll see you on the other side."

Marissa sniffs and rubs her hands over her eyes as Prometheus summons a fickle flame on his fingertips, touches the dry grass and kindling, and blows on the sparks to accelerate the blaze.

The smoke drifts high into the night sky as a trio of birds sings nearby. The crackling sparks, the roaring flames, and the tumbling waves reach a crescendo as Sarah disappears into the fire that exultantly laps at the star-scape overhead.

Without knowing why, I look up at the constellations until I can focus on the Big Dipper, and a sudden wave of solace drifts over me like a soothing bath of warm water. Gazing at the Great Bear offers an internal perspective I cannot explain. But at least it spurs me into action.

Although I'm the one who brought her here, I know who summoned the tsunami and the meteors. They worked together, and Cronus and Oceanus will pay for this. I bite my lip and watch the sparks flutter skyward, blink out, and flash against the myriad stars, adding Sarah's essence to the universe.

Wiping the tears from my eyes, I watch as Prometheus tends to the flames. Giving in to despair would be the most reflexive reaction, but now armed with direction and knowledge, a twitch in my thigh spurs me to stand and formulate a plan.

"Did you really mean everything you said?" Marissa asks. "Even that part about her being the only reason you exist?"

I nod. "Every word."

"That's a lot for someone who never really loved her, you know."

Biting back a retort I decide, instead of reacting the way I should, I'm ready to ask her to guide me. "I need something from you, something I can't explain. Princess Ariadne gave me this gift, and it's basically how I became a Titan. The problem is that using the gift consumes energy, which comes from one of two sources. One of whom just ... you know."

"So you want me to teach you how to tap into it?"

As my lip trembles, I ponder the situation, tilt my head, and sink my feet into the wet soil. "Tell me how to harness emotional entanglement. Now that you can communicate with her, you can help me do it too. Without that, we'll lose the war, and the world will end."

She grimaces, curls her fingers, and lets out a slow sigh. "No pressure, right?"

"Which brings me back to you," I say, directing my attention to Fire Guy, who prods at the flames, leans his stick against the rock, and folds his arms across his chest. "To understand how to fight this war, I need the ability to predict what the Titans might do next. Give me the rundown, saving the best for last."

He inclines his head as though he's been expecting the question, then raises his brows and glows with the firelight warming his backside.

"Warning," he says. "The Titans have unmatched powers. Combined, only the Olympians can stop them, but even that's in doubt. Wild card or none, you'll need to be prepared to lose."

"I've already lost," I grumble.

"Atlas," he begins, "possesses raw, untamed power. World-bearing strength and intelligence. Landing Mount Everest on your face will be like flicking a flea to him, only he's already mastered the art of reasoning with the flea so that it will not land on him.

"A ruthless tactician and lover of Phoebe, Coeus, is the most inquisitive of all the Titans. He plays games of logic by asking the right questions until his enemies are ready to concede, and if they don't, he smothers them with pressure.

"His sister, Phoebe, whose name means *Bright,* harnesses the power of light, although she does it differently than you do. While yours comes from energy, hers comes from the cosmos. She can blind opponents by refocusing beams of light, bend their rays to create disorienting shadows, and even set you on fire like an ant under a magnifying glass. You won't be able to use your Shade against her."

The waves below slosh around in a hollow cavern where the largest rocks have formed a fragile cave that may be home to nocturnal animals. The sound echoes in my soul as I listen to Prometheus.

"Crius, 'the ram,' uses his strength and virility to best his opponents. If he hits you hard enough, he'll knock you into last weekend and then have lunch. But he's evolved so that he doesn't even need to use his body. He can trigger landslides just by planting his foot in the right place.

"Known as 'the high one,' Hyperion embodies the sun and the moon, having fathered Helios, Selene, and Eos. He uses their gravity to direct tides and can even influence the weather to create advantages and disadvantages on every side.

"Contending with that won't be so easy, especially when he combines with Oceanus, the embodiment of the seas, who uses the power of water. Creating waves out of nowhere is only the beginning of his powers. Water helps breed life, but it can also extinguish it. Naturally, I've had more than a few run-ins with him. Once, during a sparring session indoors, he launched a wall of water at me, which I flashed into steam, blowing off the roof."

"Water has physical limits," I say. "One thing I learned from an engineer a few years ago is that it's not compressible, which makes its volume predictable—thus the pressure."

"His sister-wife Tethys is associated with fresh water, a matronly woman who has given life to many children. But what she gives she can take away. She can dehydrate troops to weaken and kill them, just as she is able to smother them."

"She and her brother must've been busy," I ponder, not intending it as a joke.

"Iapetus, the father of several Titans, including me, is what you might call a wild card. He's got powers, of course, but his advantages come from his unpredictability. The problem with unpredictability rests in how he knows what you have prepared for, and throws you off balance. So the key to fighting him will be to expect him to deceive you, and to fight back with something *he's* not prepared for.

"Rhea is the mother of the Olympians and travels on a chariot drawn by lions, whom she deems sacred. She's known for her matronly nurturing and compassion, which you might not expect to come in handy on the battlefield. Don't let that deceive you, because her attributes can be unnerving, and that can cause your downfall. Her compassion can weaken you if you let it."

"Mnemosyne's name means *memory*. She and Zeus bore the nine muses, and she celebrated the cult of Asclepius. She can cause you to forget who you're fighting for, or conversely, to remember prior alliances, which can be terrible news for you."

"I have a feeling she'll help more than hurt," I say, without knowing why. As though my faltering memory tries to access a dark corner of my brain, I can still sense something different about her. If she can remind opponents of past alliances, reason dictates I can turn her power on herself, thereby making her change teams.

Marissa is wide-eyed but groggy as she watches the flames flicker and die into red-hot coals after having consumed the last of Sarah. "These people are insane," she remarks. "How are we going to defeat them?"

"No idea," I admit. "Even if I can hone my Light and Shade abilities, it's a lousy matchup."

Continuing to introduce his fellow Titans, Prometheus erases all emotion from his face and continues, "Theia, sister-wife of Hyperion, is also a goddess of light. Her name gave rise to theism and theology, belief and the study of gods and goddesses."

"If she's the mother of the sun, the moon, and the dawn," Marissa reasons, "she must be related to the Triple Goddess. I know some things about Wiccan religion, so if you need help with her, just ask." She's looking at me as she speaks, although her tone suggests she's also addressing Prometheus.

"Your understanding may be flawed," Prometheus says, "but any words of wisdom may be helpful.

"Next is Themis, 'Lady Justice,' whose robes and scales I understand symbolize the criminal justice system. As her name suggests, she's known as a defender of the poor and oppressed, but she's also flawed in how she determines guilt or innocence, because she's not blind and impartial as the iconography suggests. Her bias can lead to cruelty, but enemies can use that against her. Her powers let her exact punishment for any perceived misdeed, and the penalty for treason is bloody execution, which means we've both got targets on our backs.

"And last of all," he continues, "Cronus, the self-appointed leader of the Titans and one of the most powerful beings ever to have existed. He betrayed and castrated his father, Uranus, the supreme god of the cosmos, and usurped his throne to rule until the Olympians defeated us and sent us to Tartarus. Cronus can redirect comets, rearrange the constellations, summon meteors, and cause eclipses. And although rumors claim he can manipulate time, I've never seen him do it. If he wants to destroy you, he will, and you stand little chance of defeating him."

"That's all?" I say, trying to count how many Titans he's mentioned. "Twelve of them not including you. Considering the Olympians once defeated the Tians, I like our chances."

"The Olympians marshaled troops to fight for them," Prometheus says, gazing out at the lapping waves and the winking stars that are reflecting on the water, "The idea is to use numbers to overwhelm the Titans and use their own powers to fight back. But you and I know that Erebus has numbers on his side."

Absorbing this information causes an ache in my joints and a throbbing headache. Rubbing my forehead with my thumb and index finger, I scan our destroyed surroundings with the realization that Sarah is nothing more than an unfortunate casualty of war. The flames dance above the coals into which the pyre has fallen, sending showers of red and yellow sparks dancing in the night like illuminated spirits carrying Sarah's warmth and energy. The odds are perhaps worse than winning the lottery multiple times, but I can't give up now.

"We're going in as the underdogs," Prometheus admits in a muted voice.

Not yet ready to trust him, I gaze at his forlorn expression, as though he's already admitted we're going to lose. I ask, "You say 'we' a lot. But for you, 'we' used to serve Erebus. Who's to say you're not a spy?"

As if expecting the question, he settles his hulking shoulders, sets his hand on fire, and blows the flames out with one heavy breath. "I'm risking everything. I wasn't one of the original twelve; before the first war, I was loyal to Zeus, yet I joined the Titans. My biggest mistake. The Olympians don't have everything right, but overall, they promise more stability than the Titans. And maybe that's all that matters."

Marissa looks like hope is growing at the edges of her expression, though she must know we're going to lose before we can win. There's no avoiding it. We're like prisoners being marched blindfolded to our doom, never trying to step out of line because we know our destiny. To find peace, I look up at the seven stars of the Big Dipper. And when a spark from the pyre curls around the handle before flickering and dying, life flutters back into me.

22
Tragedy

Everything aches, from a throbbing behind my ear to a sharp stinging in my big toe, from when I'd crashed to the other side of the chasm while trying to save Sarah and Marissa.

Marissa has become morose since the storm subsided. The blast generated a massive wave that destroyed the coastline, while the intense heat instantly vaporized a million gallons of seawater, creating a ferocious gale of spray and mist that combined with the already airborne dirt. As the wave condensed, the resulting flash floods carved out a network of muddy deltas that poured into the broken rocks. To describe the attack as shocking would be a vast understatement; it happened in the blink of an eye, preceded only by the white-hot fireball that had sent us scrambling. I may never forgive myself for letting Sarah go, and since Marissa has grown silent, I have no one left with whom to discuss it. No one mortal, at least. And although Prometheus took care of the aftermath, he hasn't yet earned my trust.

It feels so uncomfortable looking at Marissa that I drop it to focus on where I'm walking. With a radius of destruction at least ten miles across, the journey is proving arduous. As I am sidestepping a deep fracture that swallowed tufts of yellowed grass and soil, I find myself slipping in the muck, trying to right myself, and then stumbling on a twisted bit of brush root. Grimacing with pain, I hop over a boulder that has been split down the middle. Its minerals reflect the dying stars overhead, glimmering in the night like sparks of a dark memory.

"Not much longer now," Prometheus shouts, at least a hundred yards ahead of us. I suspect he's levitating over the treacherous terrain, which persists further in from the coast. A mile takes us more than half an hour. But two miles away from the shore, the rills are less pronounced and not as deep, suggesting we're nearing the point where the condensation started.

"You never told us where we're going," I say, sounding like I'm accusing him of treachery. "Might have been important."

"The way I remember it, I rescued you and your friends from drowning in the city. The topic of our destination simply never came up. You could have asked whenever you wanted."

I bite my lip and curse under my breath. Two hours into our march, Marissa's eyes gloss over and she wilts. She slows her pace even more, her shoulders sagging, and she has a frown on her face. When she pauses, I can almost hear my heartbeat murmuring in the silence. If I had anything to talk about, I wouldn't hesitate to bounce ideas off her, but the panic and hurt in my heart and brain have made logical discussion impossible.

If her expression affects me in any meaningful way, it might be that it's making me also want to sleep. Yet at times, life's nightmares inflict such deep trauma that sleep also feels impossible. Scowling, I glance at a hole in my shoe, where a spot of blood trickles across the white canvas and mattes at the frayed edges. The last few days had turned a new pair of shoes into abused foot coverings that do little to keep out dirt, grime, and water, and the soles let the sharp rocks into my arches.

Although Prometheus sees I won't ask another question, my expression prompts him to nod sharply and shrug. He keeps his voice flat as he speaks, never showing any emotion. "There is a camp nearby," he explains, "a good place to rest, to exchange intelligence, and to plan tactics. Three thousand men patrol these shores, holed up in a circular valley a mile or so inland. They will have seen the blast, but have been mostly immune from the damage. It seems Cronus missed."

"He was aiming for me," I say, my voice stoic and uninspired. I slow down, letting Marissa close the distance between us. I glare at Prometheus for a moment, trying to find the phrasing to express my emotions—yet failing. "Are you trying to be aloof, or does sociopathic behavior come naturally to you?"

"The One," he mumbles, keeping his voice low. "You know how he communicates to his servants; he senses negative attitudes. Your innermost struggles, fears, anger, loathing ... it feeds him power. I'd recommend you take the same approach."

Rolling my eyes, I lean towards him. "Great idea. Let me get back to you when my shrink tells me I need to be more *pothitive,*" I groan, faking a lisp to mock him.

"You have a shrink?" Marissa asks, her voice weary. "Other than Miriam?"

Frowning, nodding, I glance toward her. "You know one of the best things about marriage? Psychiatric care you don't have to pay for."

"I see."

After a half-syllable chuckle, I amend my statement: "Well, you *do* have to pay for it, but in other ways, if you know what I mean."

"Real sick," she says, glaring. "I didn't expect Sarah's death to be a joke to you."

That hits harder than anything Becky has ever leveled at me, but instead of internalizing it, I fight back. "You're one to talk in your trance over there. But I guess you and Sarah were never entangled."

Ahead of us, the rocks and weeds merge into a craggy ridgeline that zigzags through the coastal steppe, smoothing as it approaches the rocky shore. Ascending its gentlest flanks, I feel the pain digging into my legs even as a new level of remorse reaches my brain. Atop the ridge, the grasses grow thicker, interspersed with a rugged line of aged shrubs whose roots stick out of the sandy soil.

"How many?" I ask, turning my attention back to Fire Guy.

"Three thousand, give or take. They're going to be prepared for a ground invasion, but they know I'm coming."

Marissa rests her palms on her knees, panting from the brisk ascent. "Troops? I guess that means war."

"The Olympians might be wrong about many things, and have many flaws—among them arrogance—but they're no fools," Prometheus confirms. "They've marshaled great armies to fight for them, sending immortal representatives as commanders."

"But why all the way out here?"

"You wouldn't define it as *out* here, if you understood the history associated with this place. Nearly two and a half thousand years ago, when the Persians invaded, a terrible battle took place here. The invaders had us on the run, our numbers too thin to plan a strategic counteroffensive. The Persians had a larger number of men, were better equipped, and had an unmatched bloodlust. But this was our home. We fought until eventually we drove them back. But not before thousands lay dead."

"*This* is Thermopylae?" I ask, stumbling upon the name but sure I'd watched one of those 'based on a true story' retellings of the famous battle.

He shakes his head. "Same war, different battle. The Persians were ruthless."

"Let me guess," I say, "You were there."

"I was on Mount Olympus," he admits. "The leaders knew what was happening but discussed matters of greater importance. Zeus had me making promises to a politician to help militarily, to front reinforcements for the troops up north."

"The Persians are still ruthless," I say, summoning just enough energy to climb the last few steps to the ridgeline. "Only now they're called Iranians. And they're trying to build weapons that can destroy entire cities in a matter of seconds. The US and the rest of the Western world monitors them."

Prometheus points to the valley that stretches out below us as Marissa crawls up the last two steps, stands up, and gazes out at it.

We see flickering lights glowing in the black field, emitting smoke and sparks that climb right up to the heavens and blot out the stars overhead. Fire Guy forms a spark in his fingers and spins it into a ball of flame as Marissa stands shaking next to me.

Thousands of allies might be a good sign, yet it portends doom in some corner of my brain. Clinging to hope can only offer a vague sense of relief, a warmth that suppresses feelings of anger and despair.

Marissa can feel it. Her facial expression turns from wonder to exhaustion the longer she looks. "There are so many here," she whispers, her voice wavering. "So many stories to tell. A man whose family waits for news that will never come, just a pawn in a bigger game. Fathers, sons, grandchildren too; clutching spears, taking arrows for the greater good, never to be honored for their sacrifices. This is not a place of victory. It is a burial ground for the vanquished."

Prometheus cultivates his fireball in his outstretched hand as if venerating the smoke it emits, before he launches it skyward. A hundred feet overhead, it bursts into a dazzling pyrotechnic display that would fit perfectly into Philadelphia's storied Independence Day traditions.

Rather than admiring the spectacle, Marissa closes her eyes, lowers her head, and puts her hands on her hips. Her trance lasts twenty seconds before her eyes spring open and she glances toward the inland hills miles away. Then she shifts her attention to the place where a delta might have formed on the shoreline, if we could see that far.

"Shhh," she whispers. "They're coming."

"Who?" I ask, following her eyes and seeing nothing but the solemn darkness surrounding the camp.

"The armies of Erebus," Prometheus says, keeping his eyes down and his tone glacial. "We're flanked. And the enemy saw my announcement."

"Great job, pyromaniac." I glower at him.

"It happens now," he says, letting the seconds tick away.

Twenty seconds later, faint pockets of light erupt at both ends of the valley, lurching forward like candle flames flickering in the night. Ten more seconds. The lights intensify, arching into the black sky and speeding toward the camp like a million flaming stars. The troops have little time to react. From up here, we can hear their muffled screams, yet the clamor fills my eardrums anyway, vibrating at the base of my spine and chilling my nerves.

In an instant, Prometheus is hovering in his spot, holding out a hand for me to join him, and waiting for Marissa to grab a hold. Instead of taking it immediately, she hesitates, closes her eyes as if in prayer, and then gives in. Fire Guy's grip is hotter than the white coals left over after a campfire has gone out. When he's secured us both with one hand, he hovers out over the camp, shoots a fireball toward the coastal company, and then sends another toward the hills, letting the troops know they're cornered.

Keeping my eyes on the action below, I wait. The screams below us grow louder as the flaming projectiles scatter into the soil, igniting new blazes. Hurried footsteps scurry to ready the forces against an attack.

A man screams as a fiery arrow plunges into his chest. The advancing troops launch another volley, while steel weapons clink together at the outskirts of the camp.

I dig deep for any hint of energy Sarah has left in me, but I cannot find anything to beat back the assault. At least ten thousand eyeless creatures with droopy skin and missing teeth or limbs march in lockstep to ravage the garrison.

As an explosion rocks the camp's outer limits, the Olympian forces form ranks to defend against the assault; however, the invaders swat away spears, plunge swords through abdomens, and slice off limbs as they advance relentlessly over the waiting line.

"They're getting crushed," I say, breathless, as Prometheus summons a fireball to fall towards the coastal flank. It explodes on the ground behind the line, spraying a fountain of bloody, flaming bodies away from the blast's epicenter while he readies another attack.

"You going to just hover there like a referee?" he says. He floats downward to deposit us on firmer ground. "Launch your lightning sphere."

"*What?*"

"Don't tell me you forgot."

"Oh God," I howl, as a flaming, poison-tipped arrow vaults past my ear close enough for the fire to singe my ear hairs. "Guess I'm a tad rusty."

"They're dying," Marissa says, her voice sounding helpless as she sprints toward an overhanging wooden structure.

Once she's found refuge, I battle through the fleeing troopers. Each is taking up blades that might not be ready for the battle.

Prometheus is asking me to fight, but I can do nothing except watch. Although I'm trying to summon the will to attack by imagining Sarah's smile, her amber hair and the crop of freckles on her cheeks, it does nothing except plunge daggers of regret into my heart. I'm too feeble for battle and nothing I can do will counter such evil.

Beside me, a man in a loose-fitting white tunic and black pants mumbles as an arrow streaks through the air, pierces his shoulder, and rattles like a rubber spring doorstop. Seemingly unperturbed, he races toward the front line with his wound leaking blood around the poisoned arrowhead. Trying to keep up with him, I watch arrows scour through the air, many making plumes of dust as they land in the dry earth.

Another arrow vaults toward his head and at the last second, the darkness crowding within my heart lashes out at it, and the arrow dissolves in a cloud of soot inches from his face, causing him to halt and stare at me.

When another volley brings smoke and toxic vapors nearby, I watch it skitter through the dirt. The soldiers wield longswords along the line, clashing with the heavier armor the dead troops wear. The Olympian troops gradually gain momentum and push back, hacking away arms and legs from the zombie army, who continue as though they can't feel any pain. Their shrieks and screams penetrate the night as they leverage their numbers to keep the upper hand. But they are ill-prepared for me.

Prometheus bombards them with fireballs to disperse their ranks, sending flaming bodies flailing into the ground. He glances at me, watching me dissolve errant arrows while he rises above the fray to aid the backline troops.

When the man next to me charges at a faceless enemy soldier, he grips his sword tighter, lops off the invader's head, and goes for another strike. The opponent sidesteps the attack, seeing it coming, but when he races to parry, he meets a cloud of coal ash that bursts into flames when an arrow pierces it. The defensive strike paralyzes the dead man, just long enough for my partner to slam the hilt of his blade onto his cranium, further disorienting the enemy. The soldier, whose mop of golden hair makes me think of him as 'Blondie', and I set our sights on the five zombies racing to fill the gap.

Rage flashes through me as I build a shockwave of black dust that overtakes the enemy, eroding them to nothingness as it settles. Without understanding how I'm doing this, I keep my attention on the lines as hundreds of eyeless souls march on me, each of them collapsing in demise when they inhale my essence.

Blondie flourishes with my help. He brandishes his sword like a pro, lopping off limps and slicing into ragged, rotting flesh as the foe, realizing it has reached a stalemate, retreats screaming and howling to reform their ranks.

Spreading out helps them gain better precision, but my allies cut many of them to pieces as they stream through, breaking bodies as they go. When one of them squeezes between me and a burly soldier, the dead man turns his head and grins as though his invisible eyes can see. I return my attacks on the advancing army. They stream in by the hundreds, never stopping when one of their own falls.

We're moshing in a field of thousands, sweating, bleeding, and screaming as we give ground. Fearing that we've lost this flank, I fall back, gather what energy I can muster in my fingers, and shoot out a weak wave of light that stuns our attackers. The Olympian army hacks them to bits until they refocus, and push us back.

Screams erupt from the center of the camp. A sudden gust of wind swirls in the night, scattering our forces and the dead. They turn back with petrified faces when a soul-stirring melody sounds in the battlefield behind me. A rainbow of colors streaks into the sky, vanishing in a blaze of colored sparks.

This confuses our adversaries, and when another massive fireball mushrooms over the battlefield far behind me, the screams and howls grow distant as our enemies scatter into darkness.

My heart pulses with fury as I watch Blondie chase a lanky dead man, his legs falling to pieces as he scampers away.

Victory has never felt so hollow. Trying to make sense of my surroundings, I take in the charred inner camp, whose fires have ignited many other blazes that are consuming tents and wooden structures. When I set my sights on the building Marissa entered, my fingers tingle.

She sits cross-legged on the clay floor without seeing me, shaking with fear. What she's just seen will tear her apart for a long time, but when I see what she's crying over, deeper regret fills me.

A pair of bodies, one male and one female, lie side by side before her. Tears form in Marissa's eyes, and when I settle to my knees next to her, hoping to offer comfort, pain sears my soul. Dead soldiers and pieces of limbs are scattered throughout the camp, but the two spread out before Marissa carry a ghostly essence that lingers in the air.

Their faces are pale and forlorn, framed with blond, curly hair and bangs. The light in their eyes dims as their souls waft into the rafters, escaping into the heavens through the cracks.

After ten silent minutes, Prometheus appears beside me, standing firm, his fingers blackened from the fireballs. When I see his ashen face, a feeling of pure hatred blurs my vision. He looks somberly at the two defeated fighters, his hand over his heart, trembling.

Understanding the two fallen heroes' significance requires no words. Their spirits have said it all. Like unseen vapors drifting skyward, they flutter over the scarred, beaten camp, where hundreds of soldiers lie dead with countless more servants of Erebus mangled nearby.

You are a traitor, Kerry Gearhardt.

The voice rolls like a ground tremor.

This is how defeat tastes.

Prometheus can feel it too. He looks away from the fallen fighters and I wrap my arm around Marissa's shaking shoulders.

"They ... how?" she mutters through tears.

"The enemy had a sizeable force and was better prepared," Prometheus says, keeping his voice even.

A woman kneeling across from Marissa struggles in the arms of her man, who is trying to escort her away, but her voice comes lucid and strong. "Goodbye Iris, Goddess of color and light."

"Amen," I whisper.

"Zephyrus," another man says, his voice morose and his face lowered. "Each time the west wind blows, we will remember your sacrifice."

"I don't understand," I say. "God and goddess."

Marissa nods. "Casualties of a bigger war. The enemy is changing its tactics as we speak. This is a sight we'll need to get used to, no matter how much it hurts."

"You know them?" I gasp.

"I *feel* them. Like we all do."

"The question is," Prometheus ponders, "will we let those feelings undermine our values, our passions? Or will we honor the fallen with heroism of our own?"

His tone strikes an air of finality. My heart trembles as my chin lowers toward my chest. I have confronted two separate battles in one night, and the pain is accumulating. If there is any light still within me, the darkness in my soul is slowly extinguishing it. Although I'd never met Isis and Zephyrus in life, their spirits reside within me; we are united in our struggle for a common cause, whether or not they knew it. The fate of the universe is insignificant in comparison to the future of Sarah, Becky, and Ian. If I don't find Becky and bring her back to her true home dimension, space and time will collapse, and the Titans will emerge victorious to enslave what remains of humanity. And that is a defeat I cannot endure.

23

Letting the Satyrs Run

Sunrise paints the eastern horizon in hues of blue, yellow, and orange that glow through high wispy clouds, creating an ethereal effect over the rocky coastline. A flock of blackbirds speeds along with the wind a few hundred feet up, changes direction, and loops back to survey the scarred, smoking battlefield.

Although commanders are still counting the dead, early estimates have pegged the number of casualties at just over a thousand, a full third of the regiment. Counting enemy fallen proves more difficult, since severed limbs outnumber bodies two-to-one. Between Prometheus having incinerated many, and me destroying body parts, we'd held our own despite the numerical disadvantage. Erebus's army of the dead dying again defies all logic, giving The One a more decisive edge.

"That about does it," a man says, tallying the numbers on a sheet of papyrus by hand. He glances up when he notices me staring. The officer wears a tight armored tunic belted around his waist and a thin woolen robe draped cross-shoulder, under an alloy breastplate. His armor bears a half-dozen dings and scratches, along with bits of spattered blood. Combing a hand through his wiry hair, he raises his eyebrows and checks his math once more.

Another man bows before him and awaits orders. The commander gives a curt smile, bends at the waist, and studies his cohort's expression.

Lines of sorrow cross an expression of loyalty and composure—desirable traits for a warrior.

"Captain Zistalmus," he states. "Be ready to receive allied generals within the hour. Prepare an arrival ceremony, but keep it brief."

"Yes, Commander," the captain says.

When the commander looks my way again, I sense questions forming in his mind. We lock eyes and give briefings that require no words—just feeling. "You," he says after a tense thirty seconds. "The men say you fought gallantly. And there's a rumor going around, too."

I wander over to him with a fake smile, dispensing with the formalities and pleasantries for brevity's sake. "I was only trying to help Prometheus. Sorry I couldn't do more."

"You may be part of the reason we weren't destroyed or didn't suffer significantly greater losses. I shall commend you at tonight's ceremony. What is your name?"

The Olympian commanders could use the time to devise better strategies to counter the increasing problems of war, the enormous Titan army chief among them. Instead, we're having a ceremony. The commander should consider himself and the gods lucky none of the Titans showed up, because they might have enslaved or dismembered our entire infantry. "No commendations necessary. Some people call me Larry, although I've heard someone refer to me as Kerry, Conveyor of Light and Shade, if I remember right."

"Thank you for your service, Larry," he says. "The ceremony is at six. General Apollo and his commanders will be here, taking in a special satyr play to honor Zephyrus and Iris. Consider it a team-building exercise, meant to strengthen our ranks and improve morale. And it's mandatory."

He doesn't seem interested in my abilities, or the rumors going around, and that may be less an oversight than an admission that we should celebrate everyone's abilities in equal measure. Without Blondie, I wouldn't have had the courage or energy to fight; the commander should give him all the credit. Still, I have no idea if Blondie survived. If they expect me to give an acceptance speech, I'll try to dedicate the medal in his honor.

"The Titan army surprised you," I say. "We might owe everything to my companion, Marissa, because she saw it coming before anyone, giving us more time to organize a counterstrike."

The commander shrugs. "You can call me Archus, among Apollo's most trusted commanders. And Prometheus was late to the party. I expect him to report an explanation in due course."

"*We* were late," I admit, "because the Titan Cronus launched a meteor at us, causing us to lose one of our own. Prometheus simply did the honorable thing, helping us to say goodbye to our companion."

"The Olympians shall honor your fallen companion," he says. "But warning us was well within Prometheus's abilities, which is cause for demarcation."

"You rank higher than a Titan who serves Zeus?"

"We must all be accountable," he says. "The same goes for every commander we have. We will host a contingent of at least ten others this evening. We will see you at the ceremony—don't be late."

"Right," I say, trying to find a way out of it. If Archus has it out for Prometheus, perhaps he'll be keen to whisk Marissa and me to another dimension where we can lick our wounds and salve our wounded feelings.

Now that I've agreed, he makes a tight V-angle with his right elbow, straightens his hand, and crosses it over his chest. I opt for a military salute, hoping he doesn't take offense, but as he shows no sign of displeasure, I turn to search the camp for Marissa.

Scanning a long, gentle hill, I watch as a column of white and black smoke swirls toward the high clouds, towering over a makeshift heap of casualties and enemy body parts. A fitting funeral might have involved a mass grave, but I assume the troops had been traveling light, carrying only armaments and food. The smoke drifts and thins toward the column's peak, allowing the prevailing wind to stretch it into an anvil shape that seems to absorb the sunshine.

While many of the structures near the center of the camp are in the early stages of deconstruction, a group of weary men and women work together, flipping wide, knotty boards and hammering nails into cross-members. After the ceremony, the army will disperse, breaking into smaller regiments assigned to other regions.

Among the structures being disassembled, I spot a wooden-fenced paddock meant to keep the frightened horses corralled in order to feed them. The trapezoid-shaped building sports a central shade structure where the horses can eat and drink to keep up their energy for long rides. If their modes of transport are this archaic, I suspect that enlightening them about technologies might be a challenge. Then again, I carry nothing, and the commander has already clarified that my talents are nothing special.

Near a double gate into the paddock, a throng of weeping women in dirty, loose clothing talk in somber tones. I spot Marissa emptying a wooden bucket of water into a trough, and make my way toward her, avoiding the men rushing past with supplies, tools and lumber to build the presentation stage.

Marissa doesn't look up. I could surprise her from a mile away if she couldn't communicate by other means. When I'm less than twenty feet away, she looks at me without a hint of a smile, watching me stumble over a half-buried fire ring hidden in the sand since just after nightfall.

"What's up?" she asks, her voice wavering. She drops the metal-banded bucket at her left side, wipes her hands on her jeans, and waits for my explanation.

"We're in for a special presentation tonight. Ten more commanders supporting Apollo will be here, and they want to put a medal on my chest."

She frowns, shakes her head and pulls a strand of hair behind her ear. "You think you deserve it?"

I utter a humorless chuckle. "Hell no. But we have to go. I suggest we sit together."

That's good enough for a smile. "Are you asking me on a date, *The Kerry Gearhardt*? I wouldn't miss it for the world."

"More or less." I stumble. "I don't know anyone here, and neither do you. And Prometheus will entertain the guests by swallowing fire and belching smoke signals."

She raises her eyebrows. "Actually, he's leaving before the presentation. I would have expected him to tell you."

"He's—that *damn coward.*"

Shrugging, she resets her expression. "I'm sure he has his reasons. You can't expect a player as important as him to stay in one place when bigger battles are being waged around the world. I hear there's another group assembling near Memphis—the one in Egypt—because it carries more Greek significance."

"I'm not sure that's true," I surmise. "Wouldn't be wise to spill battle plans, especially when the Titan army is backed by one of the most merciless deities in the entire universe."

"Then you can tell me the true story tonight," she says. "Don't spare anything."

"What are you doing until then?"

"What does it look like I'm doing? We're readying the horses for the long ride, packing essentials, extra clothing, taking weapons inventory; important evacuation steps. And that's not to mention the paralysis from getting our asses handed to us and the paranoia they'll be back before night-fall."

"Don't you think it's a better idea to make plans to help me?"

"That's what I'm doing, Kerry. But you know, working has a way of dulling emotions. Maybe it's not the best means of healing, but we have little choice now. I didn't know Sarah that well—we didn't hang out on a regular basis, but I can tell she's the key to the whole quest. And maybe we can both help you find your wife and son by preventing the Titans from destroying everything before then."

"I mean," I begin, grimacing, "that we can make better use of our time by flitting off into a different dimension, to find Becky *before* the war explodes."

She looks stunned, though unwilling to go along with my suggestion. "They need our help. After the ceremony, we'll go where we're needed and when Prometheus comes back, he can help us in future battles."

"Now *you* get to call the shots?" I attempt to camouflage the insistence in my voice by trying not to make it sound accusatory.

"We merely differ on how to solve your crisis," she says. "Just be-cause we disagree doesn't mean we're adversaries. That type of thinking is detrimental to a working society. Just look at the last fifty years. Cutthroat capitalists railing against organized labor, calling them communists, when they both serve the same purpose. Groups wanting equality calling everyone who disagrees 'anti-this' or 'that-phobic.'"

"Maybe when the stakes are high, you need to stick to your principles, right or wrong," I counter.

"And we both are." She eyes me with one brow raised while resting her hands on her hips, then she accepts another bucket of water from a woman carrying it along the side of the horse paddock. "The men need your help. Show them what you can do, bond with them. Even if you can't stay with them for the long haul, getting to know them can make a difference."

I watch her heft the bucket of water and carry it to the trough. The liquid splashes over the sawn plank edges with every step she takes, and now that she's diverted her attention to the task at hand, I can seek out Prometheus to warn him of Archus's plans to chastise him.

I search unsuccessfully for hours, letting myself mingle with the common troopers. Seeing the wounds in their sides, their dented and scratched armor, their shocked, sad faces, makes the situation more difficult. Movies documenting war rarely show the devastating emotional toll on both victor and vanquished, and now that it's right in front of me, I must deal with it myself.

They crowd around me in groups of five or six, expressing dismay about the ambush, and thanking for me helping stave off the Titan army. I'd make powerful allies if I stayed, but knowing I must say goodbye just as we've built a camaraderie makes me feel I'm betraying them. If I depart now, would I be any better than the Titans?

I sit on a nearby stone perch next to a pile of charcoal and ashes six inches deep, talking and listening. I'm watching the stage take shape and this reminds me of simpler times, when I was nothing more than a construction laborer with big dreams. Construction requires teamwork, from the architects to the simple laborer, and if any one piece is missing then the whole project fails.

When one of them asks me to help support a wooden truss, I go over to join the effort. We grunt and juggle these into position for much of the afternoon, and when we finish the stage, we roll heaps of lumber to where they will erect a semicircular seating area. The pine members, twisted from heat and moisture content, build up into a makeshift gallery that will overflow with men and women in less than an hour.

After inspecting our handiwork, I spot Fire Guy prowling the perimeter of the construction project, admiring the hands-on labor, his arms folded across his chest.

He waits for me to approach, and before I can chide him for leaving, he offers me his hand as though expecting me to trust him. While his hand feels warm, I'm in no danger of burning.

"Good work," he says. "You'll ride out of here tonight with Commander Archus and his sixty troops. I'm going to mingle with the Titans to gain intelligence and misdirect them. You're a capable leader, and they're in excellent hands."

"Ah shucks," I say, not trying to hide my sarcasm. "The commander doesn't seem to think I'm all that special."

"You must understand his position," he explains. "When you command a hundred soldiers, you must avoid any suspicion of favoritism. It can destroy morale, and this company needs that more than anything. He understands your abilities by now and might compel you to use them in the future. Show him loyalty where you can. I'll meet up with you in a few days—give Marissa my good wishes."

"So that's it? Get out now before the commander lets you have it for failing him? Maybe it's best he doesn't get to hammer you in front of everyone."

"Commander Archus might not seem the ally you hope he is," Prometheus counters, "but right now he's all you have. Do everything he asks without complaint. I imagine you'll be meeting other commanders this evening, maybe even Apollo himself. Be everything they need, just like you did with Sarah."

I watch him walking away. After thirty seconds, he rises above the ground and speeds off to the south.

The crowds begin to arrive, and I feel my frayed nerves chilling the base of my spine while I wait for Marissa to join me.

"It will be alright," a man reassures a woman. She is wearing a twig as a hair tie atop her head, and a long white dress that gathers filth around the hem, but otherwise asserts its dominating white sheen.

"And I thought you would turn tail and run," Marissa says, resting her hand on my shoulder and sitting down in the soil at the end of a row.

The side aisles contain the surge of bodies competing for position in the chaos, and soon I find myself observing the nearest faces eager for the commander's speech. A woman bumps my elbow, locks eyes with me, and weaves around my feet while a tall, muscular man lets her lead the way to the front row. Percussion music thumps in the background, carried aloft by towering swells of atmospheric harmony that underscore the somber tone.

"Take your seats," an older man says from center stage, resting his hands at his sides. "We'll begin in a moment."

"Still think it's a waste of time?" Marissa asks.

"We'll be getting Prometheus back in a few days," I whisper. "I guess he's got some treachery to do."

"You know him," she says without smiling. Relaxing her feet, she exhales slowly as the music swells and then peters out as Commander Archus takes the stage.

"Thank you for being here," he announces as the clamor fades and the audience becomes attentive.

"Not like we had a choice," I sneer under my breath.

"We assemble tonight as a proud fighting unit, having just waged a costly battle against the Titan army. We didn't know they were coming. But now we're gaining intelligence so we can better predict their moves, in order to gain the upper hand. I ask you to have faith. We will emerge victorious in the end.

"Let us offer our sincerest gratitude to those we've lost, to honor their sacrifices. They will forever guide us on our journey to defeat the Titans, and although they've descended to the great underworld, their memory remains with us.

"Before the performance begins, I must commend several noble men. "First Class Major Hark Cestus Philosophus, you have been given the great honor of representing your troops on this stage. For a job well done, please approach the stage."

The audience watches as Hark makes his way down the central aisle and stands next to the commander with his hands clasped together at his waist. A freshly laundered tunic is wrapped around his body, tied together with a bright red hand-knotted sash.

"Major Philosophus, I present to you the Valor in Battle Commendation. Your actions inspire us all. Please say a few words."

Hark clears his throat, and straightens his back as he faces the heavens. "None of this would be possible without the men in my company. I dedicate this medal to them, their loved ones, and those we fight for across the world. Thank you for everything you do."

The music swells and dies to a pattering drumbeat before Archus speaks again.

"The next commendation goes to Carlton W. Markham, infantryman and father of three daughters who tragically lost their lives less than a week ago to a cowardly enemy attack. Infantryman?"

Carlton rises from the back section of wooden seating, walks to the stage along the side aisle, and bows his head before the commander. When he speaks, his voice exudes sorrow and weariness, yet there is a resolute determination in his words. "We all have someone dear that we fight for, someone close to home. My three girls are the reason I live, and I will never stop serving on their behalf. I'm not a brilliant strategist or bold fighter, just a man with a greater purpose."

When he's finished, he bows to the commander again and limps back to his seat. Beside me, Marissa sighs and closes her eyes.

"And last, Kerry Gearhardt, Conveyor of Light and Shade. Defending those who are outmatched, even when not asked, requires immense spirit and courage. Your contributions are invaluable. You fight with great tenacity and a gift most of us don't understand. I present to you the Medal of Excellence."

Paralyzed, I struggle to move my arms and legs, and in that moment Marissa nudges me, propelling me to my feet. All eyes are on me, as I, an outsider, make my way down the left aisle to the stage. The commander locks eyes with me, holding a medallion in his right hand, and offers a wry smile as I step onto the stage to accept an award I feel I haven't earned.

"A few words of gratitude, if nothing else," the commander whispers as I struggle find any words at all.

"I ... I guess I don't have much to say," I mumble, realizing halfway through that I'll need to amplify my voice. Penitence weakens my presence, and nothing I can say will heal the wounds of battle. "I lost someone too. Last night when the Titan Cronus summoned a meteor that destroyed the cliffs to the east of here, the impact stirred up a storm, and Sarah, my friend, fell. She is the reason I'm here, and Marissa has been my dependable spiritual guide. But nothing would have mattered … couldn't have … without the soldier I fought alongside last night. When I saw him about to take an arrow, I lashed out in defense. And when he recognized me as an ally, he rallied enough strength to fight on. Had he not been there, I would not have been able to summon the necessary energy to do what I did. I fight for you all so I can find my wife and son, the two people who matter most to me. Thank you for welcoming me into your ranks. We've only seen the beginning, but we'll fight for the truth."

"Thank you for those powerful words, Kerry."

I'm halfway down the aisle before he finishes his sentence. "May the gods bless you with the energy and wisdom to return to your family and friends."

The audience applauds louder than I could have expected, and in the tempest of drums, cymbals, and melodies, I settle down next to Marissa and try to ignore the stunned expression she turns toward me.

Musicians dance onto the stage from both sides. They wear strangely equine costumes, lumbering in on two feet and shimmying to the beat. Their furry outfits accentuate certain body parts, barely concealing their exaggerated nether regions. Humming in tune with the music feels unnatural, yet an unspoken grace infuses the performance, bringing tears to my eyes. Marissa is swaying back and forth as she watches a goat-horse hybrid launch another performer up to the rafters, catch him, and spin him into a dizzying spiral as the audience laughs, cries, and cheers all at once.

Next, the satyrs begin a melancholy chorus, pulsing to a hollow rhythm underlain with solemn horns and rueful strings. Their dexterity is something I don't question, and as they finish, they launch into an exultant piece praising the gods. They hum and chatter, vibrate, swirl, and stomp their hooves on the wooden floorboards as their song draws to a close. And with a heavy kick of the bass drums, the crescendo comes to a sharp conclusion and the performers dart from the stage.

The crowd roars with delight, and as the music stops they begin filtering away to prepare for the exodus.

Marissa whispers in my ear as she stirs next to me. "I didn't know you could be so poetic."

I shrug. "Being married to a bibliophile has its benefits."

"Thank you," she says. "You're a good leader indeed. But I didn't deserve the praise—I'm only an occult dealer with spiritualistic skills."

The crowds return to their camps while Commander Archus meets with the eleven other commanders wearing colorful suits and tunics with strips of black paint on their high cheek bones. The one woman, wearing a fine linen peplum tied with white satin sash, slinks behind them. The commander summons me to join them.

"This is the one I was telling you about," he introduces me as I see Marissa walking away to help the women pack. "Superb fighter, uncanny ability to manipulate shadow."

"I'm a Titan," I mumble, locking eyes with the female commander. "Descended from Crete."

"Kerry, this is Clarissa Dalmyus, commander of Apollo's seventh infantry unit, one of the best."

He then introduces me to the tallest man, whose hulking forearms ripple. "Commander Amun Cortland-Smith, of the sixth defense unit." He waves toward a shorter man who wears a wooden scowl on his dark face. "Chief Commander Salam Sapporo Ingreshi, Kaplan Saint Charles of the fourth infantry unit, Baroque Haramabad, of the eighth, and Seth Richland of the third. These are the brightest stars on Apollo's side. Many other Olympians oversee similar groups. Together, we command twenty thousand soldiers. We may be few compared to the armies the Titans have assembled—care to tell us about them, Kerry?"

Without realizing that I'm swallowing a painful gulp, I try to summarize the makeup of Erebus's army, emphasizing that many of them are already dead. Erebus may have a million loyalists besides the twelve power-mad Titans.

After I'm finished, they brainstorm possible ways to maximize any edge we may have and develop a strategy to deal with anything the Titans are likely to throw at us. As the hours pass, I rub my droopy eyes, find a quiet spot to curl up, and fall asleep gazing at the Big Dipper and the Milky Way.

Betrayal, loss, and terror permeate a short, restless sleep, and when I open my eyes, I see Marissa standing over me. She is ashen and pale, as though the worst of nightmares has spoiled her slumber too. She lies down next to me, and I hear her heart rate settle as she drifts off, leaving me alone amidst the shambles of battle. Sarah stands within the destruction in my dream, whispering the single line she's so often used to encourage me: "*You know how to find me.*"

24

Dolos the Apprentice

Commander Archus's barked orders rise above the din of soldiers and support groups clamoring to leave. Having split the forces into smaller battalions, Archus could either be making a grave mistake or employing a cunning tactic, in hopes of dividing the Titans' forces.

Although I base any strategy on my knowledge of the construction industry, I consider this a risky move. If Erebus sends the Titans to find us, he will annihilate the entire company, using comparatively few resources to secure victory. Nonetheless, the Olympians must have placed their trust in Archus, or else they'll allow him less leeway. If the Olympians have faith in his military expertise, then perhaps I should, too. I hope to share some ideas with him, but the chances he'll listen to me seem slim.

The troops rally in the darkness, and the same squad that built the stage are now disassembling it. To travel light, they are leaving the lumber behind, ignoring my tongue-in-cheek suggestion to build something diversionary, like a giant horse. Had I mentioned that within earshot of the commander, he'd have taken back my medal, and that would have been humiliating.

After an hour of sleep, Marissa and I have awoken, groggy from the sounds of preparation. The commander is promising to lead the troops on a day's journey to the island's north coast. It is a perilous trek through jumbled rocks, poisonous reptiles, and arid desert.

Before we get up to help, Marissa grasps my forearm and pulls me closer. "Look, I don't know if you felt it," she says, her voice quivering, "but I have a feeling this will end in disaster."

I lift my eyebrows to feign alarm, breathe in and then exhale my reply: "Same feeling, but probably for a different reason."

"There are a thousand voices in my head, Kerry," she says. Her voice sounds weak and frightened, but no less sure of the message. As she speaks, she pulls her knees up to hug them to her torso, as though to defend herself from an imminent strike. "A thousand people died right here. And the survivors are all saying some variation of the same thing, that we're going to get demolished."

"We have some good minds on this," I counter, trying to sound encouraging.

Since we fell asleep, workers have rekindled several fires to provide light. Their graceful puffs of smoke drift upward toward the sky, where a vat of Mediterranean air builds a cover of dark rainclouds. When the sparks sputter and blink out in the night, we fall silent.

The gap in the conversation strikes a chord of worry that can only grow. Marissa looks into my eyes for a moment and then away to where a scarred tree supports a lean-to that houses food supplies. A canvas tarp shelters the darkness inside and what appears to be stair rungs carved into the tree. A man with a basket pushes through the tarp cover, glancing around and a moment after disappearing behind a wheeled cart loaded with weapons and supplies, he goes into the tarp again. He repeats the process several times.

"What do you suggest?" she asks.

Me?

"I doubt the commander will listen to me, and he probably shouldn't."

She shakes her head, wide-eyed and serious. While she watches the stranger load the cart, her expression changes from sad to grim. What lurks there now I can only describe in metaphorical terms: A tide of blackened regret chars the remnants of rational thought, and the deeper the inner monologue, the darker the stain becomes.

"I mean, for me. I've seen many things, but I can't cope with this darkness."

"You just take it one step at a time..."

"It's like, you've read the history books, but those things always happen to people in faraway places. And you never have to experience it yourself, or feel the way they did, just sitting at your desk, in luxury. You might even think you're emotionally intelligent within reason, but nothing prepares you for it. It feels different when you're living it. The burdens are greater, and the stakes are higher."

"Empathy can be a powerful ally," I say tentatively, without knowing how she might interpret it.

"I thought my spiritual intuition served me well," she says, her voice softening. She relaxes her arms and lets her feet slide away from her, straightening her knees and hunching her back. Placing one palm beneath her outstretched leg, she stares at me for a long time, glancing back and forth between me and the man packing the cart. "Maybe I thought it was a cute power, but now I'm realizing it can destroy my mental health. How do you keep it in check?"

I only shrug. The clouds over the eastern horizon are growing darker the farther inland they drift. The camp smoke reeks of death and decay, joining the clouds to paint a dark portrait of despair resembling the dusky brushstrokes of eighteenth-century art.

"I don't really see it that way. Act now, internalize later. Becky always says that's a poor strategy, but it's the only way I can cope with things nobody should ever have to live through."

"And Sarah? We haven't had time to talk about her, but I'm sure you feel it now. The entanglement. And I know *you* know there's a reason for it."

"What reason?"

She shrugs, but it makes her shoulders sag. She says nothing, only closing her eyes to push away the tears swimming there.

"Excuse me," a woman interrupts, looking somewhat impatient, yet with a forced politeness. She looks at Marissa, straightens her back, and speaks, her voice sounding like charcoal on parchment. "Do you think you can help with the horse feed?"

"Right," Marissa says, struggling to stand up.

To steady her, I offer her my hand, climbing also to my feet and dusting off my jeans. Still damp with sweat and filthy from mud and battle, they rub against my thighs like gritty sandpaper. The woman leads Marissa toward the horse corral, whose gates stand wide open behind a pair of firepits spaced fifty feet apart. The flames dance higher when a young man tosses in bits of wood from disassembled buildings. As he pokes at the fire, it grows brighter while the other, fifty feet farther away, dims.

"I guess I'll find the commander," I say.

Finding him isn't easy. Entering a messy barracks, I find a dismal-looking soldier treating his own wounds. He cringes at the sting of icy water and closes his eyes. I nod to him as I pass by, glancing at clothes-strewn cots, piled with blankets, and small ration packets of half-eaten food. On the other side, next to a rough log-framed door, I see a man in a tight tunic crease his elbow in a V-pattern on his chest, his fingers pointing upward. He is gaunt and looks weary, yet exudes loyalty. Commander Archus stands opposite him, in a shadow a few feet from the door.

After dismissing the soldier, he eyes me and invites me into his shadowy lair to converse with me or explain the secret salute I'd seen two other people giving him.

"I want you to tell me more about your powers," he commands me.

I hesitate, not quite knowing how to describe them. Without even remembering how I got my abilities, how does he expect me to explain how they work?

"I can't really control them," I stammer, trying not to sound hopeless. "Best I can tell you is they sort of feed on emotion and energy. When it's based on hope or love, I can summon light. But when it's rage or terror, it's dark energy."

"And you use them in equal measure?"

"I don't use *them*. *They* use me."

He has no time to reply. An anguished scream outside the barracks sends the camp into chaos. This can only mean one thing: The Titan army is back.

The woman's shriek hangs in the air before a shockwave shreds through it, making the fires flicker and the buildings groan. I'd felt the ground trembling an instant before I heard it. The plank walls of the barracks building topple as the pressure wave expands, buckling the compacted earth and sending jagged cracks in every direction.

Archus stumbles toward the door frame to steady himself, shouts for the soldiers to take up arms, and darts away. I sprint in the other direction, past the disorderly cots and bleeding, terrified men. Once I'm outside, I realize what we're up against.

The sky looks like it's bubbling as the clouds boil away, ripping apart the heavens piece by piece. When the wave subsides, I feel shock and grief that mix into a chaotic emotion darker than any rage I've ever felt before.

A split second later, the stars themselves blink out and a caustic darkness falls over the camp, extinguishing the fires and pulsing like a bubbling vat of tar. Men sprint in every direction, throwing armor over their shoulders, gripping swords and shields for a battle unlike any they've ever encountered.

Rather than the orderliness that Commander Archus strives for, the general atmosphere is one of deep disquiet. The black soup permeates throughout the camp, depositing hundreds of grimy black specks into the churned-over dirt. These grow up out of the darkness into bodies, wielding jagged swords in each hand and baring bloody, serrated teeth.

When they strike it is as a well-coordinated unit. Women scream, scurrying away, even as the men prepare for the assault. An older woman a hundred feet away from the barracks attacks one of them, hitting and plunging both arms into the oily mass of flesh and teeth. Her screams carry in the night as the creature rips her arms off, devouring them bones and all.

Seeing this, a man shrieks, holds his sword above his head, and charges. The creatures destroy him before he takes ten steps, and when they do, they seem to multiply. Gathering my horror, fear and regret into a fuming ball of emotion, I let myself expand into a cloud of dark dust, and as I hover over the lurching, sticky bodies, a foreign burst of energy slams me in the heart, causing my cloud to glow.

The creatures launch themselves at me, reaching slimy hands into my core to coax out every bit of rage they can devour. Merciless squeals pierce the night, and with one blast of pure energy, they fall into soup. The ball of light glows toward me, inching into my extremities to soothe away all the dark that I have become. And when it fades away, the light pulls me upward into a pure white haze as blood spills, arms thrash, and the creatures tear apart the soldiers' bodies.

Scrambling to join in the fray, I seek to escape the fireball, but it pulls me in with its immense gravity. A second later, I black out.

Sarah pulls me into a warm embrace, and her steady breathing is a balm to my soul. My cheek tingles with the touch of a strand of hair turned almost white in the driving sun. She moves her lips as if to speak, but no words come out of her mouth.

Emotion paints this picture with a stark array of contrasting colors, as if every photon delivers a sensation deeper than the most expressive art. The healing energy crackles around us.

When Sarah pulls away, I can feel the glow on her skin. She's becoming the light, vanishing into the sun, leaving me alone in an endless realm of blurry green and brightness.

Without feeling mechanical or forced, light and nature combine into a single node of limitless energy, growing in me and through me until I can no longer differentiate between thoughts and dreams, wants and needs. Organic and eternal, the brightness flashes, leaving behind the faint silhouette of a woman wandering into the light.

I don't know where she's going, but no matter where, or how far the distance, I know we're connected forever. She doesn't need to talk for me to understand. Everything she is now becomes me, filtering through me until I'm both myself and her. Her spirit loses definition, and before I know what is happening, I'm transcending it all, as though every atom is floating out of my body.

The battle rages on. The oil-stain creatures operate as one unit, thrashing through whole groups of men with little effort. One of them glances at me as I take shape beside it, wrapping tendrils of light around its oily neck and severing it. Oil splatters to the ground, causing another creature nearby to attack.

But when it flings its sword at my heart, the blade melts into red, viscous liquid in its hands. Baring its teeth, the creature retreats, giving way to its more powerful ally, a five-story-high skeleton with bones composed of many smaller bones. The monster flexes its mighty power and transforms in an instant into a man, dark and muscular.

He lumbers toward me as my light touches his skin, yet instead of eviscerating him, the light feeds him with more energy. Reaching down into the basement of my emotions, I summon a cloud of black dust to erode him, yet he still inches closer and prepares to bludgeon me with a strength I cannot counter.

"Learning new tricks all the time, Kerry, Conveyor of Light and Shade," it taunts. "Those powers serve The One, and they always will."

As though he's controlling my thoughts, I let myself bow before him. The power leaks out of me in an instant as the screams grow distant. The oil-creatures pursue the men into the night, but before the stranger finishes with me, the soured air reabsorbs every one of them into a cloud of oiliness that slides toward the eastern shore.

"I'll never serve him," I grate out, powerless to control my own extremities.

"Rise, Kerry," he says. "Remember your place at his side."

My heart trembles.

Rise.

And I do. Every molecule in my body gains steam, pushing me higher and higher until I overpower him. Looking down and intending to flatten him, I let my thoughts propel him away. When he sees my essence, he lowers himself to the ground, doubles over in pain, and vomits.

Just one surge of energy will do it. It will rip him apart, scattering his blood into different dimensions as he flees. But before I lunge in to strike, he vanishes into a flash of black, leaving only a chilly dust devil in his wake.

The real me drives me down, pulls me back to my original form, and re-forms me with the truth of my own mind. The battle has ceased and again the Titans have won. Everywhere I look, blood and limbs taint the dirt with black bubbles of tar. With hundreds more dead, we must still reach

for something we can never attain. If the Olympians succumb to defeat, the world will crumble. And if the Titans prevail, I'll never see Becky and Ian again. That thought alone is enough to coax me into this war, to insert myself into every battle, because everything I've ever known and loved depends on i
t.

Wherever Becky is, her reality might also be falling apart. Imagining her succumbing to the dark invades my soul with a knot of torment unlike any I've ever experienced before.

I'm unstable, and eventually the power in me will engulf Marissa if the oil creatures have not already ripped her apart. As Prometheus has gone to spy on the Titans, I'm left to grapple with it alone, with no one to guide me except Marissa.

The fog and smoke dissipate, parting in the middle like a flap in a linen shroud. She walks slowly toward me, arms hung low at her side, stepping through the aftermath of the battle and weeping.

We stare at each other for at least thirty seconds, and before I summon the courage to speak, she moves slightly. I'm surprised she's alive, but she looks neither shocked nor confused.

"They're dead," she says, her voice steady, yet rasping. "I can deal with the dead. I know what they're thinking. We must warn the commander now, because if we don't stop them, it will mean the end of the earth, the sun, the planet, the galaxy. The entire human race reduced to slaves."

I gawk at her, my heart growing heavier with each word she speaks. Although she is outwardly quiet, I can sense the turmoil within her. She stands to lose everything, too.

As the smoke from the now-extinguished fires dissipates, the true scale of the destruction comes into focus. The troops lie dead in their own camps, which are now just heaps of splintered, gray-tinged wood and limestone boulders. An isolating silence covers the landscape. After a few minutes, the clouds part, exposing the heavens, and the moonlight bathes the landscape in an ethereal blue light, coating the leafless tree in a cooling glow. Power surrounds me; if I can tap into it, I can fight the Titans.

I must do it. There is no other way.

25

The Final Apparition

The battlefield lies desolate, pocked with miniature craters, scarred with burns, and imbued with the scents of death and decay. It is dark, and the air carries the cries of grieving mothers, widows, and friends. A bloody hammer with a bent and mangled claw is half buried in the dusty ground under a thin sheet of wood, its shattered edges splotched with oil. Trampled under the feet of hundreds of fleeing, dying warriors, the fiber sheet lies flush with the dirt.

Surveying the damage, I rest a single foot on the board and try to understand everything that has happened. Marissa, once raptly surveying her surroundings, now walks with her shoulders slouching and her arms dangling at her sides. For a long time she says nothing, only letting out an expressive sigh when I say I'm ready to follow the survivors into the wilderness.

"I can sense them, Kerry," she says, her voice calm yet full of pity. "All of them. Never going home."

"Home," I repeat. The misery strikes somewhere at the base of my brain, tugging stubborn tears from my eyes. "It's a luxury that some can never fully appreciate. They're lucky."

While this may warrant a shocked expression, she understands the nuance my tone, seems to internalize it, and finally shrugs. She grimaces and dabs at her watering eyes with her collar. "And their loved ones?"

"It's never so simple," I admit. I've seen death before—tragic occurrences that have hit me deep in the soul. Yet something about this battlefield plunges far deeper still.

"They cry out. Pleading with the gods for mercy. For redemption, as if *they* must live with the weight of their transgressions."

Raising my eyebrows, I utter a raspy reply: "How does sin square with paganism?"

She waves her arm as though motioning towards the sea, and its cool maritime breeze. "Transgression doesn't have to mean sin. We all make mistakes; none of us are immune."

"You can speak with them," I remind her. "Tell them they're heroes to be honored forever. You can—"

"It doesn't work that way. When they speak, I listen. And right now, they're telling me we've already lost the war. We just don't know it yet." She is murmuring toward the end of her sentence, leaking a deceitful poison that devours my spirit.

"We have something the Titans can't prepare for," I say, remembering how I have grown with light even though the demon god eroded my dark energy. "I can't control it, but I'll learn how to harness it."

She nods and frowns. "And you're not the only one fighting. I think you can learn from those around you. Learn their skills, or at least combine with them. They all have things they're fighting for, not just you."

I whisper. "I won't let Becky and Ian disappear from reality just so the dead can know they're not alone."

"You must," she says. No expression of compromise touches her face. Her words are sharp, yet low, a vocal tactic she might have learned from Becky if they'd ever met. "Because what they're telling me is that we're at a severe disadvantage. The enemy knows we're on our heels and vulnerable. The more we lick our wounds, the weaker we get, and the Titan army thrives on discord as much as hate. Running from them is what they expect us to do. But we can't do much else."

Screwing up my face as though she'd just suggested something absurd, I attempt to organize my thoughts. "You're suggesting we launch a counter-offensive when we're this depleted?"

She shakes her head to dismiss my surprise. Flexing her back, she tilts her head and allows tufts of her curly hair to brush her shoulder. "You're going to have to build a strategy on your own. Rally allies, build a defense, and stand your ground. And because they want us to make even bigger mistakes, they won't expect it."

I shake my head too and smirk. "You're getting all that from the dead?"

"You got a better idea?"

Dammit. I relent, biting my lip to exorcise the pain of being wrong again. "Commander Archus is going to love this one."

"I'm thinking we call on one of the goddesses. The hell with Archus; he's only human, after all."

We all are.

I don't need to remind her that everyone we've dealt with so far suffers from the curse of humanity and the propensity to be wrong. Am I any better suited for this role than anyone else? Blondie would make a better leader than me. At least he has direction and selfless emotion behind him. No matter what I doing, I'm never able to expunge Becky and Ian from my memory, and that makes me even more susceptible to error.

"That's hitting real close to sedition," I say.

"The commander doesn't have to know. Besides, I never swore an oath to serve the Pantheon."

"They still know treachery when they see it," I argue.

"Then don't let them see it."

Why must everyone make so much sense when I'm so determined on another direction? Had I learned debate in high school, I might make a better case to defend my positions; however, I cannot deny her logic.

I've built my career on logic. Keeping track of inventory and procurement, managing a system to track labor and material usage, while adhering to construction documents requires negotiation skills and a subtle sense of pride. Even if your decisions result in extraordinary drawbacks, making plans and sticking to them is supposed to lead to success, and flying by the seat of your pants is the quickest way to failure. But now that I'm losing the battle of wills, I am only left with to question the personality that allowed me to succeed. If I let Marissa convince me to change the game on the jobsite it would cost time and money, but here, I have no other choice. It's an unsettling truth.

Frowning and huffing out a frustrated sigh, I scan her expression, which keeps changing, making it difficult to read.

"I don't suppose you know how to contact a goddess," she says.

"No clue..." I begin, catching myself while glancing up at the heavens. Though cloaked with dust, smoke, and clouds, the stars shine somewhere in the ether, reflecting the emotions of the living. If I can somehow reach out toward the cosmos, I might be able to contact someone close.

Reflection. Since some matter reflects or absorbs light, and light behaves as both a particle and a wave, then all matter must behave similarly. My theories are sometimes wrong, but they also sometimes serve me well.

Somewhere up there behind the clouds and smoke, the Big Dipper rises above the dusky horizon, taking up spirit and soul. Pleading with the heavens has never before connected me to the Beyond, but now it just might.

"Maybe I do," I mutter, remembering the Great Bear.

I don't know how, but I'm sure this will work.

"Great," she says. "Do you have a plan for that?"

I don't bother looking at her, but out of the corner of my eye, I see her gazing into the distance, waving a subtle finger at the black horizon to our north where the defeated army has fled.

Allowing myself a moment to get my bearings, I begin gazing up at the puffy clouds, begging them to part. Marissa interrupts me by tugging at my sleeve.

Before I know it, I'm confronting a new enemy, a darker reality hidden from my view. The horizon seems to bleed out colors of sinister black, a morphing shade that rises to stand amidst the battlefield like a shrouded ghost.

In the distance, a cry pierces the night a sign of a soldier in distress, as diamond tears shatter on the ground. The figure approaches like a cold front, whipping up a frosty gale that whirls around plumes of particles and smoke. In its wake, the remnants of waning fires suffocate, emitting twisting towers of smoke that rise to the clouds.

The morphing figure takes on the shape of a man, menacing and dark. With terror flashing through me, I sprint toward him, hoping to stave off a brutal execution. Trying her best to keep up with me, Marissa pleads with me not to take such drastic action. Yet if I fail to save the soldier, I will regret the mistake. It will infiltrate every decision I make with a paralyzing 'what-if.' What if I hadn't been late? What if I hadn't reacted too slowly to prevent Sarah from falling to her death? What if Ian had never died?

But this provocateur of evil will not win.

Marissa sprints along behind me, panting as I build an attack strategy. Instead of multiplying, the man stares me down, the deep black in his eyes punctuating the night like a pair of bullets.

"LEAVE HIM ALONE!" I scream.

The ground vibrates as I zero in on him, the dark energy pulsing in my heart, ready to attack. Instead of retreating, the adversary gauges my trajectory, stands firm, and mouths something into the silence. The tremors in the ground form the words, interspersed with my hammering footsteps.

"He ... taken care ... eternity ... you must ... remember ... dreams."

"I'm not letting you kill him!" I shout.

Marissa pleads through labored breath as she tries to keep up with me—"Kerry."

"Titan of Light and Shade," I finish, launching a condensed wave of black powder at him and watching it swirl around his waist and his shoulders.

He emerges from the storm whole and looking angrier than ever. His black eyes glisten with reflections of flame, coating his expression with hellish remorse. Mounting no defense, he seems to invite my attack, using it to strengthen himself. I reach into the depraved, defeated parts of my soul to summon the bleakest energy I can muster, pressing it into the air like a sword.

The man's belt is a stricken, frayed piece of black tanned leather around tattered, pleated robes. A thin black cloak flaps in the breeze behind him, diffusing firelight and outlining his clothing in a faint orange. In his left hand he wields a bowed scythe, whose blade catches the amber glow like a molten slat of hot steel. He is using it to push me back with a pressure wave of his own.

As he rotates his shoulders, I can see what lurks behind him: A pair of long, feathery wings covered in black soot and dirt. They arch with a skeleton of bones radiating to the tips of his wings. The curved ridge supporting their weight arches high behind his head with horn-tipped pinnacles of black prodding upwards like the devil.

"NOOO!" I scream when he lowers the scythe and bends at the waist.

"Kerry," Marissa repeats in a soft, fragile voice, "Don't you know who he is?"

"It's Erebus!" I shriek.

The ground mumbles as his wave of dark energy keeps me at bay. *"I am not. You may call me the Personification of Death."*

The Grim Reaper.

"He's already dead, Kerry," Marissa says, weeping.

I know she's right. My shoulders slouch and I am filled with the darkness that defines half of my Titan name. I'm no match for him; the reaper can defend against any attack I send his way. A power like that can only come from the gods.

Realizing what this means, I shudder, trying to understand why he looks so unfamiliar. He's a collector of the dead, an emissary leading the souls into the underworld to face judgement. His power renders my abilities ineffective, no matter how dark my emotions become.

Closing my eyes, I reach out to him, feeling the words leak out of my soul one syllable at a time, inaudible to all but him. *"You've seen him. My son. Becky. Sarah. You know them. Why must you take them from me before they're ready?"*

"Kerry Gearhardt," the ground rumbles, *"Your power derives not from your ancestors or even a princess, but from those you love. Do not take it for granted. Use it for good, or you shall never see them again."*

His words ascend through my feet, rattle through my legs and knees, and produce the most heart-rending sorrow that a human can suffer. The bleakest agony and the brightest hope both come from love.

But what can this god of darkness and death know of love?

As he straightens his back, his wings flutter, their feathered tips brushing at the soil near his heels. With his arms curled in front of him, he takes a withered, opal-blue globe of memory and light into the blackness of his robes, and bows to me.

"Titan of Light and Shade," I repeat, as though he can hear the words I speak.

A slight hesitation confirms he's listening, and when he turns his back to me, his wings spread out behind him, spanning at least five feet to either side. He arches his back, curves his wings, hunkers down on his haunches, and blasts up into the sky, leaving a hallucinatory halo of black in his wake as he vanishes into the night without a trace.

Tears mark my face as I turn to face Marissa. When she sees my misery, her face falls; she now feels what I feel. The remnants of Sarah and Ian speak to her in a foreign voice I cannot hear.

She rests her hand on my shoulder, pulls me closer, and permeates into me in a way I cannot explain: sorrow, fear, hurt, memory, and hope combine into one enigmatic feeling that carries electricity sparking to my fingers. She's passing her knowledge into me so I can experience how it feels deep inside. And when it's over, the power leaves a sterile vacuum.

26

Vengeance of the Erinyes

B y now, the armies have advanced miles into the wilderness and, even if we apply basic logic and math, we might take days to catch up with them on foot. But they need us sooner than that, because the forces that hunt them are well organized and bent on destruction.

We waste no time exiting the blood-soaked battlefield. Although it has been hours since the satyrs' performance, no light has risen on the eastern horizon; any estimate on the actual time of sunrise would be guesswork, since we don't even know what time zone we're in. In the Mediterranean latitudes in the summer, night lasts from around 9:30 p.m. to 5:30 a.m. Considering the feel of the air, I'm wagering we're near the predawn glow. And if we move now, we'll make up more ground than the slower troops can.

The air hangs dense and warm, with a humidity level I'm used to. Weariness sits deep within me as I try to gauge Marissa's stamina. Although her breathing is light, her body language suggests we'll only make it only a mile at this pace before she collapses. In other words, we'll need rest, which will delay catching up with the warriors.

When Marissa squeezes her eyes shut, I see a tear leak out, and she melts into a silent sob. Rather than saying anything, I let her emotion carry her, till she wipes the dirt, sweat and tears from her palms onto her jeans leg, stretches her back, and looks up at me.

I can sense the sky clearing, and the lighter it becomes, the farther I can see. The cloud cover is advancing over the island, pushing off to the northeast and ushering in a slight cooling breeze. The moon is still behind clouds; moonlight scatters into a pale blue glow, casting bleak shadows and illuminating bloody, abandoned weaponry and damaged armor. At this location, the footprints all point in the same direction, a thousand pairs of feet trampling the dry steppe, crushing the golden grasses to dust.

"I don't suppose you can see a bright side," I say to Marissa.

She breathes hard. "I don't think Garfunkel would have any words to describe what we've seen."

That describes my general luck. I wonder if I'm the only one who has ever felt that in such a real way. Even when I set out to solve problems at work using search engines it mostly confuses me rather than giving me sage advice. With no one else to help us, Marissa and I must rely solely on each other.

"Why did you react that way when Death took the warrior?" I ask her.

"A bit of a loaded question," she says, raising one eyebrow. She's sitting in an uncomfortable sideways position, her left leg stretched to her side while leaning on her right hand. "I just knew you weren't seeing it right."

"Wouldn't be the first time," I admit.

"Nor the last."

I chuckle. "You still think so little of me? Why are you still here? And why was I wrong?"

"You viewed him as an enemy when he was only doing his job. You couldn't stop him because they were both already dead."

"Uh…"

"The dead give off a certain vibe," she explains, "that's hard to describe; you just know it when you feel it. And you didn't—there's nothing wrong with that."

"But you didn't hear him using the vocal trick I've only heard one entity use: The One. He speaks to me in my own voice, or by vibrating the ground. Even if that wasn't him, Death at least learned it from him. And that's a big problem."

"Why's that?"

"Because The One *is* the enemy. Consorting with the Titans to enslave humankind and rain havoc on the world."

She shakes her head. "That's presuming too much."

"Any yet probably not presumptuous enough," I argue. "I don't know why he's doing it, but I'm going to find out."

"One more thing we need to accomplish before we can find your beloved."

"Sometimes you gotta take a sack so you can advance the ball down the field," I say, but in reality I know very little about football, having only learned the terminology and logic by listening to the color commentators while my friend Juaquin and I had watched the Chiefs play. I might be wrong, but if a play breaks down in a predictable way, a blocking scheme may open later in the game, which the offense can then exploit.

"You think you can do it?"

"I don't think I have any choice," I say, my voice clipped. "He's going to be coming for me because he knows I've betrayed him. You don't even want to imagine what he sends."

"That might be an advantage for us. You never know."

"I know he's got bigger plans," I admit. "And he's going to count on us making a mistake."

"Got any other ideas?"

I shake my head.

The air pressure has shifted as we've been sitting here. I'm kneeling as though I'm about to propose, and the hard earth is digging into my knees and buckling my toes. As the pressure moves, I sense a wispy plume of dust lifting away from the scarred battlefield to chase it away, and fear paralyzes me

.

The dust pulls itself into a dark gray face, its lips curled in a derisive sneer and its slit eyes peering at me in the harrowing moonlight. The ground vibrates and my own voice echoes in my brain.

You fool. You will never get away with treason.

I seal the emotion out of my heart, squeeze my eyes shut, and let silence resume. Still, darkness swirls through my every thought, including Ian's fate. If I hadn't learned from Prometheus how to betray him, I might still struggle.

So be it. Live by the sword, die by the sword.

He's coming.

The face in the sand disappears and the breeze settles. Groaning, I stand and stretch my legs, offering Marissa a hand up. She shakes her head, gets to her feet and begins walking. Minutes fade into memory with each step, as if this moment will soon pass away. I can see waves lapping against a distant, rocky shore, reflecting the pale moonlight as the clouds scatter and drift apart.

The clinking of metal on metal sounds far away. Another army approaches, this one targeting me. We have nowhere to run, and no one to fight on our behalf. To secure victory, I'll need to detach my soul from my body once again. The problem is that I cannot control my Titan abilities, so I can't rely on them to save me. The One is right: We'll never get away unscathed.

My stomach churns, bracing for disaster. I nonverbally convince Marissa to sprint in line with the footprints in the dirt. We make it less than the length of a city block before we hear bloodthirsty howls and guttural grunts assaulting us with the ominous chords of death in the opposite direction.

Crunch.

HOWL.

We're flanked. Preparing for the onslaught, I suck the darkness to the bottom of my stomach, summoning images that are enough to make me retch and sob at the same time. The storm rotates like a hurricane in my heart, and when Marissa sees what I'm doing, she trips on a protruding root, stumbles face-first into the dust, and gapes up at me.

Moments later our adversaries appear, forming parallel lines a mile long to sandwich us in the middle. The mechanical chinks reverberate across the barren landscape, signaling the other army to issue attack orders. A deafening roar erupts as the two forces converge around us. I stir clouds of dust at my feet, spinning faster than a tornado and whipping up debris. Shattered rocks, corrosive dirt, needle-like brush leaves, and even poison-tipped arrowheads swirl in the wind as I envelop Marissa in a protective embrace.

Sirens wail from the mechanized army, their impassive voices echoing in the warm, humid air. Thunder rumbles as both forces close in on us. Summoning every bit of darkness I can muster, I prepare a voiceless response to Erebus.

I'm the one standing in your way. Come at me.

The spears from the dead army reach us first. The gust from my storm erases a hundred of them before they can move. But the dead only form the front of the line; farther back, a vicious array of beasts and brutes hanker to feast on my flesh, as much as the metallic monsters claw at the ground to the south.

Marissa screams within my protective gale, her voice growing raspy at the end of a long, torturous syllable. When I scream too, I cannot hear my voice.

The robot army comprises a dozen zinc-plated steel wolves, galvanized to prevent corrosion—a sign that Erebus has anticipated the Shade in my soul and has worked out how to counter it. If darkness cannot defeat them, then logic dictates that light cannot vanquish the dead, either. This is a battle I cannot win alone.

The wolves' metal teeth chew on the humid air, seething with mechanized hate. When one pounces on me, the storm only deters it by pushing it out to a quadrant of my cyclonic defense. Gathering all the darkness into one force-blast, I launch it the other way. The dead soldiers are re-forming themselves and materializing again as the wave subsides.

Eyeless zombies prod at us with spears, hurling raspy insults our way. Pain erupts as the galvanized wolves bite into my back; when they back off, satisfied at provoking agony and drawing blood, the army of the dead roll us over.

In moments they have surrounded us. Worse yet, I can no longer control the storm. Trying to conjure enough energy to create light isn't easy; I try to visualize happiness and joy, but only blackness pervades. The deceased feed on my energy.

Behind the faceless drones, ten fifty-foot-tall skeletons march, flattening their peers as they go. Behind them, arrows fly through the gaps in their ribcages. Hissing and growling penetrate the din behind them, as a dozen androsphinxes, manticores, and ghouls prowl the frayed edges of the group.

Backing the cybernetic wolves, I can feel the Shades imbibing the darkness, sending rivulets of energy through the humid air. Darkness is no match for darkness; Houdini himself could never escape these odds.

My body materializes as my attempt at light sputters out. The arrows from the dead fly by without inflicting harm, but the skeletons wield ten-foot swords, cutting and hacking through their less-skilled counterparts like machetes through jungle vines. A sword streaks right toward my abdomen and halts less than an inch away from my sternum.

With her eyes closed, Marissa is disorienting the dead soldiers, causing enough distraction to make a skeleton stumble. Its bones rattle to a halt and it crumbles from five stories high. Sand blinds me as the heap of dried body parts trips another skeleton. Bloody-fanged chimeras with black talons launch over the front, sinking their lion's teeth into my flesh as the machinery-driven wolves lash at my back. The Shades behind them form a viscous black haze that obscures them as they slither through the steel bodies, seeking to erase me.

A flicker of light glints in my soul as blood congeals on my forearm. The night rains in pure chaos while the mechanical beasts scatter; the skeletons tumble into titanic heaps of debris, and the chimeras sprint away.

Hope is so fleeting that I cannot conjure enough energy to combine with the gods. Erebus's forces remain undisturbed; they reform their ranks even as a halo of light circles overhead. Lightning forks through the sky, surging into the steel siding of the massive wolves, disabling them. Then the gods redirect energy to the Shades, but the Shades form a solid wall of sooty black, and the light merely flashes on it.

The gods try another defense, circling in the heavens, a dozen bodies disappearing into streaks of light.

The Shades retaliate the only way they know how—by eroding the distance around and above them, sucking the swirling gods into the fray. I launch dark energy at the reconvening forces opposite the wolves but cannot produce enough of a wave to cause any damage. The manticores and androsphinxes claw at the ground, scoring my arms and abdomen with bloody teeth. Seeing this, the gods launch a pressure wave that pushes them back.

But they are no match for the Shades. Their light extinguishes one by one as the shades rip through them. Horror fills me as the light fades away, and the gods vanish as quickly as they arrived. They've defeated hundreds of the enemy; they may have made the battle easier, but it won't be enough to help me win this fight.

Alone, Marissa and I face the adversaries that have converged, ready to lash out with a vengeful stroke powerful enough to eliminate us. Agony sears through me as Marissa again closes her eyes. Mirroring her, I settle down and present myself as a prisoner of war. Erebus will not have his armies destroy me from afar. He'll want to watch me suffer firsthand.

I cannot escape—I must succumb to the darkness and the vengeance I've earned. We draw our hands behind our backs, feeling the zombies slap primitive iron bands around our wrists. I open my eyes as the commander of the army steps forward; I recognize him in an instant.

27

Tyrants and Traps

Why do I remember him? This question enters my mind and lingers there, inhabiting all thought in the moments before the enemy speaks. When he breathes, he sets off trailing puffs of thin, gray smoke, wafting into the blue predawn glow where the brightest stars still twinkle. His muscular chest, covered with a network of tattoos, rises and falls as he crosses his forearms and flexes his biceps. A mane of grizzled hair hangs near his ears, and when his voice rises out of his trachea, the surrounding air seems to flee.

"Kerry Gearhardt," he says, sounding far too cordial. "Do you remember meeting me?"

I stare at him, allowing the silence to squeeze my stomach. I can only guess my expression, but it must reflect my rage and anguish.

"I wonder if your trip to Hades was productive. Was destroying his tower an odious task? I wouldn't have questioned your loyalty had you not betrayed your master."

"You're insane," I spit, aware that my lip is quivering and my ankle throbs.

Next to me, Marissa has her head lowered; dark strands of mangled hair are matted to her face, caked with sweat and smoke. With a frown, she looks up at our captor and then at the massive armies he commands. She lets out a labored sigh and shifts her perception to the hundreds of dead, eyeless warriors who stand at ease behind him.

"If two thousand years in a dungeon doesn't drive a prisoner mad," he replies, "I'd consider him to be stronger than the typical human, even ones with nascent talents such as conjuring Shade or focusing Light."

"So you've heard about me," I say, testing him. "Let me give you my autograph. Mind if I sign it 'yours truly?'"

My face may be incapable of expressing humor. Rather than smiling, my jaw slides downward and my eyes bear the burden of weary anger.

He doesn't bother rolling his eyes.

"It is interesting you have not yet spoken my name," he says. With a subtle wave of his arm he summons a burly dead man standing six inches taller than me. The servant wears a tunic and a black cape that does not cover his bare arms. He approaches me fast, yanks my hands toward him, and ties a fraying strand of twine around my wrists, as though he fears I'll break through the handcuffs. Continuing to Marissa, he says nothing. His eyes contain the same smoke and fire evident in his master's demeanor, yet I detect an air of servility behind the hardened mask. He'll never rise above these mundane tasks, but it's not his fault.

Marissa grunts when he pulls the rope tight around her wrists. Her voice catches in her throat.

"Careful, Tiny," I warn.

A pitiful ball of twine is supposed to bind me? I'd find the attempt comical and inane, but then again, no matter how deep the wretchedness, I cannot coax the darkness out of me. I worry that, left untended, the caustic sludge may burn through my internal organs, leaving only the charred remnant of my soul.

"Your silence tells me you don't know or don't care who I am."

"Assumptions," I groan, rubbing my wrists together to loosen the twine. "You know what they say."

"Assumptions are apt observations based on context, are they not?"

I'm not interested in the discussion. Instead of trying to think up a witty comeback, I glance sideways at Marissa, who shuffles her feet in the sand while directing a penetrating gaze at the crowds of dead men and women surrounding us. If I know her, by now she'll be conversing with them in a simple, intimate manner to uncover the basis of their alliance with the Titans.

"You may call me Coeus," he says, relaxing his shoulders and waving his fingers at the ropes scurrying around my wrists. As if reacting to a mundane spell, the ropes tighten against my skin, sawing livid red lines into my flesh. The bindings sting as though soaked in acid, making me flinch.

"They're enchanted," Marissa whispers, without breaking eye contact with the dead army. "Deceived by a spell so powerful they can't comprehend their own loyalty. Yet they hold fast to it like members of a cult."

"Very observant, Miss Marissa," Coeus remarks, flexing his biceps and cracking a wry smile. "Too bad your skills will wear themselves out. They cannot turn; when you're bound to someone in death, you serve him forever."

She looks down in shame, pulls her feet together, and sighs.

"You can become a powerful ally to—"

"Are you going to take us somewhere?" I interrupt, knowing where his conversation is going and trying to derail him.

"I don't need to," he says. "Your master will be here in a moment to harvest your soul, reclaiming your skills as his own. I shall watch with great pleasure. Traitors deserve a most cruel death, don't you agree?"

The ropes gnaw at my flesh, tangling with sweaty arm hair and ripping it out by the roots, and I groan in agony. A smile of pleasure parts Coeus's lips as he watches me twist the ropes, which only further tightens them.

But his grin transforms in the blink of an eye.

Overhead, vibrant streaks of light paint parallel tracks across the now pale-blue sky like a formation of fighter jets riding the sun's morning rays. One streak swirls into a cornucopia of light, creating a tight vortex that ends at the feet of the wolves as they stand idle, as though awaiting orders from Coeus.

The cyclone shimmers and then fades, leaving behind a woman with golden brown curls waving in the wind. She carries a compound bow with a quiver of arrows strapped against her golden, angelic wings. Wearing a tight, halter-cut top with a shapely V-line neck, a pair of silky harem pants, and a pensive expression, she closes her eyes, and summons a horde of animals out of thin air.

A pair of moles scurry around her leather-strap sandals while a flock of seabirds and avian predators form themselves into an attack front overhead.

With a mechanical clicking and whining servos, the metallic wolves lurch into motion as deer, moose, and tigers gather at her sides.

"You will let Kerry Gearhardt go," she commands, her voice stern yet solemn. Her enormous wings spread out behind her as she pulls an arrow from its sheath, centers it in the bow, and aims it at the Titan's heart.

"Your troops are no match for us, Artemis," Coeus says with a smirk and a shrug.

"We are here to take Kerry and Marissa," she says, fluttering her feathers as she narrows her eyes. Her aim might be precise, but a moment before she lets her arrow fly, her army multiplies. Hundreds of humanoid avians bolt from the sky, wielding weapons of their own. Seeing this, the eyeless zombies launch hundreds of arrows skyward.

As most of the projectiles miss, the harpies launch a more precise volley, cutting down dozens of dead men before the giants, cyclopes, chimeras, and sphinxes charge. The wolf machines emit chattering, mechanical howls as they attack their enemies. A giant bull moose charges the nearest construct, but the attack is hopeless. Before its magnificent antlers slam into the wolf's metal hull, the monster's serrated, galvanized teeth sink into the creature's neck, twisting its head clean off.

But the animal army surrounds the mechanized wolves even as the dead warriors launch new salvos at the swirling avians.

Coeus still holds me hostage, magically tugging the ropes ever tighter with his fingers while watching the battle rage. The androsphinxes lack ranged firepower, posing a challenge for the dead army. To improve their odds even further, the harpies aim at the thirty-foot tall giants. The arrows penetrate into the giants' sides, yet they continue to march unfazed. A cyclops plucks a harpy out of the sky, rips off her wings, and drop kicks her a quarter of a mile. The harpies change tactics in a flash, aiming their arrows at the cyclops's beachball-sized eyes.

"Let them go," Artemis repeats.

"You surely don't believe your arrows will slay me," Coeus says, his voice remaining flat.

"We will kill you," she warns, raising her voice into a fiery tempest that echoes across the land.

"Very well," Coeus counters, "let the Shades devour your friends." He nods towards the wolves, pulls the ropes tighter around my wrists, and bares his teeth.

The Shades huddle beyond the wolves, a deadly force waiting for orders. Their sooty clouds shift and flutter like tides of angry black smoke and volcanic ash.

"You know what it's like to succumb to the Shades, Kerry," he says. "Your body erased piece by piece, the most painful death imaginable, and after that, you become nothing."

The Shades cannot overpower me because I understand my skills better than Coeus does. When my shadow ability kicks into gear, I am immune to the Shades because I *am* one. And, if I'm lucky, I can fuse with inner light, which should repel the Shades.

Now, however, I have no spark in my soul, no energy with which to weaponize it. The Shades lurch in shifting black waves of soot behind the carnivorous metal wolves, rising like an oil stain on paper. Even as the blinding sun scours them, they rip at the heavens, feasting on dozens of harpies. The ground beasts don't retaliate for fear of being absorbed themselves, making them easy prey for the twenty-foot-high mechanical predators.

These turn the animals to carrion as Coeus smiles. Despite this, Artemis stands resolute to rescue us before The One True God of Darkness arises out of the landscape.

Darkness curls around a subtle rise, where rocks intermingle with desert brush and yellowed grasses. The murk strips the plants of life, spreading out miles at a time. Before he can poke his horned head out of the cave, the hill collapses, sending dust clouds a hundred feet high.

In this moment of confusion, Artemis releases the arrow, watching it fly straight at Coeus's heart.

He never sees it coming. The arrow plunges into his chest and he howls with agony, ripping the projectile from his flesh and flexing his bulging biceps. Unfazed, Artemis readies another arrow, but Coeus has made a disastrous mistake.

Ripping the arrow from the wound has invited particles of dust and bacteria in to infect it. He rages and pulses as he flings strands of rope straight at her, but the twine cannot wrap itself around her waist and she readies another arrow.

Realizing we're free, I coax Marissa to run along with me. A pair of muscular harpies hover over us, swooping low to lift us into the sky. Together we fly over the melee as the Shades and wolves tear Artemis's armies apart, while poison-tipped arrows from the warriors pick the avians off one by one. A moment before we disappear, the black horns protrude from the hill, gather more darkness, and send out a pyroclastic cloud that devours the entire ground army in a gloomy, dusty blur.

You shall never escape!

The surviving avians lurch higher into the heavens as the myriad stars coalesce around us. Energy pulses through my veins as we swoop past a red giant star, soar between its planets, and fade into the ether.

You are mine forever.

Gasping and panting, Marissa and I wrap our arms around each other. Whitecapped waves crash against a grassland dotted with clusters of basaltic rock pillars that rise at least thirty feet high. The sun shines through a cloudless sky, warming our skin as our rescuers, the harpies, flutter away toward the light.

Now resting on the central deck of a wooden ship, I feel the heaving of the waves going up and down. A large swell crashes against the port side of the ship, sending a plume of ocean spray over the parapets, creating a stream of saltwater across the deck.

Tears well up in Marissa's eyes as she realizes what has happened. Pain sears through my wrists as I examine the marks left from the ropes on her arms. Her blistered skin bubbles, as though flaming acid had soaked the bindings. She winces in pain as I hold her tightly. Wheezing and crying, she presses her hands against my back and drenches my shoulder with her tears. "It's impossible," she whimpers.

Our savior appears behind her, lowering herself to the deck of wooden planks that rise and fall with the waves. Artemis peers deep into my psyche before she speaks, as though sorrow fills her heart. Her entire army of birds, animals, and nearly all her harpies succumbed in the battle, yet she has delivered us safe from harm.

Unable to express my emotion to her, I simply stare, nodding my appreciation as her wings flutter to rest behind her. She has slung her bow over her shoulder in order to travel. I read both admiration and loss in her face as she steps closer to us.

"You ... you saved us," I manage to murmur.

Behind her, towering canvas sails, yellowed by the sun, billow with the maritime breeze, carrying us westward toward the rocky island shores. A few sailors are busy tying up heavy ropes, lashing them to the taffrails and laboring to steer the vessel out to deeper ocean waters.

"We could have used your troops when Erebus wiped out two thousand of Commander Archus's men," I bite out. "Why didn't you come then?"

She closes her eyes, wrestling with the weight of defeat. "You are too precious to give up. Your gifts are unmatched, a great asset to the Olympian army."

"This war started because of me," I admit, squeezing my eyes and gulping in pain. "And I can't even control my gift. It's like a curse takes over and I only know when it's coming by sensing the energy in myself and in the air around me."

"We were en route to your aid," she says, resting her palms at her sides and looking bitter. "The Titan army was well-prepared and headed us off. Most of us escaped, but we suffered heavy losses."

My heart rate increases. Beside me, Marissa's wheezing subsides. Her face is black and blue; she is gazing into the seas around us as though in search of fish or marine mammals.

"All this for me," I say. "I don't think I'm worth it. And I have a few things to do that don't really aid your war effort. How did you find me, anyway?"

"You gazed into Ursa Major and Boötes, didn't you?"

I nod but keep my expression closed. "How do you know?"

Her wings flap behind her, straightening her shoulders and causing her hair to whip in the wind. "A mutual friend warned me. I can feel her powers waning now, yet her spirit persists even so. She was a wonderful and loyal ally."

My eyebrows arch high on my forehead as she speaks. Though what she says embellishes the facts and neglects certain details, a sliver of it rings true. Artemis crosses her arms, spreads out her wings, and prepares for flight.

I can't bear to ask the only question I can think of, yet it seems to show in my face. Seconds before she launches herself off the ship's deck, her last words ring in my heart:

"My beloved Callisto."

I swallow as a baleful tear wells in my eye. "Vanessa."

28

Sailing with the Argonauts

The toiling crewmen are only a mild distraction; every few moments, Marissa breaks away from our quiet conversation to watch them work. A young man no older than twenty carries a steel-banded bucket from the galley, and begins mopping the deck. Nearby, two sailors discuss personal affairs related to love, or piracy. Although Marissa seems interested in what they're saying, they carry on as though they have not noticed her.

To keep out of their way, we isolate ourselves near a stack of wooden crates marked with Greek lettering I don't care to read. The nearest box, a three-cubic-foot container, lies at the end of a row, separating us from the hazards of traffic.

"I don't suppose you were ever going to tell me about Vanessa," she says after at least twenty minutes. Although her tone is inquisitive, I hear a slight hint of sadness in her voice.

Turning my gaze from the rocky coast, I look into her eyes for a second before uttering a statement I don't genuinely mean. "I don't really remember her. Although reason indicates she was a good friend."

"But it's not reason," she says, "is it? I haven't known you long, true, but I'd say reason doesn't rank among your chief priorities. You cared about her. I can see it in your body language."

"Like I said," I manage, looking back again at the shore. "It's been a long time and too many dimensions. And she's dead—nothing more."

"Your words are like ice," she chides, "crystallized by regret. If you don't want to tell me the whole story, I won't protest. But there's clearly something darker there."

A few hundred feet above the rocky coast, a group of seabirds is flying, gliding on the turbulence. Although the rocks and distance make understanding the geography a challenge, I spy eddying currents in the shallows between monstrous pillars of rock, coated at the base by layers of green algae and lichen. A mile away, a narrow inlet carves a canyon in the rocks, and a cape juts into the sea. The land above the rocks comprises grasslands and some rudimentary farmhouses, one or two dispersed in groves of olive trees. Each of the boulders jumbled at the water's edge carries evidence of its own story. A few seals lounge in the morning sun before splashing into the water to chase their next meals.

"I shouldn't remember her at all," I say, dropping my chin, "because she died in a different dimension. If I ever figure out why I remember even that, I'll let you know."

"I think you've been through far more than you're letting on. Can I help you remember it, or would that only make matters worse?"

I shake my head, casting my eyes to a reef three hundred yards away. Its black-tipped rocks seem to rise and fall with the waves, plunging deep into the sea where numerous marine creatures gather around their base.

Before I can reply, a sailor approaches us and rests his elbows on a crate. He has foreign markings and tattoos depicting mythical sea creatures. Curling on his chin, his dark scraggly beard is at least eight inches long. His wide-set azure eyes seem to have been bored into a wooden face, carved with age lines wriggling around them.

"Sorry, I'm interrupting," the man says. "What's your destination?"

I stammer: "Don't know, really. We just escaped a battle."

He gives a friendly nod. "Welcome to the *Argo*. Can I interest you in some sardines?"

Marissa gasps, faking a smile, but as I do likewise, she tears away her attention from him, biting her tongue and looking at me as though a painful truth lingers on her mind.

"Are you the captain?" I ask him.

"You're looking for Jason," he replies. "In his private chambers, second door on the left. Right now he'll be planning a fishing expedition, charting the known waters to determine where the fish are."

I look over at the galley. A wooden stairway in the hull planking forms a dark rectangle in the sunlight, with a dingy gray hue seeping down the panel walls. Tiny round escutcheons secure the railing. The stairway descends seven or eight steps, less than a full story, that lets seeded glass transom windows feed light into the rooms. Wide enough to accommodate loading and unloading cargo from the hold, the stairway teems with life. Carrying what I assume are food rations in a burlap sack, a sailor stoops out of the hold, while a younger man descends the stairs.

In the center of the galley, a thick mast rises forty feet, supporting an expansive white canvas sail, its center decorated with a red pictogram of a Trojan warrior. Tethered to a cross post by wood-rimmed grommet holes, thin, sturdy ropes guide the sail into the wind. A semicircular platform rings the base of the mast on the galley roof, with a long looking-glass mounted on an ornate, carved railing. The helmsman, a muscular man in his forties, glances at us as he steers the craft with two oars, keeping a consistent distance from the shore.

With each wave that the boat bobs over, a knot tightens in my stomach, making me nauseated. Marissa seems unperturbed, her expression even.

When the crew member struts away, I make way for the stairway myself. Marissa darts between two men carrying shoulder-loads of supplies while four more work to untangle a mesh fishing net. I steel my nerves, descend the steps, and rap on the door.

It opens immediately. Jason is older than I'd envisioned, perhaps in his mid-fifties, with a bushy gray beard and a dark expression. He wears a simple pair of black trousers tucked into knee-high black boots, and a long-sleeved shirt under a dark brown coat. His greasy hair is combed back into a knotted ponytail that tapers between his shoulders.

"What's your purpose aboard this vessel?" he asks as he ushers us into his quarters. An antique map lies open on a slanted reading table. The table's beaded ledge holds a few errant writing and measuring tools. The table has heavy wooden feet, branching off under the top like squared tree limbs. It is banded with a polished black walnut strip. The table juts into a hardwood wall, creating a paneled void filled in with upholstered seats. Jason motions us to a pair of stools opposite his bench, sits, and turns his attention back to his maps as he waits for us to answer.

"I don't think we have one," I mumble. I don't want to irritate him.

He eyes me between glances at his map while he clutches a stylus between his thumb and middle finger. "Everyone has a purpose."

"We just escaped the Titan army," Marissa explains, looking down at the burning red rashes on her forearms from the enchanted rope.

"You're involved in the war?" he asks, straight-faced and rigid.

If he knows about the war, he probably knows who I am. I decide to test this idea. "The Olympians say they need me, although I don't know whether I'll be much use. I'm trying to rescue my wife and son from another dimension. I don't want to be in your way."

"That would make you the one they've been talking about," he says without changing his expression. Gripping the stylus, he pulls a straight-edge from the ledge and traces a light line along the shore, crosschecking whatever numbers he has marked in the margins. "We don't get much news here, and even that is often second- or third-hand if we're lucky. The Titans must not consider us important."

I frown and straighten my back. The back wall of this tiny room has a fold-out cot, at the foot of which rests a cushioned box seat built into the dark, paneled wall. Overhead, a simple canvas curtain allows slivers of sunlight to shine into the room through the pair of transom windows.

"Who do you travel with?"

I hesitate to answer him. Is he trustworthy, or someone who will turn on us for monetary reward? Deciding to play it safe, I fold my hands into a V-shape at my waist. "Doesn't really matter much at this point."

"Then would you mind describing how the war is going? Judging from your looks, I'd say less than ideal."

"We're holding our own," I lie, shrugging. "More or less holding the line, though the Titans have assembled an epic army. They aim to supplant the Olympians to retake control of the universe. They have experienced tacticians, but we may have something even better."

He scoffs. "You? 'Kerry Gearhardt, Conveyor of Light and Shade' might have a nice ring to it, but you're out of your element. Are you sure you don't want to sail the seas with us?"

"I have other priorities."

"Such as?"

"I've got to find my wife before she's destroyed ... and my son, before the dungeon of death erases him." Between those sentences, I squeeze my eyes shut, flex my muscles, and try to calm my nerves. "You might question why I'm involved in the war ... the dimensions are unraveling because of the Titans, and a paradox. If I don't make it right, my wife will remain trapped forever in a dimension where she doesn't belong, and our son will never return to us."

"Well, when you say it like that," Marissa sneers. "Maybe Sarah's death wasn't so tragic after all. It's not like she ever mattered to begin with."

I can feel her scathing eyes digging into me without glancing her way. Instead of tuning in, I let my gaze fall upon a tapestry crest tacked to the wall just above the cot. A checkered pattern of blue and white like the Greek flag is centered, above which a massive bird of prey sinks its talons into it.

"You're still entangled, you know?" Marissa raises her voice, causing my nerves to simmer.

"What do you mean?" Jason asks, frowning and dropping the straightedge back into the ledge.

"You want to explain it?" Marissa jabs at me.

Rolling my eyes, I stammer: "It's a supernatural bond connecting a woman called Sarah and me across time and space, as though we're of the same stardust."

He lets out a sigh and regards Marissa between glances at his map. Near the shoreline on the map, I can just see bony fins and venomous eyes, next to a single word scrawled along the broken coastline—sirens. "Sounds like a conundrum for Apollo," he says.

"I've never met him," I say, keeping my voice emotionless. "Artemis delivered us from harm and brought us here to recuperate. The Titans are making large-scale plans for war, because they're losing badly. I don't suppose you can lend your ship to the effort."

"*Argo* is a merchant vessel," he says. "We have munitions suitable to fend off pirates, but not for war."

"Real heroic," I say accusingly. "You *were* a hero; now you're a coward, hoping to get rich. Good luck with the Sirens."

Marissa gulps. "Sirens? I thought they were a myth."

I scowl at her. "Aren't we all? Scholars, historians, poets, and playwrights will write about all of this centuries from now. That is, if the universe survives. They might even name a constellation after us."

"A bit of an optimistic view," Jason says, "considering you're already on the cusp of defeat. We'll serve the gods if called upon. Until then, we'll keep a low profile. Now, if you would, I must take the steering oar."

He stretches his back muscles, reaching his palms toward the low ceiling in his chambers. He scowls at us as he opens the door, then stalks along a narrow hallway and into the cavernous hull of the ship. The constant rocking and swaying have subsided, giving my stomach a rest. As Jason leads us up the stairs, he shouts to a man carrying a thick rope into the galley, glances up at the sail, and hurries toward the steering oar. The man at the oar steps aside, allowing Jason to adjust the course. The wind has slackened and the current is carrying the ship farther away from the shore, out of the Sirens' reach.

Jason barks orders to adjust the sails for the shifting wind, leans on the oar hard to starboard, and gazes into the still, shimmering waters.

Marissa and I move to the rail to keep out of the way of the hurrying men.

"I don't know why I lashed out that way," she whispers. "Don't think I meant it."

Shaking my head, I reply, "You say everything you mean. I can see why people shop in your store. If it isn't the pagan memorabilia, it's the passionate woman behind the counter."

"Uh ... thanks ... I guess?"

"Don't mention it."

Before I finish speaking I see a shadow moving below the surface of the water. Marissa and I stare into the depths where a long, spiny appendage chases the craft through the water; it slams into the hull of the ship, before either of us can utter a single word.

The men let out a volley of shouts as the ship vibrates.

"Hard to port!" The captain's aide cries. "Put on speed!"

"Harker, Daines, man your posts!" Jason yells.

Again the tail slams hard into the boat, splintering wood and causing the deck to lurch underfoot. The impact knocks Marissa over and to stop herself from tumbling into the sea, she grips a thick rope tied to the rail and reaches for my hand.

Regaining her balance, she steadies herself as another crash loosens nails and showers the water below with more splinters.

"Ready the harpoons!" Jason urges, as six men sprint toward the stairway and disappear into the shadows. "She taking on water, Brae?"

"Negative, Captain!" the hardened voice replies.

"We can outrun her," Jason decides, keeping both hands on the steering oar and staring straight ahead.

Men scurry from bow to stern and back, preparing for the beast's next attack. When the tail smashes into the hull, it sends me sprawling onto the deck to roll around in water from a toppled bucket. I reach out to Marissa, who is still grasping the rope, and see her eyes pleading with me to stop the monster. But I can do nothing.

However, the creature soon retreats, moving away through the water like a supercharged torpedo. But I know we're not safe yet.

As I stumble to my feet, Marissa, still clinging to the rope, points in horror at a dark vortex swirling half a mile away on the starboard side. The ocean spray whips into a frenzy as the whirlpool grows.

A man screams as he tosses a net overboard, trips over its ropes, and spins to face the abyss. Whipping my back to rise to my feet, I stagger toward Marissa, seeing her eyes go white when the churning saltwater assails us. But before the vortex can draw us in, the torrent suddenly dissipates.

Now a dozen horned heads rise out of the depths, coiling and whipping in the breeze like a nest of angry, two-hundred-foot-long serpents. They bare massive, serrated fangs and their black eyes gleam at us.

A single jolt of the mast causes the wind to whip us closer to port. To compensate, Jason leans on his oar while growling out curses. The monster sucks in vast amounts of seawater and sprays it out over a square mile.

Its jowls show sticky strings of venom and its heads stretch skyward. When the heads slap back onto the water, a hundred screeching voices rend the air, bruising my eardrums. I stagger backward, hoping for a burst of energy I can use to deter the beast. But it has locked onto the *Argo's* scent.

Wood splinters again as the vessel creaks, responding to the power of the steering oar. The entire deck vibrates when a massive head with a two-foot-long horn splashes up above the waters, spraying us with its stringy venom.

Some of it splashes onto my skin, and I recoil. The wounds from Coeus's twine bindings bubble an angry red. As the venom seeps into my blood, it produces dark hallucinations of Becky and Sarah fighting over me.

When Ian intervenes, Sarah slaps him, her hand mark glowing with red and orange flames. I try to separate them, but my skin freezes and the fighting becomes a nightmare. Ian lurks deep in a dark room; the only sound he emits is a helpless murmur that makes my heart ache. In his dark corner, he moans and cries as the gun in his right hand rises. He moves it round to the back of his own head, gazes at me through sodden eyes, and pulls the trigger.

BOOM!

The ship shudders as the monstrous serpent head crashes into the deck, breaking off sections of the hull and railing into the frothing sea. Overhead, the dozens of smaller heads move in a coordinated dance as they eye each of us in turn. I dive out of the way as the neck whips through the air to coil around the mast. The craft lists hard to starboard. Jason shouts at the top of his lungs as the foot-long horn swipes past his face.

The beast now sharpens its attack. The serpentine neck twists around the mast like a forty-foot-tall rod of Asclepius as its spiny back saws it in half.

Overhead, the sails teeter as the hulking mast gives way, the top half, suspended from the cross member with ropes, flapping in the wind as the lower half points, broken, toward the sky.

Rage finally fills my veins. The many-headed monster's serpent heads gather in clouds of black and poisonous rain from the sky. As I jump to Marissa's defense, I dodge a massive splash that crashes over the deck near her feet. To prevent her going overboard, I pull her sideways, rolling us toward the center of the deck, in front of the stern where Jason fearlessly maneuvers the vessel like the experienced navigator he is. He looks over at us as we roll away, Marissa hitting her knee into my crotch and smacking her face against my forehead. I can feel her nose twisting as she rolls off of me, completely soaked by the ocean spray. She gets to her feet and sprints off toward the galley, leaving me to deal with the monster alone.

The next head comes down to crush part of the taffrail even as its hulking form creates a towering wave that again tilts the whole craft toward the starboard side. As the wave rushes out, the head submerges to scrape its serrated horns across the keel.

On the horizon behind the monster's waving heads, a twenty-foot-tall woman wearing a long black dress hovers above the waves. She is carrying a gem-encrusted staff and is howling with rage, her voice rebounding against the rocks, to which we are drawing ever nearer.

The woman directs her monster's heads to assault the ship in unison, but Jason spins the bow back toward the open waters of the channel, and I can hear voices singing from the rocks. The enchanting sound is a counterpoint to the monster assailing us.

Then Becky is suddenly standing on a jutting rock, dressed in her blue and white chevron dress, her hair in a silky, plaited ponytail. Her clean face reflects the cool blue light as she dances and sings to entice me. *"Kerry,"* she says, her voice echoing in the mist, *"You have found me at last. Come, let's retreat to the bedroom for a blissful evening..."*

"Kerry?"

I spin round to face Marissa. She is holding a wet rope, and she's dripping with saltwater as she limps to my aid.

I look longingly back at the rocks, but Becky has vanished. My nerves prickle as Marissa hands me the length of rope, looks over at the ruined mast, and makes a decision we both may regret. She fastens the rope to the taffrail and wraps her hands around my waist, then she hurls herself overboard, carrying me into the churning sea. Immersed in the chilly waters, I feel panic tear through me as I struggle for breath. Marissa gasps as she pokes her head above the water, gripping me tighter with each passing second. Abandoning the crew of the *Argo* feels like a betrayal, but it may just help them to escape the many-headed monster—because it's me she wants.

I can hear her hissing my name and at the same time I can hear Sarah pleading with me. We watch the broken ship trailing away into the storm as we cling to a detached piece of the hull, ready for the monster to tear us apart.

You know how to find me.

29

Between Scylla and Charybdis

Debris from the *Argo* floats on the salty waves and separates into a multitude of wooden shards that are impossible to avoid. Although the section of hull we're clinging to is supporting our weight, it's too flat, and in this gale the waves are crashing over it. Freedom will be a freezing struggle for us.

Rage compounds my agony. The saltwater stings the wounds from Coeus's twine, and my throat is raspy and sore. I give my emotions free rein. "Why the hell did you do it? You've sentenced us to death!"

Marissa is lying on the craft and using her palms to paddle toward a larger piece of debris made of railing and shiplap that has gathered algae. "The ship is going down," she snaps. "Didn't you see it?"

"KEEERRR!"

My blood turns to ice as I recognize her voice. "Becky!" Flopping like a fish toward the edge of our makeshift raft, I stick my boots in the water; despite the strong current, I'll take my odds of swimming to her.

"SHUT UP!" Marissa shouts at Becky, continuing to paddle away from the rocks.

"I'm going to save her!" I cry, desperately paddling in the opposite direction. But her strength matches mine, keeping us in place as the raging monster squeals and roars at the escaping ship.

"You're going to die!" she yells at me. She pauses, allows her face to slacken and assumes a mournful expression. "That's not Becky. It's something pretending to be Beau."

I gape at her, still trying to counteract her rowing. "Beau?"

She is trying to navigate our raft out of the path of a large wave, but the swell slaps over our soaked bodies. She is gulping as she tries to right herself. The saltwater has washed away all that was left of her makeup and she looks downright pale.

"Long story," she yells.

The monster is still lashing at the surface over a mile away, but she looks like she has changed the focus of her many heads; now she's shrieking toward the bluffs. One head turns toward us, enraged. Her necks are whipping around in the gale. Marissa is still trying to row us closer to the monster, and I have to challenge her wisdom. I'm hurrying to fashion an oar from a fragment of debris to help us move faster towards the shore. But the current is too strong.

"Tell me later!" I howl.

"You see that chunk of wood?" She is dog-paddling us towards a clump of floating debris. "Grab it!"

"KERR..." Becky's voice is singing what sounds to me a charming melody. The monster is climbing onto the rocky cliff using its fangs as pickaxes. "Come make—" sings Becky.

"Kerry!" Marissa shouts. "She's trying to kill you. That's what these Sirens do. Now cooperate or we die!"

"I'd die for her eight days a week," I gargle. I'm reaching for the bobbing plank, but it slips out of my hands. Marissa slows the raft to try to help, by reversing her paddle, which means a lot of exertion against the current.

But as I grab the splintered wood with both hands, the splinters gouge bloody scratches across my skin and I worry that if sharks call this channel home, they'll be here to feast on us in a matter of minutes. Then I reason that sharks may be steering clear of the enormous monster for fear of becoming a side dish.

"PULL!" Marissa screams.

Wincing from the pain in my hands and wrists, I wedge the fragment of wood away from the clump, dragging it across the frothing surface for Marissa to grasp. Then I see a second fragment and convince her to row towards it. "Just a few more feet..."

SPLASH!

The sound reverberates across the surface of the sea. As the monster claws away at the craggy rocks, I gauge the direction the explosive noise is coming from across the channel. The *Argo* is sailing into disaster.

An eddying current is now dragging us away from the rocky shore at a rate of a few feet per minute. The singing from the jumbled rocks grows distant as we helplessly follow the ill-fated ship. Muted cries from the deck sound between massive waves that are moving fast enough to smash us back against the shore where Becky's imitator awaits.

"Got any plans?" I yell.

But Marissa had seen it coming before I did. One of the monster's heads is raised over a hundred feet high as it clings to the rocks, craning to see the source of the explosive noise. The ship's sailors are trying to avoid the other monster. As the huge wave pushes us fifty feet closer to the shore, my muscles tense as I wait for the backwash to carry us back out to sea.

The channel here is only three or four miles wide, which should afford the ship a passage that avoids both beasts, but the current has taken them too near the opposite shore.

I watch the doomed ship while using all my strength now to help Marissa row toward the center of the strait, though we're weakening, exhausted and hungry. Rather than pressing on, I watch the ship navigate the crashing waves.

Then we see the second monster: It lurches out of the waves, its massive cylindrical body like that of a blue whale, but easily four times the size. Its mass would surely create a tsunami if it fell into the water, but it still swims. Fifty-foot-long fins propel it through the swells, and when it lunges higher, it shows hundreds of spiny tentacles surrounding its circular maw and double rows of serrated teeth. Its two saucer eyes are each twice as big as a beachball.

As it porpoises in the waves the monster's backside comes into view, a network of fish scales encrusted with spiny barnacles and jagged coral formations. The dark eyes zero in on its prey as it rises above the waves and opens its fanged mouth wide enough to swallow the entire ship.

Splashing back into the water, the fangs rip through the *Argo*'s hull, slicing the vessel in two. Tendrils splash out of the water to encircle one half of the sinking ship, carrying it a hundred feet high before dropping it into its maw. When the hull falls into the jagged teeth, it shatters. The other half of the ship submerges beneath the waves as the monster spits out an anchor, sending it flying a quarter of a mile towards the opposite shore, where the other monster leers at its lost prize.

With their screams extinguished, the remaining *Argo* crew try to swim away from the creature. Pinched in two of its tentacles, the ship's bow now drops all the way into the monster's mouth. Its movements churn up water that washes us back toward the rocks where 'Becky' waits.

As the ship's debris floats away atop twenty-foot waves, the massive body sinks back underwater, the monster inhaling a mouthful of seawater as a chaser for its wooden meal. We watch in horror as the desperate crew flow in with the gulp and the beast swallows them whole. At least fifty crew members have been eaten like a snack, and the debris stretches over a mile away from the site where the *Argo* met its doom.

I feel a terrible regret deep in my abdomen as Marissa, ever focused, is steering us away. I'm relieved that instead of chasing us down, the monster gradually slips back under the water even while the dozen-headed snake creature prowls the opposite shore.

Now that the turbulence from the *Argo* is spent and the gale has subsided, we're free to paddle our makeshift raft toward the center of the channel and away from both of the massive creatures. Marissa's breath sounds raw as she powers us through the waves, urging me to help her. We separate ourselves from the beasts and move out into open waters, where the channel's mouth is at least twenty miles wide.

After at least thirty minutes of hard paddling, I spot a village perched atop the coast a mile away, sheltered in a rocky cove. Its dense thicket of trees looks inviting, at least as a suitable refugee camp. We row to the rocky shore, and clamber off our craft and up over the rocks, hoping for shelter.

About halfway up the cliff, we gaze back at the place where the monster destroyed the ship. Only a few fragments remain upon the waves. From inside the cove, we cannot see the many-headed monster on the rocks, nor can she see us.

We climb in silence, reaching a grassy ledge overlooking the cove, from which I reach down to help Marissa to get up after me. A shepherd is tending his flock a quarter mile away in a field in front of a whitewashed plank fence and a wood-sided barn, and he ignores us.

The sheep are bleating while returning to their field.

Marissa is exhausted and dehydrated. She combs her hands through her salty hair, frowning and hesitating as though I'm about to say something to divert her attention from her injuries.

Ripped fabric is stuck to her skin, absorbing blood from an injury to her torso, and she winces whenever she moves. She is dabbing at a two-inch-long gash on her left cheekbone, careful not to apply too much pressure. She ignores my injuries, which are only the now-healing wounds from Coeus's twine, a dozen tender bruises, and a wounded ego.

"How bad is it?" I ask.

"You might thank me for saving your life," she snaps.

"We did it together. What the hell were those things?"

She chatters her teeth and her lips quiver. "I don't even want to know. Next time I try to save your life and you protest like that, I'm letting you die."

"Why are you so angry?" I ask.

She scowls at me, and continues as though I hadn't spoken. "It wasn't supposed to be this way. Had I known joining you would mean we'd both lose a friend while fighting for our lives over and over again, I would have hesitated. I guess that makes me the fool."

"Now we're on solid ground, let me first say I'm sorry. I tried to warn you, but I don't even remember most of what's happened to me. It's like my memory of it has been washed away by the effects of time travel, or worse. But, no matter what, I'm going back for Becky. You understand?"

"That wasn't *her*, Kerry. Don't *you* understand? They were Sirens, imitating her to lure you to your death, just like they did in the ancient tales."

I wince and let silence settle in as she struggles to ease the cloth from her stomach. After ten full minutes, I gather the courage to ask her: "Who's Beau?"

"I don't think it's life-threatening," she says, ignoring the question. "Maybe a potential nasty infection if we can't find medical help soon, but I'm charging on anyway. After that, I never want to see you again."

I nod, feeling lame, and for another ten minutes I watch her tend to her wounds, along with the shepherd who is watching us from behind his fence. The grassland stretches into rolling hills along the shore, studded by pockets of shaded woodland. In this quiet, isolated little place the inhabitants probably don't worry about the bigger cities; these must feel like they're on another plane of reality. Although rustic may not be my style, I could imagine living here if I had to.

Marissa's voice is quiet and somber and her lip quivers. Her tone is slow and tactile, as though driven by a distant motor. "Beau was my boyfriend two years back. I was going to marry him. Little ceremony in a big city, with only a few friends and family there to witness it. I wanted to wear a frilly black or purple dress, because, you know the whole white before Labor Day except at your wedding is so cliché and overused."

"Maybe it's just in keeping with a holy tradition," I say, to which she responds by rolling her eyes.

"Anyway, he was cool, had more tattoos than unmarked skin, muscular, always wore tight black T-shirts and even tighter jeans. He had a mole above his lip that I liked to kiss sometimes. But he had a darker side."

"Right," I say, trying to smile as though humor were at all appropriate.

"I rarely saw him without a drink. We had wine sometimes, a beer or two every night, and hard liquor when we went out. I always walked him home, about six blocks away from my shop, when he was too snookered to talk. It was fun, and I never told him to slow down. But when his family put him up for treatment, all hell broke loose. He's never coming back because of me. I can't forgive myself."

"It's not your fault." Even my empathy sounds unnatural, but I say it anyway, because she's on the brink of tears again.

"It always was. He hit me one night, right here. Of course, I thought it was the whiskey talking, so I almost put it behind me. But then he screamed at me, ranting like a maniac, so I told him to walk himself home and sleep on it.

"He drove instead. Seventy miles an hour on I-95, right under a tanker truck. I often wonder what would have happened if I'd urged him to get help sooner, or at least walked him home one more time to brave whatever punches he threw."

"I guess that you're stronger now," I reply, lowering my voice. "We're going to survive this because of you. I don't know your background or any of your personal relationships, but you're a strong woman and you're far braver than I am. And despite your look-how-occult-I-am appearance, you're a good person."

She nods dismissively and curls her lip as she dabs at her wound. "You want to know why I explored paganism in the first place?"

I hesitate, biting my lip and thinking of the two enormous monsters destroying the *Argo*.

"Religion. I see religious people defying their own faith by engaging in the same evil they claim envelops the rest of the world. And then they go to church on Sunday, acting like grace alone can save them ... like, who is Grace, anyway, and why don't they depend on Jesus instead? They're no better than anyone else. I saw the truth. One god of gods, so loving and gentle that he smites his own children, condemning them for all eternity. Maybe I should be relieved there are so many gods. But I'm not, because this doesn't even feel real to me."

Her words sink into me like poison. Becky always depended on religion to get her out of the worst predicaments. Marissa has chosen the opposite path. Yet, despite their opposing views, they are share similar traits. I know Marissa will stick with me until the end, because I've already seen Becky commit to doing the same.

30

The Army of Erebus

I've always boasted a superior sense of direction—part of my ability to discern where I am in time and space—but when you get lost in interdimensional time, these abilities become distorted and corrupted. Time jumps have messed up my bearings. I'm guessing it's morning, but the angle of the sun makes me think it might be afternoon. Worse still, I can't tell where north is. I realize we are lost yet again. I scowl and help Marissa cope with her injuries while she tries to ignore me.

This village nestles in a crease in the hills, settling into a meandering valley whose stream has disappeared, either evaporated or diverted. Perhaps twenty people call this place home, and one of them, the shepherd, is not welcoming toward us. I catch him glancing at us once or twice as we sit near the cliffs, planning our next move. Either he speaks no English, or he merely refuses to let two mysterious travelers interrupt his ruminations.

Marissa has her left hand placed on a rounded stone halfway stuck into the earth, its domed surface coated in green and yellow lichen. Leaning back, she spreads her fingers, perhaps wondering if anyone will come to retrieve us. By now the gods will have learned about *Argo*'s destruction and may have assumed we've survived, but every moment we wait, our danger increases.

"How are you feeling?" I ask, rubbing my neck.

Either she doesn't want to talk about it or she feels that we've discussed everything we needed to. She mumbles and crosses her arms. "I've been better."

"They're going to find us. I know it, somehow."

She sighs. "This is a war we can't win. We've seen what the Titans have up their sleeves. Where are *your* powers, Kerry, Titan of Light and Shade?"

When people around me offer irrefutable points to demolish my defenses, I often shrink into silence rather than fighting back. I can't defend myself, and Marissa knows it. "Uh..."

"That's what I thought. You can't control whatever gifts you have, and therefore you can't fight. Poor position from which to debate, much less go into battle."

Glowering at her, I wish I could shred this argument, but again I have nothing.

"You supposedly have abilities, too," I say. "But so far they're also not always effective."

She shakes her head and stretches. "You might call my talent tactical. It isn't based on energy like yours, and it's already proven favorable. I sense what that Titan we ran into says may be inaccurate. In their spirits, the dead fear that they're on the wrong side, that if they lose, they'll be sent to Tartarus forever. It just isn't enough for them to switch teams."

"*Teams?*" I say, biting my lip. "It's easier if you think the fight is between good and evil, light and dark, but reality isn't like that. In the end, either there are no sides ... or there's only one. We depend on the Olympians because we must, but don't assume they're humanity's only hope. That may come down to us, like it or not."

"What are you saying? That good and evil don't exist?"

I shake my head. "They're just not as distinct as everyone says. Listen to the way people talk. There's always this nefarious *they.* Because someone else is always responsible for what's going wrong. It's easier than taking the blame, or admitting that you've made mistakes along the way. Good and evil *do* exist, but sometimes good people do horrible things, and evil people sometimes act honorably."

"You don't believe the Olympians have the right ideas?"

"Do you?"

"I don't think any gods truly do." She closes her eyes as though pausing to feel the wind sifting through her drenched and matted hair, which is sticking to her neck, shoulders, and face. "Maybe if all religions get together and propose an ultimate god that takes in all aspects of human nature, we'd at least have a start. Until then, no matter what happens in *this* war, there will always be another one."

Although I understand what she's saying, I'm not entirely convinced. War isn't always based on religion, or even territorial desires. A pastor I once heard tried to explain warfare in simpler terms by saying that no one ever wins. If war always results in loss, then why does it remain so popular? Whoever coined the phrase 'people are naturally good' might have more accurately stated that people ignore each other's needs and that often leads to violence. But then again, I'm no preacher, and my ideas may not suit a religious discussion.

"Tell me more about the real enemy, then," she says, watching a car putter along a narrow, dirt road through the village, approach a dead end, and wait. Seeing a modern car after riding such an old-fashioned sailing vessel offers a jarring contrast, proving that we've been in a modern dimension the whole time.

"It would seem the Titans have teamed up with Erebus, the personification of darkness. He's the only one who can command such a vast army."

"Great..." she says, stretching out the word. "I'm getting the classic 'bad feeling about this' vibe."

"I don't really know the logistics of how it works, but most of his slaves made a choice. And that's the real power he has over them. His numbers may be in the tens of thousands, living and dead, and not just humans: giants, cyclopes, gorgons, sphinxes, chimeras, pretty much every monster you've ever dreamed of. Not to mention the Shades—the most powerful allies he possesses. Shades are the detached spirits of the dead. To most people, they're invisible or they just resemble smudges. Those spirits you always see ghost hunting TV shows faking may be the closest thing pop culture has to them. They've given themselves so fully to The One that they can absorb you. In essence, they rip your spirit away from your body as they absorb every atom and molecule. You therefore cease to exist, forever. Not even as a memory."

"Sounds lovely."

The idling car stays far longer than it should. The driver is either lost or waiting for a particular person to show up. He watches and waits beyond dark-tinted side windows, set far enough back into the seat to hide his features in shadow. The car is an older model Mercedes. It bears the trademark hood ornament, chrome-tipped double exhaust, and enough power to make a Mustang Cobra owner blush. It's a silver, boxy behemoth on the outside, plush and comfortable on the inside.

I've seen enough corny spy movies to imagine the driver might carry a black briefcase stuffed with bundles of crisp hundred-dollar bills. He might even be wearing sunglasses and a black suit.

"I don't suppose you can communicate with the Shades," I say, lowering my voice.

"It might be more complicated than normal but it should be doable."

The driver's side door pops open and we are near enough to see he is an older gentleman with salt-and-pepper hair and a chiseled face, wearing a T-shirt, cargo shorts, and white tube socks with red stripes around the rim. He's thin and agile, yet age has hunched his back and caused his skin to sag around the knees. When he gets out, he stares at me and asks, "You're Kerry?" in a gravelly, high-pitched voice. "I expected something more impressive."

At the mention of my name, Marissa gets to her feet. I stand too, waiting for him to explain how he knows me and what he's doing here.

But he doesn't. He simply motions us to his car, expecting us to get in. I think that a mass murderer would never drive a vehicle this refined, and this stranger is too old to overpower me, but I am a little cautious in following him. I limp through the ankle-high grass toward him and grimace as the pain digs into my calves.

"I was told you'd be here."

"Who are you?" I ask.

An annoyed look of surprise covers his face as he holds open the passenger side door for Marissa. "You don't recognize me? Damn shame."

What the hell? A sudden urge to hit him passes over me as I swing open the back door and climb into a tan leather seat with enough leg room for Wilt Chamberlain. I don't bother with the seatbelt.

"Still got the sass all these years later," he mocks me. "What do you say we grab a bite? Talk about life, love, philosophy, physics, you name it."

"You're not Secretary Harley," I say, remembering his face and as-suming he would look much older now.

The stranger shakes his head, slams the door behind him, and starts the motor. "Of course I'm not. But I knew him, in another life."

"Right," I say, rolling my eyes. "Of course you did. I assume you've got a nice bridge to sell me. Probably related to a Nigerian prince or two."

"Same guy, same attitude. I expect you to punch me later."

I scowl at him. "Just tell me who you are, how you knew I'd be here, and I'll worry about breaking your nose later."

"I talked with a Fire Guy a few hours ago. Told me to pick you up here because he heard about a shipwreck. A Titan saw you coming here, and as for who I am ... well, let's just say you can call me Cy."

I groan and punch the back of his headrest. "Cy's dead."

"What makes you think that?"

Oh my God.

I don't know—another piece of a puzzle. I have a dim memory of him protesting as I walk with a tongueless, eyeless woman into a dungeon. But that was maybe a dream rather than a recollection, or else I wouldn't have remembered him dying. A common cultural myth that has outlived its namesake states that shared false memories become a staple of common knowledge, because human memory is subject to cognitive bias. Have I become a victim of the phenomenon?

"Cy's dead, but he's not," the stranger explains. "The Swan does not fall. He flies."

"You?" I can't believe my ears. But if he *is* Cy, I know one way to test him. "What was the theme of that hotel restaurant we ate at?"

"A silly, anachronistic representation of ancient Memphis," he says, rubbing his chin. "Doesn't matter how accurate it is, as long as it invites people in to spend their money, thinking they'll come out looking like Egyptians."

"It really is you," I gulp, and feel sadness welling up inside. "I swear I saw you die. You were just ... how did you get here?"

Convinced that he's talked me into believing him, Cy only gives a curt nod and frowns at me in the rear-view mirror. After he negotiates a three-point turnaround, he drives slowly along the dusty road and explains.

"After I'd spent some time in the underworld, Hades told me Zeus wanted to talk to me. At least that's the way Zeus explained it. See, the underworld rearranges your memories. He said the Titans had escaped, that you'd had something to do with it, but that my guardianship of you was worthy of another shot. So he put my spirit in this dapper body until the end of the war—a first step to reincarnation. If I help you to help them win the war, I get to stay and ruin more people's holidays. The first time I met Fire Guy, by the way; a real piece of work. That's the story and I'm sticking to it."

"I'm lost," Marissa says.

Cy merely raises his eyebrows at her, resting his hands on the top of the steering wheel as he leaves the village behind. When he speeds up, dust rises behind the car. "This can't be her," he says.

For once, I know who he's talking about. "No, she's helping me find her."

"I'd assumed you already did."

My chest feels tight and a sour regret eats away at my ribcage with every flourish of memory. "I kind of did, but then I left her in the wrong dimension. She's lost and can't find a way home because of me. Because I've created the mother of all paradoxes."

He gapes at me as I relate the story. "You know, Zeus is going to kill you. Great guy, I'm sure you'll get along."

"Is that where you're taking us?" I ask.

"First, introductions are in order," he says, glancing back and forth between us and the curving road as it meanders through the valley. "I'll start. I'm the former king of Liguria, in Italy, transformed into a swan after my best friend fell into the river, and now I'm back to help Larry win the war that started because of him. Larry calls me Cy. And you are?"

Marissa rests her hands in her lap, and gazes out at the grasslands and isolated homes rolling by. The landscape is interspersed with isolated rustic homes and a few trees. "I'm a dealer in occult artifacts and paraphernalia, part time Spiritualist. Marissa."

"Occult, as in hexes, spells, and lost magic?"

"Much of it based on pagan symbology," she adds. "But they were right about many things. Modern religion adapts plenty of pagan traditions, despite persecuting them and labelling them as evil."

Her words suddenly make sense. My entire life, I've learned how Christians are persecuted, never considering the other side of the coin.

In the silence I decide I must ask Cy an important question. No matter how I phrase it in my head, it always sounds self-absorbed and shallow, and not a little ignorant. Instead of asking, I've been passing the time looking at the scenery. After twenty minutes of bumping along, Cy turns onto a paved road that follows the crest of a ridgeline. Golden grass and sunshine stretch as far as I can see on my right, while on my left, the land ascends to rolling green hills along the coast. A dingy gray fog obscures the sea, but that's ok; if I ever see that channel again, it will be too soon.

Now, I must trust Cy once again, because without him, Marissa and I will be nothing more than refugees watching the world descend into utter chaos before destruction. Without him, I never could have rescued Becky.

"Got something on your mind, son?" Cy asks.

He looks nothing like I remember him, but now that he's reintroduced himself, his personality has an uncanny resemblance to the aggravating man I once knew. "You said Zeus reincarnated you. Tell me how that works."

"I'm afraid it's not the time for that. We're due for a meeting."

"I think you know what I'm talking about," I say, "and we've got time."

But he changes the subject, electing to talk about the weather and the climate in this region. If I'm following him correctly, we must now be somewhere in modern day Greece, along the Adriatic coast. He is chatting lightly, trying to cheer up Marissa. Thirty minutes later, we're rolling to a stop on a forgotten farm, where a single, abandoned barn with a partially collapsed roof sits in the shade of a large elm.

The yard has rusted scraps of metal, everything from obsolete farming implements to decaying truck axles. Ringed with an old fence composed of rotten supports and runners, grayed from years in the sun, the farm looks like a tight twenty acres, a flat expanse featuring a forgotten chicken coop of rusting aviary wire.

Inside the gray-tinged barn, I can almost see the decay rising through the fallen roof through a ten-foot hole. Cy parks the car, checks his watch, and leads us through a side door into the barn through a human door beside the folding overhead door operated by a hand crank. An X pattern of aging two-by-fours bolsters the doors, carrying flecks of ancient red paint.

Gloomy shadows fill the interior, a two-story edifice of timbers succumbing to insects and dry rot. Insects always attract spiders. Thick cobwebs hang low from the dusty rafters over the mezzanine and down the walls like ancient silk curtains.

Cy leads us to a far corner hemmed in by a waist-high picket fence possibly used to corral goats or sheep. The dirt floor has tufts of thick straw that smell sweet. Near the edge of the enclosure, sharing an exterior wall, is an oblong food and water trough with pieces of straw overhanging its edges. Newer looking boards cover the three-foot-deep manger.

"After you," says Cy, peering into the pit.

The trough's darkness seems to bubble, as though it contains an interdimensional disturbance. I grip Marissa's hand, fall into space, and come out into a field of carnage where fires rage and darkness reigns.

Pain pours into me like molten lead. Horns blare, warriors scream, and heroes are born.

Scores of arrows vault through the skies and rain down on the company of soldiers. A man nearby has the appearance of a commander, and nods at me as Cy materializes. The army forms a front of spears while arrows and other projectiles volley between them. Multitudes of reanimated undead soldiers with no eyes battle beside a hundred giants and cyclopes, carrying various launching mechanisms from simple catapults to complex trebuchets, preparing for the onslaught of the Olympian army.

As I ready myself for combat, Marissa takes my side, steeling her nerves as Cy stalks away. Steady roars echo in the fray behind both fronts, and then the battle begins in earnest.

BOOM! BOOM!

A chorus of explosions rock the ground as the giants launch heavy stones through the sky to pummel whole groups at a time and screams erupt everywhere. The commander approaches, gives a cordial nod, and offers me an elegant sword. He smiles. "You'll find it complements your style."

I swing it in my hands, letting thoughts of Becky from the forgotten realms of my brain begin to stir. When I open my eyes, the sword is glowing, its shining blade vibrating as though charged by a million volts. At last, I'm ready.

Cutting through the first enemy is easy. His bony abdomen splits when the blade hits it, spilling dust and sticky, maggot-infested innards at my feet.

I swing the blade again, destroying an emaciated man a foot taller than me. His sagging skin offers little resistance. Memories of Becky course through me as the battle rages and explosions erupt all around. For now, we are winning.

31

Campe Reborn

The blade glows brighter with every swing, every detached limb imbuing it with greater spirit as though the mere gift of the sword has reawakened the energy held deep within me. When a zombie with a head of decaying hair concealing his brows charges me, I slice the blade right through his abdomen, toppling him like a load of bricks. Undeterred, he grabs at my ankles to pull his torso through the dust, ripping his shirt on a knobby trunk of underbrush.

Marissa is wide-eyed and silent, even as enemies surround her. I can feel her doing something, especially when she focuses on a group of tall undead men and women who wield blades and shotguns. With a ripple in the air current, she's reaching out for them in spirit, hoping to convince them to change sides, even if temporarily.

I don't have time to study what she's doing. Before I can evade them, the undead split into two smaller groups and four or five come my way. The leader is a woman carrying a rifle strapped to her back. When she 'sees' me swiping my sword toward her, she draws the gun, bolt-loads a slug into the chamber, and aims it at my head. "Say goodbye to the legend," she shrieks. Meanwhile Marissa is focusing on the five of the enemy who are surrounding her.

The only woman in her group has a half-bald head that reflects the orange glow from a nearby fire started by a recent explosion. The other half of her hair hangs in loose clumps, and when I see why it looks so loose, my stomach leaps. Though time has long since cauterized the wound, an oblong chunk of her scalp dangles over her ear, revealing a decaying soup of muscle and skull. She chews on something, then grimaces at Marissa, and yields.

The woman attacking me is pressing the barrel of the rifle to my forehead, squeezing the trigger while baring a row of razor-sharp, bloodstained teeth. She loses focus when the chamber clicks, allowing my blade to smash into her shoulder. She looks taken aback, flexing her biceps, where a tattoo of a handsome man shows in the soft light.

"The legend strikes back," I say.

She howls, points the gun at my face again, and prepares to fire. But I see it coming long before she can pull the trigger. On my backswing, I allow my grip on the sword to slacken. The wild swing causes the tip to puncture a lone soldier's chest behind me, and when I pull it out, the undead woman locks the bullet into place. But my dark energy is at work, and she lowers the rifle, turning it on herself.

Watching her body cascade into the dirt, I yank my sword loose from the attacker's ribcage. I turn to see how Marissa is doing. A slight flick of her wrist tells me she's doing something helpful.

A man in front of her turns his head toward his comrade, and instead of digging his claws into Marissa's flesh, he attacks his closest companion, flaying his neck with his fingernails. No blood seeps from the cut—only a gelatinous ooze of mud and earthworms.

Sizing up his 'kill,' he bares his teeth and screams, biting down on his victim's neck, gorging himself on the worms while sawing through the rotting flesh with his canines.

Marissa now turns her attention to a group of women launching flaming arrows every-which direction in this target-rich environment, where the projectiles are likely to hit someone. Knowing that her skills can't match mine, she must take a different approach to fighting, using her own talents to make up the slack.

Within a few moments, she has convinced another zombie to turn. He commits suicide by lying face-up while legions of his own men trample him. Marissa focuses on another while a poison-tipped arrow comes out of nowhere, aimed straight at her head.

I deflect it, but I'm so far away that my sword won't do the trick and I briefly black out, before seeing the arrow thud into the earth, ripped in half.

"Thanks for that," Marissa says.

"What do you think you're doing?" I shout. Before I see it coming, something huge lumbers toward me.

"What does it look like I'm doing? And watch your six, Kerry!"

I spin my body around, meeting the six-foot-tall shin bone of a giant cyclops. The undead all stagger away as it approaches. He roars as he reaches down to pick me up, squeezing my shoulders in his vise-like grip. I struggle to break free, but it's no use.

My sword clanks to the ground beneath my feet as I am raised seven stories, where the monster's huge eye glowers at me. He opens his mouth wide enough to bite my head off, but the moment I feel myself entering his jaw, my body turns to light.

He groans, making a chattering sound like a hungry stomach growling at the thought of food. He won't get his fill because what he doesn't see is the air around my head growing black. He roars in pain, flicking me away in rage, clutching at his now-toothless mouth. The fall from seventy feet is tempered by my dark energy outburst taking weight from my mass, and I land on my knees while the cyclops kicks at me, luckily missing as it continues to roar.

An explosion rips through a company of our men even as Marissa attempts to negotiate with wave after wave of attackers. Although a few of her spirituality-bursts hit where she intends, most fail and she's overwhelmed again, needing my help. But I'm still battling the cyclops even as another thunders into my field of vision behind him. Together they flank me. I dash for my sword, feeling my energy pass into the hilt as I prepare to slash at the monsters' knees.

The energy crackles in the blade, emitting white light, and the sword cuts through the first monster's legs with ease. Trying to clutch at his wound, the creature trips on his own brother, toppling both onto a company of undead marching toward Marissa.

The monsters lock onto one another, ignoring me for just long enough. The one I hit with the sword bites at the other's neck and ears as they wrestle in the mud and grass, flattening two more of the enemy.

Readying my sword for another strike, I reach high over my head with the tip pointed downward like the sword of Damocles in the banquet hall. Marissa is trying to influence a seven-foot-tall man ready to attack her, but he lurches when I sink the sword into his back, pull it out, and slide at the other cyclops in one motion.

Screams erupt from behind the Olympian lines as mortal warriors flee from a hulking creature gathering mass within their ranks. The monster grows out of the ground like a soupy green mush, assembling itself into the figure of a woman eight feet tall. She wears a knee-length dress, torn and resewn around the midriff, and her form twists against invisible ropes as it rises.

Unable to devise a strategy, the soldiers nearest her gather ranks and attack her waist with spears. She wears a knee-length skirt, torn and resewn around the midriff, where a dirty and bloody belly button emerges. She raises a pair of swords and parries her opponents easily, her height proving to be an asset as the men fail to make a mark.

Another group of soldiers join in against her, but she sees them coming and her blades cut through men left and right as she tears through the troops. They could use my help, but before I can get over there, I see a pair of winged goddesses land before them, flaring their wings. The green woman instead attacks the goddesses, who deflect her blades and disarm her.

Retreating from the goddesses who are protecting the soldiers, she stretches up and flicks a glance at me as she easily disarms a rifleman aiming at her head, using the gun to blast holes in the lines. Armor flies and men fall still as she kicks at them, battering them with her feet and fists.

I'm still in danger. Although the angry cyclopes are fighting one another, waves of the enemy are scurrying over and around their flailing bodies like army ants. They zero in on me, an army of three-foot-tall nymphs wielding rocks, longswords, and handguns. One of them launches a rock at my head, and when I duck to avoid it, the projectile explodes into a cloud of loose shrapnel and I am surprised to feel the resulting pressure wave barbecuing my back and searing my flesh.

Marissa screams as a dead man has her in a choke hold, and the nymphs are climbing atop one another, aiming silver-plated cowboy revolvers at my face.

A trio of blasts and a puff of smoke later, I feel a white-hot bullet whiz past my ear, where it hits an Olympian soldier.

Our entire line collapses and the nymphs pile on top of me, clawing at my flesh and hair, screaming in my ears. I buck one of them off and she flies six feet up into the air, into the path of a light blast from one of the goddesses.

The goddesses are flapping their giant wings with enough fury to whip up a dust tornado, which crosses the path of the green sludge woman, temporarily immobilizing her.

Olympian soldiers are capitalizing on this, cutting at her thighs with daggers and swords even as a monstrous BOOM echoes across the battlefield.

The shotgun blast hits the woman in the knee, and she shrieks in agony while the flying goddesses wrap strands of white light around her shoulders. She pries a blade away from a soldier, screaming as she holds it aloft. A half-second later, the weapon sinks into her own leg, amputating it at the knee.

Undaunted, she fights off a dozen soldiers at once, parrying with the sword, and killing three more.

Meantime the nymphs tumble over me, slicing at my forearms and thighs as they batter me from all sides. Screaming and trying to bat them away with my hands, I feel the pressure build inside me before it comes to a head. A second later, they are launched twenty feet away as a glowing halo of white spreads through them.

Twenty fifty-foot-tall composite skeletons march from behind their lines, stepping over the blast of light as it dissipates into the crowd of attackers. The nymphs try to reform their ranks amidst the skeletons, but their interference renders any teamwork inadequate.

The army of bones won't be so quick to succumb. Feeling out their trajectory, I squeeze my sword, hold it high like a samurai, and wait. The skeletal leader unsheathes a blade over six feet long, holding onto the silvery hilt. I watch the steel flicker in the light of the fires as another explosion hits behind the lines.

The armies press us, locked in a deadly dance. I see Marissa fall to the ground, wheezing as the blast wave reaches her. She shields her face with her hands, breaking eye-contact with a zombie who lunges toward her with a hook-shaped staff eight feet long.

He sags as the blast reaches him, falling back into the mayhem. Legions of dead warriors, giants, cyclopes, nymphs, and skeletons are now marching toward us in greater numbers.

A dozen soldiers surrender after another explosion cuts through our forces. The winged goddesses continue to wrap the one-legged eight-foot woman with ribbons of light as she flails on the ground, twirling her sword in a tight circle that removes limbs from bodies as it spins.

Olympian screams fill the atmosphere as the dead army overwhelms us. In no time, The One True God of Darkness himself may arise from a crack in the landscape to devour us in utter darkness.

Marissa covers her head with her arms as fists grab at her clothes. I attempt to launch another light halo, but I'm outmanned. They are carrying her away as I scream her name.

"Marissa!!"

Before I can move toward her, pain roars across my back as flames boil away the inflamed skin where the shrapnel has pierced my back. I howl as the agony plunges me into darkness so deep I cannot fight my way out, and I stumble to the ground.

I can see them carrying her away as she bites at their hands. They wrap strands of poisoned twine around her wrists and ankles as they tie her to a white stake ten feet long. Fire dances at Marissa's feet as the eyeless dead men and women hoist the stake into a vertical position.

Her screams dissolve in the smoke as the orange and blue flames lick at her feet. Laughter surrounds her, and I rush to her defense, but not before the goddesses yank them into vortexes of light.

Pain propels me forward, and I move like a cloud of black fog. More of them reassemble around Marissa even as the goddesses draw the first ones away. I'm going to have to watch them burn her at the stake. No—I dig down into the depths of my soul with every ounce of agony and rage I can find.

Tears are sparkling in her eyes as she bores into me with her gaze, and suddenly, I'm floating away in an amber haze.

"You know how to find me, Larry. I know you. From across the galaxy, a hundred billion suns and planets separate us, but we still connect. Because we must."

"I'm only one man," I say, "a defeated soul. The Titans are going to rip me apart and eat me for breakfast while Erebus looks on. It's over."

"Your allies fight on your behalf, because they must. Appeal to them. Find your way home."

"Sarah," I rasp.

Marissa has disappeared and the undead army surrounds us. Even though a thousand of them lie defeated, their army has emerged victorious. I watch my blade fade into darkness as my eyes begin to close.

I am imagining the aftermath. It will be severe, and the Titans will analyze this battle to strengthen their numbers and their strategy. My abilities are nothing in comparison to theirs.

I'm no match for the Titans alone, but I know I have allies.

Then there is a sudden flash of orange and red light, and a hulking behemoth emerges. The enemy panics at the sight of him.

He kneels, and picks up my limp body to carry me away from the carnage onto a ridge overlooking the destruction. Through the darkness and the haze of smoke, I see large numbers of dead bodies, and a much larger force surrounding an army.

Prometheus presses his hands against my chest and tells me not to move.

"You gave it everything you had," he says.

"I'm..." I moan, grimacing as I try to lace words together. "No hero. They took her. They're going to burn her alive."

"Patience. You know a funny thing about fire? It seeks oxygen. Fire needs three things to ignite in nature: a spark, fuel, and oxygen. If it lacks any of them, it dies. I stole their flames as I passed. They can try to spark the blaze again, but they've got a bigger prize."

"Me," I croak, wincing in agony.

His warm hands press at my back where the pain feels like it's eating at my flesh. A single nod tells me everything I need to know. The war will not end until I'm dead and the Olympians will assemble a greater army to meet them again in an all-out battle for the world at large.

"You." He hesitates. "And maybe me, too."

He applies a pressure pad to my back to soak up some of the blood and charred skin.

"I think they suspect something is up. Mnemosyne and Theia gave me a weird look when I was leaving."

"What..." *groan...* "are you doing with them?"

He shrugs. "Gathering intel. Feeding them false information regarding the strengths and weaknesses of the Olympian army. They attempt to use their mortality against them, a tactic you've probably already seen play out."

"Why?" I ask, doubling over in pain.

"Why indeed? It seems your betrayal of Erebus is inciting revenge. I was there when they defeated your ancestors, the Titans of Crete. Do you remember them?"

I shake my head, moaning as tears leak from my eyes.

"Merope, Lady of the Six, had a special bond with you. By now I wager you know why."

I have no idea. At the base of the incline where we are, the undead army spreads out. They will revel in victory while we lick our wounds, giving them ample time to plan for the inevitable Olympian counterattack. Zeus will lead us valiantly, hoping to avenge our fallen brothers and sisters, and though I've never met him, his legend has remained firm over the centuries, even as belief in him crumbled.

"Your friend Marissa must know, then," he notes, reacting to my expression. "She fought well, too, even turning some of them against each other as I understand it. The Titans will try to manipulate that ability. Rest assured, it doesn't get any easier from here."

"What are they planning?"

"I don't think you're going to like it," he mumbles, still tending to my back.

"Tell me," I growl. "I can take it."

Sorrow suffuses his face. I know what he's about to say will destroy me again, and no matter what I do, I cannot look away from it. His lip quivers for a moment as he breathes, "Philadelphia will fall."

32

Ambrosia of the Meliae

My heart sinks through my chest, falling like a boulder onto my stomach. The somberness of Prometheus's tone does not soften the blow. No matter what I do, I'm not immune to the trauma of war.

Philadelphia is my home; the city I love, even after moving away.

"Take as long as you need," he mutters.

"I'm going to *kill* Cronus."

Prometheus nods. "To do that, you must learn about him—as much as possible. And none of the Titans know everything."

I growl. "When were you going to tell me?"

"I'm afraid there's only one man I trust to tell the complete account recorded in Olympus. The problem is, he's busy planning the next fronts for the war."

"Take me to him."

"Not a great idea," he says, looking across the desecrated battlefield. The Titan army must have Marissa tied up somewhere, but I cannot see any nascent fires where she disappeared. I'm frustrated that my injuries are delaying her rescue.

"The war runs through me, and the Olympians know it," I say. "Consulting with me might be the biggest advantage they have."

He hesitates, looking skyward where the moon is engaged with the stars in a coordinated cosmic dance, forever twirling around this peculiar ball of rock and soil we call home. After poring over the details in his mind,

Prometheus emits a raspy sigh and relaxes his shoulder, a sign he is relenting. "I take it we're not leaving your friend."

I shake my head while trying to sit up. Overcoming the scorching pain in my back and legs takes all my energy. Prometheus offers me his hand, and taking it, I feel heat prickle on my skin.

With little effort, he rises to his feet, pulling me up as he goes. "We're going to need a strategy."

My lip quivers as the agony, now imbued with more oxygen, slices across my back. "You plow right through them with your flamethrower hands, and I'll follow. They'll be too afraid to attack."

He says, "I'm thinking something a little more subtle."

"Look at this, a Titan who's built a reputation on being in your face with flame," I mock, "suggesting restraint. These really *are* the end times."

"I don't think you're going to like my idea," he says, but with resolution. The thing about explosive pain is that it floods your body with adrenaline, deactivating the logical centers of the brain. If we're to save Marissa, I'll have to go along with him.

"Fine," I say through gritted teeth.

"There are Shades in their midst. It will probably scare the Tartarus out of the survivors, but then again, they've seen the Shades already and one more won't matter. The enemy would expect to have your support."

Humph. "Nice try. I can no better control that ability than anyone not named Jesus can walk on water."

Raising an eyebrow, he turns to me. "Who is this Jesus? A friend of yours?"

I force a smile. "I guess you could say that."

"So you can't do it?"

Replacing my smile with an ugly frown takes far less energy than it should, ignoring the common axiom that frowning takes more muscles. "Oh, I can do it, but I can't predict when it's going to work. It's a collection of dark energy, and I'm sapped right now."

"You know they're probably torturing Marissa right now, and if they don't erect a gallows, they'll burn her alive. Don't even get me started on Sarah's fate. Or that of your family: your son, caught in a limbo he can never escape, your beloved wife trapped a dimension where she doesn't belong…"

"I never told you about that," I rasp.

"Observation," he counters. "It's too bad, when the fate of your loved ones, your city, your world, depends on a power you can't use when you really need it. I guess they call that irony."

His suggestion slams into my gut with every word. He'll be lucky if I don't use that dark energy to wring his neck. But then again, the lecherous freak show probably has a plan for that, too.

"I won't promise you glory," he grumbles. "There's a good chance this entire operation will fail, or you could end up enslaved as a Shade forever. The Shades cannot turn from Erebus; they're bound to him for eternity. But you already know that."

My fist gathers into a ball and punches into his face. As though unsurprised, he simply turns to look into the crowds. The throng of undead, the cyclopes, the giants, the nymphs, mechanical wolves, Shades, and that gelatinous monster woman surround a few hundred survivors, keeping them hostage as leverage in the war, which indicates that the Titans expect a counteroffensive. Their leaders will perfect a strategy, careful to account for any unforeseen complications along the way, which means they are in an isolated group. If I can turn myself into a Shade, I should be able to slip through them, untie Marissa, and find a portal without garnering much attention. Prometheus, on the other hand, can't do any of that, but at least he can fly.

The plan emerges in my head as I study the battlefield. Indeed, the commanders and generals have mustered a tight formation a few hundred yards from the dying green monster woman. Their strategic location is not without its flaws. They will detect large-scale disruption among their armies and prisoners and look to put a stop to it, and that will create a blind spot.

The Shades confer in a soot cloud a hundred yards from where a dense circle of zombies are holding a group of survivors captive. I should be able to enter through that gap, far away from the leaders, *if* the other Shades don't see me.

"I'm still going to need an energy boost," I say.

"Very well," he says, grinning. A split second later, his hair is on fire and he's squeezing my hand in a fist of white-hot coals. I writhe in pain as the image of Ian floundering in an abyss that he's created floods my mind. I can still hear his childlike voice murmuring in the dark, while a million tiny spiders scurry toward him.

I picture Sarah slipping from my grasp, falling into the mudslide, and then her body burning on a pyre Prometheus built with his own flaming hands. And when my mind shifts to Becky, these pictures fall away.

She stands there in her blue and white chevron dress, delicate and dreamlike, shrouded in a darkness I cannot dispel. I can feel her heartbeat matching mine. A thousand miles apart, yet one flesh, emotionally entangled from the beginning of time itself.

Blood. Severed hands, defeated men and women, broken swords, scuttled pistols, and blast craters. All are scattered across the surface of the trampled grassland. If the battlefield can feel, it must sense my response.

The darkness draws me into the crowds. Eyeless undead can still sense my movement. Some of them look away from the group, focusing their attention on the black-stained mob of Shades, perturbed.

I can only evade capture by pretending I'm among the Shades, and my trajectory is a path through them—a foot-wide gap that zigzags through their smoky mass. Floating through it will require me to condense myself into a solid form. Passing through them like an added puff of smoke would sound the alarm because they will feel my emotions if we touch.

A surreal sensation creeps through my current form as I slither through their detached souls. Through those few inches of separation, I can feel their distant heartbeats.

Tethered to The One forever. One purpose, one mind, one heart. A never-ending continuum of thought and soul. They believe the One will emerge victorious, giving the Titans free rein to make peace across the universe.

Prometheus had launched himself skyward, flying south away from the battlefield while keeping high enough to avoid being seen. He made it three or four miles before rising so high that he would look smaller than an ant at a great distance. Far above, he circles the battlefield, focused on that one point where I've guessed Marissa may be tied up.

The Shades speak in a foreign, wordless language of vibrations and mismatching emotions. Marissa could speak with them on that level, but if she did, they might tear her away from her sanity.

She is captive in a camp of twenty zombies. It would be easy for me to erase them bit by bit, but in doing so I'd be absorbing pieces of Erebus's loyalists, and to keep myself free from his influence I must stay away from them if I can.

They have erected the stake in a heap of dry grass and kindling. The nails embedded in the stake support some thick twine ropes made of shredded, braided bark that must burn her flesh when she moves.

I stealthily approach them like an oil slick on water, moving like a river of steam over broken, battered ground. They have erected the stake in a heap of dry grass, kindling, and balls of wood-shavings as fine as cotton. The nails embedded in the old, splintering wood support thick twine ropes made of shredded, braided bark that must burn her flesh when she moves.

She looks unconscious, unmoving, but breathing. The army has given up lighting the fire, conversing amongst themselves in a foul, Greek-tinged language that sounds rotten and discarded, as though every thought is a forgotten relic of time fossilized to keep its secrets.

But they can sense me. With every drifting move I make, I feel their attention shift as I form a column behind Marissa. She moves when I release her from the vertical mast, absorbing splinters and sawdust as I erase it. I don't dare erode the twine for fear of harming her. The stake is thirty feet away from the closest warrior, an emaciated man who's turning his head back and forth between the stake and the group, as if uncertain whether to raise an alarm.

Prometheus's descent comes without warning. Dropping from ten thousand feet faster than an eagle catching its prey, he emerges like a column of smoke, nods at me, and emits a fiery cloud that fogs the area. After ten seconds of fumbling her body, he lifts her and the ropes binding her onto his shoulder, breathes life into me, grasps my blackened hand as it emerges from my mist, and skyrockets away from the battlefield before the watching army can move a muscle.

Perfection. My body has little time to emerge, even as the image of Becky's simple smile and tender lips pokes through the black canopy shrouding my heart. In the blink of an eye, the scene evaporates, and we hurtle through space faster than the speed of sound, until we emerge on a hard stone floor.

Lustrous columns crown a flat-topped hill amidst a low, sprawling city that stretches from the distant mountains to the shore. A million points of light glitter like golden flecks of metallic paint on a black canvas. The stone pylons rise over thirty feet to support cracked, decorative beams spanning from one end of the citadel to the other. Pediments of the edifice depict gods, goddesses, and storied battles from millennia ago. Nude skin and hair in braided knots are interspersed with fluttering white gowns. Cloth covers the men's groins as they fight for survival.

A stately goddess greets us, looking stately and sublime. She wears a wreathed crown embedded in a sheath of shiny blonde hair atop her head. The hair curls into golden ropes down her back as her silvery robe ripples an inch off the cracked and weathered limestone floor.

"Welcome, Prometheus and Kerry, to the Pantheon. I trust you want to meet with Arch General Zeus. Please follow me."

She turns and glides across the floor toward a dark gap between two of the stone columns and I glance into the blinking stars overhead. She leads us through the gap without saying a single word. A brief blot of darkness precedes an ornate room with tiled marble floors. Gilded curtains frame seeded-glass windows, through which distorted bulbs of starlight reflect off the tile. Twelve thrones form a perfect circle around an embedded star-shaped pictogram. Only one figure dominates the room. The goddess excuses herself as we look on at the ghost-white beard of the Arch General, his gold-flecked robe resting against his leather-strapped sandaled feet.

"Approach," he commands, his voice low and gravelly. "Thank you, my servant Prometheus. And what a pleasure to meet you, Kerry, Conveyor of Light and Shade. Make yourselves comfortable."

A few feet away, within arm's reach, an ornate pedestal table supports a delicate China dish containing bunches of grapes. Zeus motions toward them, allowing me to partake. My stomach growls as I pull dozens of the green and red fruit free and roll them in my hands before chewing them two at a time.

"I bring news from the battle," Prometheus says, turning down the corners of his mouth. "It was a thorough defeat, although we did rescue the human, Marissa, from certain death."

I swallow a grape whole. God, what happened to her? Did we lose her between the dimensions? Seeing my expression morph from shock to dismay, Prometheus waves his palm at me to comfort me.

"Without greater numbers we stand no chance," Zeus mourns. "But you didn't come here to discuss battle tactics, or you would not have brought Kerry alone. What is on your mind?"

Prometheus raises his eyebrows at me while I swallow grape juice and chew. "Please ask him yourself," he says.

I gulp down the grapes I was chewing. "I want to defeat the Titan Cronus. I can't help do that without knowing more about him. Can you give me everything from his birth till now—please?"

He gives me a sideways glance and sizes me up, peering for a moment at the reflected starlight behind me. The light in the throne room is shifting like a breeze through candlelight, ensconced in a chandelier high above.

"You may not like the story," he says. "Please refrain from vomiting on our polished floor."

I grimace. "I can take it."

"Cronus is the son of the first gods Uranus and Gaia, born over four thousand years ago, long before the gods established Athens as the capital. The legend has been passed down through hundreds of generations, keeping the basis intact throughout.

"He was an inquisitive child, quick to learn about the great cosmos his mighty father ruled. But he wanted to learn more, to become a legend all his own. His mother and father gifted him with powers, and he long experimented with moving enormous masses, deflecting asteroids and comets, eliciting glowing praise.

"But when he reached the age of maturity, he espoused ideas his father did not support, including wielding his supreme powers to make the universe a perfect place of harmony. Uranus disapproved, calling the idea sadistic and undemocratic, but ultimately allowed Cronus to continue experimenting.

"His powers grew, and one evening, yearning for change and r-eflecting on everything he considered good, he manipulated the spin and orbit of a distant planet now named after his father. That change in mass resulted in a change in gravity, attracting many moons and distorting space-time.

"Eager to tell his father what he'd accomplished, he approached Uranus and claimed an ability to manipulate time.

"You may hear the root word *chronos* in his name, a stark coincidence if you don't mind the expression.

"It was true. He proved it to Uranus, earning his father's ire. They had a terrible fight over using his powers in this way, but when his father gained the upper hand, Cronus fell wearily, retreated to his room for the night, and returned long after his father had fallen asleep. Armed only with a vitreous porcelain knife, Cronus entered his father's quarters and castrated him in front of his mother.

"Uranus's blood rained down on the earth, sprouting a grove of sacred ash trees inhabited by a race of ash nymphs, women literally born from the blood of Uranus. After we defeated Cronus and his eleven brothers and sisters and sent them to Tartarus, these nymphs provided us with the ambrosial food from which we exercise our own powers for the good of the universe."

I contemplate this revelation for at least two minutes, during which both Zeus and Prometheus gaze at me in plain hopes that I haven't yet gone mad. Understanding his past might reveal a weakness, but all I see is power taken to the extreme, an unquenchable hunger for control.

He can use gravity to distort time, hurl asteroids and meteors at the earth without breaking a sweat, and I can never match his strength. The longer I consider his powers, the more anxious I become, until an idea takes shape.

The light again flutters overhead when a stronger breeze extinguishes some of the flames. How *did* the builders light candles on a chandelier forty feet high without a ladder or scaffolding?

"Prometheus," I say, swallowing the sweet aftertaste of the grapes, "you spent two thousand years with him. How are his eyes?"

"Why do you ask?"

"I want to know if he's as sensitive to light as the other Titans. If a man peers into darkness for too long before glancing at the sun, he can go blind."

"Cronus is no mere man," Prometheus says, shrugging. "He's a Titan. And one of incredible power."

"With incredible power comes incredible responsibility," I wager, referencing an ancient quote neither Prometheus nor Zeus have ever heard. "Tell me the truth."

"He may have a weakness, but he's not a fool," Zues admits, stroking his beard and for once looking interested in my line of reasoning. "He knows you'll be looking for an advantage and will seek to mask that flaw."

"I think I know the way," I say, not quite believing the words I'm speaking.

Becky once explained how men can be physical beasts as well as emotional, but that brawn rarely coincides with disciplined learning. Cronus may have mastered incredible power by studying the physical characteristics of the cosmos, but that doesn't mean he's fluent in matters of the heart, or the pursuit of justice.

The idea takes shape faster than I can deduce its flaws, and when I speak, I rattle off the sentence faster than I can breathe, garnering shocked stares from both Prometheus and Zues. "I'm going to pit him against his sisters, Themis and Theia, and castrate him. See how he likes it."

33

Disaster

There are bleak thoughts, and then there are *dark* thoughts, the kind that pull you into realms crowded with their own demons. I'm unsure how to handle my own words.

But Prometheus looks less surprised than I expected; he crosses his arms and drums his fingers on his tattooed forearm. The markings run from his elbow, past his wrist, and onto the back of his hand. His ink may have once portrayed long-ago battles and victories, but now it looks like blackened scars from old burns. He wrinkles his nose for a split second, waiting for Zeus to put his ideas into words.

"After he led the Titan rebellion, we put him where he belongs," Zeus says, his voice patient, yet alarmed. "This idea comes with several drawbacks, chief among them being that he will be expecting revenge."

"An eye for an eye," I growl. I know I'm using a misunderstood Bible quote to justify my idea, but I don't care. The longer I think about it, the more my fingers shake.

"Tartarus is what Cronus deserves," Zeus says, frowning.

"And yet he has escaped already. So secure—"

"Which would never have happened without your help. Am I correct? You could have ignored the demands of Erebus.

I snarl with an aggression I don't know how to channel into rationality. My fingers shake, my arms and legs vibrating as I shout at him. "You don't know what I've been through. Don't even pretend to understand who

I am. I had no choice. You sit up here in your marble tower in all your hubris, commanding a war you think I started because you're supposed to be the good guys? I don't give a damn what you say."

"We know your value, Kerry. Don't underestimate ours."

"You believe this?" I raise my eyebrows, turning my attention to Prometheus, who has so far chosen to show little of where his loyalty lies, leaving me nothing to work with. I want to draw the anger out of him, so I won't feel so alone in attacking Zeus, but he's staying silent. If wisdom is his motive, fine, but if his reticence is servility, I'll punch him with a fist of light while he's not looking.

"That is no way to address the gods," Zeus growls. "You'll do well to remember your duty. You must go back to your home. I understand the Titans will gather there, and when they do, we have a surprise for them."

Clenching my fists, I feel my throat tighten. "NO! HOW DARE YOU BRING WAR TO MY CITY?"

"The Titans are bringing it," he says in a stern voice. "It's your city, so fight for it."

"I'll be back," I snarl. "I can do lightning too."

Prometheus ushers me out without saying farewell to his supposed master. I have countless questions, but he interrupts me with an elbow to the ribs.

"Your temper is misplaced, Kerry. If you want to use anger for justice, point fingers at those who are responsible. You'll get your chance, because you will lead the army we've assembled in Philadelphia."

"What about you?" Without turning my head, I feel my throat rasping with shame.

"I'm needed on another front. You have good men and a small contingent of Olympians at your disposal. If you want to turn our fortunes in this war and save your family, you have all the energy you need." He hesitates, indicating he's chosen to hold something back. I'm good enough at reading between the lines to understand what he's *really* saying.

I have a duty to the Olympians, Becky, Ian, Sarah, Marissa, and the entire universe. But without knowing how to fight, I'm alone. Zeus and Prometheus are forcing me into a battle I'm ill-prepared for, and that doesn't bode well.

"So that's it? It's goodbye now?" I glance around at the spacious foyers and promenades, searching the shadows. "And what have you done with Marissa?"

"We left her in Philadelphia," he says, his voice low and solemn. "By now, she must be awake. Go home—we'll meet again."

"You're damn right we will," I bark.

He leads me into a shadow between a pair of columns. The shadow beneath the frame flutters as I stare into it.

Prometheus frowns as he looks up. His expression has a familiarity I could grow fond of if I didn't want to punch him first. I say nothing more as I back into the archway, narrowing my eyes and grimacing as pain swells through me.

The light-speed rush through time sends me swirling past stars and planets. A million points of light gather into a hazy disc at the edge of my perception. And then, darkness.

Philadelphia is on fire.

In my worst childhood nightmares, the apocalypse in my imagination would seep like oil stains over barren, cracked earth, the light of fires flickering under starlight as a million voices mutter discontent and agony, always on their guard should a band of desperate, rogue scouts seek their sustenance and food—guns always loaded under their dusty pillows as they sleep under the stars, seeking the relative ambiance of remoteness. A lifetime of Bible study makes you expect certain human reactions. A selfish zeal that permeates all personal interactions as people look inwards towards their closest relatives without placing trust in strangers. That tale-older-than-time-itself nightmare where in dark epochs people show their darkest sides. I know what to expect.

But I am wrong.

Fires scorch skyscrapers across the city, bathing the city's crown jewels in red-orange light as smoke rises into the sky. The people are at war, but not with each other.

I hear their screams, their exhortations to fight back against a common enemy. Where is the army Prometheus has promised me?

I gasp as a man gallops toward me with twin swords hanging to his ankles. "You're here!" he says, grinning and nodding at a flaming twenty-story high-rise several blocks to my right. "We've got your command post prepped. Market Street, two blocks from Independence Square. Talk to Miriam."

He hesitates while I size him up. Unsheathing one of the swords, he hands it over to me. I test its weight by swinging from side to side. Why should I carry a sword? It makes about as much sense as giving a piano to a ship captain.

"Kerry!" someone a block away shouts, pointing a handgun at a zombie staggering toward him. "Good to see you again."

I'd know his voice anywhere. Even if he doesn't say another word, I can hear him complaining about referees, downing a beer, and ranting about how Kansas City always gets away with penalties because of their superstar quarterback. It's my friend Juaquin.

"What are you doing here?" I stammer.

"You mean besides looking after your friend? Looks like I'm—"

Quin is firing at the undead man, hitting him square between the skin-wrapped eye sockets. From the zombie's scaly lips comes an incantation which I can't make out over the ringing in my ears.

"—fighting a battle."

"You?"

"Crowds of us," he remarks. "These creeps never knew what hit them."

Suppressing the urge to groan, I cock my head to survey the shambles of a toppled building. I judge the trajectory of a massive flaming projectile aimed straight for the skyscraper Bones Holdings had constructed all those years ago. Panic robs the breath in my lungs as I force out her name. "Marissa—where is she?"

"Just around the corner. She's got a winged fairy lady helping, hiding where the enemy can't find her. She'll escort you to Market Street."

Turning on the balls of my feet and glancing through the corner of my eye, my heart freezes as the meteor explodes on contact with the glass exoskeleton of the tower, raining flaming detritus down on the tarmac. Screams erupt all around me as I sprint across the street, dodging a flaming arrow, and leaping into the shadow of a long, rectangular overhang at the foot of an aging residential high-rise. All the lights inside save the always-on emergency lamps have long since gone out, allowing the abandoned building to sink into blight. A block away, two men decked out in camouflage, helmets, and armor face a wall of soldiers marching shoulder-to-shoulder through the streets, inching backward as they fight. Behind them, a thousand car horns lament their stranded drivers. Cornered, the soldiers open fire with automatic weapons, mowing down soldiers by the dozens while jets scrape the skyline to direct the military's hodgepodge reaction to the assault.

"The hell you did!" one soldier screams at the other.

"Hell of a shot!"

Sinking into the dark, I feel Marissa before I can see her. Despite her trauma, she remains defiant. Her eyes flick back and forth from the goddess to the stranded cars.

A city enveloped in chaos cannot feel quite so apocalyptic without volatile traffic jams that imply it might be better to flee on foot. Thousands of people have similar ideas, and many of them had not left home without their guns and knives. One young woman wields a decorative katana, cleaner than the one the soldier had just given me.

Even so, my sword feels right in my grip, complementing the energy in my hands and redirecting it through the silvery blade, which vibrates with my power. I let it rest on the ground next to me as I kneel where Marissa is sitting.

She bites her lip and stands up. A spot of blood flecks her skin on her left check, while a nasty bruise festers at the corner of her mouth. She groans at me when I look her over. "What are you looking at? Never seen a pissed-off occult dealer?"

I can't say that I have.

But we don't have time to chat. I guide her along the blood-spattered sidewalk, dodging the throngs of people fighting for their city, or battling their way to safety. One woman screams while she unloads a nine-millimeter magazine at an undead foursome. They lock eyes on her as they return fire, pelting her with bullets as they fight through the gridlock.

Seeing the carnage unfold, a man flips them off through the windshield and, pounding his fist on his horn, hammers the gas pedal to the floor to run them over. They buckle when the car's bumper pins them against an idling moving van, loaded to the hilt with supplies on their way to another city.

"When's Washington going to help us?" a man asks no one in particular as he sprints through a hail of bullets and arrows. A group of enemies breaks formation, hurtling toward the lobby of a tall office building. Marissa shrieks as she sees him die right before our eyes.

A row of cars crashes together as the force of something violent and massive propels them forward. Drivers with whiplash fall against their horns as their cars pile atop one another, crushing the bottom vehicles in an expanding wave of cars smashing through the streets. Residents flee from the source of the mayhem.

Like a fifty-foot-tall bulldozer, a wave of sooty water, crushed asphalt, and mangled steel shoots out from the source of the blast wave. I can see the perpetrator standing atop a parapet, surveying the carnage below with a keen eye.

I turn to face him, filled with the agony of watching my city burn.

A twister of fire and red iron careens off a nearby tower, burying a dozen cars in heavy slabs of concrete, steel, and pipes. When the building's skeleton fails, I see the upper floors topple first, breaking the lower floors as the whole mass falls.

Ten blocks away, another building succumbs to the same fate. The dead and living servants of The One fight in unison, moving through the city like elite strike teams, gunning down people in the streets and making my heart sink even further.

We know we'll never reach Market Street running through this; by that time the Titans will have reduced the city to rubble. The cross streets in front of us are walled-off, buried in twenty feet of wreckage. Cars lie crushed below the concrete and steel, their drivers wheezing their last agonizing breaths.

Even during the Revolutionary War, Philadelphia never faced such chaos. If Washington has forsaken the city, Congress will experience the wrath of the whole country. But then again, the country has given them enormous power, and an uprising won't prove any more inconvenient than swatting a housefly trying to land on a sandwich.

Rage pours through me as Marissa skids to a halt behind me. The living and undead servants of The One are closing in on us. They have us trapped.

A block away, another building fire-balls into an ear-splitting explosion, and then another. Helpless, a handful of gods and goddesses swirl over the mayhem, launching targeted strikes of light and pressure waves at the Titans, who are still razing the city.

Behind us, a sinkhole opens, filling with dark water, suds, and kitchen gunk, and rapidly expands. The abyss devours curling slabs of asphalt and concrete, three cars, and a dozen fleeing spectators.

As the enemy force launches flaming arrows, white-hot bullets and fire at us, I swallow every ounce of energy I can muster, power it all into the sword, and see it catch the wave of destruction before it reaches us. The bullets and arrows melt away as the glowing sword absorbs them all, drawing in more power.

In my counterstrike, I chase them back toward the collapsed buildings blocking both approaches to the intersection. The streetlamp and traffic-light pole crashes into the street, wounding several of them as it falls into a puff of concrete dust.

Channeling my rage, I begin to slice through them, even as more of them crawl over the destroyed buildings. Battling through them all, I keep my rage and energy focused into the sword, deflecting attacks and chopping off limbs at the same time.

Marissa can't do anything, but she doesn't need to. Staying aware of her surroundings, she tiptoes past a pile of debris clogging a storm drain half-buried under tons of brick. A pipe lands next to her, emitting a loud iron clink as it drives divots out of the asphalt near the drain.

More enemies launch attacks and I absorb them all, but I can see the enemy forces increasing. A gigantic wave of river water slams through the canyon, flushing towering piles of rubble away from the street corner. Marissa sees it coming and wraps her arms around a barber's column just as the wave slams me against a building, flipping me head over heels and trapping me against the brick face.

She gurgles my name before the wave pushes onward, carrying wreckage along with it. As I flip right way up and keep my head above the water, I can see stranded citizens watching their city crumble. As the wave subsides, the sky opens up like a gash, revealing a black hole. Then the black fades to an orange light that comes gleaming through. It's big enough to swallow half the financial district.

The gods react by blasting it with light and destruction, forcing it into the riverfront piers, causing a titanic explosion that rains down steam and ash like confetti.

The Titans aren't finished yet. A fire hydrant pops off the bolted plate anchoring it to the sidewalk and lets out a jet of water fifty feet high. Only one thing can cause that kind of pressure surge in the city water system—steam.

When water is heated, it expands in volume a hundred-fold, forcing extreme pressure throughout the system. With this level of pressure, the entire system can give way. In line with my expectations, utility hole covers pop out of the streets, carrying thick masses of coal ash like a viscous black sludge invading the water.

A dozen Shades are riding the pressure wave through the pipes, devouring mounds of debris as they go, even as more destruction rains from above. The hole in the sky is closing, but the ground vibrates with the blast of another meteor; the shockwave rolls out through the streets, crumbling concrete and asphalt and carrying citizens away.

The entire city is being sacked, and I'm watching it unfold, helpless to prevent it. The gods and goddesses streak away to help another front north of the city center, leaving Marissa and me alone with Titans.

I use my rage to regain my balance. The blast wave and the flood has wiped our enemies off the map too, but I know they'll return in greater numbers.

The energy within me collects into the blade of my sword, and I hold it up to send a jet of light skyward like a beacon to attract all twelve Titans. They'll know right where to find me.

Battling through it takes more energy than I can create on my own, but now a premonition of losing Becky and Ian pours through my veins like acid, eroding the essence of my soul, and the dark energy that sits just below the surface rises into a cataclysm I cannot control.

I feel the dark energy pulsing through me, emptying into the hilt of my sword. It splits atoms as it hacks through the firestorm. Gathering Marissa into a tight embrace to protect her, I am piling up bodies, and before I know it, I'm emitting my own shockwave as the light leaves my eyes.

We feel it shooting away from us, destroying buildings for ten blocks in every direction. The Titans will think they've bested me, yet I can feel the tug of memory coursing through my cranium like ebbing crimson ribbons of a long-ago time.

MEMORIES:

Becky's hands press against my back as she kisses me, releasing years of passion and longing into one moment. My body aches and writhes as we wrap our arms around one another. The world surrounding us fades into black and gray, leaving just the two of us locked in our little slice of fleeting eternity.

I dare not peel my eyes away from her, but I know that once I open my eyes, she'll be gone. Nothing can prepare me for the chord of agony it strikes.

She vanishes into smoke as embers fade into nothingness, leaving only the ashen face of our son. He's stricken with a stabbing trauma that cuts him deeper than his eyes can show, but I feel his soul hollow out as he gazes at me, fading into black as the world disappears.

Ice-cold hands grip mine, clammy and disorienting at first, but eventually supplying me with warmth as the ruins of Philadelphia come into view. Skyscrapers two dozen blocks away have been reduced to powder and the stench of death and filthy water fills my nostrils.

Marissa's tears only show a fraction of the dismay I witness: Dead bodies lie in every direction, in burned-out cars, buried under mountains of rubble, and in untold numbers of smashed vehicles. Many have escaped, but I can do the math. Cronus has killed hundreds of thousands of the people of Philadelphia.

I'm going to destroy him. Hate consumes me as I survey the ruins of the city. My fingers are trembling so much that I drop the sword, hearing it clank in the dust and broken concrete beneath my feet. This feeling of righteous anger is enough to change a man from the inside, but if I act on it, would I be any better than he is?

Directing all my rage onto one person might feel cathartic, but only I know the real reason it explodes within me at all. By pointing at Cronus, I don't have to blame myself for setting him free, albeit in an act of desperation.

Finally, I understand what's happening. My many dimensions have merged into one disjointed reality that threatens everything I think I know about time and space. Every dimension is one: Becky is still lost in a parallel reality, Ian is still murmuring in that dank, cobwebbed limbo, searching for a way out, and somehow, Sarah is still dead.

All by my own hands. I have taken too much life from the world, cutting too many stories short, all because I meddled with time—for Sarah. And it has done nothing but cause destruction for everything I call home, the heart and soul of a city I love.

I can blame Cronus all I want, but the true enemy dwells within me. And that's a reality I can never escape.

34

The Ancient Titanomachy

Marissa wheezes in the dust and smoke, wincing through watery, tear-filled eyes as she surveys the aftermath of my outburst. My heart has gone dead, resting in a dormant slumber so deep that I may pass out at any second. Falling to my knees amidst the ruins I have no energy left to fight, but the silent battleground remains. The untold thousands of dead surround us—men, women, children, and old people—and every sight causes agony to build within me.

"God," she whispers. "I can't believe you did that."

I knew I possessed the powers of a Titan thanks to the princess of the light, Ariadne, but none like what I've just unleashed. My outburst has leveled several city blocks, but surely the Titan army would have smashed them anyway.

"At what cost?" I mutter, breathless. "We lost—everyone did. The war's over. And time itself is on the brink of destruction."

The skeleton of a high-rise, once faced with opulent glass, sways behind her, a few blocks away. The concrete decks crumble, leaving lopped-off corners hanging by bent corrugated decking steel, ready to drop several stories at any moment. The framing settles as the wind picks up, blowing thick plumes of dust and smoke across the Delaware into New Jersey.

"It's not over," she says. "Not while the Olympians are around. You need to have faith."

Faith? Coming from a woman who has thrived on the absence of faith for a lifetime? If I didn't feel so demolished, I'd utter a derisive laugh, but all I can do is frown direfully.

I may never know how I managed to crush several square blocks of the city I love without harming Marissa, but I can't bear to think about that. She doesn't seem threatened—in fact she looks encouraged.

"I know a secret," she says, wiping sweat and tears. "These Titan assholes might believe they've got unlimited power, but I've seen cracks in their ranks. If we can somehow exploit them, we can win."

I don't even care about winning. Victory might taste sweet after a game, but doesn't feel appropriate after war. While one front might achieve their goals, they lose whatever helped them win.

"I've got to find her..." I gasp, inhaling smoke. "I know she's here, because every dimension of time is here."

"What?" She raises her eyebrows, glancing toward the wrecked financial district a half mile away. The fallen towers emit plumes of thick black smoke into the sky, sparking lightning that strobes in the soot.

I recall the last time I saw Becky in our home dimension. The memory is foreign and distant, like a long-forgotten relic, yet it still resonates with a frequency the sparks agony in the center of my soul. "The past," I sniff, coughing and bending over to rest my hands on my knees, "the future, the present. It's all here. I don't know if it's the same way for you, but the paradoxes I've created might be trying to right themselves."

"Huh."

Her body language remains mute, but I can see a fragment of new hope in her eyes, interspersed with confusion.

"We've got to find her. Now. But I don't know where to start."

She hesitates. "Don't you want to know what I've seen? For all their phenomenal powers, the Titans *have* a weakness. You haven't seen it yet because you don't know how to connect with the enslaved—the conscripted."

"I don't care about that." I shrug.

"You have to. Don't give up this easily. Before they captured me, and started torturing me, I saw something. Just a brief flicker of fear in a dead man's spirit."

"That's not possible."

"I thought so too, at first. And then I saw it again, stronger, like a suppressed light. The armies outwardly show perfect loyalty to their masters, but there's restlessness deep within. If we can show them a better way, we can turn our fortunes."

"Maybe after we find Becky—"

"If the dimensions are merging like you say, then time is losing stability and may collapse around you. There's only one way forward now."

High above the ruins, storm clouds gather. The ground quakes; panic swells within me as the street begins to crumble. Smashed cars buried under rubble a block away cascade into the hole that is opening wider and wider, swallowing millions of gallons of water, mounds of concrete and granite, particles of glass, and chunks of twisted iron.

You will never escape, my servant.

I lower my voice. "Do you hear that?"

Marissa shakes her head. "But I do *feel* it."

Moving closer to her, I struggle to my feet as she pulls me up by one hand. I feel my bones vibrate as something sinister tugs at every cell within my body. "He's going to enslave humanity," I exclaim.

"Well, that's a little steep. I just wanted to say he seeks to defeat the Titans, too. But maybe you should tell me who *he* is and why he's talking to us in this way."

"Erebus, The One True God of Darkness," I begin. "He enlisted the Titans as part of his plan to take over, because he cannot do it himself. He dispatched his armies to fight with the twelve Titans because he wants to overthrow the Olympians. The Titans almost won thousands of years ago, without The One running the show."

"I don't follow."

"The Titans gave rise to the Olympians, but the Olympians feared their power and thought they had the wrong ideas. So the Titans confronted them, which sparked a rebellion. They had the Olympians on the brink, but ultimately lost. As punishment, Zeus cast them down to Tartarus forever. The One made me release them on the condition that I'd see Becky again. But I never thought he'd go this far."

"Do you think he will now?"

I gulp, and smoke fills my lungs. Coughing feels like razor-sharp gravel scraping my throat. I grip Marissa's hand for a moment to steady myself, eyeing the fallen traffic lights and the murky water carving canyons in the broken asphalt, and allow rationality to return to my brain.

Does Marissa really think we have a chance? Even though she's not saying so, I can see that glimmer of hope in her. She's never been dishonest with me. Even now, humanity carries traces of light, no matter how dark the world grows.

Dabbing at an ache in my gut, I narrow my eyes, looking up to see a circle of light pulsing above the city, like a circular throbber on a loading screen. The rotation slows, and two winged beings descend into the wreckage, zeroing in on us.

I glower at them, but before they can see me, I watch as chunks of concrete weather into a coarse sand next to a buckled column, whose rusting rebar slices at the darkness. They can sense me, homing in on the emotion pouring out of me.

The angels land on sandaled feet to stand amidst the ruins of a city that helped found Western democracy, based on Ancient Greek ideals.

Five feet apart, they step closer to me, frowning and careful not to trip on any of the detritus. Equaling my height, the angel on the right looks shapely and fit. She wears a billowing white dress that ends just below her knees. Long and slender, her arms jut into voluminous sleeves fastened to her plunging neckline via a pair of golden rings, which gather the white cloth into sheaths. Her hair flutters as though there's a light breeze, and slung over her back, a dainty bow hangs next to a leather-bound case of feathered arrows.

To her right, the other woman stands six inches shorter and curvier. She wears a white and golden one-shoulder dress and a crown of white daisies over her dishwater blonde hair, concealing a bony shoulder. Her short sleeve blossoms with color and a silver clip fastens the back to the front.

"I am sorry I could not help more during our last encounter," the woman with the bow and arrows says. I cannot remember who she is.

"Your relationship with Callisto led me to you."

"I think her name was Vanessa," I say.

"Yes. She is a loyal friend."

"Is?"

She nods. "Beginning a new life as her spirit wanders the stars. That's how I know her now."

Seeing my reaction, she hesitates, glances at her companion, and frowns again. "This is Demeter, goddess of the harvest, daughter of the Titans Cronus and Rhea."

"Some call me Deo," Demeter says. Her melodious voice is sad. "We must bring you to safety now."

"I need your help," I croak, glancing back and forth between them. "I … I need to find my wife, but I don't know how … I know that only way I can save her is by helping to defeat the Titans."

"The war is not going well," Artemis says, her frown deepening.

"I have a plan," I blurt out, beginning to think out loud. "But we need one hundred percent cooperation from all the generals, commanders, and Zeus himself."

"We have been hoping for a new lead," Demeter says, narrowing her eyes, "and your help will be appreciated."

"But I'm not giving you anything if you don't help me to find Becky and our son."

"Let us meet with the Pantheon," Demeter says. "I believe we can help you with your wife, but collecting the dead is not something we can do. I hope you understand it isn't because we refuse, but because we cannot."

"You're goddesses," I croak, my face going red.

"Come now, Kerry," Artemis warns. "Share your plan with us when we are with the Pantheon."

"Marissa's coming too," I say. "She's a big part of what I have to say, and we may need specific information from her."

"Agreed," Demeter says, holding out her hands as though to welcome us into a group embrace. Clasping her soft hands around Marissa's tattooed one, she tilts her head back and launches herself skyward, disappearing into the pulsating light. When Artemis offers me her hands, I take a deep breath, and plunge with her into eternity.

Ten of the Olympians are gathered around a heavy, inlaid table with a single, carved-granite leg centered in the expansive tile floor. The room can seat at least fifty of the affluent and powerful, of the philosophers, of those who sometimes challenge authority. The patterned walls, backed with red felt, feature intricate hardwood carvings and rise to a coffered cathedral ceiling painted in chiaroscuro and depicting a circle of gods and goddesses, in the center of whom is Zeus.

When I see him seated at the table with his beloved Hera at his right, I feel panic rise. He gazes at me with a baleful expression that seems to separate his political acumen from his personal emotions toward me; perhaps I am the only human male who's ever challenged him.

Marissa walks over to the table first, pulling out a chair and running her hands along the beaded rail. Going over my plan in my head, I join her while looking around at the faces still afflicted with the grief of losing two among their number in battle.

"Kerry, Conveyor of Light and Shade," Hera says while her husband strokes his white beard. "Please explain your plans. We can then pass them on to our generals and commanders, who are even now recovering from a string of heavy defeats."

"If we don't gain the upper hand, the fate of the universe is at stake," I say, shaking. My fingers tremble as I rest them on an inlaid pattern of Greek geometry in the soft, buttery wood of the table. "I must find my wife, Becky. That is my price for helping."

"Your wife is dead, Kerry?" Hera asks.

I flush, and Marissa rests her hands on mine as I try to soothe the fiery sting of Hera's question.

"No, I don't think so," I say.

"You'd know it if she were." Marissa whispers, causing me to whip my focus to her. Her voice is almost silent as she continues: "Entanglement."

"I left her in the wrong dimension of time," I explain to Hera, "but now that our shared dimensions have merged, I know I can't waste a moment. But I have a plan to defeat the Titans once and for all."

A few of the goddesses bite their lips or lean forward, while Apollo gazes in stunned silence. Zeus continues to stroke his beard while Hera stares hard into my face with soulful eyes, which sparkle with every beat of my voice.

"My friend here says she has seen cracks in the loyalty of their armies," I begin, glancing at Marissa, inviting her to share her knowledge.

"How do you know of this?" Athena asks Marissa in a firm voice.

"Some describe me as a spiritualist," Marissa explains, her voice drawing out near the end of her sentence. She takes in a deep breath and then continues: "I know you don't believe in the various pagan sects, or any of the founding principles of Taoism or Zoroastrianism, but I trace my abilities to Wicca through these, to shape my understanding of spirituality. I can commune with the dead. And since our enemies employ legions of dead soldiers, I have communicated with some of them.

"In them I see a range of emotions that are only covered in a thin veneer of loyalty. They have shown me sorrow, bitterness, and even a hope that they can break free. I've already seen three of them turn on their comrades before being torn apart for treachery."

"You're sure of this?" Hera asks.

Marissa nods.

"I believe we can exploit it," I explain. "I also know that Cronus has a weakness, his sisters; I plan to pit them against him. Because he leads the Titans on Erebus's orders, we can use Hades to confront him while we undermine their army's loyalty."

"How do you plan to do that?" asks Zeus in his booming voice, placing both palms on the table.

"I need to get caught. I believe Theia and Themis will react if I overwhelm their forces with a controlled blast of darkness. And when they confront me, I'll let them deliver me to Cronus. And that's where I will spark a vicious debate, knowing Cronus will react with anger, forcing them to blind him temporarily."

"What of Hades?" Zeus says. "Did you not help to topple his tower?"

I ... *what?*

I don't know how to answer his question. "You're saying he's dead?"

"He's not dead," a sneering voice says, crackling with venom. "At least not yet. My reign over the underworld may have ended, but I'm still alive for now."

"You need to retake your kingdom," I say without hesitation. "Gather the soldiers you need."

"You don't understand," Hades says, pushing away from the table and scowling. "The embodiment of darkness covers all of Hades now. The armies have been stripped of their armor, overtaken by evil. It is no longer my domain."

"But if we can convince the dead slaves to rebel against their master, you will have a powerful army at your disposal. And I wonder if there are not still other souls partial to you? Creatures? Monsters?"

"Daemons," Apollo interrupts. "They do not answer to Erebus, but you could convince them to stand with you." He directs his attention to Hades, allowing his gaze to linger.

"It's a risky plan," Hera says after thirty seconds of silence.

"We are all at risk right now, anyway," I argue.

Hera nods, wrapping her dainty hand around her husband's powerful, tattooed arm. "I concur." Casting her gaze upon Marissa, she asks, "How sure are you of this ability?"

Marissa forces a smile, grabs my hand, and breathes in. As she speaks, I make out the five-pointed star in the circle and remember what she said about it so long ago. Protection. "My ability is strong. As to whether it will work, we won't know until we try."

"If you help me reunite with Becky," I say, picturing the welded washers in her palm like an oxidizing photograph fading with time, "it will work. But I want my son to be reincarnated."

"We cannot do that—"

Zeus cuts her off. "If your plan works, it will be done."

Hera scowls at him as though he's broken a sacred pact between them. But he only exhales and glares at me, perhaps remembering our earlier argument. I've won him over, and that's all that matters.

"Report to your commanders, generals," Zeus orders them all, his voice growing sturdier with every syllable. He returns his gaze to me and sneers, "You will report to Apollo's company, which is combining with Ares's infantry, on the island of Crete."

Crete is the birthplace and homeland of the Six, my Titan ancestors. And also the home of King Minos and Princess Ariadne, who gave me my abilities. It doesn't seem like my home, but if my roots run deep, I may be able to tap into the energy needed to use my powers. I'm now worried that Marissa's plan is sketchy at best, and whether Theia and Themis will resist my temptation. I am concerned that the entire plan will collapse. But my hope of finding Becky again hangs by a thread, which is enough for me. If it works, we'll live in happiness forever. If it doesn't, we'll just have to watch the world burn.

35

Titanomachy II

Without further warning, Apollo scoots his chair back from the table, causing a deafening scraping sound against the marble floor. He doesn't even bother glancing my way. Instead, he nods at one of the other Olympians while everyone but Hera and Zeus also rises. Low chatter echoes through the elongated room, bouncing off the cathedral ceiling. I stalk by his side as he hurries out the door. Apollo with little exertion shoves it open as Marissa hurries to keep up with us.

She grabs me by the crook of my elbow and takes me aside a second or two after we cross the threshold "You aren't going to tell me I can't come with you?"

I raise my eyebrow. "Why would I do that?"

"Because it's a battle? And because my skills won't stand up to heavy bombardment and I'll just hurt you? Or because I'm a woman?"

"Uhhh."

"That's what I thought," she says, with a coy smile. "I just needed to hear you say it."

One elongated single-syllable word of hesitation is all it takes to reaffirm I'm not the typical sophomoric hyper-masculine construction worker who needs to 'mansplain' basic problems and solutions. I can't decide whether to feel empowered or insulted.

"To Crete," I whisper.

"Can't wait."

Apollo hurries toward a nondescript door into a corridor that has a chair rail affixed to the wall three feet above an intricate base mold. The handle is a forged pewter C-shaped pull rod bolted to a coved iron escutcheon plate. As he yanks it open, blackness greets us. He rushes into the void, disappearing while Marissa stares after him. I guide her through the portal, even though this kind of travel hits me like a recurring nightmare, and we speed through a galaxy devoid of stars or life.

Dry grass crunches beneath our feet. We have landed on a rocky precipice overlooking a treacherous gorge at least five hundred feet deep, that zigzags through a dusty landscape flanking a barren, domed peak. A coat of thin snow caps the summit, blending with the high, wispy clouds behind it. Green brushes and tiny splotches that might be wildflowers dot the foothills where vast numbers of soldiers await their leader.

Apollo stalks toward the canyon rim, raising his right hand to signal his army to hold still. Many miles away, the enemy occupies a wide, grassy plain over a mile behind Ares's infantry, preparing to march. From the rim, I can see them forming a front in expectation that the Titan army will divide their forces. The major problem with this setup is that the enemy far outnumbers us. Apollo's company inhabits the rocky slopes of the mountain, pressing into crevices and crouched behind green and tan brush for camouflage.

When I glance around, I meet the eyes of a petite female archer wearing a thin helmet garnished with gold. She nods at me, lowers her gaze, and pulls an arrow from her quiver. Behind her, riflemen lock and load their guns and check their sights. At least two dozen men and women anchor themselves to the slopes of the gorge via ropes and belays, hunkering down with what look like incendiary devices, meant to launch explosives at the enemy. Everything a modern battalion needs to destroy an army of evil, yet they still outnumber us.

Flanked or not, it will be easy for our adversaries to win, which I hope means I'll be captured sooner rather than later.

The Titan army spreads out when they see us. Ready to open fire, they form ranks, turning their backs on the setting sun, twenty degrees above the hazy horizon. The atmosphere flares with rays of yellow and orange sunshine as they prepare for battle.

Twenty feet away from us, a man with a tactical scope sizes up the enemy, hunching against a backdrop of limestone and tufts of yellow grass, raises two fingers and then a fist while gazing through his scope. A leader translates the man's message into words.

"The enemy is preparing to fire mortars. Take cover or pre-empt?"

"Do not give away our position," Apollo says. "They may see us, but they don't know our configuration, which creates an advantage. Take cover."

Ten seconds pass while a sultry breeze lifts from the chasm like bubbles of heat from a river of lava. Eight more seconds. The wind disturbs the brush, and the archers hunker lower into the mountainside. Five more seconds. Then three.

WAR.

The first salvo takes the form of a dozen rockets whizzing through the sky as loud as jet planes, charging us like comets. When they explode against the rock face a few degrees from where we stand, the launchers send volleys ripping back through the sky while the archers wait for the enemy to get within range. The bombs explode across their front with blossoms of flame, sweeping dozens of combatants off their feet.

Minutes pass before the archers loose their arrows, then thousands of projectiles arc through an expanse of blue, raining down on the enemy like a swarm of angry wasps. As the launchers ready another mortar salvo, Ares's men lurch toward the enemy flank in melee and ranged combat. The riflemen above us busy themselves scouting opponents and picking them off one by one. Before they've dented our forces, we've cut down hundreds of them.

But we're still outnumbered.

I am hunkered beside Marissa when one of Apollo's commanders approaches me, carrying a silver-hilted sword hammered out of flawless stainless-steel. "Commander Kerry," he says, nodding. "Your weapon, sir."

"Don't call me *sir*, or even '*commander.*' We are equals."

"Are we?" Marissa speaks up. "Then maybe you should both listen. We have a problem."

I glare at her, raising my eyebrows. "Such as?"

She hesitates, relaxing her shoulders and letting her eyelids droop. "Maybe ten to twenty percent of their army is dead, and I can't get a reading on another ten percent. Which means we're facing a diverse army..."

The rifles drown out the last few words of her warning, but I understand her meaning. Forces that varied will require a greater diversity of attacks, and because we are shorthanded, it's a tall order. If we're to enjoy any chance of success, the battle will need to wind down faster than we anticipated.

"Slow down the attacks, Commander," I order.

"Sir—Kerry? I highly suggest we—"

"We want them to think they've overwhelmed us sooner rather than later," I respond. "It will mean we save ourselves hundreds of lives while getting to their leaders faster."

"Which Titans do we expect to command this army?" the commander asks, glancing up at Apollo, who surveys the battle scene while the rifle blasts ebb.

"They have two other battles at present," Apollo says. "That will mean four leaders, because of the importance of this fight. Our intelligence suggests Theia, Hyperion, and Themis will accompany Cronus. Prepare accordingly!" he orders the commander. Then, glancing at me, "Kerry, please consult."

I swallow. "If it's Hyperion, he's going to distract us with light and, judging from the sun's angle, they have a tremendous advantage there. I know how to play Themis and Theia. When they arrive, Theia should predict each move we make and detect our hiding place. And if I know Cronus well enough, he'll attack the mountain with meteors, to cause a landslide. We have less than thirty minutes to get off the mountain."

"Commander," Apollo says, "alert your company. March through the gorge and meet them head-on. Kerry, you will loop out and meet their west flank, while Commanders Archus and Typhus take their men east through the foothills. Coordinate your status as you march."

"*Sir...*" I begin, trying to engage him on a more personal level. Before I can express my thoughts, the cliff face across the gorge explodes, sending a cascade of fighters plunging to their deaths. "Sir, with all due respect, they expect that I'll be here, and will therefore—"

"I know that, Kerry," he says, sounding impatient. "You have three hundred men. With us dividing, they will expect you to command the largest force, thereby minimizing their numerical advantage. Trust me, I've been doing this longer than you've been alive."

"Brilliant strategy," Marissa says. "I go with Kerry or none of this works. Deal?"

Apollo nods, signaling for us to move. I march away from the cliff face while my forces gather behind me. "Onward," I yell, raising my sword.

My three hundred soldiers, a mixture of men and women dressed in robes and tunics, wearing their breastplates high, are already sliding their visors down over their faces. The sun dips closer to the skyline as we march through the brushlands in the foothills, taking the path of least resistance like a stream. Our descent takes us forty minutes, during which I glance at the sky every so often to gauge what the Titans are doing. So far, everything remains silent. When they arrive, I'll know it. Then again, they might already be here, timing their appearance for when we emerge on their western flank.

"Ten minutes until range," I announce into the radio. "What's your six?"

"Do you even know what that means?" Marissa whispers.

"No idea."

"Great, they gave command to someone who never even plays first-person shooter games. I can't say I blame them."

"I have, too!" I say, remembering the times when Quin and I would strategize before and during battle against an expansive alien civilization bent on destroying humanity forever.

Ten minutes pass faster than I could have anticipated. We round the base of a pyramid-shaped foothill with three hundred soldiers ready for battle. Armed with semi-automatic rifles and a small supply of grenades, spears, arrows, and swords, our company stops when I raise my fist. To gauge whether we're out of earshot, I wait fifteen seconds before announcing orders.

I lay out a simple battle plan: "Form up. Guns up front, all sixty of you, followed by spears and swords, with archers in the back. We're going to fan out on approach, keeping even fire so they can't focus their retaliation. This will be a fight for our planet's future. Remember that. The enemy will never surrender, but we can still emerge victorious. On your mark!"

Marissa keeps close to my side while the soldiers form ranks. Less than three minutes later, they're ready, and before I launch them into battle, I look at the spiritualist. "How many dead here?"

She shrugs. "A few hundred, give or take. I still can't figure what makes up that last ten percent, which has me worried."

"Mechanical," I answer. "They're going to be hard to bring down and will chew through us like we're nothing."

"Alright, slight strategy update," I announce to the troops. "Focus grenade attacks on the mechanical animals. I'll provide cover where I can. Ten seconds."

I count down, pausing on three, and gulping before two and one. "GO!"

In unison, our three hundred warriors sprint toward the base of the hill, cresting a small rise where the opposing army awaits. They have created a wall of bodies a half-mile long, shaking spears and wielding ranged weapons.

They unleash their weapons on us as we sprint toward them. I run with my sword held aloft, Marissa keeping pace in my dust. The warriors scream as they fan out, earth-shaking detonations and blasts echoing through the chaos as they go. Just before we reach them, the sun explodes into a blinding white orb shrouding the island in an agonizing white. Hyperion has made his appearance.

In simultaneous motion, rocks and fireballs rain down, pockmarking the mountainside with craters and fiery explosions that emit mushrooms of flame and black smoke into the sky. Battling against the light is impossible, but before long the sun dims, hiding behind a thick gauze of smoke as the entire landscape goes up in flames, fanned by winds blowing northward. I settle into my domain as the gunmen battle on all fronts. A dozen enemies die in a split second, while our arrows slam into the craniums of eyeless undead behind them. They screech with cries of war as we blast them apart, but they also volley their attacks effectively, cutting down a dozen riflemen before a single grenade goes off.

Our soldiers, carrying spears and swords, now run into the fray as the gunshots die down. We have spent all our ammunition in a few moments, making too little impact on the enemy. Marissa's estimate of a few hundred dead may be spot-on, but they're so mixed in with the army that she'll need time to communicate with them. She hides behind me as I advance into the commotion.

Enemies spurt out of the smoke by the hundreds, slashing and hacking at us to whittle our numbers down, while Cronus continues bombarding the mountainside with projectiles from the sky.

When the meteors enter the atmosphere, the compressing air heats them until fan-shaped plumes of smoke, dust, and fire erupt by the dozens. If he were a decent marksman, he might wipe out our entire force.

Yelling scours my throat as I cut apart enemy soldiers, slashing my sword in a figure-eight motion, and I can feel my emotions growing darker. Remembering Sarah and Becky causes my sword to glow, and as it does so it speeds up as though propelled by its own burst of energy, independent from the power in my body. I slice fifteen of them apart as my forces fall one by one. Screaming lets the power in my veins loosen, and when I reach concentrated energy, I form it into a ball of forked lightning that sparks off the tip of my sword into dozens of the foe, who fall dead in an instant.

Still hacking away, I feel a sudden gust of hot wind coming from down the slope. A host of Shades emerge on us seconds later, ready to devour us all.

They hesitate for a moment before beginning to swallow swordsmen. Mechanical servos whirl in the black space behind them, ready to pounce at a moment's notice. Emitting more light than the Shades can counter, I advance on them, cutting down ten enemy swordsmen as I go.

Marissa slinks back as I march forward, still protecting her with my light, as a mass of troops converge around the last of our unit, my three hundred having diminished to only thirty. I feel the Shades focusing their power on me, converging into a superstorm that sparks with lightning before my eyes. A menacing shroud of black covers the landscape as mechanical wolves chew up the remainder of my troops.

Only dim echoes of my humanity spread through my mind as the lightning forks off my sword tip to join in with the Shades. I growl as they approach, watching them eat their own forces as they advance.

Yes, I know you.

Please, not again!

In the name of Zeus...

I roar as every ounce of energy I can muster pours into my sword, impaling the super-Shade with millions of volts. And then I hear it—and feel it.

Dad. Daddy. Visions of running on the beach, tossing a frisbee back and forth illuminate my subconscious mind, as if conjured from thin air. Ian laughs, spins, and flings the disc as far as it can fly while the wind carries it into the lapping waves from a personal watercraft. *"Go get it,"* he calls, as if daring me to battle the demons of the deep. His voice grows darker as the storm rages within my heart. *I did it. I'm no longer human. I have transcended. And soon you will too, Dad. Join him, with me.* He exhales, his eyes drooping with sorrow, and ink-black stains streak down his pallid face. *The One!*

Ian.

God, no.

I scream as my Shade son rips me apart atom by atom, turning my skin to mush. "NOOOOOOOO!!!!!!"

You feel me now, my servant. Become your destiny and your life will be complete. You will live with your wife and son forever in happiness.

The darkness lurches. And then it all fades away as a flash of dark energy races out of me, blasting a vast, blackened crater where I once stood. The last thing I can hear is my sword clinking at my feet.

My adversaries surround me as my mind reforms itself within my pulverized body. I feel as though flaming plumes of sawdust and glass are cutting through my every pore.

"You're good and captured now," a calm but menacing voice says. I can sense only an amorphous blob of color and light nearby, but I already know who's talking.

"Cronus," I rasp. "Can't say I'm surprised."

"You are defeated, Kerry, Titan of Light and Shade."

The light grows brighter as the shapes sharpen into blurred images of men and women standing around me. One of them—a woman with long blond hair curling to her waist and a white robe fluttering on the scorching breeze—says, "You have fought bravely. You should be commended for your efforts, but we now must inflict on you the punishment you deserve."

"Themis," I say through gritted teeth. "I'm glad you're here." Pain saws through me, and I spit out dust and blood.

"And Theia, and Hyperion," Cronus says. "It is the end for you. We shall take you to The One."

"What do you think should happen to me?" I ask. "Cut out my entrails and burn my body on a cross just to watch me suffer, and then send a meteor down on top of me to clean up?"

"Something like that," he says, grinning.

"We are not cruel," Themis warns, her voice as sharp as glass. "The treason you have committed is worthy of a noble death before your master. It will be painless."

"But then, how will your brother get his jollies?" I tease, although the pain is numbing my nerves as I spit it out. "What do you think, Theia? Does such cruelty match up with your religious values?"

"I do not make the rules I live by," she says. "We are just."

"But your brother just said he wanted to rip off my testicles and feed them to the zombie Typhon, didn't he? You should put him in his place."

"Your diversionary tactics will not work," Theia says, but her voice is growing crooked and sallow. "Let us make for his lair."

"The hell we will," Cronus growls. "I want to watch him burn."

"You will get your chance to see him die," Themis croaks, waving her hand in an attempt to dismiss the tides of his anger.

"He'll still be alive when he meets The One," he barks.

"Good one!" I say, trying to sound callous. "But you forgot your maniacal laugh. Doesn't that help you feel all-powerful?"

"Your taunting will not be effective," Theia says. "We have planned for your outburst from the start. We structured our whole battle plan to capture you, and be assured that nothing your little friend says will turn the hearts of the dead."

"Well then, what are we waiting for? Let's go."

"Patience," Hyperion warns. "We must travel to the entrance at the banks of the Styx by flight. I shall carry you."

With little warning, Cronus launches himself at me, curling his meaty fingers around my throat and shoving a rusty blade into my gut. "An incision here and there won't kill you," he whispers, goading me to attack him.

I try to summon enough energy to block him, but I fail. No darkness, no light, just a stripped-down version of me, suffering like never before. The torturous throes of agony hurl themselves at me rapid-fire, burning my intestines to cinders.

"Cronus!" Themis warns.

"Feel it. Kerry. All that pent up rage and aggression. Tell me how this blade feels in your gut."

I scream, shattering my lungs and shredding my throat with enough defiance to erase my voice.

But I recognize the right moment as he lunges forward again. To immobilize him, Hyperion sends a blinding wave of light straight toward us. I close my eyes as Cronus's blade slashes across my flesh, drawing a hot line of blood upon my stomach. Rage floors me, but now that my plan is in motion, I cannot speak—I can only act.

His moment of disoriented confusion causes him to stumble, and in that split second before his hands let go of my throat, I draw energy from him. It is a caustic brew of blackness and light that sets my veins on fire. Bringing all the courage out of my heart, I wrap my arms around his neck and squeeze, combining the light and the dark into a compressive headlock that could very well kill him. He fights back by punching me in the ribs, but I don't release him.

Together, we fall to the dusty earth, pounding at each other with bloody fists until I straddle him, channeling all the energy he gave me down into my fist. With one vicious strike, I slam my bloody fist into his crotch.

Howling, he throws me off, launching me twenty feet and pouncing on me as I roll to a stop at Themis's feet. She fends him off by holding up one hand, bringing forth a contortion of air pressure that locks him in place. I launch myself at him, growling as I go, but Theia captures me in a rope of light before I can reach him.

"Your plan has been foiled," she snarls, tightening the rope around my throat and causing excruciating pain. "We will take you to your master now."

"That's where you're wrong," I say.

Theia and Themis glower at me, curling their lips into ugly sneers, but saying nothing as Hyperion approaches to fly me to the gates of Hades.

"I have no master, and The One has his hands tied. You'll never make it."

"We shall leave now," Hyperion says, wrapping his lanky hands around my arm.

Light does a funny thing to a Titanic gift in a human body; as soon as he touches me, I glow with enough power to disorient him. I channel all the light into electricity, zapping all four of them with a single burst of energy.

Theia sees it coming before it happens and summons a grounding compression to catch and absorb the lightning, but it does not work. The fight is not over yet.

Cronus rises to his feet, snarling with terrifying rage as he bears down on me, but four streaks of light encircle him, blasting Themis, Hyperion, and Theia off their feet. When the four streaks of light have merged into one, I see my feet leave the ground even as Theia tries to pull me back. The two opposing forces might tear my body apart, but a fifth channel of light disorients her, loosening her grip as the gods carry me to salvation.

My sight vanishes as darkness crowds my heart. Ian is a Shade. That fact has rocked me to my core, shredding everything I thought I knew. A Shade. A servant of The One True God of Darkness, Erebus himself. My plan is unraveling, and before I lose consciousness, I see Sarah's image fluttering over the southern horizon like a misty, undulating beacon. I have found her.

36

The Trial

*T*he valley of the daemons burns with the fires of war. Low-lying brush plants, turned ashen-gray, burst into flames and emit toxic smoke as the Spartan armies trample the dry grasses underfoot. When the first Spartan attacks, the daemons multiply, staggering out of the underbrush by the score to overwhelm the opposing force. Within minutes, hundreds lie dead with deep cuts and gnawed flesh. Angry red lacerations cover every inch of exposed skin. The daemons rip Spartan helmets off, and when the force grows thin, the dead replace them, leveling the battlefield.

Screams rage through the lowland as the fires spread, scurrying up the steppe-ridden slopes and along the dry creek. More daemons pour out of the shadows, enforcing agony and dismembering multitudes of eyeless undead. Soon a thousand dismembered corpses lie strewn about the dry riverbank, their limbs sawn off by serrated teeth and razor fingernails. Some victims have had their intestines ripped out through zigzag gashes in their abdomens. They scream as the daemons remove their heads, carrying limbs and vital organs off into the night.

The massacre gains ground as thousands more zombie slaves pour into the valley from the highlands, under the angry stars blazing down from the underworld heavens.

When the Spartan commander dies, he issues one last edict to the slave armies: Fight to the end and never retreat, no matter how steep the losses and how visceral the pain. He doesn't even feel the jagged blade before his head bobs *forward, bounces off the ground and rolls to a stop with his baleful eyes stealing one last glance at the deadened night, forever devoid of wind and clouds.*

After hours of vicious warfare, the battle ebbs as the daemons corral the remaining undead into a dense knot beside the dry creek bed. Even without eyes, their faces plead for mercy as the daemons spare them.

The man overseeing the battle stands on a balanced rock perched at the rim of the ravine, flexing his weakened muscles as the daemons await further orders. He hikes downward while the blood-curdling screams diminish into wayward howls and murmurs of agony.

General Hades, the former ruler of the underworld, descends as the hordes of daemons part. He walks between them as they salute in their own way, by baring their bloodthirsty teeth and hissing in their zeal.

"Spare us, Lord of the Underworld," a waning old one grinds, his timbre wavering with swells of agony, "for we have erred."

Hades is not impressed. He parts his lips to excoriate him, but then holds himself back. "You have expressed eternal fealty to Erebus, a debt not so easily paid. You now commit treason against him, and for that, he will act with severity."

"Forgive us, Lord—"

Hades, the dark-cloaked horned gentleman, gazes at the emaciated man, chiding him with a misery-laden croak. "You must never use his name again, or refer to him as The One."

The daemon cocks his head and cranes his neck, seeming to ask how Hades plans to enforce it.

Hades understands the expression in a flash, correcting himself as he rasps on: "We shall hear it if you do, and then the pit of Tartarus will be your fate. What say you?"

"We have not repaid our debts," a female daemon drones, her spiderweb hair fluttering on a variation of air pressure. "Our Lord will not free us from servitude unless he suffers defeat."

A grimace and a sly smile cross Hades's lips. "It will be done. We march to his lair now—follow and witness the architect of your freedom."

Organizing the dead armies does not prove difficult. With the help of the most vicious of the female daemons, the bloodthirsty Keres, Hades shepherds them into rows, a block of single file lines stretching from the top of the nearest bluff to the rocky shore of the creek. The leader of the Keres hisses at the nearest emaciated undead, whipping him into submission with razor-like claws at sonic speed. He screeches and moans as a fresh round of pain torpedoes his veins.

Marching to the Lair of Erebus takes several hours as the prisoners of war number near a thousand men and women. The trek takes them over uneven ground, through rivulet channels, arroyo gorges, and grass-covered highlands before they reach the river. The Keres lead the way, baring their bloody, blackened teeth.

When they reach the banks of the mighty Styx, they pause, awaiting transport to the other side. The dead men and women cannot swim or wade. The River Styx is a corrosive liquid that would eat their souls away. Hades flies across.

Without waiting for orders, the Keres pull up stones from a shallow part of the river, causing rapids. In single file, the dead march across as Hades watches from the opposite bank. After another hour, the troops have mustered on the shores of Erebus, less than a hundred yards from the black walls of the abyss. The dead dare not enter, but the Keres escort Hades into the blackened den to hunt for the horned, black-robed figure who has enslaved the Underworld.

The Keres reach him just in time for Hades to hold up his palm, speaking into a giant wall of smoke that takes the shape of the horned darkness. "Erebus, embodiment of darkness, your reign has ended."

The shadow roars with laughter.

The Titans are reducing your forces to kindling and corpses. They shall rule the cosmos and celebrate the day you Olympians fall!

"Cronus is weak. Your strategy has failed."

Cronus is but a tool.

"Come out of your lair and see for yourself where the loyalty of your followers truly lies. You cannot control them forever."

SLAVES!!!! *His thunderous voice rolls through the rocks, air, and dust like blast waves from a nuclear explosion, carrying notes of death and destruction. The shadow sizes Hades up, rears back to attack with his horns and staff, but instead collapses into a ball of ash. He then detonates as a light bomb, carving sections of boulder from the walls and ceiling, which fall with deafening roars that echo through the chamber.*

Fire ignites in the dungeon, a soupy mass of liquified rock and bubbles of white-hot gas bursting into the chilly air. When the smoke cloud condenses into the horned frame of a seven-foot-tall man, the Keres howl.

"You see, Hades," he rumbles, "I have already carried out my plans. The dimensions of time have melted into one, so the mortals can never escape. They will learn their place or perish in the new universe I have made."

"Surrender."

"It cannot be undone, you fool!" Erebus erupts in laughter. "Humanity is under my control."

"Think again," Hades croaks. "A young woman with spiritual foresight has broken your spell. Gaze into your orb of darkness and watch as they betray you en masse. Your defeat is near."

The mirthless laughter of Erebus echoes throughout his den, causing another blast of light that shears gigantic boulders off the ceiling and sends them tumbling into the firepit of lava. "DIE NOW!!!"

The skeletons rumble together, five stories tall and relentless, ready to erase Hades. But he has one last order to issue the Keres: "Destroy the lair and drag him out to face his eternal torment."

With that, he turns on his heel and strides away, leaving the Keres to do the dirty work. They build columns of stone as fast as the skeletons can shake them down, and when Hades departs, the throng of undead soldiers leap into battle to aid them.

The battle rages for twenty minutes, after which thirty percent of the undead army lies in pieces, and piles of splintered bones carpet the cavern floor. The Keres leaders, two tall females wearing tattered cloth capes over their loins, climb up their assembled towers, wedge explosive devices into rock crevices, and crawl down to flank their enemies once again.

Erebus flees, billowing into smoke as he hurries away toward the Styx, pursued by the Keres and with the undead armies on his tail. As the explosives detonate, he launches himself into the river, where he dissolves into a black oil stain that floats away downstream.

The Keres give chase, carving trails through the wavering grasslands as they hunt him down, casting a net into the stream to trap him at last.

When Hades reemerges, the domed cathedral of black rock has crumbled, shrouding the entire landscape in plumes of dust and smoke. The One has no choice but to return to human form, and when he does, Hades slaps glowing chains around his wrists and ankles, sapping him of all the powers of darkness he wields. And as his power flames out, his control over the remaining undead loosens. So falls The One True God of Darkness, and as Hades escorts him away to Tartarus, the dead evaporate into mist, their souls freed for their final judgement at the feet of King Minos while the Minotaur watches with sympathy.

Marissa pleads with me to let go of the hatred swirling in my heart, a black soup of emotions that bubbles in my bones and flesh, yet I fail to quell the torture. Everything I once knew lies in ruins, a discarded heap of shredded feelings and memories ripped out of my brain. She cannot possibly know what plagues me. Not even the tragedy of Beau can compare, nor can her darkest nightmares. I'm alone, defeated, and destroyed.

Ian is gone forever, prowling the world as a Shade, eternally isolated from his beaten, bruised, and gunshot-wounded body. I cannot bear to think of it, of what remains of him, and not even my tears can give him justice. I am banishing hope to a place from whence nothing can return.

Twenty minutes pass as Marissa rubs my back and shoulders with her palm, the pentagram tattoo on the back of her hand moving under the Cretan starlight. I'm ready to give into the shadows at last, to become a Shade forever, yet some foreign energy sparks in me yet again.

Prometheus circles the battlefield in a fiery jet of smoke above the soldiers of the Titans, who are destroying the remainder of the Olympian army. The ultimate defeat lies before me. I am the one who freed them. The dead gave up when Marissa convinced them to surrender, and for that betrayal, their own comrades ripped them apart. But I still don't believe it. How can the slaves of Erebus surrender now? And what happens with the Shades under his control? Do they cease to exist, or are they condemned to wander the hinterlands of the underworld for eternity?

I am too miserable to work it out. The only purpose that has guided my journey from the very start has crumbled—Becky remains lost somewhere I can never find her, Ian is a Shade, and Sarah only exists as a spark in my heart.

As he lands, Prometheus sends a flaming cascade of boulders onto the Titan army. The Titans will have seen him arrive, and will kill him when they learn of his treachery. But he's played his part well as a spy for Zeus. I can only glare as he smiles at me.

"I bring good news," he says, abandoning his usual tactic of muting his emotions. "Erebus has been defeated and sent to the depths of Tartarus for all eternity, stripped of his powers. And his slaves are free. That leaves only the Titans, and we're going to catch them and put them where they belong."

"What about you?" I rasp.

"Zeus has granted me a pardon. I'll be free to assemble a new breed of six Titans. And I want you to be the leader."

"I'm not immortal," I mumble, letting my expression show my misery.

Marissa circles her arm over my shoulder, as though hugging me will make me forget the sorrow that has invaded every part of my being.

"It is not required."

"I don't need this anymore," I groan, hot tears scorching my cheeks. "It's over. There's no Titan in here." I clutch my fist against my chest and heave.

"Zeus is coming here to grant your wishes," he says, raising his eyebrows. "He'll defeat the Titans and give you freedom if you want it. He will be here at any moment."

My shoulders lurch as I moan in self-pity. It feels so unnatural and distant from my spiritual nature that it only brings more disgust. This torture began when I started traveling through the dimensions of time, and I want out. Prometheus's six new Titans must find someone else, because I will never forget the hurt that has split my soul in two.

"So, Zeus promised something," Marissa says. Her voice is wavering but her tone is sincere. "He said he would help Kerry find his soulmate and revive his son."

"He's a SHADE, God dammit!" I wail. "He can't be reincarnated."

Prometheus frowns and looks at his feet. "As I understand, that is correct. The gods don't refuse to deliver on that promise; they simply cannot.

On rare occasions, mortal human beings don't even make the cut, but for Shades, it's impossible. You understand what that entails, Kerry."

"I'm going to be a Shade right there with him," I grate. "How can that be when I promised Becky eternity?" I search my pockets for the welded washers, but they're gone. Somewhere in all the battles and time jumping, I have lost the little welded symbol. I can deal with a lost artifact, but I can never forgive myself for breaking an eternal promise.

"I'm afraid I don't have all the answers, Kerry," he says sounding dreary, "but you have helped save the world. You will be remembered for that."

"I don't care if I'm remembered, unless it's by Becky, and that's only if she can look at our time together as something like a blessing, if blessings even still exist."

"Human beings are resilient creatures," Prometheus says. "They were designed that way. When Gaia gave life to earth, she set humans apart for their capacity for virtue and wisdom. Didn't you see the way your fellow citizens battled? They refused to give in to evil. And that proves that when pushed to the brink, humanity forms unbreakable bonds, not irreconcilable hatred."

"People are animals," I growl. "Cy taught me that a long time ago."

"Perhaps he was wrong."

With that, he tilts his head sideways, watching a white circle of light float down from above us and take the form of Zeus himself. Prometheus gives him a cordial nod, steps back, and launches himself skyward, emitting a jet of orange flame in his wake.

"Kerry, Conveyor of Light and Shade," Zeus remarks, reaching into his left sleeve for a shimmering bit of metal and presenting it to me as a gift. "I believe this belongs to you."

I break down again into sobs as my fingers touch the cold, electrically-welded steel rings. He's making me a promise, yet it still belongs to Becky. It always will.

37

Fall of the Titans

The foothills spiral into darkness like foul water circling a drain as Zeus carries us up, away from the battlefield, as fast as a rocket. When I look up, the pinprick stars swirl overhead, looking like one of those time-lapse images of the heavens. Marissa closes her eyes as he vaults us above the mountain, settling us down on a rocky ledge over-looking the destruction. Pocked with burn scars and heaps of corpses, the foothills darken as the seconds tick by.

When he allows us to settle onto the ground, I shed a single tear as I observe the battlefield. Marissa's eyes narrow, as though she's checking to make sure she's alone, or offering a soulful prayer to the Triple Goddess. She goes into a trance-like state as Zeus addresses me.

"Wait here, I will bring news," Zeus says.

I snarl to stop him, causing only a second of hesitation. "What about my family? We had a deal."

Only a single, quick nod, and he shoots off like a firework, forking lightning through the sky.

We can see little from our altitude. The Titan armies and our defeated troops look like a carpet of ants, occasionally illuminating with flashes of light and glowing bursts that might be pressure waves. But no meteors rain from the sky. If Cronus were leading the battle, I would see fireballs raining from the firmament to set the earth alight, reducing the mountain to rubble.

"Son of a bitch," I growl as Marissa remains still. Her body language suggests she's communing with the dead, but does it work if they've only been dead for a few hours?

At any moment I expect the black-winged figure of Death to swoop down from the sky, to collect their souls to carry to the underworld. Yet the mountainside remains still. At the foot of the hills, light flickers and dies, flashes again, and collapses into a black pit before exploding outward in a wave of pressure. The Titans are facing their last stand, and aided by their vast army, they outnumber the ten Olympians that are battling them.

Flash. *Boom. Rumble.*

It sounds distant, yet so real. Another series of flashes precedes a short moment of silence, followed by an enormous ball of lightning that sets fire to the brushland, emitting an ear-splitting rumble that carries on the harsh wind up the mountainside.

Another arc of lightning brings more bursts of thunder while flashes of light and pressure waves are visible in the night. Continuing to track the mayhem, I witness the flashes drift east, gaining speed and growing sparser as lightning bolts chase them. The Titans are on the run.

My heart hammers in my chest as Marissa pries her eyes open to witness the spectacle. She then closes them once more for another breath of conversation with the lost spirits. If I knew what she was saying, I'd perhaps chime in with my own words of wisdom, yet ... my heart is scarred with hatred. I hope the Titans burn. I hope Zeus and the Olympians feed Cronus's testicles to the chimeras, and I hope it hurts.

Lighting forks again, blazing across the sky, producing roaring thunder as the Titans flee. With every moment, the pressure waves and flashes precede longer periods of darkness until the signs of battle disappear.

We wait for Zeus to return, for at least forty-five minutes, sitting quietly in the warm summer night while enduring our grief. It blinds me to whatever reality may lie beyond. An unspoken solitude captures the moments in vials of memory, storing them for later access, yet those memories can never carry the same amount of misery that made them.

If Ian cannot be reincarnated, I will never be whole, and Becky will have forgotten we ever had him—because he died in a different dimension of time and has become a Shade. It won't take long for acidic memories of this moment to tear my brain apart, concocting vicious hallucinations potent enough to drive me insane.

Conversation might at least bring relief from my inner demons, and when I see Marissa raising her head to peer over the cohorts of soldiers in the valley below, I know she's present enough to talk.

"What did you say to them?" I ask.

She shakes her head and looks away before lowering her eyes. "I only listened. It's complicated."

"Seems like we might have all night," I say, sighing.

"Some of it I can't tell. Call it an unspoken trust ... or visions I can't fully explain. Yet I can sense lingering themes of gratitude. For the Olympians, and even for you. It's never enough to overcome the sadness and sting of loss, but it's something. And maybe that's enough."

"I don't deserve any thanks," I say. "I did it for selfish reasons. I opened the mother of all paradoxes to save the woman I loved, broke time, and freed the Titans. And the gods are still pissed, which they should be."

"I wouldn't say that," she says. "You taught me a lot about life tonight. Courage and conviction in the face of impossible odds, despite what you've lost. If it can get through to a stubborn fool like me, I'd say the chances are good you hit them where they can feel it."

I groan in agony at the memory of Ian as a Shade. "Is it enough to replace what you lost? What did you say his name was?"

"Bo," she whispers. "Of course it isn't. But you still give me hope. And maybe when the world reaches its darkest moments, hope can be the medicine that separates life from death, victory from defeat."

"We lost," I say in monotone. "We lost everything."

She raises her eyebrows and rests her tattooed hand in the crook of my arm, where the starlight reflects off her skin, casting jagged black lines against the backdrop of the sky. "But what did we gain?"

I gaze at her tattoo as I attempt to assign emotion to her words. "Protection."

"I see you're finally coming around to the way I see things," she says, emitting a single-syllable laugh midway through her sentence.

"Praise the Triple Goddess," I say, frowning.

"Maybe not quite," she admits. "I don't need to convert anyone. Only convince them that servitude isn't the only way. Which you could probably say about most things in life, including construction?"

She strikes a chord of truth.

Should religion maintain its 'right way,' or should it evolve? This type of thought may provoke a strong reaction from Becky, but what if every religion shares basic moral values despite millennia of discord? Could this commonality enable humanity to attain what some call transcendence?

"You want to make a bet?" she asks.

I sigh. "Lay it on me."

"Your son is proud of you. Even if he can no longer feel you the way you usually feel close relatives, entanglement remains a solid concept."

"Or a cockamamie theory," I blurt out, regretting it in an instant. Scientists build hypotheses on the evidence, standing firm until a more complete understanding arises, and science may one day find evidence to confirm the idea of soul entanglement.

For a long time, I mull it over. Meaningful thought and pragmatism have always been a way to keep demons at bay, at least long enough to start the healing process. But the loss of a child won't heal no matter the countless hours of meditation a psychiatrist may recommend. Even if I live to see Becky again, it will be a long time till Ian and Sarah's deaths no longer hurt me the way they do now. It might take me to my deathbed.

After at least another half-hour, a rocket streak of dust and smoke rises out of the battlefield, approaching the ledge where we are waiting. Zeus arrives faster than I consider possible, and he's carrying a companion. Another streak of firelight erupts from the valley floor an instant later, and he lands before me, carrying a limp body with him.

When he drops the captive to the ground, rage uncoils within me, ready to strike out. I have enough energy to kick his body ten feet, yet I hold back, and my foot only makes him groan in pain.

"How does it feel?" I spit, kicking him again, rearing back to energy-punch him in the jaw. Marissa's hand isn't strong enough to hold me back, but when I feel her touch, the warmth of her fingers absorbs some of the power.

"Kerry, I deliver to you Cronus, the ruler of the cosmos and a Titan of time. What shall we do with him?"

"Kill him," I snarl.

"Kerry," Marissa interrupts, frowning.

"No ... let's make it hurt. Let's make him undo everything he did. But I want you to bring Ian back, Zeus. You owe me."

"A Shade cannot be—"

"DO IT, YOU ASSHOLE! Torture Cronus all you want. Just make sure he remembers while he's burning in Tartarus that actions have consequences."

"Indeed," Zeus says, glaring at me—the intended nuance bypasses me, but I have given up on rationality—"but perhaps we can negotiate terms."

"Like a treaty? The hell with it."

Cronus uses this opportunity to speak, although he doesn't dare look at me. His voice is outright cautious, carrying a calm tone while his muscles wane in the moonlight. "You've heard that I can manipulate time."

"Get it over with," I say, glaring at Zeus, "or I'll do it for you."

"You will untangle his dimensions," Zeus orders Cronus, holding a firm hand four feet above the Titan's mouth. "Untangle them so that he knows how to find his beloved wife, and to before his son became a Shade, and we shall bear leniency."

I growl. "He doesn't deserve leniency."

"Tartarus won't be so awful," Cronus says, squirming. "I have a few friends there."

"You shall be stripped of your powers to control time and the cosmos," Zeus says, laying out the terms of his punishment. "In exchange for your manipulation of time, you will get to keep your fingers and toes and endure only moderate pain and suffering."

"Just kill me," Cronus pleads.

"DO IT," I bark.

"This is the deal I offer you, Kerry," Zeus says, the timbre of his voice rising into a tempest. "Take it or leave it. I expect you to make a wise decision."

"Fine," I growl, kicking Cronus in the shin. "Make it happen."

"I'm a bit weak at the moment," he complains. "Maybe if you give me a boost?"

He's suggesting I lay my hands on him, which I'm more than happy to do. Kneeling on the rocky outcrop, I close my eyes and dig my fingers into his scalp with enough pressure to draw blood. When I feel a spark of energy pulse through my fingers, I let it seep into him, one precious drop at a time as I claw my fingers through his hair until they're bloody.

"Yes," he says, ignoring the pain. "Now let me work."

Cronus closes his eyes while flexing his muscles, gathering the cosmos in his hands as he spins it like a baker swirling a ball of dough. Ten minutes later, he opens his eyes, looks up to the heavens, and relaxes. "It is done. Wait four hours for everything to finish aligning and, in the meantime, let me give you a hint on how to capture my traitor brothers and sisters."

"We will track them down," Zeus promises.

Before he is finished speaking, Prometheus lands on the rock, glowing like coals at the end of a bonfire.

"*You* are a traitor," Cronus growls upon seeing him. "You will die screaming."

"I will pardon my loyal servant for his crimes," Zeus says, curling his lips into a sneer.

I tune them out while I rest my head on Marissa's shoulder. If he changed everything, why does it all feel the same? Unless he was lying. Rather than dwelling on it, I let the sting of remorse prowl through my head until I can only produce heart-wrenching tears. In moments, I give in to a restless sleep.

Wings flap overhead and rustle against the grass and dust at the hooded figure's feet. His black robes filter enough starlight to highlight the jagged edges, making the ensemble fade into shades of gray. His skeletal face carves a white crater in the night, punctured by faint, glowing eye sockets when he raises his scythe blade. *Dad. No. Please don't leave me. Brianne! Dad.*

When he raises his bony hands to his face, he lets the hood droop, revealing a scarred, bald scalp where the wounds of fire and warfare had touched him thousands of years ago. When he speaks, his voice echoes in my soul, morphing into the sounds of Ian's helpless wails. He utters only one sentence, which will reverberate in my soul for a millennium: "Be free."

When I awake, a predawn blue permeates the east, touching the thin clouds with hues of light yellow as the sun lingers below the horizon. Marissa rests with her head on my shoulder, having given in to sleep. When I move, her eyes twitch.

Zeus approaches from the head of a rocky trail that curves with the mountainside. Prometheus is explaining something to him in an inaudible murmur, which ceases when he sees that I've awakened.

"Good morning," he says. "Are you ready for a miracle?"

"This is a one-time only opportunity," Zeus warns. "For your service, I give you this one gift."

When his hands turn, the sky turns upside down, and the dazzling stars dance at my feet, trapping me in a reflective void cut off from the world. A chilly mist gathers out of the vacuum, spinning a tight spiral as gravity gives it form. My head aches as the memory of poison-tipped arrows punctures my calves. The mist swirls into a cyclone of fog, melting my heart. Every second stretches toward infinity.

As though I'm peering through a mirror of time, eyes emerge from the mist, followed by a gaunt face and his dark, shaggy hair. His eyes are closed, and when his naked skin appears out of the fog, my heart soars. And then, motion. He breathes, heaving and shivering. Zeus fashions him a robe from a strip of his sleeve, wrapping around his broken body as he struggles to peel his eyes open.

"Ian," I gasp, reeling. "Tell me you can hear me."

"Hi, Dad," he whispers.

"And one more thing," Zeus says, pointing to the conical mountain-top in the distance. "Courtesy of Prometheus."

The stars flutter and blink as the sky turns orange and red. The ground trembles as the air itself bursts into flame, sending embers and sparks swirling toward the heavens and evoking distant memories where the flames danced around Sarah's lifeless body. I can feel her screaming my name as her fingers slip out of mine, letting her fall into the shattered, flooded river of mud.

The fire grows with every passing second, radiating a sphere of yellow-orange light that flickers as the embers engulf the landscape. Like white-hot coals emerging from the flames, feathered wings take shape, spreading in front of the inferno like a graceful bird.

In the blink of an eye, a pale freckled face framed with auburn hair graces the wings, transforming into a beak. Sarah's image unfurls, her still-flaming wings flapping in the night. She rises higher and higher above the mountaintop, releasing a trail of billowing smoke as she ascends.

I can sense Prometheus grinning as I stare into the shimmering light, transfixed. "Allow me to introduce the Phoenix," he says. "If you'll consider joining my quest for cosmic justice?"

"A Titan," I breathe with tears in my eyes.

"A Titan."

Marissa's eyes flit open at the disturbance, reflecting the now-distant glow of Sarah's golden aura floating away into the cosmic night sky. For once, she seems at peace. I may never be normal again, but this moment will forever burnish the memory of loss and sacrifice into my heart, supplying me with the will to reclaim my life.

38

Titans for the 21stCentury

Tears soak my cheeks as Prometheus extends his hand to help me up. Once I'm on my feet and stretching my legs, I offer similar help to Marissa. Shaking her head and grimacing, she stands by herself and looks at Zeus as though to question his sincerity.

Dawn brings warmth, a fleeting feeling of comfort that expands in my heart as I look to the skies, searching for any sign of the Phoenix. She has the right to travel the world if she chooses, which wouldn't surprise me.

Although my back and legs ache, I can help Ian up. His skin is clammy, yet confidence escapes through his eyes. He pushes a hand against the rocky ground to assist me, stumbles to his feet, and pants as he glances up at Prometheus and Zeus.

For a few moments, Zeus looks away, glancing from the distant valley to the conical peak, pausing at the other side of the rocky gorge where we landed. He offers a courteous smile, then addresses Ian first, while speaking to both of us.

"When Cronus manipulated the dimensions, he tangled two strands to match you into the right realm. From here, you can find your way back home. Good luck, weary travelers."

"I'll send him a card," I choke, not meaning to sound humorous.

Ian issues a dry chuckle.

"And now I believe Prometheus would like a word. I have pressing matters to attend to at a gathering at the Acropolis. Give your wife my greetings," he says, then launches himself into the sky and disappears. I watch his smoky contrail blaze across the firmament, while feeling Marissa's hand wedged against my back as though to help me remain standing.

I can't say a word; the only thing I can do is wrap my arms around my son, squeezing him like a boa constrictor while tears leak from my eyes. For a moment his hands rest on my back, relaxing as the seconds tick by. He says nothing, wiping away the tears and staring out at the valley while Prometheus gathers us into a tight circle.

"If you have a moment for a detour," he says, glancing at me before switching back to Ian, "I want to introduce you to a few people."

I grimace and shake my head, raising my eyebrows to look at the fading stars as the rising sunlight whisks them into darkness. "I've got to find Becky."

"A few moments, and then I will help you find a portal home. You must think critically in order to return to the correct dimension."

"Then make it quick," I say, glancing at my wrist as though I'm wearing a watch. Before I feel his heavy, hot hand in mine, I reach into my pocket to grasp the welded washers, absorbing energy from them.

By craning his neck and squeezing, he takes flight with all three of us in tow. Carrying us across a field of dying stars into a constricting channel of radiance, he guides us through time at the speed of light.

"That was weird," Ian says, panting.

Marissa eases the tension with a mischievous smile, which makes him raise the corner of his mouth in reply.

The ground beneath our feet is soft and marshy, a layer of grass roots and mud overlaying a bog two inches deep. Grasses extend to the horizon in every direction, rising to my elbows before the landscape swells into a pair of shallow hills like a windswept prairie at dawn. A yellow-orange sun low on the horizon burns, blurring the grass as its light bends around the individual blades of yellow and green.

For a moment we are alone, but when I inhale the sweet country air, four other figures emerge in the grass as though they're growing out of it. All of them stand taller than me by at least four inches, even the women. They approach in measured steps, glancing at Ian first, then Marissa and me, and exchange familiar smiles with Prometheus.

Prometheus grins at me while motioning to a woman at his right with long, wavy locks curling down her back, a neat arrangement of flowers tucked behind her ear, and a dainty gold pendant hanging from her neck. Her warm green eyes promise a sense of newfound hope, and her steady demeanor draws my eyes to the gold medallion she wears It is a glowing emblem of a golden orb, with four gilded rays protruding from the top right of the disc, and the artifact spreads warmth through my veins.

"Kerry, Conveyor of Light and Shade," Prometheus says, his voice crackling with crisp energy, "I would like you to meet Eos, daughter of the Titans Hyperion and Theia, and goddess of the dawn. She's an old friend and an all-around better person than her parents."

She leans forward to rest her hand on my shoulder, shunning the typical first-meeting handshake, and causing my shoulder to glow. "The pleasure is mine, Kerry," she says.

Next, Prometheus waves his arm at a hulking figure to his right, whose wild hair whips in the breeze like tattered strings from a flag. He gazes back at me and his height grows as a long serpentine tail uncoils behind him in the grass. He flexes his pectoral muscles and swats at the long cloth of a purple cape. His gemstone eyes reflect the dawn, scattering purple and blue light around his head like a misty halo. "This is Ophion, a former ruler of Earth and an elder statesman, as wise and cunning as they come."

He then motions to another woman, this one taller and more slender. She wears a crown of leaves like a Native American headdress above her tan face, and her opalescent eyes flicker in the morning light as she gazes at me as though longing for a distant secret I don't even know myself. Her green dress has short saccharine sleeves that look like thin moss. Turquoise strings of beads are sewn to the square neckline and waist, flowing like rivers in the cooling breeze. Leaves and berries adorn her shoulders, soaking up the morning sun.

Prometheus smiles as he introduces her. "Kerry, meet the Oceanid Dione, daughter of Oceanus and Tethys."

"Pleased to meet you," I say, reaching to shake her hand. She hesitates, grabs it, and pulls me into a quick, comfortable embrace.

"Finally," Prometheus says, "allow me to introduce my brother, the father of all animal attributes and defender of life. This is Epimetheus."

Epimetheus stands taller and lankier than his brother, and his golden crop of finger-length hair waves in the sun. His bulging biceps bracket a washboard torso, and a tattoo of a rhinoceros crosses his left shoulder. He gazes at me for several moments before extending his hand for me to shake. His grip is light and uncertain, but when he gets the hang of it, he grips me more fully and pulls me into a big man hug.

"My friends, please meet Kerry's companion and friend Marissa, a guardian of spirits, and his son, Ian. Kerry is a long-lost descendant of the Six Cretan Titans, a man destined for greatness."

They smile at Marissa and Ian before Prometheus continues: "Kerry, I formally invite you to join the five of us, the new Titans of the cosmos, formed with Zeus's blessing." He notes my pained expression and waves his palm. "You will have your own life. We live in our own separate domains, relying on each other only when we need help. When the other eleven Titans join Cronus in Tartarus, the universe will need heroes ready to pitch in. Do you accept our appointment?"

I stare at him while glancing at the other four. For more than a minute, I can't speak. I expect my expression carries the full weight of my emotions. My legs twitch as a nervous tic of pain wriggles through my veins, and my skin feels cold with adrenaline. "I don't think I'm cut out for it," I say, "but if you insist."

"Excellent," Prometheus says, glowing. "We are the New Titan Order."

Marissa's eyes light up. "Neato!"

Prometheus laughs while I glare at her through weary eyes. The first dad joke I've heard in a different dimension, and it came from the self-proclaimed dealer of the occult and lover of spirituality.

When the introductions are complete, Prometheus notes the time by glancing at the rising sun, rests his palm on my outstretched hands, and flexes his muscles. He takes us far away and the green and blue landscape disappears into night amidst a sea of glittering stars.

A moment later, we emerge in the destroyed streets of Philadelphia at dawn. Smoke still rises from a thousand dying fires, choking what remains of the city in a hazy soup of smog that ebbs each time a light breeze blows.

Bidding us farewell, Prometheus flies away, leaving us alone amidst the rubble of the city I once called home, where bodies are still buried in the ruins, trapped in cars, or rotting in the storm drains. It reeks of death, but when I look around I see pairs of eyes peeping from the shadows to greet us. Dozens of humans and animals emerge, gazing upon us with wary expressions, trying to discern whether we are heroes or enemies. Judging by what remains of the landmarks, I assume this is the old-town segment of Market Street, where I once met a man on a street corner and shared a pastry with him. I recognize the corner the moment we arrive. Its toppled green-cross signs poke out from a haphazard pile of crumbled bricks, dust, and glass. The building's roof might lie in five different ZIP codes by now, torn away during the destruction, trusses and all. A few columns of ash-covered steel are sprouting up amongst the rubble, trembling in the morning sun.

Amidst it all, a woman stands alone with a straw broom, beginning to sweep up the colossal mess as though she knows where to start. I gaze at her for five minutes until a lightbulb clicks in my brain. Marissa recognizes her before I do. Together, we stop at the broken, glass-covered sidewalk embedded with a metal curtain wall strip where the storefront once stood. She peers at us and drops the broom, snakes her way through the disaster and greets us with solemn hugs.

"It's good to see you again," she says, her voice strained with weariness, yet crisp and friendly. "If you have come back for your final healing session, Kerry, I'm afraid I need to clean up first. My apologies."

I rest my palm on her joined hands and force myself to smile. "You make a compelling offer. But I have unfinished business myself."

"I understand that, and good luck," she says. A rat scurries out of the wreckage and darts for the haven of a storm grate.

"I want to say thank you," I say, gulping in shame. "What happened here is pretty much my doing, but I will make it up to you. I promise."

"What happened here cannot be blamed on one man," she says. "Maybe in some way, we all played a part. But I might be the only person in this city who's truly seen your heart. You are a good man."

As we wander away from the historic district, feeling dismay at all we see, none of us can speak. We dart into a side street where the parking garage stands as sloped, pancaked concrete decks ringed by crumpled aluminum railings. Across the street, a jumbled pile of bricks, glass, insulation, bare pipes, bits of broken sheetrock, and sparking wires fills the alley. A moment later, we enter a familiar side street and cross to a corner where the two walls meet, and the black stain still exists. It has resisted multiple attempts at cleaning and sandblasting, and it only makes sense that portals should be durable. After all, the dimensions they hold together are. Hoping it still works, I turn to face Marissa, gathering the courage for a last goodbye.

I try to bring the right words through my tears, and fail. She slings her arms around me and closes her eyes. "I'm going to miss you," she says. "Pay a visit sometime, will you?"

"Thank you," I whisper. "For everything. For helping me learn and grow as a man. For turning our fortunes in the war ... for all of it."

"Don't mention it," she says. "And don't forget to bring your lovely wife when you visit. I'd love to meet her."

I turn and place my hand on the blackened brick, grasping Ian in my other fist as the portal whisks us through the heavens, until our feet connect with gravel and sand.

The lake strikes a vibrant balance, of cobalt between azure sunshine and verdant forested hillside. A few couples relax on the beach or swim in the shallows. A pair of jet skiers skims the choppy surface of the water.

As far as I remember, each time I landed here I made first for the island, yet now the cabin has vanished, and trees are growing where it should be standing. I turn to face the lake house, uncertain of what dimension we have stumbled into. What if I knock on the door? Will the crazy man with the gun answer, threatening to blow me away for trespassing again?

I decide to try my luck.

Remembering the house better than I do, Ian leads the way up the beach, through a section of matted grass and toward a black wrought-iron fence standing six feet tall. He scuffles through a patch of gravel past a cooling unit and a gas meter, around to the front of the house. I feel my nerves spike as hope pours through me.

It feels like home—a proper home. A place to stretch my feet, curl my arm around my wife's waist, and watch the fire crackle in the hearth. Comfort. Ian spins the handle, pushes open the door, and rests his hands on the oval kitchen table.

She scrambles up from the sofa, disturbed from an afternoon slumber, a confused look on her face when she sees Ian. But as she looks at me, she glows. I reach my hand into my pocket, feeling the cool steel turning in my fingers, walk over and gather her in the warmest embrace I've ever given her. Tears wet her cheeks when she pulls away, rests her hands on my shoulders and kisses me. "I waited a long time for this," she sniffs. "Decades. What made you choose today?"

"It's funny you should ask," I explain between multiple kisses. "I'm sure I got pulled away again—no, you won't remember that, and it's probably best not to try explaining it right now."

"Ker—"

I kiss her again, letting my tongue slip between her lips for a split second. When I pull away, I gaze at Ian, trying to decide how to reintroduce them.

He does it for me. He pounces on her like a lion cub wrestling a sibling, hugs her and whispers, "Mom," over and over.

"I want you to meet our son, Ian," I say, wrapping my arms around them both.

She gazes into Ian's eyes for a moment as if to memorize his face, deciding that he resembles me, and opens a dormant path of memory in her mind. "Yes," she whispers. "I remember. So handsome."

My heart feels like it's beating a million miles an hour as I gaze out at the sparkling waters lapping against the sand like fine wine on a warm summer's day. This moment will live on in memory for the rest of time. The most joyous, complex emotions are flowing through me like a nourishing flood. The energy causes me to glow, and when Becky sees it, she smiles as though she always knew it was there, lying somewhere below the surface of my heart and just waiting for the right moment to burst forth and carry her away.

I don't want to move a muscle because if I do, and she disappears again, I'll never forgive myself.

In case the energy and emotion aren't already palpable enough, I reach into my pocket, pull out the welded washers, and hold them aloft in my palm. Tears flood her cheeks as she curls her fingers around them, burying her hands in mine and kissing me like never before.

A moment later, Ian interrupts us. "I guess I'd better get home. Care to show me the way, Dad?"

Not right now—but he's right. This is the wrong dimension and leaving him here would be another enormous mistake. Besides, he needs to see the woman he loves. Brianne.

"I don't want to go," I mutter, kissing Becky once again. "Save a spot on the couch for me, will you?"

"Of course," she says, her tone flat. "Just promise me this time you'll come back?"

I nod and smile before facing the door, with Ian leading the way.

Now that I must escort Ian home, a memory pops into my head. A man I came across on the street before I met Marissa. The sparkle in his eyes now seems familiar enough to choke me. The doting, fatherly love for his newborn daughter felt so wholesome, even as people ran through the streets in terror after a building crumbled and fell. Her name rings in my head as I lean to pull the front door closed. Vanessa.

I can only smile as the warm memory pours through me like a vivid pool of mercury and chardonnay. The Great Bear, Callisto.

When I pull on the door handle to close it behind me, Becky's voice sounds from beside the sofa.

"Ker?"

I grin as the loving nickname swells through my soul.

"You're still in trouble."

Glossary

Ambrosia—the food of the gods, which gives them their powers.□

The Argonauts—heroes who sailed with Jason to Colchis in search of the Golden Fleece aboard their ship *Argo*.

Artemis—goddess of the hunt and protector of all animals.

Big Dipper—part of the constellation Ursa Major, or the great bear, named after the goddess Callisto, who was transformed into a bear.□

Calypso—A nymph who detained Odysseus. Her name means 'to cover,' 'to conceal,' or 'to hide.' □

Campe—the female monster who served as a guard in Tartarus for the Cyclopes and Hecatoncheires, whom Uranus had imprisoned there.□

Charybdis—Scylla's companion monster, who sucked in seawater to devour ships.□

Chiron—A wise centaur and a son of Cronus—the brother of Zeus.

Coeus—a Titan, the god of questioning and intelligence.□

Coronides—two nymph daughters of the giant Orion. When the land of Boiotia was struck by drought, they sacrificed themselves to the gods. Then in pity, Persephone transformed them into comets.□

Cronus—the son of the primordial god of the sky, Uranus. According to legend, Cronus castrated and murdered his father to assume control of the cosmos.□

Cy—the nickname of Cygnus, a king of Liguria, who died of sorrow after the death of his friend or lover Phaethon. Zeus transformed him into a swan and placed him in the heavens after his death.□

Deimos—The personification of fear in Greek mythology, and brother to Phobos. Deimos is also the name of Mars's smaller moon.□

Dione—a sea nymph goddess, or Titanide, a daughter of the Titans Oceanus and Tethys.□

Disaster—from the Greek words 'dis' for 'bad' and 'aster' for 'star.' The Greeks believed that some stars could signal destruction.

Dolos—the god or spirit of trickery and guile. He was an offspring of Gaia and Aether, or Erebus and Nyx, and an apprentice of Prometheus.□

Entanglement—the physical phenomenon where pairs of particles, which are also waves, interact over vast differences of time and space, per a long-running discussion between physicists Niels Bohr and Albert Einstein.□

Eos—the Titan goddess of the dawn, known for opening the gates of heaven each morning to herald the arrival of her brother Helios. She is the daughter of the Titans Hyperion and Theia.□

Ephialtes—also known as Epiales, a daemon and personification of nightmares.□

Epimetheus—the brother of Prometheus, a Titan god of afterthought and excuses, who was later tasked with repopulating the earth. He delivered traits to all animals.

Erinyes—the graceful ones, known in English as the Furies. They were the goddesses of vengeance in Greek mythology.

Eris—the Greek goddess of strife and discord, and the name of a dwarf planet in the Kuiper Belt.

Gemini—the half-brothers Castor and Pollux. Castor is the son of Leda and Tyndarus, the king of Sparta, while Pollux is a son of Zeus.

Harmonia—the goddess of harmony and concord, the opposite of Eris.

Hecate—a moon goddess of Greek mythology often depicted holding a key and a torch and accompanied by dogs.

Hestia—the virgin goddess of the hearth and home, the firstborn daughter of the Titans Cronus and Rhea, and one of the original twelve Olympians.

Hypnos—the personification of sleep.

Io—one of the mortal lovers of Zeus, a priestess and servant of the matron goddess Hera (the wife of Zeus). When the affair was discovered, she was transformed into a heifer to keep her safe. Hera tasked the giant Argus to guard her.

Iris—a goddess of color and light.

Meliae—the ash tree nymphs, they were born from the blood of the castrated Uranus and were considered the wives of the Silver Race of Man and the mothers of the Bronze.

Melinoe—a goddess of nightmares and madness. As a daughter of Zeus and

Persephone, she was known to haunt mortals and communicate with the spirits of the dead, giving her a connection to the underworld.□

Moirai—the Fates, three sister goddesses responsible for granting destinies to mortals at birth.□

Nyx—the goddess and personification of the night, she was born of Chaos. She is the mother of several primordial powers, including Sleep, Death, the Fates, Nemesis, and Old Age.□

Ophion—an elder Titan god of wisdom, who was later overthrown by Cronus and Rhea.□

Orphic Eschatology—a set of religious beliefs and practices in the ancient Greek and Hellenistic world, associated with literature ascribed to the poet Orpheus, who travelled into the underworld and returned.□

Pandora—the first female human created by Hephaestus on the instructions of Zeus. She is famous for opening a box or jar containing all the ills of humanity and releasing them into the world.

Paradox—from the Greek word paradoxon, which means 'contrary to expectation.'□

Phobos—the Greek god of fear, a son of Ares and Aphrodite, and the brother of Deimos, the personification of fear and terror. Phobos inspired the name of Mars's larger moon. Ares is the god of war in Greek mythology and Mars is the corresponding Roman god of war.□

Prometheus—a Titan god of fire, although not one of the original twelve Titans. He is a son of the Titan Iapetus.□

Pyre—from ancient Greek, it is a structure made of wood for burning a body as a funeral rite.□

Satyr—half-man (or woman), and half-goat (or horse), known for its love of music.□

Scylla—a monster occupying a narrow strait, with many serpent's heads.□

Shades—the spirits of the dead in Greek mythology.

Sirens—birdlike spirit creatures who mimicked loved ones to lure sailors to their deaths on rocky shores.

Thanatos—the personification of death. He was often the last vision of soldiers dying in battle, and is otherwise known as the grim reaper.□

Titanomachy—the war between the Titans and the Olympians. The Olympians betrayed the Titans to gain control over the universe. After losing the war, the Titans were imprisoned in Tartarus, along with Prometheus, who later earned Zeus's forgiveness.□

Tragedy—a Greek performance play featuring satyrs, often inflected with sadness.□

Triple Goddess—from paganism, a powerful archetype found in many spiritual traditions, representing the three phases of a woman's life: maiden, mother, and crone.□

Zephyrus—god of the west wind.

The following sample chapters of the next book in the series, as follows, are early drafts and will not reflect the final text

Plato's Forms

*A*nother *Dead Body.*

The new *Philadelphia Daily Phoenix* tries to weigh the occurrence by reporting another tragic death as if bodies haven't been turning up daily for the past year. Ho hum. Just another dead person.

But this is no ordinary body. When I consume news, I make a habit of scanning the first few paragraphs rather than just the headline to gauge my interest in the story. One name jumped out at me: Former mayor Archinson, or as I call him, Archimedes. The victim. According to the *Phoenix*, authorities uncovered disturbing evidence of foul play.

True enough, the "authorities" these days are little more than paid bounty hunters hired to take on dirty tasks such as bringing in "criminals" dead or alive. Often, the perpetrator is dead. The bounty hunters run under the auspices of The Freedom Brothers, a well-funded organization governing the city by unconventional practices, which often include money-laundering, bribery, slander, and outright murder. They keep the city in check, at least in the eyes of Harrisburg and Washington.

To me, the circumstances call for careful consideration of all the known facts. No one ever elected the Freedom Brothers. They command a city of 100,000 people. A prominent band of invested citizens has risen over the last year, calling the Freedom Brothers a vast criminal enterprise. And while the description fits, the new group, which calls itself United Philadelphians for Progress, isn't much better. In under a year, UPP has taken credit for the murders of at least three FB officials, ostensibly to reestablish democracy in its United States birthplace.

Not surprising. And there's nothing I can do about it. If I run off to Philadelphia without her consent, Becky might kick me out for good.

I love her. She maintains a curious sense of humor and style throughout our travails, often chiding me, using that cute little smirk when she knows something is bothering me. And the current state of Philadelphia keeps me up at night. Wondering whether Marissa has kept herself out of FB's attention is only secondary to sweat tremors that wake me at all hours. Citizens in terror. Gunshots. Monsters. Titans. The chilling cries of mourning mothers, husbands, and children haunt my dreams.

Becky has warned me six times that "doom-scrolling" is detrimental to my mental health, but she's suffering, too. Her memories of Ian remain incomplete, as if lengthy periods of his past have been erased from existence forever. I try filling in the holes where I can, but I face the same problems. A week ago, Ian called for the third time and Becky didn't even recognize his voice. After hanging up the phone, she retreated to the bedroom, buried her face in the pillows and sobbed for ten minutes while the moon-washed waves of the lake lapped upon the pebbly beach.

She reaches over to turn the lamp off without my approval, pecks me on the cheek, and rolls toward the hallway while I scan the article.

It should surprise me what has happened to the city I've always loved. In truth, I find that those post-apocalyptic dystopia thrillers miss an important characteristic of humanity. While the typical movies show totalitarian governments raining terror on the hapless citizens of society, the reality is even more chilling.

Although Philly has begun rebuilding from the destruction, its population remains less than ten percent of what it was before the Titans sacked it for their own nefarious ends. The competing criminal enterprises let chaos run rampant without helping those who suffer. So long as the image of justice and order prevails, Harrisburg doesn't care. Lawmakers often say the city deserved its fate, or that the people should have expected that electing fools could never achieve the desired changes. The concept has merit, although, the not-so-shocking cruelty brings headaches that transform my face into something Becky would rather not see, and that somehow makes me angrier.

And if Harrisburg doesn't act to bring order to the city, why should Washington? The Senate pretends Philadelphia doesn't exist, either out of convenience, disdain, or because it provides no funding to keep the power-hungry parties sated. Six months ago, a member of the House of Representatives referred to Philly as "the former City of Brotherly Love." Ten years earlier, that little wisecrack would have caused nationwide outrage. Now it's not even a blip on the radar. Because what Philadelphia became represents a more-nuanced version of what became of the nation.

Increasingly, politicians serve their own wishes, using ever-heated rhetoric to get elected and untold sums of dark money to keep their campaigns going strong while they do nothing to solve the nation's problems. Bickering and finger-pointing have replaced well-reasoned solution proposals for popularity.

Some days I imagine that if I were anyone important, I could run for office and change everything from the inside, ignoring the proverb that "absolute power corrupts absolutely." When that thought does creep into my mind, I wave it off because I've convinced myself that I'm better than today's politicians. But if I did get elected, would I be better after a year or two? While I consider myself a good person, I'm not ready to exert so much faith in my own moral values.

When I reach the last few words of the article, a tribute to Mayor Archinson, I toss my phone on the floor, roll to spoon Becky, and when she shrugs me off, grunt and shift toward the window, looking into the woods. A pair of cars curls along the windy avenue into the forest, skirting the scenic lake while dodging a few night-owl tourists wandering back to their cabins or bungalows on foot.

I sigh and try to will myself to sleep, but my brain conjures images of Philadelphia from the past and the present, congealing into a mass of blackened anger and weariness while the echoes of grieving mothers wilt in my ears.

Hours pass. Becky has begun snoring, letting her shoulders rise and fall with each breath and twitching every few minutes, as if a disturbing image floats into her subconscious. Maybe if she wakes up, I'll ask what's bothering her, but I know her. When she realizes that I've failed to sleep, she'll elbow me in the ribs and lecture me in the morning.

Laying in bed is useless, so I decide to arise, put on my slippers, and sift through the pile of mail that has accumulated in our black metal roadside mailbox during the week. I don't make a habit of checking often. My excuses don't amuse Becky, but why should I go out there to bring in nothing but glossy ads, dubious credit card offers, and fake get-rich-quick schemes? We pay our bills via new technology, assuming that "big brother" has no use prying into the financial lives of an average couple trying to stay as far away from the big cities as possible.

My soles shuffle on the soft carpet as I walk, the drawn curtains allowing blue moonlight to filter into the living room. We usually deposit the mail on the bay windowsill next to the plush recliner I use to escape reality by watching delusional kids' shows depicting the world as just. It may be propaganda, but if it sets my mind at ease for only a few hours, maybe it's worth the risk.

Sighing as I sit down, I grasp the letter opener in my left hand while searching in the dark for an envelope. The first I shred on sight. Regardless of who it's from, I can feel the fake cardboard credit card inside with my fingertips. "Why do these clowns still send snail mail?" I grunt to myself as I toss the shredded envelope aside. A few ad mailers make me feel better. Two pizzas for the price of one at our favorite Erie pizzeria, Romano's. This one goes in the 'worth saving' pile.

A half dozen ads go into the garbage heap before my fingers find the edges of a thin, hand-addressed envelope from Philadelphia. I recognize the return address as Miriam's shop on the corner of Market Street, but the lettering seems cleaner and more elegant than the old seer's should. I gulp as I cut the letter open to reveal the dogeared corner of a photograph printed on copy paper. A single sheet of paper awaits in the envelope, so I flip to the page to read the same penmanship on the back of the envelope. Excitement leaks through my veins as I read the written text:

Found this: I could use your help Kerry, Conveyor of Light and Shade. Come quick and I'll buy you dinner.

No other words, not even a signature. I'd consider it rude, but then again, the letter might as well be an InstaText sent through the USPS's ridiculous network. If the woman who sent the message had left a connection number, I'd send a snarky reply by recording myself saying "good one," and then forget it.

But it has a photograph.

Flipping to the front side of the page, I perceive remorse clinging to my senses before my eyes can make sense of what I'm seeing.

Cracked, pitted pavement, stained from oil, tire skids, and chewing gum create a jarring backdrop for the scene. Mayor Archinson himself peers back at me through helpless eyes. His weary, aged face hides distress and anger, as though resolution has trained the darkest of emotions out of his mind's foreground. Behind his head, a spot of crimson blood, dried and clotted, trickles toward a fragment of a white line that doesn't resemble paint. Deciding the white must be a rubberized crosswalk coating, I let my eyes scan the foreground.

Clutched in his right hand, he carries a thick, rubber-banded manila envelope stuffed with papers and photographs, the contents of which have spilled out onto the street. What little the photograph shows is hard to discern. The scene is dark, but enough residual light glints off the glossy surface to hide what the photos reveal inside a gauze of white. Minor details jump out at me. The corner of one photo may be a pediment from a Greek-styled building. I study it for several moments to determine its origin, then let my eyes wander to a hand-typed message addressed to the National Archives in Washington, D.C. The choice of font and size is unreadable, even for someone with perfect eyesight, but my vision is sharp enough to detect what the title alludes:

RESEARCH MAY UNCOVER THE LOCATION OF AT-LANTIS

"Atlantis," I grumble, as though unsure of myself. Atlantis never existed in the first place, a fictional island said to have disappeared forever, as Homer described it. For centuries, researchers and explorers have tried to uncover where the island's ruins lie, meeting certain degrees of failure every time. Dozens of missions have come back inconclusive, and even the most promising, an exploration backed by data and an enormous monetary gift has exposed only snippets of information and a ridiculous-looking Sonar image purported to show sharp lines and columns. Scientists claim that straight edges don't occur in nature; a disproven myth that has somehow outlasted many conspiracy theories.

When you look at nature with a keen eye, you see straight edges everywhere you look. The central 'veins' of leaves dart from the tip to the stem. Basalt dries in hexagonal columns under misunderstood geological forces. Various minerals form crystals in perfect geometric shapes, including the famed Platonic Solids. Water ripples in streams, especially those in small laminar flow conditions, from crisscrossing straight lines like a lattice of waves.

I toss the photograph aside, wondering what she might have meant by 'needing my help.' My research skills amount to digging through project specifications and documents, comparing construction materials and equipment to decide what fits the requirements most closely while analyzing cost savings.

"Right," I whisper. "Another mindless conspiracy."

Disinformation campaigns have labeled conspiracy theories as "proof" for many decades. Their proponents love to point out famous conspiracy theories that have been proven, often citing evidence that is at best circumstantial.

The media have been complicit in spreading these iffy stories forever. I take a moment to gauge my trust in the *Philadelphia Daily Phoenix*. The outlet claims to be the city's sole remaining source of truth, using the coincidental fall of the *Enquirer* as evidence that only the *Phoenix*'s editors are untrustworthy. Aside from the fact the *Enquirer* failed was because the city itself failed, the *Enquirer* cited facts based in thorough research to tell their stories.

The *Phoenix* instead deals in suppositions made by talented journalists and editors wishing to strike the right emotional tone through manipulative language. I've seen it in a variety of stories, including a feel-good piece about a fresh farm-to-table produce supplier feeding the many struggling citizens remaining in the city.

For this propaganda to take hold, people must rely on a single major outlet, and the *Phoenix* has used coercion and bribery to suppress competing sources, judging by my own eyes and ears. Basic research divulged various connections between the editors and FB movers and shakers.

If I can't trust the *Phoenix* for the whole truth, why should I invest even a fragment of trust in an unconvincing photograph? I can think of only one reason.

The UPP ordered Archinson's assassination to throw FB off track. The *Phoenix* reporters whitewashed the evidence left behind for a reason: The Freedom Brothers don't want the information in Archinson's hands to go public. They couldn't sanitize it because they didn't arrive on the scene first. Whoever took the picture had. Which means she's in trouble, and indeed needs my help. If the FB hasn't already dumped her in the Delaware River, I'll consider it a minor miracle.

I choke up when I wonder who may have sent the letter and mutter under my breath. "What the hell are you doing, Marissa?"

"Ker?"

I look up to see Becky standing at the entrance to the hall, her frizzled dark hair cascading to her shoulders in waves, laying limp along her gray robe's fluffy collar. The robe descends to her knees, allowing a glimpse of her lower thighs.

"Uh, good morning." I croak.

"Return to bed and let's discuss it tomorrow."

I follow her to the bedroom, lay down, settling into a comfortable snuggle while she dozes off. The demons return when I close my eyes. Meteors crash to the earth, exploding into mushrooms of orange and yellow flames, emitting clouds of black and gray smoke as they descend to destroy the city. Amidst it all, the sneer of Cronus infects the scene with the poison of rage. Did the Olympians ever corral the other eleven?

I've heard nothing in over a year. I know only one way to find out.

The Last Ptolemaic Ruler

The suspicion of weary eyes falling on me invades my demeanor with a stark warning as the shade from the deciduous trees across the road obscures the sunrise. From the hallway window, I may witness the yellow glare on tranquil waters before the boats and personal watercraft disrupt the peace. Then again, the flitting, restless gaze is more than sufficient to disrupt my morning rhythm.

How long had I slept after Becky had lured me back to bed? I don't keep track of time while I'm trying to fall asleep. The very act of focusing my mind keeps me awake at the best of times. But when something so disorienting worries me, tracking the passage of time is the least of my problems.

"Good morning, honey," I croak without so much as turning my head.

A random, minute swish in the silent air suggests she's blinking, and when she does that, she's usually concocting a way to pry me out of a stubborn frame of mind. Rather than being borne of stubbornness, my mind has constricted into digesting what Marissa's letter *really* meant and how I might go about replying to her.

Mail delivery no longer works in Philadelphia. The Postal Service no longer operates an office in the central city, making those unlucky residents sneak out to the western suburbs to take advantage of its services. And since addresses have become useless locators, any incoming mail stays in storage at the suburban station just in case Philadelphia residents know they have a letter incoming and wish to retrieve it.

I doubt Marissa will be anticipating a snail-mail expressing my disapproval. If she wanted to reach me through InstaText or the good, old-fashioned cell call, finding my number probably wouldn't prove difficult. No, she expects me to come visit. Because she wants my help to break the gang's stranglehold over city governance.

The newspapers claim the city population has risen north of one hundred thousand, a far cry for the million-and-a-half plus that called Philly home before the Titans sacked it. Partisans and government officials from outside the city often deride any attempt to estimate the total number of casualties, as if those lives ever mattered to them. The level of scorn given those who remain is another matter. In remote job site meetings, I can get away with expressing empathy for the survivors once or twice without attracting unwanted attention.

Job site coordination leadership has shifted offsite over the years, allowing me to manage teams via real-time videoconferencing. While the technology has existed for decades, it has advanced to include a virtual world, where team members can don the goggles and show me the issues compared to the construction documents without so much as clicking a button. Keeping team members productive involves daily one-on-one chats, which often break off from the team meetings by excluding those who don't need to hear the information we share. This ability has succeeded in keeping me far away from the city. While most of our work surrounds Harrisburg and Pittsburg, I hear rumors of Philadelphia projects from time to time, including a yet-to-be-approved development which promises to construct a thirty-story mixed-use product with commercial and residential components in the heart of the former financial district.

"How did you sleep?" Becky prods, resting her dainty hand on my shoulder as I gaze into the shade outside.

She leans to tap her toe on the lamp behind her to turn it on. We invest little in the trendy tech products unless they offer valuable convenience. The ingenuity of the design eliminates the problems of motion-sensors, which would be a major nuisance should we roll over during the night. Now that we don't have to fumble through the dark for a switch, we can sleep in peace until we need the light.

"Well," I start, not planning on offering an answer.

It takes two seconds for her to exhale, perhaps a sign of relief. "Deep subject."

"Yeah. Something like that."

"What were you looking at last night?"

Never one to break the ice with marital small talk, she gets right to the point, which sometimes proves unnerving, even when I expect the tactic. Planning for it is one thing, but putting the preparation into practice often leads to failure, because I'm not great at expressing half-formed thoughts without stumbling over awkward phrases or useless filler words.

"Oh, it's just another Philly thing where the gangs are wrestling for control. You know the shenanigans."

"Indeed."

"Yeah," I mumble.

She inhales and gazes at me while I turn away from the window, prop up the pillow behind my head, and look into her eyes, kissing her once on the lips. "What's going on this time?"

"I assume saw the news already."

She closes her eyes, communicating a solemn mourning. "The former mayor?"

Becky has never lived in Philadelphia. A longtime resident of Harrisburg, she worked in education when we met, staying in school leadership roles throughout our long separation. I still don't even remember how we ended up owning this lake house, but it's home now. Becky excels at sharing in the heartache when someone memorable dies, even without personal connection.

Mayor Archimedes's death would have made national news in any other era, but now he's just "another dead body." And Marissa wants me to help figure out his secrets before the gangs can lay claim to it, destroy it, or worse.

"Did you ever meet him?"

"Not personally," I recall. "He was the one who got Secretary Whitworth into public service, realizing his dreams and all that."

"And you still haven't introduced me to him," she whispers.

"Time and place," I argue. "Not really the point. Because Arch was considered a visionary, drawing the respect of many, despite party affiliation.

That's good leadership, which unfortunately seems to have fallen on deaf ears."

"Then what has you so worried?"

"Marissa found him. Before the FB or UPP did. And he was carrying a document with purported new information about Atlantis. Which means her life is in jeopardy."

She rolls over and buries her face in my chest. I can feel her curled hairs tangling in my chin stubble as I breathe in and out, watching her head rise and fall with my breathing. I glance at the television resting atop our eight-drawer dresser, its elongated shadow falling over the intricate X-pattern inlays in butternut hardwood. A handcrafted luxury piece that could fetch a thousand dollars new, Becky had paid just three hundred for it and worked to revitalize it herself.

She always had a good eye for detail, a trait that attracted me from the beginning.

"So that means you're planning on going to Philly," she says, matter-of-fact.

"I'm thinking about it."

"Acting like I don't understand how you feel again? You know better than that."

I have nothing to offer in self-defense, so I utter a sheepish sigh while eyeing her handiwork. The straight-grained inlays lay perpendicular to the grain in the surrounding wood. Cutting hardwood with that kind of precision can't be easy, especially if the woodworker wanted to keep it intact over a lifetime of use. Quality craftsmanship is so rare these days.

"You know how I feel about the city," she warns. "It was dangerous when we met, but now, I don't want you to even consider going."

"I have an adequate system of self defense," I hint. "They better bring it if they want to get at me."

"Who's they?"

Damnit. She knows my clever retorts about what I call the 'nefarious they' by heart. Falling into that trap is humiliating, but instead of reacting out of anger, I grunt in confusion.

"Not like you don't know."

She sighs again. "You've already decided. Tell Marissa to be careful. And would you visit Reading on the way? Your son needs a man-to-man."

"Ian?"

She can't hold back the grin. "No, your *other* son, the illegitimate one you had with..."

"Of course I can. It's on the way. What does he need?"

"He'll tell you," she says. "Because he trusts you."

"He trusts you, too."

This time, she fakes a smile and lifts her head so she can gaze into my eyes to prepare for a kiss I hope will never end. Instead, she whispers. "I know that."

With this busy an itinerary, I'd better make good time to reach Philly by nightfall. If the city is dangerous by day, the real peril arises after sunset, where it will be harder to cross the razor wire-topped fences ringing the city undetected. Gang members man the perimeter at night, ostensibly a public safety measure. But the guards serve a dual purpose. By restricting travel into the city, they can keep tabs on whatever opposition may arise, making it easier to temper before it gathers a head of steam, thereby extending their power.

Dressing, showering, and brushing my hair takes only thirty minutes this morning. I pass the time on the highway to Reading listening to 'oldies,' rock music I loved in the mid 2010s. The rhythm never gets old. The journey takes a little over five hours in minimal traffic conditions, where the most efficient route involves tolls. I don't bother speeding.

Reading is closer to Philadelphia than Becky is comfortable with, but Ian is a grown man and doesn't need parental protection to defend himself. When most of Philly's surviving residents fled, many chose to settle in Reading and Scranton, causing crime in those cities to skyrocket.

I pull up to Ian's townhouse after two in the afternoon. Pangs of hunger compress my stomach at the last minute, but I can suppress the urge to eat for a few more hours. And that's if Ian doesn't force-feed me with Brianne's legendary meals.

"Dad!" he shouts from around the corner, as though he could sense me coming.

"How's life treating you?"

He pulls open the door after two minutes, kicking something metal out of the way before greeting me with his trademarked grin. The kid isn't much younger than me, and he looks just like me. "Mom said you were coming. You eat leftovers?"

I can't refuse.

He leads me in through a crowded entryway, a three-foot square of irregular shale tile hemmed in by strips of silver where the carpet stretches into the living room. Wire rack storage shelves flank two walls, carrying boxes of bric-à-brac, important papers, childhood memorabilia, and assorted cookware. He reserves the bottom shelf for the copious supply of dog food, enough to feed the ravenous beast that might as well rival the legendary Cerberus in weight. The dog's dishes are blue-painted aluminum bowls with white paw prints at intermittent intervals. I can hear the animal panting as it lumbers down the stairs while Brianne calls it.

"Bernie! Stay!"

The Dog's name is Bernie? That name can't have been Ian's choice. But Brianne is a complicated woman with eclectic tastes, and could have derived the name from tennis, politics, or just wild thoughts.

"Brie made a delicious lasagna," Ian says, his demeanor never slipping from cheerful. Still, hidden trouble must persist in the back of his mind, or Becky wouldn't have sent me.

"That'll work," I say.

Parents often yearn to dig the trauma out of their kids. I consider it to be a natural parenting technique with its own drawbacks. Instead, I find that allowing Ian to voice his concerns when he feels the time is right allows more trust to prevail, leading to greater rewards. And while Becky doesn't always agree with my approach, she's understanding enough to let me try until the trauma gets the best of him and she must step in to curtail the damage.

"You want to know something?" he says.

I savor the meaty lasagna and the crumbly cheese before mumbling. "Hit me."

"It's actually two things. I found out something that could be dangerous, and I didn't want to bring it up with Brie before I discussed it with you."

"And what's that?"

"It's a funny thing. I didn't even know I was doing it. But the other day, it started snowing."

I screw up my face and offer a fake grin. "In August."

He nods. "Next thing I know, the neighbor's falling down the steps, getting out the snowblower without knowing what did it. I figured out it was me because of another problem I'm having. Brie's pregnant."

"Well, damn," I grin. "Congrats, man."

"See, we're not very well prepared. And scared out of my mind. The snowstorm went away when I forced myself to see things clearly. And returned as a cyclone when I let the dread overcome me."

"What?"

"I guess I have powers. But I thought someone had to give you yours. And I don't recall anyone giving me anything."

"Makes sense," I say, thinking fast. "I'm a descendant of the Six, which means you are, too. The problem is, you must try to control your emotions, because they drive it."

"That's what I understand, which makes me even more nervous."

"It's manageable," I say. "Figure out how you got it. Experiment in a controlled environment so you don't hurt anyone you love."

He nods and eyes the growing pile of dishes in the sink. If my intuition is correct, he might be considering using his gift to wash them for Brianne, since I'm guessing she'd assigned him the task.

We eat in relative silence and then settle into a chat about the complexities of daily life, the increasing danger long-time Reading citizens fear every day, the consequences of raising a child in perilous times. I can offer him little reassurance. Ian understands that any such sugar-coating will do little to solve the problems, but that leaning on me can at least lessen the emotional loads associated with it.

Three hours later, I'm heading out the door, hugging him and Brianne goodbye, sneaking past Bernie's enormous paws, and heading for my car. Storm clouds gather, growing gloomy in time as I drive away while Ian watches from the porch. The rain begins falling in sheets, lasting twenty minutes until I approach the Philadelphia suburbs.

Nightfall is only a couple of hours away, but I may be able to sneak through one of the less-trafficked gates without raising many suspicions.

The chain-link fences have already deteriorated with age, bearing signs of suburbanites attempting to burrow into the city proper. Long stretches of fence bisect parking lots, zigzagging between aging residential buildings and tearing through once-peaceful parks. The park nearest the gate hosts a gathering of protestors holding signs condemning the opposing factions in the city, since the chaos affects them, fence or no fence. A man in dirty khakis smokes a cigar, flicks it through the fence and issues a decaying toothy grin as he watches its red glow peter out in the weeds on the Philadelphia side.

The citizens show no interest in stopping me, but they watch me until I can no longer see them. I elect to park my car in an abandoned lot someone had bulldozed, pushing hulking chunks of rebar and concrete into towering piles that hide my car. Taking the rest of the journey on foot is not without its pitfalls. The destruction makes the trek plenty dangerous without the city's controlling interests leveraging support and inflicting violence on innocent civilians. At sunset, I find my way to the wide section of Market Street approaching the historic district, when a familiar face peers out at me from a makeshift cave. The ruins of the architectural masterpiece create a tantalizing cover for anyone wishing to avoid eye contact with the gangs. I stare at her for a few moments as she waves me into her temporary residence, welcoming me with a knobby handshake.

I stutter as she whispers in the darkness. "Are you ready for your final healing?"

Acknowledgements

The third book in the *Revelation* series came together a lot faster than either the first or second books did, despite sporting a bigger plot. As with *Reflection*, I hammered out the book's first act without writing a detailed plot. More authors identify as "pantsers" than you might expect, while I adopt a hybrid approach. I find that writing the first act gets the ball rolling, and once I discover where it's going, I draft a basic outline for Acts 2 and 3.

By now you have noticed that *Reflection* ended on a minor cliffhanger. The plot intentionally left a few strands tangled, and when I typed the last period, I already knew I had a major piece of the plot to resolve. Because the dimensions of time follow set rules, I realized that Kerry left Becky in the wrong dimension at the conclusion. The Titans' escape at the end leads into *Reincarnation*, and they have gained strength while assembling a monstrous army.

Now that you have finished reading *Reincarnation*, I offer more exciting news: A fourth book in the *Revelation* series is coming. It should be a lot of fun, even dabbling in the amateur sleuth bag of tricks. As of writing this note, I haven't penned a single sentence yet, so the final product may differ from what I've revealed.

As always, I want to thank everyone who contributed to this book in any way. First, Jeanine Henning designed the unbelievable cover art. She's a first-class designer, and I'm blessed to work with her. Joined by her promising protégé, Angela Tuson, Tarryn Thomas once again assisted with the editing, helping to polish the final product. I want to thank the professional team at Atticus for introducing more interior design options and for being easy to reach with technical difficulties.

I have had the pleasure of interacting with many writers over the last year, and I thank them all for helping to navigate the treacherous waters of marketing and promotion. Thanks also to the Boise Public Library, Brian at Kuna's Book Habit, Maria at Green Avenue, and the various Barnes & Noble managers who were gracious in organizing store events.

Fellow author Bernard K. Finnigan is a reliable beta-reader who pulls no punches, helping me to improve my story. A wonderful group of Idaho writers, Treasure Valley Authors, have been amazing, giving numerous marketing ideas. We all support each other, combining our talents into a cohesive, growing group. Merri, April, Jeanette, and Chris know the marketing business as well as anyone. I have also been fortunate to belong to the Murder Mystery Mayhem writer's group, formerly known as Idaho Sisters in Crime. Sherry is a fantastic leader.

I want to thank my family for accommodating a hectic schedule and the peace of mind necessary to craft stories like these.

Finally, a writer never gets far without readers. It's a humble pleasure to interact with all of you, and I express heartfelt gratitude to everyone.

-bm

About the Author

Brad Mathews bends genre rules by creating dynamic, unorthodox characters thrust into criminal investigations.

He is known to use abstract imagery to construct striking realities that build into suspenseful mystery tales.

Mathews is Certified in Plumbing design, and his extensive Building Information Modeling experience gives him a unique ability to detail mechanical and industrial settings in his novels.

Mathews resides in Boise, Idaho with his family.